Kathrin

Raising to Love

Kathrin

Raising to Love

Georg Engel

K A Nitz

ALBANY, NEW ZEALAND

Kathrin: Die Erziehung zur Liebe
first published in German 1918

This translation into New Zealand English
Copyright © K A Nitz 2019
All rights reserved

ISBN: 978-0-473-49723-1

FIRST BOOK

I

Do you know where the cavern of the winds lies? It opens up somewhere at the end of the world. And on the twilight evening in which the "Heron" shot out from the peaked waves of the narrow English Channel into the grey waters of the Atlantic, the North Wind had the week's watch right then, and crouched at the broad stone table, and smoked with delight. The swathes of smoke which he puffed from the short pipe stump did not disperse, rather they gathered and became dark clouds in the low hanging sky. Meanwhile the other brothers of the grey head, the East Wind, the South Wind, the West Wind, all lay in their corners and slept. They did not like the eldest, for they said brother North was a murderer. They did him an injustice however. Though the old fellow simply possessed the rough fists which shattered the solidest beams like glass, in his shaggy chest the morose heart often hammered in fear that nothing else occurred to him but this one roaring song of destruction which he had learnt in the ancient days of his youth. He would also rather have coaxed and wooed like the flaxen-haired South Wind. But, the devil, it did not work for him. And when he tried to laugh, over there on the other side of the horizon somewhere a few houses or churches collapsed.

"It is a heavy burden," the North Wind said, and at the same time he opened up an old, strangely yellowed book, "it makes you tired when you want to keep order in your business, and not travel along rushing and un-concerned like the youths do."

With that he moistened his hulking forefinger, and passed arduously and wistfully over one of the dark pages. The pages of the folio, however, did not lie still and dead, as is the custom with men's books, rather they lived. And on them, the waves put forth their play; sun, moon, and stars passed across the sky; the white cliffs shone, and fluttering swarms of seagulls whirled over the masts and funnels of the ships which glided along on the inscribed sea lanes.

"Yes," the old one suggested as he scratched about with his nails on the white, glittering image of the "Heron", just as the three-master had reached the great water, "a spruce ship. Captain Hennings. Eighteen man crew. Women's clothes flitter, yes, even a piping little child's voice cries out. Fetch the devil, it is nothing to me, I follow only the mood which rules my head and hands. Pity — pity."

With that he moistened his finger more, and erased the white vessel with a strong swipe.

On the page, the waves fell against each other like blue mountains of glass, the smoke of his pipe passed over them, and the "Heron" sank trembling to the depths.

"So", the old man said, and chucked his book under the table, grumbling.

***

Up to now a rare star had sporadically blinked over the roaring, watery desolation, now it seemed to the swimmer as if to the left and right thousands of garishly phosphorescent lights were spraying up from the depths and from the seething haze above him. They danced, they shot all about, and became more and more avid and bloody. Whenever a wave met his head, it thundered at the lonely man who was setting his last manpower against that unfeeling universe in which his brain was numbed and wreaths of blazing roses whirled over him in circles. The stupidest and the most elevated things held his mind zealously ensnared. A sad, insane residue of human things. He screamed at God, not desperately and imperiously, but following the tradition impressed on him that there must be something which strode through death and destruction unchallenged. And besides that, the thought clawed at him that with the leap overboard his father's watch had slid from him. It had been a so-called egg watch, surrounded by a thick, darkened silver cover. And now, as a new blow hammered at his head, he even calculated that a watch which was protected thus must continue ticking unerringly on the sea floor. Truly, he heard its beats. They laboured, drilling, burrowing, and yet regularly in the tumultuous cavities of his ears, and the uniform, restless noise began sending him to sleep and breaking his will to live. The poor wheezing chest, crushed by the black shackles of the water, began spewing out senseless words. Compulsive desires, a long way from the laws of the community to which he now belonged, took power over him.

Why did he weigh down his left arm, half of his power of resistance, with this ridiculous, long-silenced bundle? When the sun had still played about him, when human voices had sounded about him, when he had felt joy over eating and drinking, sleeping and waking, then this little packet had been a child. An undeveloped, stupid, dirty thing which once sat on the roof of his cabin where it had scrimmaged with a puppy over a bone. Richard Sell could barely think whether the little sprog had been a boy or a girl. It was no concern of his either. And now he was lugging it with himself over the black fields of death? Certainly for no other reason than because it was customary to snatch from the ravenous mouth of the sea its floundering morsels. He would have probably acted towards the little ship's dog exactly the same. But in the end, this acquired readiness to help was a dangerous stupidity. Was the damned packet not becoming heavier and heavier until it was gradually reaching the weight of the enormous beach boulders back by his home town? Was the beastly bundle not huddling up to him as if in there a pair of thirsty suckling lips wanted to slurp the last frozen drops of blood from his veins? The devil fetch all those odd commandments. They did not concern him in the least anymore. He was a spat-out man whom the spirits of death had tossed in the air on a damp, black shroud, and let fall down again.

God have pity, the egg watch on the sea floor was ticking so mercilessly, it was smashing down with cudgels his last rational thoughts. No, no, he was doing it, he was tossing the bundle which he hated so grimly away from himself the next moment. The little passenger must also have long since gone silent or been frozen. Why in all the world did he still have a superfluous pity towards a heap of rigid bones and sinews? And how dirty the thing had been. The small misshapen face had also hosted a number of disfiguring pimples. Quite certainly, the wet cradle formed the right place for the ugly monster.

An enormous hollow towered up, rushing before the swimmer, it washed down with a crash, and the paralysed man cried out for the first time in fear of death, and clasped in despair for his companion.

Yes, a cradle — a wet cradle — it rocked so gently.

"Such a thing has never occurred on the 'Green Herring'", a terrible voice boomed, although it was visibly endeavouring to bring to light a certain contentedness. "First you had to break apart the stupid fool's arms so that he gave away his treasure. And what now sticks in the thick woolen blanket there? A little tot. And stark naked."

"Yes," the ship's boy, Bob Swanegel, said, who stood in bare feet next to the hammock, and kept the netting in a swaying motion, "it is naked, and it is a girl too."

"Boy," the square-built Captain Kohlrausch shouted, not being able to hear, and hence striving at least to make himself understandable to his fellow men in the clearest way, "boy," he roared, and shook his massive head of grey locks, "what are you saying?"

"I am saying that it is a girl", Bob Swanegel established, and at the same time, he lifted his stubby nose, and looked so clever and considered until his skipper was once again seized by a boundless admiration for this much experienced, worldly wise, young man. "A girl", the boy whispered quite quietly, and moved his lips in that strange picturing way, which signified a truly refreshing thing for the deaf man, however.

The rascal remained the only one with whom the hard-of-hearing man could have a proper conversation. He was thus a great treasure for the herring catcher, his bullhorn for the rest of the crew, and the Captain thus endeavoured to constantly remain in the favour of his charge.

"A girl?" Captain Julius Kohlrausch repeated, completely paralysed over the strange visitor to the 'Green Herring'. "How do you know that, Bob?"

"I have checked her", Bob instructed him emotionlessly, and looked at his skipper derisively from his twinkling red eyes. "She has pimples on her face, and if you strike her on the back, she rolls her eyes."

"Jesus," the skipper stuttered, and squinted needily into the corner, "what do you give the poor worm? We have no milk on board."

The boy deliberated for a while, then he raised his right leg, and rubbed with his bare foot on his torn grey trousers. Finally he lifted his stub nose again, and had worked it out with his formula.

"You must stick your finger in her mouth," he commanded finally, and put his hands dismissively and comfortably in his pockets, "little children need nothing more."

"Good," the Captain concurred, and he sighed with relief, "do that, Bob. And then clothe the tot in a shirt of mine, but one of the dirtiest, you hear? It is not decent that the thing lies so naked before us, because it is, as you say, a girl."

Again he emitted a sigh like he was wont to after the difficult fulfillment of a duty, and then bent over the hammock.

In there a young fellow of perhaps twenty years lay in the warm, red and white checked bedding. You saw for a moment nothing more of him than a round head almost shorn bald, and it seethed fiery red and hotly about the cheeks and forehead of the recumbent fellow, for the fists of Captain Kohlrausch also had not spared those body parts of the fished-up man with his attempt at re-animating him. The fine slender nose, of such a noble form as you would barely have trusted a young insignificant mariner to have, appeared to be quite shrunken in both nostrils, a certain sign that the sea god had already planted a quiet little place on the green meadows of the sea for the lost man. Long dark eyelashes twitched uneasily over the closed eyes, as if in doubt over whether they should not finally drink from the blue light which streamed in mildly and benevolently through the round little cabin window.

"This is a quite quiet picture", the master of the 'Green Herring' finally affirmed after a further period in which nothing of importance had occurred. "Who knows whether there are means which bring men to speak. Or do you know one, Bob?" the Captain added in the distant inkling that the solution to such a difficult puzzle could not remain closed off to his highly gifted charge either.

And see there. Bob Swanegel's learnedness did not fail this time either. Considering, he passed the back of his hand under his nose, to then bring forth convinced and self-assured, "There in the corner, Captain, stands our broom. You must break off one of the brushwood stalks, and tickle him about his nose with it. Then he will speak."

"Yes, then he will speak", Captain Kohlrausch cried, highly delighted since he considered that means of getting information to be quite inconceivably beautiful and simple. "You have a notable head, Bob Swanegel."

"Yes, I have it from my mother," Bob confirmed earnestly, "the old lady is assistant to the town midwife, Wurm, and goes to her briskly with all sorts of things at hand."

The Captain lowered his eyes.

"Shut your mouth," he commanded bashfully, "and leave me in peace over the old women. But tickling is good. And we want to perform the act now, straight-away."

Master and student strode busily about the prosecution of the difficult case. And Bob Swanegel executed his task so perfectly that a loud sneeze was really heard from the hammock. At the same time, the recumbent figure stretched and, at the foot of the place of rest, a crowing child's voice began screaming.

"So," Bob said contentedly, "she is also perking up. Just listen, Captain, it is a nasty old tot. It chortles like a hen when it finds an earthworm."

Straight afterwards, however, the young worldly wise man was frightened back from the white and red checked pillows. For there a pair of brown eyes had opened, as empty and deep and lacklustre as if they were just two dark holes.

"Ugh the devil", Captain Kohlrausch now stuttered too, completely bewildered, as he sank back with embarrassment into a bow of greeting. "It is a right beautiful day today. But don't take it wrongly, who are you?"

Only, the dark pits remained dull and without emotion, just the mouth, shaded by a fine blond fuzz, began murmuring and stammering without will.

"What is he saying?", Captain Kohlrausch stepped closer in suspense.

"He is saying 'egg watch'", the ship's boy passed on unperturbed.

"Aha." The herring catcher obligingly bowed once more; he held this first utterance of his guest to be an appropriate introduction. "I am Captain Kohlrausch of the 'Green Herring'", he began. "Two hundred tonnes. Sail and steam. We are taking something useful to Amsterdam and then to Kiel. No, no, remain lying at ease, my dear Mr Eggwatch," he calmed the ill man who was seeking arduously just then to sit up, "nothing further will happen to you here. It is merely because of the damned ship's journal in which I must record your revered arrival. You can thus tell me quite quietly and slowly, and Bob Swanegel will then write everything into it, for even if he draws quite large letters, they are very readable though."

Meanwhile, the shipwrecked man had pulled himself together somewhat more. His first movement was to his heaving chest as if he held something hidden there. But it was only a slow, cutting stitch which passed from there towards his back and pricked every single word as if with a sharp nail. Such a strange pain, never felt before, tormented him, a pain which drove the young life back into consciousness though. With boundless astonishment, the recumbent man surveyed his strange surroundings as well as both the unfamiliar faces, until finally an embarrassed smile appeared on his pale lips, and the slender figure bent forward to fasten a look of incomprehension on the screaming creature at the foot of the hammock.

Strange, why then did such a whimpering worm remain shackled to him forever and eternally? He did not think he had ever been bound up with such an unclothed squaller. In addition, a tormenting choking fear came as if he had lost something.

But what?

He was missing something precious, something terribly necessary for life! Just what could it be?

And with a muffled sigh, the exhausted body sank back again into its pillows. Just a single word stole anxiously and full of secret awe from between the clenched teeth, "Eggwatch."

"Well yes," Captain Kohlrausch said, "that we know now."

Towards evening, Richard Sell awoke again. He in no way felt the comfortable relaxation of all his limbs which a long dreamless sleep confers, he had rather the feeling as though a wrecking bar had been worked quite unconcernedly between his teeth. And rightly, when he reluctantly moved his head, he noticed that he was not deceived. Before him, in the space sparsely lit by a small oil lantern, stood an adolescent boy whom he must have already seen somewhere once, and the boy was endeavouring to push a spoon incessantly into the mouth of the recumbent man. A hot, pulpy mass was thereby collecting on the lips of his charge, but which did not hinder the boy from continuing with a monstrously serene face in his activity. And yet, how beneficially these first hot drops warmed the limbs still shaking from the cold. How they struggled against the stiffening which had tied up his sore chest heavily and unbreakably until then. The wordless feeding lasted for a while. Greedily and mechanically, the recumbent man swallowed the wholesome meal, and an open envy seized him when he had to notice how his protector finally turned to the foot of the bed to dispense his offerings there with the same sober irreverence.

"Where am I?" Richard Sell whispered, as he tilted his head a little towards the sloping wall of the ship; he recognised distinctly the noise of the spraying waves, and the gentle rocking of the hull filled him with the strangely comfortable feeling of habit. "Where am I?"

"Here", Bob Swanegel responded after considering for a while with displeasure, and at the same time he struck the spoon against the brown pot.

"Yes, but I meant — —", the rescued man continued urging.

But the conversation was thought by the ship's boy, who basically represented the intellectual hegemony of the 'Green Herring', to be a completely superfluous waste of time at such a late hour. The work of feeding washed-up people did not stand in his apprenticeship contract either.

"It is already ten o'clock", he hence added dismissively. "Jochen Riesebeck has long since been lying in our berth. That tall old rogue always lets his legs hang down when he sleeps. And then I cannot find my way to my place. Adieu."

With that he struck the pot once more, and straight afterwards shuffling steps announced how Bob Swanegel was stumbling up steps to the familiar place of his rest.

The foam beading past splashed and swished incessantly. At regular intervals, the impassive man sensed the dipping and rising of the small ship, and the dreary little light of the oil lantern obscured the objects of the wooden room with its flickering.

It became quieter and lonelier. Before the open eyes of the young helmsman, from which sleep fled, many coloured balls began gliding along across glittering lines. A strange ball-play of his daydreaming. Beginning and end wanted to join up, imagination began ordering the contemplative man again in the ranks of the living. Insistent questions over where-from and where-to arose in him, and as his eyes were filled by the quiet harmonies of the iridescent balls, his spirit groped its way back into the community from which it had been cast out of for a long time. White and black collided, light and dark. More and more carefully, the undecayed disposition of the young man strove for a foothold and certainty.

How was that though?

***

It was not such a long time ago at all that Richard Sell had trodden for the first time the planks of the 'Heron'.

Wait, wait, you must count them off on your fingers. Quite right, eight days at most could have elapsed since then. And when the slender, just qualified helmsman stepped over the gangway of the anchored three master, his entire family consisted exclusively of the limping black Hans who up to then had only learnt the one word, "give". Admittedly, some maintained the raven also often misspoke when it tossed the insult "thief" into the world in quite inapt places. But Richard Sell did not need to place any weight on this particular view. For it was established, the few groschen which he had inherited once from his father, a sexton who had died young, had been spent to the last pfennig on his own education, and the black Hans could not possibly make references to other property. Father and mother under the ground, a well passed exam at the maritime school, the bluish black raven, and everything shrouded by the soft, almost unconscious knowledge that there was yet a world of far more spiritual beauty above earth and sea; the belongings which Richard Sell brought with him consisted of these things. Up to the gangway of the ship. But no — you should not lie, particularly if you compute so earnestly the debits and credits of your life on your fingers.

The fresh young man named one more thing as his own, a thing to which he barely dared confess, which he spurned and yet drew again to himself because the consciousness of this feeling hid in itself something too awful, treacherous, and besides that also again something secretly blissful, fortifying, and precious. You were certainly only twenty years old, but you could not help it at all in the end that suddenly a pair of blue eyes, laughing, radiant morning-stars, had rested on the being of a poor insignificant man-child. It had all happened quite unwilled and without intent. Or did it not signify a cheerful coincidence that from the side of the white three master, the proud sailing ship which had lain for a long time by the wooden harbour walls of the village at the river mouth, a light glove made of white cotton had to flutter into the water? And a sailor, who was travelling about on a tiny boat marvelling at the luminously painted vessel, should not be duty bound to wrest such a delicate web from the green, slowly flowing river to then, bedded carefully on the blade of the oars, offer it up to the owner bending down? At this moment, the joyful stars had been strung blue, thankful, and unconcerned in his heaven. Richard Sell remembered how he had stared completely rapt and distracted up into a fine pale countenance, whereby for the first time the thoughts of his own advancement, which usually ruled over him incessantly, had swirled away. Strange, you

could thus be completely torn away from the accustomed surrounds without feeling pain over suddenly not
being the central point of creation anymore. And you
had indeed been that before. The question of how you
would become a rich and esteemed man, an independent man who conquered the pressing poverty, that
question had until now whispered from every breeze.
On every ray of sunlight, nothing danced but that consideration, and there was no human face which had not
inquired quietly and silently over when the ascent of the
helmsman Richard Sell would now finally begin. Yes, if
you were poor, then you really had nothing else to worry
about. That was recognised. And now? Quite unexpectedly, on a still unoccupied afternoon, as the forests of
the sacred grove turned blue from a distance, as the
seagulls shot across the river greedy for food and as,
quite nearby on the awash wooden ramp, a pair of village women were washing their linen things; then all of
a sudden the universe should display something still
more important than the fortunes of Richard Sell?

But it comported itself thus.

"Oh, that is very beautiful", an unassuming clear
voice had uttered in response, and a fresh mouth bared
a row of shiny teeth as the drops running down from the
raised oar sprayed back distractingly onto the eyes and
forehead of the young mariner.

Straight afterwards, the bright blond head had vanished behind the high side. But Richard Sell stood in his
boat and listened to the wind. Too odd, he constantly
thought he heard a sweet, unfamiliar music which
flattered him and altered his entire being and made it
better. And yet, when he deliberated quite coolly with
himself, they were always the same syllables which
pounded to him from air and waves, from the rustling of
the bulrushes by the shore, and from the chirping of the
swallows flying past in his dream, "Oh, that is very
beautiful."

Yes, by God, it remained inexplicable. For when he had already long since climbed onto land, yes, as he strode along the riverbank restively, even still later when he was already taking in his night's supper in the small, humble fisherman's tavern, this tender tinkling constantly surrounded him and poured a joy into his heart he had never known before. His chest expanded, his eyes sparkled, and when he leant back in his chair, then his fists closed together tightly as if the power resided in him to arrest the globe in its course or turn it quicker. Yes, now something great must happen. And hardly had he lain on his rustling straw mattress in the crooked lean-to, which had been granted to him by the completely senile, almost eighty year old smoker Ott Knuth during the time of his unemployment, than suddenly a part of his practical reason, which had kept him in rein for so long, suddenly reported for duty again, and it shredded a little the glittering web of the golden net surrounding him.

He pounded violently with his right hand against the wooden wall behind which his toothless landlord tended to keep up a grumbling soliloquy half the night through. Something crackled down from the wall lining, cobwebs or a crumb of accumulated soot from the smoker, and the air became still more acrid than before as a result.

"Mr Knuth," the tenant called cautiously — for because of his high age, the social description "Mister" was permitted by the smoker in general, although you addressed him informally and a little disparagingly at the same time in the river-mouth village of Uhlenhus — "Mr Knuth, are you asleep already?"

"Rubbish," the old man chewed from next door, "don't you hear, Richard, I am singing something to myself. In that way, you can think best of all. That you must try sometime."

"Wonderful, Mr Knuth. But do you know perhaps what the name of the captain of the three master is?"

The smoker first growled a few notes of the gentle folksong "In a Cool Place", then he blew his nose, coughed heavily, and croaked in response, "Rubbish, he is a son of the merchant Hennings from Altefähre. There is money there."

Money? The young man who could not sleep pricked his ears up. The old magic word which had exercised its power for so long over him began binding him this time too.

"Where is he headed for?", he inquired further while he hastily struck the wood anew.

"Rubbish," the old man inside grumbled, because truly more of the black soot had scattered on the bed covers than he thought proper, "leave off with the damned drumming. The 'Heron' is sailing for India. Rice and sugar. There you can make beautiful profits."

"So, so."

Now the significant, the tormenting question neared. And without realising, he scratched anew at the wooden partition.

"My love who lived there has vanished", the old man sang from within a little moronically.

"Tell me please, Mr Knuth," it poured timidly over the lips of the recumbent man, "has Captain Hennings got a daughter perhaps? She is blond."

"What?" The old man struck angrily at his pillow and kicked his foot against the chest so that the worm-ridden frame creaked and groaned. "Eh, that is rubbish. Leave me in peace, and if you cannot sleep, then you should sing, Richard Sell."

"That I will too," the other offered, "but she is blond."

"Well, if you know", it sounded from within with conviction. "Blond? Then it is teacher Brassen's daughter, his eldest. Only eight days ago they married. But what concern of yours is the young wife of the captain?"

"Oh, none at all", Richard Sell apologised in a low voice. "I was just thinking." And after some time, within which his landlord practised a scale devoutly, the young man added, aghast at his own intents, "Is she travelling with him to India?"

"Now that is enough though," Ott Knuth wailed angrily, "you surely don't realise at all that you are disturbing me? But when I was young, you idiot, I did not leave my better half behind either. And at the same time she had a thick lump over her right eye. No, if you are not smooth and warm, then you guard such a thing."

"Yes, that you do", Richard Sell affirmed with a proud note as if he were himself the possessor of such a blest treasure. "You guard it — you guard it — —".

And then sleep won dominance over the enraptured man. A blond head bent over him and smiled at him, the heavens descended to be quite close to him, and the stretched-out man did not wonder in the least that all the thousands of stars on the steely sheet were simply dancing and flickering gold pieces which fell down to him in an inaudible rain.

"Oh, that is beautiful", it dawned through his senses.

***

The next morning, Richard Sell put on his best blue sailor's suit. He brushed the last speck of dust off the fine cloth, and when he stood before the remnant of a broken mirror which the smoker had nailed to the wall for his tenant, the young helmsman was irritated for the first time over his missing hair. Certainly, a smoothly shorn head just did not need to be attended to for very long, but there were in the end cases where a carefully drawn parting was not to be despised. Without considering further, the departing man pocketed his papers, and he would have strode out now decisively and heedlessly through the far too low door if a discordantly croaking voice had not arisen behind him.

"Ah so", Richard Sell recalled thoughtfully.

On the back of the only chair which was in the dark cavity, a raven was toddling back and forth excitedly, pecking with its beak at the worm-ridden wood, and bristling its bluish black feathers with displeasure.

"Yes," the parting man said, now completely clear about what a weighty decision stood before him, "yes," he suggested, and drew a little piece of sugar from his pocket for his companion, "it all happens for the sake of getting ahead. You must go high, Hans. And out there it shall go much easier."

Now the raven made a massive blow against the dry wood. "Thief", it said very distinctly.

Its master was startled. "What?", he asked in a low voice.

"Thief", the raven repeated once more with great definitiveness.

Then Richard Sell scratched with concern behind his ear.

"Nobody knows," he murmured, disturbed and as if excusing himself, "I will also tell nobody. Such a thing you do not do though. But I must attempt once in the wide world, how else can something become of me? And I must rise — I must go up, mustn't I?"

But Master Hans did not stir anymore. He sat suddenly quite anxiously tucked together and turned his sharp eyes squinting.

"I will be here straightaway again," Richard Sell called to drown out his pounding heart.

And then he rushed away as if his fortune were hurrying past out there and he had to stop it. Breathless and without being able to grasp a clear thought, he sprang up the narrow gangway, and see there, the first being he meets on the clean scrubbed deck of the three master was a delicate blond woman. She sat in the shade of the siding on a low folding chair, and the staring man noticed disconcertedly how in the lap of her white dress quite thin long gold threads sparkled in the sun. His numbed consciousness deceived him vaguely into thinking these barely visible lines must be the strands of her own hair from which her skillful hands were attempting to form a strange adornment.

Right, right, that was a watch chain. A chain of soft gold which was certainly destined for Captain Hennings. Truly, whoever wore this sparkling jewellery did not need the treasures of India anymore, he would stride along adorned like a king and was certainly immune to all adversity and any pain. It remained quite inconceivable that there was such a preference on earth. And then something wonderful happened.

The young woman raised her bright head and looked at him. "Ah, you are here," she spoke as calmly as if she had already been expecting his appearance for a long time, "you certainly want to apply for the second helmsman's position, don't you?"

"Yes", Richard Sell stuttered with effort; he could not wrest himself away anymore even with the greatest exertion of force.

"Well good," the young woman smiled pleasantly, "I will call my husband."

Only before she could carry out her decision, a firm hand had already been placed on her shoulder, and a powerful voice spoke in-between, "I am Captain Hennings, and I know you quite well. Are you not the helmsman Richard Sell who resides with the smoker Knuth?"

"Yes, Captain", the man being addressed now pulled himself together, and looked with earnest brown eyes inquiringly and without straying into the steady tanned man's countenance there before him. For now, where it concerned his future, all equivocation slid off him for a while, and the first look taught him that he was dealing with a strict and yet benevolent man. The skipper looked like someone who understood at the appropriate moment to throw the rope over his neck for luck. And that pleased Richard Sell like nothing else.

Then the talk went quickly back and forth. Truly, on the white ship, in the vicinity of the blond woman, life seemed gentler, more pleasant, and without spinning out those difficulties which had previously often knotted or even torn apart the rolling threads. Everything was ordered quite simply as if even the most insignificant thing had already been determined beforehand. To his immense surprise, the arrival learnt that Captain Hennings had already wanted for some days to be able to take the young striving helmsman into his crew. And after the skipper inspected in-depth the papers handed over to him, the pact was concluded with a handshake. Now for the departure. For the bright gleam which now and then lit up from the white dress of the woman strengthened the hired man in the conviction that he would never lose the trembling self-consciousness and boyish elation on the planks of the 'Heron'. No, he had to savour it in silence, stepping aside quietly and undetected after some time of goggling to dedicate himself then completely to his sober end goal. Back there, concealed by clouds and sea, dawned the silver cities of which he had read. The sacred river rushed past them, pearl-adorned elephants carried little temple halls on their backs, and buried treasures waited only for strong hands to be brought to light.

"So, Marie," Captain Hennings demanded, "now set the first lunch before our second helmsman. A bottle of red wine would not go amiss either."

Then Richard Soll breathed out. She was called Marie. A beautiful name.

***

The 'Heron' stormed along easily and happily. A sailing breeze blew into its ruddily swollen sail. Sheltering hands stroked the water smooth and level before its bow. You hardly noticed the strength which resided in the white racer when it shot with fluttering crests over the white humming course. Sun and moon rose, threw red and silver carpets before its path, and the days foamed behind it. But, what always remained permanent was the gentle, the thriving succeeding which adhered to everything for which Richard Sell stretched out his hands on this white ship. Not only that Captain Hennings soon recognised what an assiduous, efficiently schooled and work-happy assistant he had obtained, no, the crew too had quickly forgotten the youth of the second helmsman and followed the short orders supplied by his specialist knowledge with respect and inner acclaim. The young man knew so well what was essential, and never plagued his people with minor matters. Everything he ordered always had the appearance of a painstakingly worked through calculation which did not warrant argument over or contradiction. And the old sea-dogs experienced it charitably and did not resent the second helmsman that he tended besides that to have little conversation with them and kept apart from them. Even the scrawny, liverish first helmsman, who because of his suffering always kept a wad of tobacco and a short pipe between his teeth at the same time, secretly admired his comrades recordings of the sun and moon, and he hence thought it unnecessary to throw a cynical phrase in the path of the young man.

"Our little one understands his thing", the sailors thought amidst agreeing nods of their heads, and they looked at the second man as if at the dial of the compass itself.

And in that they judged rightly. For in the chest of the then maturing man, in the serious youth with the short cropped hair, the fine slender nose, and the sometimes hard, sometimes thoughtful brown eyes, there nature had really inserted a magnet needle which showed undeviatingly and without fluctuations the preconceived way. It always stretched towards the same direction, and its magnetic attraction to power, to wealth and eminence kept it stubbornly on its path. And yet — nobody knew how this needle also sometimes began to tremble, yes, that its entire being could be shaken as if the certain guidepost wanted to spring from its base.

Such things happened on the mild May evenings when the green and red signal lanterns glimmered on both sides of the ship, and the 'Heron', still under half loaded, as it were weary of the course of the day, glided out into the pale dusk. Then, under the silent silvery dance of the stars, shrouded and made uncertain by the incomprehensible whispering voices of infinity, those inmates of the vessel found themselves together on the high siding who had not yet unlearnt the seeking of an answer in the whispering and muttering of the elements to the depths of their own dispositions, and were depressed by their impotence because the right thing never occurred to them. In the pale magical circle of the moon, two heads then usually loomed over the side of the ship and followed thoughtfully the dark images of their shadows passing wavering and playfully between the raked up watery furrows. Sometimes the young taciturn helmsman caught himself making the wish, frightening to him, that both the fluttering shapes down there might be released from their bodies to sink with each other into some billowing realm of mist. When the like befell him, he was filled by an accusatory horror, and he moved imperceptibly away from Marie Hennings, who shared this savouring of solitude with him, as if the calm clear eyes of the young woman could read the criminal thoughts themselves in the blue night from his forehead. And yet, it was so inconceivably soothing, the nearness of the gentle, happy creature. If he recalled rightly, they actually tended never to exchange many words with one another. But nevertheless, both the young, timid persons shared the consciousness of a good understanding, and the desire for the clean paths of life was common to both, even if the sober helmsman already knew that no mortal could tread them persistently unendangered. Often when he took in the wonder of the imposed distance in such hours next to the young woman, shaking with restrained desires, and yet again and again tamed by Marie's simple naivety, she then smiled at him encouragingly, like someone who wishes to bring the hidden powers and abilities of another to fruition, and asked with her bright, calming voice, "You are always looking so far out, Mr Sell. What are you seeking there?"

The man addressed kept to himself. "For my way", he replied after some thought. "There must be something which raises me up."

Now the captain's wife stroked the smooth railing contemplatively with her slender hand.

"Are you not content with your position?"

"Oh, but yes — for the time being. But there is still so much about me which is unclear. And then — I also don't want to always remain poor and dependent, but become a rich man in a short time."

His companion hesitated. "Does so much good really lie in that then?", she responded after a while doubtfully.

But the objection stirred in Richard Sell.

"Very much, Mrs Hennings", he countered firmly, and his tone became hard and self-assured. "Then you have most of what you wish for, and need not just do without the best." He looked at her for a moment with knitted brow as if she were at fault for his hardship.

"And you must seek all that so far in the distance?", she began once more, as she shook her slender head, untouched by his rebuke and unsuspecting.

But the helmsman did not back away from her.

"Yes. for me it lies in the distance," he concluded stubbornly, "there I must seek, I will not find it nearby."

Then the blonde breathed freely and with relief. And as she turned to embrace with her eyes the little house on the bridge in which the dark outlines of the Captain were drawn, she whispered happily to herself, "I have it nearby."

"Yes," Richard Sell said curtly.

Marie Hennings would in the few days in light and sunshine which were still begrudged to her also take another happiness into her heart which was given to her like a remuneration for unobtainable and withheld things by chance or by providence. And it was Richard Sell who placed it reluctantly and quite awkwardly in her arms.

One morning — the 'Heron' was measuring out just then the Danish straits — an unusual bustle arose on board. The crew ran back and forth, informed each other through droll gestures, and the more distinctly the dogged voice of the first helmsman shrilled from one of the lower cabins and the more fiercely it blustered and rolled, the more grimly a mocking applause was painted on the broad faces of the sailors. Across the board, from able-bodied seamen down to the ship's boy, they all seemed to endorse the interruption of the usually so harmonious life on-board. The words "Brodersen", "gallows bird", and "a hellish fun" made the round, and just when Marie Hennings, startled by the general whirl, opened the door of her spacious cabin to inquire about the cause of all this unusual racket, the entrance was already darkening, and her husband entered the space with his firm, short strides. The Captain threw his cap on the folding table wordlessly, and his usually so serious and measured features also held the mean between a restrained cheerfulness and badly controlled fury.

"That is a nice mess", he squeezed out, as he gazed out the open window with his back turned.

The young woman stepped up to him and placed her hand on his shoulder. "What is it then, Albert?", she asked sympathetically, "are you having trouble?"

"Yes", the averted man responded, already somewhat less reserved, for the soft touch calmed him. "A nasty story."

"Do you not want to tell me it?", the young woman continued urging, and to make it easier for him, she also added, "why are our people all speaking at the moment about the sailor Brodersen?"

"Because he is a gallows bird", Captain Hennings burst out indignantly, and now turned around curtly to his blond wife. "Think, the fellow has smuggled a child on board."

"Not possible!" The cry which Marie emitted sounded bright and fresh as if it were to no extent given by anger or reluctance, and on her fine, narrow countenance, her most cheerful smile collected. At the same time, her blue eyes sparkled a little mischievously, as if she too could not grumble straightaway over the outrageous incident with the sailor. "Ah", she suggested in a low voice and crossed her hands over her breast. "Is it a girl?"

The Captain threw an astonished look at her.

"I don't know what sort of worm it is," he remarked coldly and shrugged his shoulders, "that does not concern me at all either. We always believed the drunken tether had locked a young dog there below. And now helmsman Wollert, whom the bellowing has always irritated, finds instead that it is one of those little human squallers."

"Albert, how old is the child?", the young woman interrupted her husband excitedly.

Only, the Captain declined to engage himself in such details. "That has nothing to do with the case", he declared, and intended just then to grasp his cap again. "The essential thing remains that we have thankfully been keeping close to land. As much as I don't like to lose a man, the fellow must leave me with his worm today. It is quite impossible to let such an impropriety pass."

"But Albert — —".

"There it stays", Captain Hennings decided firmly. "Believe me, dear child, it must be."

At this moment, there was a knock at the door, and on the "come in" of the Captain, Richard Sell carried an unclean, rumpled bundle into the cabin, which on closer observation manifested first of all as a tiny red head and a few disordered strands of brown hair. Weary dark, child's eyes looked insensibly and dully around, as if you had just then raised them violently from sleep, and a moist mouth slurred senselessly and incomprehensibly to itself.

"Yes, here we are", the father of the child murmured in a low voice, having likewise pressed through the open gap in the doorway. With ducked head, he stood before the others, and the bright seat of fear beaded over the Herculean man's damp forehead while his calloused hands wrung each other incessantly. "I cannot help it, Captain, I could not help myself any other way."

"Yes, Captain," Richard Sell now also related, "you must hear the man. His reasons are not bad."

And at the same time, the second helmsman was already placing his burden in the arms of the young woman; as something quite self-evident which was owed her and for which she had already long been stretching her hands out. Tenderly, blushing, and full of helpful zeal, Marie Hennings bent her blond head down over the much reviled living being.

"Yes, you must hear Brodersen", Richard Sell repeated more urgently once more.

"Oh, Captain, just a word," the sailor begged, whose devastated and bloated face had begun twitching, "you do not know what a state we are in — you cannot know", he suddenly cried and struck his right hand loudly against his chest so that it gave a dull blow.

The others looked on with concern. But then, as if he felt obliged to also hear against his better judgement the defence of the man accused by him, the Captain sat down silently by the side of the table, and gave the sailor the sign that he would be permitted to shake off everything which oppressed him. Then Brodersen took a deep breath. However, before he dared make the diffi-cult confession, he fastened a shy sideways glance at the young wife of the Captain as if he feared his sorrow, his common, soiled earthly woe could not be good for such ears.

"Captain," the hunched man stammered indecisively, seeming not to be standing firmly on his feet, "it is not for everyone and anyone. For what our sort experience — —".

"Make it short", Captain Hennings commanded without paying attention to the unexpressed request. "What have you to bring forward?"

And then one of those human fates was revealed over which a ray of sunlight could never play because it had been pushed beforehand into dark hollows without exit or escape. With balled fists, the man spoke as if it were unbearable to him to talk about himself and his affairs in a circle of well-dressed and clean fellow creatures.

"It was simply like this," he wrestled out arduously, "she found her way to me on the street."

"Who? — Do you mean your woman?", the Captain flared up.

The other man nodded, but he did not dare raise his glazed eyes anymore from the floor.

"As it goes. I always drank a little much, and she was one of the mam'selle's in these businesses. After that we could not part from each other anymore. But when the hardship came and the child, we often fought — yes, yes, it went that far. Finally each went their own way, I mine and she hers, until I noticed one day —" Brodersen paused. Shame threatened to choke him before the wide-open eyes of his listeners. "Well, in a nutshell," he burst out, "she could not let go of the colourful ribbons, the hats, and all the trinkets. And because I could not scrape up the necessary for that, she pulled it from the pockets of others. Until one day it went askew and she was put away for a few years. Then I stood now with the two year old sprog. What was I meant to do with it?"

"Great God", Marie Hennings whispered instinctively, and the blood drained from the fresh cheeks of the second helmsman as if he himself belonged to the foundering and outcast. You could thus plunge so low if you did not gain wealth and power?

The sailor threw his right hand forward as if he were now forcibly throwing his memories and every scruple from himself. "I had just a few clear days," he said more firmly, "and then I considered whether you would wait until the wife returns and the old lottery starts from the beginning. And would perhaps the same become of the little, innocent worm? The father a boozer and the mother still worse? — No, perhaps one can begin a new life quite far from here. Perhaps what is not completely rotten can be saved. And see, Captain, then it seized me — and then I smuggled the little one here. Yes, yes, man must have something to worry about. And now I want to beg you — yes, I want to beg you imploringly —". He folded his hands, raised his shoulders, and all that he had still to bring forth died out in a short groan.

About him it remained paralysingly still. None of those present dared disturb through human words a lost man who was seeking his dreary way amidst pain and torment.

***

Ah, the plans and hopes of those born of dust whirl in the wind. Why must what began so lovingly perish?

Why did beauty crackle up, and why did the desires shatter, the quiet, unexpressed desires which yet fill a soul and lend it shape and form? How charmingly the picture flattered the eye and memory when the blond woman sent the dark-haired child of the sailor high above her head to then jubilantly catch it again in her protective arms. How the crew grinned — yes, even the earnest Captain on the bridge twisted his lips cheerfully when the second helmsman was used to knot together again the unfastened little clothes on the foundling's back. And could you not consider it a promise for the future when you saw the sailor Brodersen performing his hard ship work with a sort of dogged joy? All that should have happened only by chance? A downy feather which just chased the sun and yet was caught by the greedy fingers of the depths?

"Pity", the north wind groaned, and turned over the last page of the story of the 'Heron'.

The blast of wind which then occurred howled and and roared like a terribly shattering cry of fear over the sea. The sky drew together like an adamantly threatening brow behind which no thought of grace resided. In the middle of the day, the night climbed up from the fury-twisted surface. A frenzy arose. The wrong thing began to prevail, and raged in mad triumph against order and reason. The sea turned into a bellowing fastness, it could not restrain its violent black walls anymore, but sent them in swelling rows against the offender. From all sides, the roaring white balls flew and buried themselves in the wooden parapet.

"We will pray", Marie Hennings stammered, and stretched her hand out seeking protection to Richard Sell as he swayed past.

She wanted just then to climb the steps to the command bridge where the Captain, enveloped by spraying shrouds, sought in unnatural calm to protect what had been entrusted to him. His hard voice rang out through the raging.

"Sell, the foresail down!" But the north wind tore up and swallowed the weak words.

"I would like to go to my husband", Marie asked once more.

Then something tore in the soul of the young man. Wildly, hungrily, he clasped the arm of the woman, and for a moment their pulses smashed together dying and yet willed to life.

And then the absurd thing happened. The firm arc of the universe shifted, that which had been floor until then turned to vaporous heads of clouds, and the black abyss sucked and devoured and choked down into itself the crunching work of men.

And then the egg watch fell into the water, and time stood still.

2

"Well, how goes it?" Captain Kohlrausch asked kindly and tapped his guest, who was sitting on an upturned basket, benevolently on his hunched back. "It is quite right, young gentleman, that you let the sun shine through your ribs. The natural warmth is the best medicine. Bob Swanegel says I should also run around naked on deck for an hour early in the morning. Because of gout. But from shamefacedness, it is for me too silly and too disrespectful. You see, a captain without trousers cannot appear with the right impression. And in an educated harbour as well! Is that not so? — Am I not right?"

Sulphurous green and emerald-coloured, the towers and roofs of the ancient churches of Amsterdam were shining in the morning light. A clamorous noise of rattling chains, hissing steam cranes, shrill ship's whistles, barking dogs, and the coarse voices of men flooded over the narrow, dirty quay, and the rumbling and rattling of wagons travelling up and down deafened any clear understanding. But the master of the 'Green Herring' found himself in the fortunate position of not being affected by those disturbances of the outside world because of his stopped ears. Broad-legged, his fists sunk in his enormous, grease-stained pockets, he stood on the wet, scales-covered deck, and in his bloated face a double satisfaction was reflected. Firstly it made you chuffed and caused a soothing and pleasantly tickling feeling when you could let the Dutch gold pieces and bank notes, which you were just receiving for a part of the catch, run through your fat fingers so prettily. And then — you also enjoyed to some extent a feeling of importance, when you returned straight from the harbour office where you had reported the rescue of two human lives. Truly no fun! In particular, when the one bundle pulled up out of the sea turned out to be a learned helmsman who could even speak a little English. On the other hand, it signified nothing that the pale young man had exhibited a strangely bent posture since the day he could crawl around the deck again, and frequently complained with lips twisted in agony of a drilling pain in his back.

"Eh, there will be an ointment for that," Captain Julius Kohlrausch consoled him with conviction, as he endeavoured to stroke the rescued man as imperceptibly as possible on the shoulder. "You must in fact know, Mr Sell," he continued somewhat more sparingly, "I have ordered the harbour doctor over here. No, no, not merely because of you," he parried in a startled way when a strangely pathetic look skimmed him from the brown eyes of his guest, "the entire crew must be examined. Bob Swanegel and myself too. For they are talking themselves here into believing in an infectious disease. And it is also quite good if you go every few years under the fingers of such an ointment steed. Why not? The man will have his bread too. And then," he added as the strongest cause for persuasion, and raised his forefinger smartly to his nose, "you need to also go, my dear Sell, to the Consulate, because of the compensation. The people will snoop about you otherwise, into all possible things, and will perhaps be immodest. No, no, it is quite good if you and the tot head on straightaway with something in writing."

When the mention of the little child occurred, Richard Sell pulled himself together from his slouched position, and as it had already often done, his gaze strayed also now, astonished and questioning, over the single living being which tied him with his past and with the fate of the 'White Heron'. Barely a few steps distance from him, next to the open cavity from which the blue and green scaled beings were shoveled out unremittingly, the little creature crouched on the moist planks and was sunk deep in a stimulating spectacle. The observer shook his head. What was the strange sprog, the orphan left behind by the sailor Brodersen, doing there actually? Look at once, the child had lain together like little bricks a number of herring that had slid away, and gradually under the tiny hands something like a star had arisen. It sparkled silvery in the sun, and whenever a new fish flew into the figure, the assiduous creature clapped her hands and let out a bright cheer. Her brown locks fluttered at the same time about her head in the purring wind, and her dark cheeks became more coloured.

"Come here, girl," Bob Swanegel said, walking past right then, and at the same time, the ship's boy set the girl patronisingly on his knee, "I must wipe your nose once again. Two indecent candles are always running out of them. I washed her today too", he added after finishing the work, while he lowered his red sackcloth into his pocket again unperturbed. "She has eaten plum jam, and then she always looks revolting."

"Bob", the girl cried, and held her nose wailing, for the boy had in his attempt at cleaning gone to work just as thoroughly as he was accustomed to do with scrubbing the deck.

"Yes, she knows my name too", Bob Swanegel confirmed with approval. "But, Captain, what will become of her now?"

"Yes, what do you think?", Julius Kohlrausch responded with concern and looked in astonishment from one to the other.

Then the ship's boy moved his hand as if he wanted to push off any responsibility for the lack of comprehension of his boss before contemporaries and posterity.

"Well, she must go with Mr Sell to the Consulate", he continued full of saddened wisdom, and shrugged his shoulders several times damningly.

"Can she go there perhaps in the shawl? And in your shirt, Captain? And I also want back my socks which she is wearing."

These reasons stirred up the soul of the master of the 'Green Herring' violently. Bob Swanegel had once again revealed unimagined expanses of life. And swaying between the admiration for his first advisor and the dawning realisation that the young German lady could in fact not undertake the visit in her half wild state, Julius Kohlrausch grasped in his pocket, loathly shoved a bank note away and drew out instead two large silver pieces.

"Here," he handed his gift to the surprised helmsman, whereby he turned away a little, for he was not accustomed to sharing out alms to the simply ashamed, "over there, my dear Mr Sell, is an old Jewish jumble shop. See, there on the corner. There you can get something cheap. No, no, let it be please," he fended off, when his guest made a movement as if the coins were beginning to burn him between his fingers, "you can return it to me later sometime. You are still young, and anything possible can become of you. And Bob Swanegel can accompany you to the dealer," he concluded definitely, "for you will surely have noticed yourself, the boy has a great understanding for everything, and you have to be astonished over his intellect. If you have Bob Swanegel with you, then nothing can happen to you."

An hour later, the Dutch doctor climbed on board. He was a fat, rotund figure in a camel-coloured hunting jacket, and about his neck fluttered in addition a short grey woollen scarf. The man looked like an asthmatic buffalo. Wheezing, he rolled across the deck, and when the Captain wanted to lead him down to his own berth so that he could first have a close look at both shipwrecked persons there, the Dutchman reluctantly waved his little black stethoscope, which he never let out of his hand, and groaned in the worst German, "Below stinks — rotten air. Man healthy only in open air — up here."

"Good then", the master of the 'Green Herring' agreed, after Bob Swanegel had made the doctor's opinion comprehensible to him. "Anyone who has a clean leather need not be embarrassed. And it will be nice for me," he whispered furtively to the woollen ball, "if you tried to give the helmsman a pep talk. The young rascal sits far too depressed."

"Looks bad", Doctor van der Bloos gurgled with a look at his impassively waiting patients, and he held his stethoscope to the sunlight to see if it had not also gotten dusty. "Tuberculosis — bad years. Main thing — quick, quick — no time."

The examination was conducted between a mountain of ship's ropes and the angled cabin wall. The sun shone brightly over the exposed youthful body, but the ill man nevertheless trembled in the wind. He was freezing. A breath-robbing feeling of fear was clenching his chest. It seemed to him as if every hammer blow which the woollen man made against his skin tore a rift in the glazed little temple which he had built in there from loud hopes for the future. He heard a fine painful rattling, and it cut across his back as if he were being wounded there by a pointed shard. He instinctively shivered.

"It often tortures me between the shoulders", he began stammering, as his eyes began pleading for mildness and mercy.

"Yes, yes", the doctor said.

"But it will get better again," Richard Sell urged, "won't it?"

"Yes, yes", the Dutchman murmured, whereby he placed his awkward head on the other man's chest.

After this exhausting consultation, he folded up his stethoscope, passed his fleshy hand without further ado onto the neck of the little girl, who was occupied right then with plucking a few flecks of wool from the stranger's trousers, then he tore the screaming girl's eyes open and passed his judgement again with the very indifferent syllables, "Yes, yes."

Hereupon, Doctor van der Bloos pulled up his sleeves, asked for ink and paper, and stumbled with Captain Kohlrausch down the cabin steps. Richard Sell stared after him. The feeling was constricting him forcibly that that man had just taken all the sunbeams away from his head and had drawn an impenetrable cap of haze over his eyes instead. For the first time in his life, complete darkness reigned about the lonely man, and no inner voice wanted to inform him to where he would now have to turn.

He was still standing dully and shivering, a stranger being in a strange world which was peopled for him with utterly isolated people, when he was called back to life by a light blow. Then he started and came to his senses. Praise God, someone wished something from him. And although none other than Bob Swanegel had reminded him of his presence, a stream of thankfulness shot towards the precocious fellow. Self-confident, cheeky as ever, the little fellow stood next to him, casually pressed a brown cap on his ear, and declared himself ready to start on the walk to the junk dealer. But first the doctor had to know 'her' name.

By 'her', the boy always meant the unwelcome female monster. The helmsman unhesitatingly stated that the child was named Brodersen. Only, Bob lifted his stub nose and shook his broad head discontentedly.

"That we knew," he assured disparagingly, "she must have a first name though."

Now Richard Sell hesitated. What was it? As hard as he tried, as earnestly as he also pondered and deliberated, no, he was incapable of recalling the first name of the child. It was lost like everything else, like everything which lived on the 'Heron'. Again the drilling sensation of being the outcast for whom all the ties to the past had been torn befell him. And with a hefty, flighty movement, he turned to the girl in the grey cloth and attempted abruptly to have a conversation with her. He sat on the upturned basket, and as he took the child between his knees so that she could not escape him, he tried to stroke his charge over her brown locks. Only, in the middle of the attempt, he paused, shocked by the unaccustomedness of the caress and repelled by the laughing gleam of the dark eyes of the child. And then something else. Quite abruptly, who the mother of the child had been stabbed through his mind, and that the lost person found herself at the moment behind iron bars. And more harshly than he intended, it burst out of him, "What is your name?"

The child gazed at him and nodded. Then it smiled a little in embarrassment.

"What is your name?", the seated man repeated again more insistently, and pressed his knees somewhat more strongly together.

But the girl did not seem to know what was desired from her, she twisted her mouth fearfully and shook her head.

"Bob", she stuttered finally, rejoicing to have at least found something.

The ship's boy, however, who had curiously attended this procedure, moved his hulking head slowly, and showed himself to be neither flattered nor astonished.

"No, girl," he suggested decisively, "that is all by the by. You can wear my socks, but my name I prefer to keep for myself alone."

And then he pointed to a tugboat gliding past which bore through the world on the front of its bow on a blue background a neatly stenciled name. Peering, Richard Sell followed the outstretched arm of the boy.

"Kathrin?", he read with a doubting lack of decisiveness. And suddenly he rose and said definitely, "For my sake, it all the same. Go down, Bob, and report there that she is called Kathrin — Kathrin Brodersen."

And thus the thing Richard Sell had rescued received a name.

Kathrin received something else from her tall companion in suffering — her clothes, her nation, her adornment. The child strode along colourfully like a strange, well-nourished parrot when she now wandered on the hand of the pale helmsman through the gabled, acutely angled lanes of the harbour city. A billowing lavender woollen dress after the crude taste of Dutch coastal residents surrounded her little body. Over it, Bob Swanegel had hung on her a long, red and white striped bibbed apron, and to complete the outfit in the finest way, a pompom hat made of the same lavender woollen cloth had been put on her head by Richard Sell as well. Broad ear flaps fell down to below the neck of the little one, and her feet were stuck into ponderous wooden clogs on which she now floated across the cobbles as if on ancient galleons. And the first attempts at walking in the strange shoes were forged with such difficulty that the tiny thing frequently remained standing, following the innate addiction to finery of her gender, to pluck from time to time delightedly at the thick puffy sleeves which fell misshapenly from her apron.

"Beautiful," Kathrin then uttered contentedly, and twinkled up to her companion, demanding admiration, "beautiful!"

And strangely, again and again the expression of her delight tore the deeply brooding man up from his thoughts. Right, right, that which moved him so, which struck his innermost being so irresistibly, consisted of the memory of the first word which he had once heard from a pale, blond woman. Had the address of Marie

Hennings not sounded similar? The wanderer shivered, and in the midst of the hustle and bustle of the street, the sorrow of a sudden abandonment overcame him anew. He confessed indeed that he had anyway made the honest decision to part from the lovely picture after a short time. For it was indecent and dishonourable to latch on to something, even if only in thought, which formed the purpose in life and the happiness of a stranger. But it was yet so pleasant, so elevating to imagine that there was a being in your hometown who spun friendly wishes for the distant one because she was just as convinced of the strength and industriousness of the other as he himself.

And now alone again. Dear God, he knew that state, he had always put up with it and had to also accustom himself to it again now. Admittedly, a marked difference lay between his old plans and the afflicted present. Now he was burdened with memory, and then — yes, the devil, the uncomfortable pain in his back. This stabbing burning and wheezing in his chest! Whether perhaps something could yet hinder him from rising out of the darkness of his current state?

The contemplative man shook himself and looked around.

"Tired", Kathrin complained, having been torn through the bustle of the streets with him during his soliloquy. "Tired." The little child stood there and pointed with her hand at the wooden shoes by which her tender feet were probably being rubbed sore.

"I see", Richard Sell murmured, and at the same time he reminded himself that these little creatures possessed a certain claim to mercy and care, yes, that they ultimately lapsed into helplessness without care and attention. "Then it's no use", he sighed, and with that he took Kathrin up on his arm and began carrying the lavender-coloured woollen bundle.

Appeased, the child slung her arms about his neck and gazed over his shoulders with dark eyes at the strange bustle of the big city. In her disposition, not the slightest suspicion stirred of how her guardian began wheezing under her burden, and how the suffering man had to wipe the round beads of sweat from his forehead several times.

"Sit still", Richard Sell ordered finally impatiently, and a confident hope whispered to him that he must soon be freed of this unnecessary torment. Oh, quite steadily, the maritime authorities or the consulate would already be worrying about the little castaway. And in his mind's eye he saw his companion already vanishing into one of those benevolent institutions which the state had built so abundantly for such cases. He imagined it without pain or remorse.

But strangely — just as the helmsman was wavering up the steps of the German Consulate with failing strength, Kathrin, quivering back before the blackness of the dark hall, slung her arms tighter around his neck, and in the ear of the concerned man, a word penetrated from the child's mouth which merged disturbingly and in a novel way into his intentions.

"Uncle", Kathrin whimpered quietly and stroked his cheek.

"Lord", the mariner stammered in shock and quickly let the child glide down to the ground. But carefully, so that he inflicted no harm.

***

The evening sky stretched blue and rosy about the confusion of masts and funnels in the harbour. The quarter disc of the moon hung down unreal and transparent like a delicate cloud in the distant ether, and the fine smoke of sleeping machines curled, in reddish breaths, into the resting windless universe. The swallows shot, laden with stalks, back to their nests, and across the surface of the oily gleaming canal, the head of a smacking fish scurried now and then. Evening calm reigned, and only from the deck of the 'Green Herring' did the drawing music of an accordion sound. Up there, Bob Swanegel sat with dangling feet on the roof of the Captain's cabin and enticed from his instrument that ballad which he knew spoke most of all to the practical disposition of his boss, "Ladewig has the Largest Purse."

"Listen, woman", he uttered at the same time to Kathrin, who huddled raptly at his side, and he pulled his case apart with all his strength. "If I now let in a lot of air, then the notes begin — do you hear? — and then Kohlrausch always receives a pain in his toe,"he added delightedly, "pay attention".

And rightly, from the cabin a pained voice roared out, "Peace — in three devils' names — who then could endure that?"

"Do you see?" Bob Swanegel said, "I know him."

In the cabin, meanwhile, his master was undergoing a time of suffering. The good Captain prided himself not a little on his fate of drawing a few pretty groschen from the pockets of rough dealers in a both clever and yet very relaxed way, but how you were to teach a suffering man that he belongs according to the sentence of the doctor in a hospital, and in addition must never again take up his former difficult profession, that was something Julius Kohlrausch did not of course know. And hence he rubbed embarrassedly back and forth on the much too narrow bench, blinked with reddened countenance into the light of the little hanging lantern over his head, and as he puffed up his cheeks from time to time, he attempted first of all to lead his young guest on all sorts of detours and wrong ways, just to prolong the difficult revelation for a short period yet.

"Yes," he boomed, and struck the table with his fist, "the girl here. I do not like her. But she is a difficult and unbreakable sort. When you take hold of her, she withstands it. She is much attached to you, meanwhile nevertheless — —".

Only, the arts of the master of the 'Green Herring' did not catch. The helmsman looked his host far too earnestly in the eye, and it was not easy to escape the young man when he inquired so urgently and ingenuously, "What did the doctor say?"

"Yes, what did he say?", the herring catcher cried desperately, and rubbed his forehead with both fists as if something special must spring from there. "Do you know what, my dear Mr Sell?", he finally unburdened himself violently. "He suggested you should recuperate for a bit."

The other man nodded ponderously. "Well, and then?", he continued the conversation unswervingly.

"Then?" — Thunderbolts, it was really demanding a little too much. How could you throw right in the face of such a young fellow that something like: 'You are finished. You are no good for anything anymore.' That was absolutely sacrilegious. No, that you must begin more delicately. — "Yes, and then," the fat Captain turned to and fro, "then you should just walk a lot."

Now Richard Sell raised his dark eyes, and it seemed to his opposite that in them a directly uncanny understanding for his mournful position was painted.

"I should walk on land?", the young man murmured, sinking down, and propped his head on his hand, "thus on land?"

"Yes," the boss of the 'Green Herring' concurred contritely, "where else, my boy? On the waves, only our Lord and Saviour managed it. Apart from that," he sought good-naturedly to console him, and scratched the tangle of his grey locks, "it is all the same where a steady fellow runs about."

Richard Sell fell silent. It was one of those pauses in which raging and embittered thoughts push bloodily onto the sharp points of life. Then the helmsman nodded a few times, and what he brought forth sounded completely distracted and distant.

"Good — then good." With a slow movement, he buttoned up his blue jacket to finally produce two bank notes. "Here, Captain," he began, and a residual of his earlier definiteness was thrust forth by his voice, "they gave me a hundred guilders at the Consulate, Dutch currency. Half belongs to you for the journey and upkeep. For me and Kathrin Brodersen. No, let it be," he parried when he noticed how his host squinted at the notes covetously and yet ashamed, "I know, you are owed more. But the other half, I must keep so that I can start on something in my home town."

"Yes, of course", the herring catcher agreed as he pushed the green notes back and forth indecisively. "But nevertheless — —". Slowly and obliviously, he dropped the green paper in his pocket, and again shook his enormous Neptune's head uncomprehendingly. "Do you want to haul the tot about now for even longer?", he asked, shrugging his shoulders, "or do you not want to drop it off at the Consulate?"

Just as this was spoken, Kathrin cheered loudly on the roof of the cabin and clapped her hands. A shrill discordant note from the accordion indicated that the little one must have taken possession of the instrument with or against the will of Bob Swanegel.

"Oops," she cried delightedly, "oops!"

But below her guardian raised his head and listened for a while bleakly to the outbreak of joy from this little human who clasped so tenaciously to him. Strange, it remained just like in the watery wastes when the swimmer had wrestled for their bare life, she was just there and did not abandon him.

"Yes," Richard Sell finally said to himself, "they wanted to stick her in the asylum of the poorhouse."

"Good," the Captain interrupted very jauntily, "excellent."

But the Helmsman rose up. "No," he corrected, "that I did not like. I had considered it. Why should one not take the thing home too? I want to take her to where she belongs. And there we will part."

"Eh yes", Julius Kohlrausch suggested, and stretched his legs out noisily. "This is noble and decent. But take care, my dear man, it becomes expensive, I know that."

And then he yawned, let his head sink down on an angle, and closed his eyes as a sign that the most difficult business of the day had now been concluded.

***

The ship was sleeping. The deck had long lain lonesome and abandoned, and only the silver spiders who were born from the light of the moon and stars crept across the slippery planks and clambered scurrying up the black ropes and masts. Up there they rocked, and appeared next to the late wanderer who singly and alone thrust his dark shadowy figure into their sparkling play. Lost in thought, he strode back and forth, sometimes raised his pale countenance up to the calm night sky, and then leant again on the side rail to examine attentively the lit windows of the harbour businesses. Over there it was getting lively. And when the wild music came from one of the open doors especially intrusively, then the man on the 'Green Herring' became more restless than before and threw his body further forward as if he intended grasping for the mad sounds.

Truly, it was about a difficult and unequal struggle which the ill man was now fighting with wild, dying strength against himself and against everything he had previously wished and striven for. It was the fight against his youth and against all the good spirits which he had offered up until now for its protection. A derisive fury of destruction thrust in over the man who had been thrown off his path. The desolate voice screamed more and more hoarsely and provocatively in his inner being,

"Why are you setting up laws for the future? Has something in the future waved to you? No, you are broken and defeated. And soon they will inter you. To what end are you thus saving the few miserable groschen which have been pressed into your hand? Why do you conserve your strength which is already on the decline? Who is benefiting from your most honest and faithful intentions? Nobody. Whether an insignificant and unfamiliar man sinks reconciled with himself into the rotting grave, or whether he tumbles in intoxicated by lust and greed, what does it matter? The weeds and the thorns will not grow an inch less rampantly over you. And does the paid pastor perhaps know whom he blesses under the hedgerow of anonymity? Ridiculous, do not deceive yourself about the latter. You are played out. You owe nobody an account, nobody — nobody — — and now at least bring it to an end both happily and gruesomely."

Thus the voice nettled and bored, and that which it sought he confirmed to it. He looked confusedly about in a whirl, and the green and silver spiders drawing their shimmering threads over the deck and masts clambered up to him and stabbed at his large, horrified eyes.

"It is true," he murmured again, and at the same time, he was already creeping across the gangway to the illuminated windows of the wooden houses, "they shall not say I departed as an idiot and coward! No, that they shall not. What striving? What decency? That is all dust once you are lying down below, and rational men laugh about such things. I want to be clever."

He was already hewing his fist against one of the brown doors, and as a rusted bell sounded above him, he began singing loudly and cuttingly. But it sounded as if a heart were breaking.

***

Out of the tobacco haze, as the door or a window is torn open, a small black wooden figure emerges now and again high on the smoke darkened wall. It is the patron saint who lends his name to the tavern, "Jean Bart with the clay pipe." A glass is often swung towards him, the drops frequently richly spray his misshapen feathered hat, and the liquid trickling down collects as a puddle in his outstretched open top boots. For the patron saint must never be cleaned, that his dignity will not tolerate.

Behind the counter with the red, green, and blue bottles, a fat, clattering organ seethes, "Hey there — my lady — don't you hear? — A glass of the sweet stuff again for the gentleman from Germany!"

"A jug, my sir," a just as dripping hoarse voice answers from behind the colourful bottles, "the Germans are a noble folk. I bet the gentleman will take a jug."

"Spumante", Dortje whispers lovingly in the ear of her pale neighbour and slings her white full arm familiarly about his neck. "Quiet, Jean, the German is a fine man, a great captain. I tell you, he will foot the entire bill."

"Dortje, Dortje, will you surely rid him of the corpse-like colouring?"

"Eh what, I am fond of him. He is a prince. Has he perhaps prodded and pushed me just once like you do, you insolent man?"

"Yes, he is a mummy's boy. When it comes to paying, then the Germans are not to be seen anymore."

"My lady, what am I saying?"

"How can I know what you are saying, you idiot?"

"I said I bet the German prince will pay for the entire store. I have seen his wallet, it is chocker."

"Dortje, come, my treasure, I am a Frenchman and know better than such German hicks what is suitable for a delicate woman. Do you hear, I will blow you a serenade on my pocket comb:

> Va t'en — va t'en — va t'en — jusque lá,
> Caligula — Caligula — Caligula!

"Bravo, bravo! Dortje, give the black-haired tenor a kiss, he deserves it."

"No, I don't want to. Don't you see how my pale prince is making an air to gift me ten guilders? He knows what is owed to his faithful girl."

"Jean Bart, how would it be with a few bottles of sparkling? We want to propose a toast to the health of the couple."

"My sir, do you hear? This is becoming a blessed evening."

"I hear, my lady. But the thing goes over my head. I would like to know whether Dortje's prince backs me up?"

"What does that mean? You are insulting my handsome captain. Look, I am drawing the golden purse from his pocket. Oh, oh — paper guilders! Will you still doubt in his noblesse?"

"Landlord — landlord!"

"My sir, the German prince is asking for you. I bet he wants to pay."

"No, no, landlord, that is a mistake. I did not invite this company. No way! I am alone — entirely alone."

"Aha, there you have it, Dortje! These Germans are always the filthiest cheapskates. They won't begrudge anyone the black under their nails."

"And you want to be a captain, you seven weeks buried corpse? You betray a poor trusting girl about your rightful earnings? Ugh, that I must not suffer!"

"Smash his head to a pulp!"

"In the air with the mangy dog!"

"Calm, my gentlemen, unclean elements have crept in here. But Jean Bart with the clay pipe holds onto his reputation. Dortje, stop with the face scratching. And you, my sir, throw the German fellow out!"

"Bravo, bravo, long live Jean Bart! Vive la France! God save old England! — Ha, how the rascal flies onto the cobblestones!"

> Va t'en — va t'en — va t'en — jusque lá,
> Caligula — Caligula — Caligula!

***

On the gangway which bound the 'Green Herring' with the wall of the quay, the man crawling back stopped for a moment. Down there in the narrow gap, a lost moonbeam sparkled as if a burning snake were hissing through the sluggish water. And startled by that, a both loathsome and yet also enticing idea crept through the wine and shame numbed brain of the tired, mocked, and humiliated man. What if he now slid down into the black cleft? It could happen so easily. Nobody would notice, and only the fiery eel which shot back and forth in the gap would then perhaps stir its limbs for a second somewhat quicker and more lithely. But then the stupid, absurd hopes foundered forever, the hopes which also tied the miserable cripple to that above, to shimmering castles in the air for which the entrance was never found. Ugh, the devil, did not the scythe constantly thrum which cut up these ridiculous threads all over the world? And did not the busy brain nevertheless always spin such unnecessary webs out of itself anew? When would the clattering loom finally stand still? Really, now was the suitable moment. Right now, when the misery was burrowing into him, when he had realised that even disgrace and vices could not completely swamp the soul of a striving man. Should he not place himself now on the plank to dive down quietly and decisively?

But as he pondered, his fingers clasped in his pocket the salvaged notes, and the old pattern shot over the reviled loom. What he held firmly there, greedily and insolubly, as if if were the lifeline which was tossed to him in the gap, was money. Such a thing could increase itself. And the stronger you multiplied it, the more powerful the might it signified. Such a note was like an oyster. It remained shut for a long time, nobody guessed that life worked in it, but suddenly it opened up and released millions of like-natured seeds. No, that was no play. In that was the most beautiful and wildest and most tantalising thing in his existence. It was so stirring to wait on the miracle of the tenfold increase in its powers. Perhaps the oyster stood on the point of bursting its shell, and with that power health and satisfaction also certainly streamed out from it. For this was all fundamentally the same. No, that tantalising waiting and hoping for the expected moment must not be interrupted. In this fearful waiting, you actually possessed all of life. The entire rich, colourful existence.

And Richard Sell decisively folded the banknote up cleanly in his pocket, mastered the burning wheezing in his chest, and toddled quietly and inaudibly down to his berth. From the darkness of the narrow space fell the regular breaths of the sleeping children. Here by the one long wall lay Kathrin as well as the ship's boy, Bob Swanegel, stowed one above the other on their beds, and only gradually did the arrival distinguish on the lower berth the round countenance of the little castaway. She had bedded her head with its curls on her rounded fleshy arm, and the peaceful creature was smiling in dream.

"Who knows," Richard Sell thought, as he sat down on the bed opposite, "who knows — the dumb thing also imagines in the end something which she does not possess. And just that pleases her, and it offers her a comfortable feeling. No, I will not give up, I will start again from the beginning. Nobody in whom it sits can ever let go of it. And disgrace and vices and sickness, they do not banish the urge, that I have seen now. You must act like the oyster — yes, yes, like the oyster!"

3

Ott Knuth — the eighty year old who in the night, to drive away time, sang so prettily and persistently to himself, whereas during the day he made almost no movement other than swatting at the flies which swarmed about his bald, trembling skull — was sitting on the cracked steps of his smokehouse and warming himself in the sunshine. He constantly crouched thus by himself, and only sometimes did he turn his trickling look to the beehive shaped ruins in whose dark cavity he had for thirty and more years hung fish for smoking. Now they had stood empty since time immemorial, for Ott Knuth received an old age pension and performed no further work than to wonder over why he was still to be found every morning on the shattered steps as the oldest resident in the village at the mouth of the river, Uhlenhus. But today the smoke-blackened dungeon echoed with such a strange jubilation that the former owner of the den had to turn his ear disturbed towards the unaccustomed sound again and again. There inside, Kathrin sat in her lavender coloured woolen dress on the sooty brick floor and emitted the highest tones of delight when the raven Hans hopped from one of her balled fists to the other. And the bird repeated these gymnastics with the regularity of a swinging pendulum.

"Look, uncle," the blessed little being often sought the attention of her guardian Richard Sell as he leant on the doorpost, "leaps — fine."

And the returnee then nodded distractedly, and his calculating eyes began counting anew the iron cross bars on whose hooks the fin-bearers had previously hung.

"Yes," Ott Knuth finally chewed, a strange dizziness having been induced for him by the eternal here and there of the raven, "now you have already been here five days," — he began counting on his bony fingers — "no, six — or five though — one does not matter for me, that you don't have to think, Richard. But how goes it for you today?"

"Better, thank you."

"Hm." The smoker swatted weakly at one of the flies taking a walk about on his skull. "Beast! — Yes, what I wanted to say," he began anew, as the giggling in the beehive found no end, "today you want to go with her thus to the orphans' councillor, Tredup?"

"Shortly," the helmsman responded; he coughed a little and at the same time undertook an in-depth inspection of the protruding fireplace. "What sort of man is the orphans' councillor?"

"Eh" — Ott Knuth led his finger to his mouth and sought to remember. Then he seemed to have found something striking which fell especially from his crumbled memory. "Looks black, like a tar barrel. As if every day were a burial for him. But otherwise he is amiable. Full of wit. And what I do at night, he does in the day."

"What is that?"

"He sings!", the old man burst out, affronted because the youth could overlook something so important. "Tredup sings."

It remained still for a while between the men by the beehive. Only the raven fluttered suddenly to Kathrin's head and began plucking at her lavender woolen cap.

"Give," it cried, "give!"

"Oh, uncle, listen", sailor Brodersen's daughter enthused.

A yacht was gliding under auburn sail along the narrow river, and a breeze passing around the corner forced a renewed wheezing from Richard Sell. He sought bravely to hide it, only, his host seemed to understand the struggling movement.

"Will you not lie in bed with the sawbones in town?", the old man inquired tensely, and in his insentient eyes, which just floated like blue jelly, a bleak darkness told that he would in no way regret the departure of his companion. The old man did not seek any permanent company and yet could not do without it. Meanwhile, the helmsman had tested the firmness of the red brick floor with his foot. Now he spurned drily what the old man uttered in concern for him.

"No," he spoke impassively and decisively, "nature will also help."

Then Ott Knuth nodded animatedly with his bald head so that the wrinkles on his neck swelled heavier over his woollen scarf and the grey strands of hair fell playfully on his temples.

"You're right," he gurgled excitedly, for nature was his goddess too, to whose clemency he felt obliged in a mysterious way, "nature is better than the sawbones. Just," — he tapped his chest meaningfully — "the damned coughing, and the uncertain years in the twenties." Snagged by an idea, he stretched his gaunt arm out and drew his guest close to himself. "I have a pot with dog fat," he whispered in his ear, "and I have an insight, too. Be quite still, Richard, we will try it with the full moon. But first now, go to the orphans' councillor, Tredup, so that you rid the unnecessary mouth from our necks."

"Good," Richard Sell said, as he twisted his mouth a little, "we are going."

So he took a step into the beehive and lifted the child up. But here he lingered once more, and as he directed his look with special tenacity at the rotten walls, he suddenly expressed that very thing which would grant his life calm and a foothold from now on.

"I want to make a suggestion to you, Mr Knuth. I would like to buy this smokehouse from you. What shall it cost?"

Only, the old man did not understand him. He raised an ear tilted to the sun and looked in wordless astonishment at the dilapidated rubbish which had previously provided him with his sustenance. And only when his pale companion repeated that suggestion once more in all seriousness did the old man stop his wavering and burst out almost fearfully over the hare-brained intentions of the other man, "But it not worth anything."

"That I think too", Richard Sell agreed emphatically. "It is only human power which makes any value from anything. Do you understand me, Mr Knuth?"

"No, Richard."

"I offer you then forty talers", the other man continued thoughtfully, whereby he strode with the little girl once more around the walls. "I haven't indeed raised them yet, but I will make an effort."

"And then you will stay here in the smoke?", the old man choked out admonishingly from his toothless mouth, for the strangeness of this remarkable decision robbed him of free breath, "a young learned fellow like you wants to sit here for fifty years like me?"

"Quite right," the man being questioned affirmed, and his voice echoed off the vaulted ceiling, "I have considered it well. I consider everything in-depth anyway. Even the smoke will do me good. It will eat away what is bad and harmful. And then — it also remains all the same where we employ our hands so long as the basic idea agrees. And it finds itself in order." He stood now with his bent forward pose right before the smoker, and offered his right hand towards the seated man over the head of the little girl. "And you can stay with me as well, Mr Knuth", he concluded, completely at one with himself. "Will you?"

But the old man emitted a grumbling laugh like someone who feels sympathy with a complete fool.

"If you are so stupid," he decided finally, "why not? But I see it well, the learned people always grasp the bad nuts."

"Shake hands, Mr Knuth?"

The old man rose wearily and shook. It remained inconclusive as to whether it was from cold or from inner laughter.

"Eh well," he grinned, "if you are fixed on it, I want to leave you to your fortune. But, Richard Sell," he added critically, "you must not tell anyone either how much I have cheated you. — Look, that would be uncalled-for to me."

***

"Come in", Mr Tredup called, for there was a knock on the white-painted door of his office, and at the same time, the tiny little man hastily slipped his arms into a long, black frock coat which hung down almost to his feet. Until now the orphans' councillor had been occupied with destroying an enormous plate full of dark-red garden strawberries as he constantly dipped one after another into a tin of castor sugar to then lead it to his narrow, pursed lips. When perforce a pause of satiation or fetching breath occurred, you could then assume that the black-clothed man used the interruption for the piping of some jolly student song, "Beautiful Minka, I must leave" or "You are almost thirty years old". And it had no effect on the calm contentedness of Mr Tredup that his being sounded as if a learned parrot were purring melancholically and without rhythm through his nostrils.

"In the black whale to Askalon ..."

There was a knock.

"Come in", the orphans' councillor called with a start, pushing his strawberries hurriedly under a protrusion of the old yellow roll-top desk, and only after he had convinced himself whether his long black cravat wafting down was appropriately complementing the sorrow which flowed about his entire figure did he rise and shuffle towards the entering visitor.

"Ah," he twanged, and whistled a little when he perceived the little lavender woollen bundle who clasped with both fists to the doorpost in a sombre foreboding, "what a beautiful, little girl. I have something for you. Yes, really, I have something", he assured once more and fetched from his trouser pocket a bag of fruit lollies, of which he as a former confectioner possessed a sumptuous supply for such occasions. "I will stick one in your mouth", he continued, and stretched his hand towards his whimpering guest in vain. "Now, you are a very lively child. What is your name?"

"Kathrin", the arrival cried, now pressing the backs of both hands against her eyes as if she could thereby be protected from the sight of the giant black fly.

Mr Tredup stuck the lolly in his own mouth instead, and considered that a Kathrin Brodersen had already been registered with him. He had already procured her papers, and everything was in order as far as the single small circumstance — hm —

Now Richard Sell cleared his throat, for in this white painted room and surrounded by the cool, sober birch-wood furniture, the tormenting feeling crept up on him incessantly that he could be required to negotiate over a living merchandise. For the first time since he had been carrying the under-age being through the world, it occurred to him how terrible it would be to determine the fate of another creature so unquestioningly. With pounding heart, he confessed to himself that he would be ready to chase this tiny child out of the sunshine so that he could hide it forever in a dark chamber. For such a public provision did not boil down to anything else. And why did he accommodate himself to all that? From no other cause than that he himself did not possess the necessary means for the maintenance of a boarder, and because he thought it more comfortable to impose the care for his companion in suffering on other shoulders.

Certainly, it was in keeping with the law, and all others were treated similarly. But the devil, as he now pushed the crying child forcibly towards the large black fly who skipped around with thin legs about the fearful child, he could not banish the shameful thought that he was disposing of something living which followed him with large, loving eyes because it had gotten used to him. Whether he would attempt the same with his raven as well?

Never.

Ugh, people acted treacherously towards each other. They had issued from the same creator's hands, but they attacked each other mutually and battered each other contemptuously like earthenware.

"She will hopefully have it well in your orphanage, St Spiritus?", the ill helmsman inquired to drown out the voice of his own conscience. "I can count on that, Orphans' Councillor?"

"Tredup", the other man introduced himself, and pulled his frock coat open delightedly. "What do you think, they have it very good, the dear little ones. Hot meals twice weekly, and every two years new winter and summer clothes. In addition, they visit their relatives once every month."

The fly whirled to the birchwood desk, threw a desiring look to the hidden strawberries and rummaged in a heap of yellow sheets of paper.

"The little Miss possesses a mother," Mr Tredup established there, and passed his hand over his mouth as if he were wiping away something unwelcome, "hm — we won't speak over that. Does she have other relatives? I must make a note of it."

"Yes," the man asked definitely, and encouragingly stroked the head of Kathrin, who was now clasping one of his legs for a change, "in Stralsund lives the mother of Mrs Brodersen. A laundress. But since she received my letter," the young man added a little ashamedly, "she has vanished from the town."

"Aha — vanished", the orphans' councillor whistled, and shoved his protruding pointed nose snuffling in the air as if he were already scenting the distant connection. "We know — yes, yes, we know. Such grandmothers do not love being reminded of their further progeny. But there are fortunately other women who do everything to receive such dear little ones."

Mr Tredup seemed now to have arrived at the main point of the conversation, at a fact which required a certain, sweet and sugar-coated art of description. For the former confectioner shoved yet another fruit lolly in his mouth before he whirled back to his visitor with his most joyful smile, letting the hundreds of folds play in his gaunt countenance. Then he plucked a few flecks of wool from Kathrin's cap and sucked in a breath with inner contentedness.

"Yes, there are still such maternal women, Mr Sell. You can really believe it. Our St Spiritus is in fact completely full."

"Full?", his guest stuttered, noticeably disappointed.

"Quite full of such nice, pretty children. Why not as well? You can think, in a maritime town, even if it is also small, an excess of this article prevails. God yes, it is sad." The folds in the starved face suddenly twisted to a sharp angle, and the narrow countenance looked abruptly as though hit by bad harvest or at a funeral. "Then these maternal women offer us a true blessing. I have, to make it easier for you, ordered the best of them here right away. She is waiting in the adjoining room. It is the former midwife, Mrs Christine Braesel, a very neat and pious housekeeper to whom we have already given three of our other children for care and board. Oh, oh," he fended off a rising objection, "you can be very happy over this position. The little room of the midwife, Mrs Braesel, looks like a well-polished jewel case. And whenever I appear to check, our dear little ones are leaping about like weasels. It is a true joy when you notice so much sense of duty. Pay attention, I will call the lady in now."

Humming, the great fly whirled to a concealed door which had previously escaped Richard Sell's notice, opened it, and called patronisingly, "Come, my dear Mrs Braesel. We all rejoice over your willingness and your diligence. This is Mr Richard Sell, the rescuer of the beautiful child. As it were her guardian. And you will now on be a mother to Kathrin, won't you?"

An enormous umbrella pushed through the door first. Then a noble woman's body followed, whose curvature was shaded by a black shawl, and finally a red-flecked countenance appeared with a pair of tense blue eyes over which a bonnet set with many glittering pearls nodded.

At first the midwife groaned a little to indicate what grievance the rising from her chair had caused her, then she curtsied old-fashionedly before the orphans' councillor and directed her motionless blue eyes to her new charge.

"Ah," she wrested from her asthmatic chest, "what a pretty girl. And the pimples do no harm either. It indicates a fine skin. Yes, yes, such a thing is rubbed by me with hare fat and vanishes after three days."

"Of course," the orphans' councillor nodded, "you understand your craft, my dear Mrs Braesel. And now give a kiss to Kathrin, for that is her name, and accept her like the ten talers for taking in. Have you any other comments to make?"

"Oh, just a trifle," the foster mother coughed, and on her red and blue speckled forehead, a serious and solemn cloud reared up, "I hear that Kathrin Brodersen is not a complete orphan."

When the midwife had uttered this prompt, she looked chastisingly from the child to the helmsman as if she were curious as to how you could rebut such a shaming reproach, and Mr Tredup also seemed gripped violently by the indicated deficiencies of the little girl so that he rubbed his pointed nose embarrassedly.

"Admittedly," he composed himself finally and also threw on his part a reprimanding look at Kathrin, "hm — yes — you are not wrong, there is certainly still a mother present, but you know — hm — a case of disability exists."

"I know." Mrs Christine Braesel pushed her body forward, and set her umbrella stiffly erect before herself. You only noticed now how, despite her dependent position, something truly enthroned and powerful emanated from her. Thus even in tiny creatures an innate majesty and dignity is often expressed.

"You will excuse me, Orphans' Councillor," she said with a quiet respectability, "for inquiring about that. But I must look out for myself. I receive support from the Welfare Administration, and Pastor Köper honours me occasionally with a visit."

"Alright," the large black fly hummed, and at the same time he flapped his coat impatiently so that Kathrin began sobbing loudly, "alright — calm down, my sweetie — you are a pious and just woman."

"Yes, I must watch out for myself," the midwife continued, moved much by this praise, "and hence I must not make any contact which could cause me harm. Right, Orphans' Councillor, it is so?"

"Without doubt — of course — it is so," Mr Tredup sought hastily to disperse these unexpected scruples, "just calm down, dear woman."

"And if Kathrin's mother would perhaps visit me, or want to meddle in my raising, no, then —".

Appalled over so much fuss, the former confectioner suddenly pulled out the bag of fruit lollies, and made a movement as if he intended stuffing the largest of them for conciliation into the broad Pharisee's mouth of the foster mother. He thought again, however, in good time and just stuck the packet in his other trouser pocket.

"But Kathrin's mother is dead," he cried bitterly, and his pointed nose seemingly pushed forward hostilely in the direction of his adversary — "only as a citizen of course, and we will make sure that you solely are able to deal with the guardian of the child. Yes, stop —", here the great fly interrupted his humming, and his protruding eyes remained fixed so avidly on the countenance of the young helmsman as if the latter were a fruitcake on which he ought to settle unconditionally. "Mr Sell, you are a serious, brave, and prudent man. And so that I do not forget, I have in fact proposed you to the court as guardian for the little orphan. It is surely quite obvious that you will accept the honour, yes, it is actually quite obvious."

"Certainly", the midwife noted. Nobody would have been able to convince her that the decision seized by her and Mr Tredup could yet be upset again by some living being.

And Richard Sell?

He stood, held Kathrin by the hand, and the sympathy for this helpless human merchandise which crept up on him made him forget his own uncertain situation, the discomfort which wheezed in his chest, and the forty taler which were hanging in the darkness and for which he had to leap to fetch down for his future.

"I am admittedly only twenty two years old", he said nonetheless indecisively, for something still bristled in him against being burdened with a care, or shortening his time for other things. For someone who did not take advantage of his days, someone who allowed himself to be distracted by incidental things, did not comprehend

the fleetingness of life, and that the most precious possession is time. "Yes, I am actually only twenty two
years old", he demurred in the hope that he would be
contradicted with strong reasons.

And he was not deceived in this expectation. The fly
hummed about him flatteringly and treated him as tenderly as the sweetest cake; grandly and indomitably, the
midwife held her umbrella before her lap, yes, the blue
and red flecks in her face chased one another, eerily and
meaningfully, as if they were warning flags which she
had drawn up against a hostile ship. How could an
already half compliant man be able to resist for very
long? And when Richard Sell left the room with the
sober birchwood furniture, he possessed the prospect of
his first firm employment in his new existence. He had
become a candidate for guardianship of Kathrin Brodersen, of Kathrin, who simply showed no intent to part
from him ever again. No, really, certain ideas of affili-
ation had naturalised themselves quite strangely in a
firm way in the child's mind. For when the helmsman
now intended leaving her, naturally under the awkward
exhortation that she should always be obedient and
well-behaved, Kathrin clasped firmly to his leg howling,
and neither the dry kiss of the midwife nor the prospect
of a fruit lolly was capable in the slightest of adjuring
the instinctive fear of the lavender coloured woollen
bundle for remaining alone and cast out.

"Now," Richard Sell heard the rebuking voice of the
midwife still wheezing behind the door, "you see that
you were a long time with a man. — Will you surely be
still? — Calm is the first thing you must learn."

***

By the bank of the river on which Richard Sell was
striding back to the village at the mouth, Uhlenhus, the
bulrushes were waving, and when one of the small
steamers cut through the narrow channel, the onrush-

ing, swelling furrows pressed the wall of perennials down before them, and the green stalks seemed to change colour in fear, and turned yellow and silvery grey. The wanderer attentively followed the course of one of these passenger vessels. Not because in the distance and with the small breadth of the harbour the appearance was roused in him that the steamer was rolling along across the land in a wondrous way, across fields and fresh meadows, no, the ill man was, despite his striving for knowledge and understanding, a mariner, and hence he believed — half in jest — in signs and premonitions. Thus he also paid attention for the moment carefully to what side the smoke of the funnel creeping past was wafting over. For if the threads of smoke rolled away over his right shoulder, then it was thus quite accounted for that his project could not remain without success. Oh, and he needed now so much the favour of destiny, he had to chase after that possibility as painfully as his sore chest would also double up with the furious run.

Whether the forty talers which he needed to begin with would not soon join him? How incidentally did you suddenly acquire so much money? And whether the smoke of the funnel hurrying past could not perhaps curl past from the right?

Right — ah, the grey clouds skimmed over in fact from the desired direction, and Richard Sell stopped abruptly and gazed after the fleeting forms contentedly. His serious features, which despite his youth were constantly dominated by a reflectiveness and a tenacious energy, brightened when he now turned to examine the blue lines of the sinking image of the town. Golden midday sun spun about the slender onion domes of the church which served the entire region as a landmark, and the red tile roofs of the houses lay under it like a slumbering herd resting about its shepherd. Yes, in them resided science, trade, and handcrafts, and above

all things money, the silver and golden blood of all un-
dertakings. The lonely man immediately began again
directing his thoughts to his goal. And as he plucked
about at the green stalks of the river's bulrushes, his
plans ordered and formed themselves, and marched towards the dawning town which he wanted to conquer.

"What does the man need most of all who wants to
get on in life?", the cool calculator asked himself. "Hm,
above everything else, he must surely possess contacts",
he gave himself as an answer. "And whom can I list for
myself in this respect up to now?" He tore a few bulrushes out and allocated each one a name. "Ott Knuth? I
know an old senile man whom I owe money as well. Mr
Tredup? He must in his life have hardly ever dispensed
anything but a few fruit lollies. — The midwife? Away
with her! She seemed frankly to be the left-behind
widow of a miser. And Kathrin? God, she was a good-
natured wild child, but her property consisted for the
time being of only a lavender coloured, woollen dress
and a pair of wooden clogs. No, Kathrin could not seriously be placed in reckoning. Who remained? There
probably remained a few good friends of his, but they
rested on the seafloor and rocked gently for eternity. It
was extremely uncertain whether their damp hands
would ever dispense gifts again. But in that Richard Sell
inflicted a wrong on the drowned people. How was that
then? For just as his memories were rambling about the
white shadow of the "Heron", the boat which shall have
borne all his hopes a few weeks before to beautiful blue
coasts, he started, and his power of imagination stepped
quite unexpectedly under a comfortable roof. Lord God,
the "Heron" must have been fitted out by a shipowner!
Quite certainly, for Captain Hennings had not been the
only owner. And that man ought to possess an interest
in becoming acquainted with the only survivor of the
proud vessel? The ill helmsman nodded eagerly in his
playing with the bulrushes, and at the same time, he en-

visaged his idea more and more objectively, and as more and more probable. Perhaps an eyewitness of the demise was even extremely welcome to the shipowner because of the settling of the insurance sum. From the common misfortune which would deliver a stately indemnification to one, but had provided the other with a sore chest, from it advantage and profit could perhaps be coined also for the smaller and nameless ones.

Why not?

You must simply try it.

And infused by a peculiar feeling of strength whose sources sprang from a well thought-through calculation of probability, the ill man strode back more lustily than before on the meandering country path next to the river. ... A few giant, white trimmed masts which had been horizontally thrown diagonally across the street suddenly blocked his path. Torn from his thoughts, Richard Sell looked up, and a strong embarrassment overcame him when he perceived how he had almost stumbled before a young girl who was sitting in her white linen dress rapt in herself on one of the spars. Despite the bright sunshine and the gentle breeze which shot occasionally across the river, she was unconcernedly turning the pages of a little book. The rays of light danced at the same time happily on her wavy pale blond hair, and on the slender face a reddish glow was scurrying. It could just as well have been called forth by the heat of the day as by inner agitation and participation in what was read. With the unexpected emergence of the stranger, however, she was startled, torn from another world, and her book fell clattering into the dust of the way. Astonished and at first a little disturbed, the young lady examined the unwelcome wanderer, and her calm clever eyes announced to him distinctly how she did not like having been separated from the important and meaningful things which floated about her soul. But then it seemed to be evident to the seated girl on closer consideration

that it would be something out of the ordinary to re-
strict an open street by a barrier that could not be
climbed over, and she tilted her head almost imperceptibly and began a few incoherent words of apology.

"Ah," she brought forth, and with time her words became clearer and and clearer and more considered, "our
people should have hauled the masts onto the little boat
down there. You see, down there. But meanwhile," —
she pulled out a tiny watch — "the midday pause occurred. If you do not want to go through our house," she
was continuing already in the calculation of the future,
"then you would probably have to climb over the wood."
And when she noticed the sickly countenance of the
stranger, she added amiably and full of harmlessness, "I
will like to offer you a hand."

Already she was rising and making an air to assisting
the waiting man. It all happened with great affectation,
yes, her offer seemed given more from the wish to be
permitted to return quite quickly to her calm rest on the
white, smoothly polished wooden trunk.

Only, in Richard Sells stirred the shame of the man
who strives instinctively for good manners. In particular
before a young girl in a clean white dress, and quite especially opposite a creature who had lingered so avidly
in the world of letters. And the love of learning and the
striving for the beautiful and unfamiliar became over-
powering in him. Where did this cool, clean being surely
like to roam about? What had been capable of igniting
in the clear, reckoning eyes that luminosity which, as he
well noted, immediately died away when she directed
her look at him?

He bent down adroitly, picked up her book, and as if
by chance, he educed the title, "Ferdinand Cortez and
the Riches of Montezuma."

At the same moment, the slender, white beams vanished for him, even the young girl in the bright dress
fluttered away, and instead of the bulrushes of the

river's bank, suddenly brown fibrous palm trees shot into the blue air. What a miracle! Even from the stretched out, single-storied ship's outfitting office of A. Guntrum, before which the ill man was lingering just then, all at once a multiply partitioned, heathen temple of colourful stones and coloured wood had arisen. The effect was so strong on the mariner of the life and deeds of that hard-hearted and yet glorious adventurer who, intoxicated by fame and greed for gold, had plundered an innocent world. And the young girl had roamed on those glittering shores, ensnared and blinded by the magnificence and the primitiveness of a virgin region?

"Yes, that is something", Richard Sell said as he liberated the book from its layer of dust and without a thought of whether his conversation would be pleasing or not. "I read the book at maritime school. It has never let go of me."

The young lady in the white dress, however, seemed to find this confession still stranger than the striking desire of the stranger to pursue a conversation to which he had not been invited. A look of assessment met his plain, blue tunic, before she took her property back from his hands. The astonishment over the unusual hobby of the simple man was quite distinctly betrayed in her demeanour.

"Certainly," she said in her cool and restrained manner, "you should also use your free time just for such instructive works. But where did you — —?"

The undertone of shock over the unexpected knowledge of such a humble man was becoming more and more audible.

"Oh," the man addressed finished indifferently as he was already climbing over the wood in front of him, "even on the 'Heron', we kept a small library with us. And you can believe me, dear Miss —".

Only, the young woman had suddenly been transformed. The well-known name of the lost ship seemed to have bridged the gap between the just then still unacquainted pair.

"Lord," she cried, and supported herself with both hands against the masts to be able to gaze now better into the gaunt countenance of her opposite, "then you are the rescued helmsman?"

Richard Sell found this recognition unpleasant. His nature bridled against being credited for an accident like it was a merit. It also did not comfort him that he was being stared at so unexpectedly by the shiny eyes as though he was a strange mythical animal.

"Quite right," he declined any further information impatiently, "that I am. — And now a good morning to you, dear Miss."

With that he doffed his blue cap, and intended to stride onwards on the path on which, if somehow possible, the forty talers should sparkle towards him. For since he could not bag them in the realm of Montezuma, he must just find them elsewhere. And indeed soon. That his future desired. But his fate was right now in league with him and stretched its hand out to him. The young woman in the white dress in fact called his name suddenly and almost fearfully.

"Mr Sell!"

Strange, she also knew that?

"Here," the man addressed said awkwardly, "what do you wish for, Miss?"

The girl stepped resolutely closer, and this time her shiny eyes remained sympathetically joined to his pallor, to his sunken chest, and to his bowed posture.

"It was surely terrible to be thrown about for so long by the waves?", she asked more warmly, and with her right hand she brushed as it were a shiver from her body. "I hope for you that you overcome the effects quite quickly."

"We will hope so", the young man thanked her a little hastily, for he did not in any way like to be reminded of his forfeited powers. "Certainly, I don't rightly know — —".

In his habit of always steering towards the next goal, he wanted to indicate thereby how little he comprehended her lingering on his suffering. The young woman, however, since her being was like his own, taught by upbringing and occupation to be on the same side of sobriety and immediacy, preempted his objection with a gentle smile. It was a row of completely uniform teeth which she exposed at the same time, and Richard Sell saw immediately with his prying mariner's eyes that two of them displayed small gold fillings. A proof of the good order which the young woman also had granted to herself. Now she stood right before him and let her bright, unassertive eyes rest on him still inquiringly.

"I am Sophie Guntrum," she thereby introduced herself unassumingly, as if this ceremony belonged to a goal which she must not abandon anymore. "My father", she continued with some pride and pointed curtly at the low, strung out building, "was one of the owners of the ship. We delivered almost the entire inner fitting out. See there inside, behind the shop windows you can recognise everything — brass rods, compasses, clocks, ropes, anchors and sailcloth. I myself worked in the office on the books. And my father was already surprised because you had until now reported to neither him nor the other shipowners. How would it be if you soon made up for this? You may have all sorts of things to discuss with him, might you not? You won't disturb him at all either, for he is sitting right now in his private office and reading the paper."

As the daughter of the businessman suggested this, she stepped to the side and performed a definite movement as if there were nothing else but agreement and obedience to her invitation. She seemed imbued in the most certain way with the idea that the business interest which she conducted with her words could not fail to make its impression on her pale companion either. And really, Richard Sell listened up attentively. The golden letters on the black iron sign over the entrance sparkled blindingly deep into his soul — A. Guntrum — Ship's Equipment — partner in a shipping company — it was all very far from the realm of Montezuma, but in the background of this name he heard it clinking with gold and silver. And he strode after such a noise, even if the sound should entice him into humiliation and danger. On his cheeks it blazed, he straightened up, and with a short remark whose meaning he had straight afterwards forgotten again, he declared himself agreeable with the wishes of his guide. Delighted over her success, although she deemed it quite natural opposite this poor and neglected invalid, Sophie Guntrum nodded. And she could not fail to choose, instead of the shorter way through the green front door, to lead her charge first of all out by a side door through the strung-out storerooms of her estate. There they strolled past all the things which pertained to sea journeys because they lent them comfort and security. And it flattered the young woman in the bright dress when she perceived how her companion, astonished by the worth and the brilliance of those wares, obviously began a calculation over the wealth dormant here.

"When you imagine," he murmured bashfully, "that here with you all the secret powers of great ships lie hidden, or when you envisage the voyages which these compasses should direct, then — —".

The two young people looked at each other and smiled. A little embarrassedly. For their power of imagination had met a point from which they could gladly and tirelessly soar. Away from the firm ground of money and from the pedestal of work, their mental vision was capable of clasping wonderful and covetable images in a shimmering distance. But both required this immovable point of departure to rise up above the sober earth. And they felt that and rejoiced, because they stood together on such a solidly worked ship of thought. And yet — right at this moment, their sailboat passed over a shallow so that its keel crunched and its planks gently trembled. Just then Sophie Guntrum led her companion past a stretched out hammock made of fine white silk netting. It was clear that this soft web must have been destined for tender and delicate limbs. Then Richard Sell was overcome by a memory of which he was full.

"Oh," he cried, as he stroked the fabric pityingly, "Marie Hennings lay in such a hammock occasionally under her awning." Now the merchant's daughter checked her step. She also grasped the fabric, but more to smooth and order it.

"I went to school with the wife of Captain Hennings," she said quickly, "in Stralsund. At the time she was a delicate, slender girl. Is it true that she later became pretty?"

If the ill helmsman was once more called to life to be a witness to the perished glory of his secret mistress, who could then have taken umbrage with him when he incautiously forgot the tone of gold for a second? And confidently, as if he ought to defend her reputation, he responded without thinking, "The poor woman was absolutely the most beautiful woman that I knew."

After this confession, it remained still for a while between the two. The merchant's daughter lingered still by the silk netting and stroked the close mesh. Then a clever, discerning smile slid over her lips, and while she did not change her place, she stretched her hand out gently and pointed to a small glass window which was recessed into the wallpaper.

"Back there my father is sitting, Mr Sell — yes, there, the bald man without the collar. It is right now the proper moment, for he has finished reading his paper.

But please do not knock, my father does not like such a thing."

The young lady in the bright dress nodded politely to him, and her shiny eyes followed the ill man attentively as he straightened up to maintain posture and confidence before the prosperous man.

***

"So, so, it is you", Mr Guntrum suggested. After he had learnt everything, folded the newspaper up awkwardly with his fleshy hand on the green oilcloth of a simple table, and still made no air of offering a chair to the man standing before him. "It is right pleasant for me that you are here," he continued, and at the same time he rocked his plump knee thoughtfully, "you will have to give your statement for the records, for we need that for the insurance. And now one more thing."

Here the large, blue eyes of the merchant, which up until then had been overshadowed almost completely by thick, heavy lids as if their owner were rendering homage to a constant doze, were directed for the first time fully at his visitor, and Richard Sell was almost frightened when he noticed this hard glimmer. Where had he perceived shortly before a similarly penetrating luminance? And what countenance familiar to him reflected in all the world the same lack of feeling for the fate of unfamiliar living beings? He had also caught somewhere once before the unmoved, indifferent voice.

"Yes," Mr Guntrum grumbled now between his teeth, stuffed a short English pipe, and looked rigidly at the weighty iron safe in the corner as if his look was alone capable of opening its heavy doors, "it is in fact so — we have here among us a small insurance for seamen who have come to harm on our ships. Hm, it is in fact so — we cannot toss out much and also want to be over it once and for all. Do you understand, my dear Mr Sell, I do not love nonsense! So now listen at once." And the large, blue eyes emerged again from their hollows and appraised the young man cold-bloodedly from head to toe. "Five hundred taler. Are you okay with that?"

"By God!"

The helmsman swayed, and the bare room skipped perilously up and down before him. At the same time, the smoke from the merchant's pipe whirled like giant numbers with human faces towards him. He saw Mr Tredup, the orphans' councillor, the midwife Christine Braesel, yes, even Ott Knuth as well as Captain Julius Kohlrausch with his first advisor Bob Swanegel riding about him and screaming in his ears, "Congratulations — congratulations — hold tight! — That is the fortune!"

Senselessly he grasped his chest to tame the dry coughs shaking him.

"It is in fact so," Mr Guntrum added with displeasure, because he realised with regret how much the claims of his visitor must have been overestimated, "you will issue me a little declaration by which you agree to no further claims. — You understand me. And now wait please."

The merchant rose ponderously, puffed a few large clouds, and shuffled in his slippers to the safe. And it was not heavenly music, but rather the clinking and rattling of a giant bunch of keys through whose clatter the fat man, before he switched the mechanism of the doors, once more tossed back, "What will you actually start with the money then now? It is in fact so — it does not concern me at all, I ask also merely for my own pleasure."

"Me — me —?"

You could have stoned the confused young man, and he would not have known in that solemn moment anything more about an entrenched plan. Everything, everything had been wiped away and suspended by the enormous experience, by the alteration of each thing being calculated. Only quite gradually, like a draining

away of his earlier sorrowful existence, did something
about the purchase of the dilapidated smokehouse
trickle forth from him. But it sounded pitying and did
without the great desire which had gilded his intentions
up to then. But precisely the modesty of the newly
chosen profession seemed to agree favourably with the
merchant.

"Look," he grunted, as he was already vanishing with
his head into the cavity of the iron safe, and the fringe of
grey hair on his neck bristled, "for that you don't need
much. It is in fact so — I will give you first of all only two
hundred taler, and the rest you can fetch in an orderly
fashion in case of need." During that he was already
counting, still in the black hole of the locker, a few fat
notes onto the iron plate. And carried away by the habit
of business speculation, the fat man continued excitedly, "It does not concern me at all, does not worry
me in the slightest, but how would it be if you reserved
the catch from a few fishermen for yourself? You must
pay the fellows something up front, that always works",
he added, and looked at his guest for the effect of this
with a grin from the side. "You must everywhere have a
little monopoly. I am very much for monopolies. Look
around, where in this town is there another business for
outfitting ships?" — He blew into the air. — "Eh, no, I
have grabbed it by the neck for myself!"

The merchant interrupted himself suddenly as if hit
by an idea, and made a timid attempt at a bow. After
that he tapped the ill man benevolently on the back.

"Listen please, it is in fact so — should you perhaps
need iron rods for hanging up the fish, kettles or metal
plates, grates, thread, absolutely the entire shebang,
young friend, then you will not go past me. Will you? A.
Guntrum delivers everything ten percent cheaper than
the competition in Stralsund. So — and do not take it
wrong, before you start, I would have myself examined
by a competent doctor just in case — Professor Reimers

is the cheapest — you must proceed safely everywhere. That is the main thing."

4

Time is a remarkable housekeeper. It runs around quietly in its circle, sometimes wipes here, sometimes hammers there, and when you first watch it, you do not believe that it has adjusted much. But if past races could raise their heads, then they would think the old man has started racing about in his little house and has turned everything upside down. Where a beech grove storming the sky rustled mysteriously, dead-straight roads are drawn today, and where you set off with boats over drowsy lakes, the plough now burrows, and the yellow hosts of rye wave their lances. Hence they tried to hang a clock on the business of the old man so that they could obtain a measure for the hustle and bustle. Only, all these works ran either too quickly or they hobbled timidly behind, and the old man continued on unworried and let them tick and strike.

The learned of all nations, however, calculated the behaviour of the old man each in their own way. The Jews kept it with the moon, the Pope with the sun, and the ship's boy Bob Swanegel controlled the bustle of the old man, whom he tended to consider to be an absolutely perverted woman, according to the form of the letter boxes which he came across before the dilapidated smokehouse of Ott Knuth. When the 'Green Herring' floated once again into the mirror-smooth harbour of the river-mouth village of Uhlenhus, the changing shape of the box always excited new qualms with the ship's boy.

"Look, Captain," he spoke to his boss Julius Kohlrausch after the first visit, "I was meant to drop off a note over there in the pancake made of clay. But Mr Sell is practical, he has simply cut a slit in the clay wall, and I pushed the paper with the news of our arrival through there. Have you ever seen such a letterbox?"

But the slit gradually became a wooden box in which very many notes and letters waited for an answer, it became a cast iron container, and one day Bob Swanegel stood as a tall twenty year old lout again before the pancake and shook his head irritatedly over the frivolity which expressed itself here so showily.

"God, thunderbolts," the boy said to himself suspiciously, and rubbed his right leg against his left, for he held this habit to be beautiful and meaningful, "if the entire thing is not a con. You hear now so much of such precarious tales. Now it has become a strung-out building with tile roof, chimneys, and a proper horse stable. Look, and they even have curtains properly before the windows. Fetch the devil, if the box outside is not made of proper brass. Here you must pay attention. For such millionaires, I have heard, carry no heart in their chests, and the sealed letter which I should toss in here makes this Mr Sell into our admiral. Thunderbolts, leased to him for five years. Would not have believed that such an eternally coughing man had such a smart mind. But in the contract, I have also written in things that will surely hurt his hair a little. Ugh, the devil, how it stinks of smoke!"

And with that he threw the envelope determinedly into the box, breathed on the brass, polished it with his sleeve a little, and said very consideredly, "Ever nifty!"

***

Yes, the old man had laboured around in the rotten beehive without rest or peace. And it had been helped at the same time by Richard Sell as if he had been tied to a date by which the old and work-worn thing must be replaced and entirely sorted out. In this way, the property had expanded and stretched, men and plans who could mutually support and further each other were found together here, and gradually it obtained the appearance that the smokehouse formed the heart and soul of the river-mouth village of Uhlenhus. The entire life and bustle directed itself to this centre. The taciturn, gaunt man in the sober, wood-lined chamber, which the others called the office, wrote a line, and at once a little flotilla sailed towards evening out into the grey misty bay. He drafted a despatch, and from the Danish coast two fishing steamers, which had been outfitted for their goal by the firm of A. Guntrum with especial care, rushed home.

Even the firm of A. Guntrum!

It was quite indescribable how its relationship to the dilapidated beehive had been transformed. The owner of the smoky heap of clay had long since no longer appeared in those clean spaces where the treasures of the fat merchant dreamt of future adventures. Miss Sophie had a long time ago drawn a final stroke under the uplifted amounts of the little compensation sum in her gloriously written ledger, and she also did not smile anymore benevolently or even a little patronisingly when a written order was received from the house of Sell, because it constantly dispersed such a penetrating smell of smoke and flounder. Instead A. Guntrum resigned himself more frequently to girding a collar on Sunday mornings. And it looked very solemn when the weighty gentleman wandered in his old-fashioned frock coat, in his right hand the bamboo cane with the Lord Mayor crook, to Uhlenhus to pull on the familiar porcelain handle of the bell there before the newly built house.

He had himself delivered the bell pull, that is, he had honoured it as a donation to his friend Richard Sell, of whom he did not rightly know whether he was his protege or his ideal. For it was clear, such a level-headed doggedness in any business advantage had not been seen by A. Guntrum before. He admired directly the imaginative way in which the young man understood how to build tangible possibilities from breakneck and extravagant plans. And the method by which the lonely calculator refused money and monetary value for his own needs to suddenly again shoot with steady hands golden arrows after a distant goal, this cold-bloodedness enraptured the experienced money gatherer ever anew to grinning acclaim.

What, however, did all the business prosperity mean against the tough battle which the former helmsman had led against the hereditary foe of humanity, against withering and destruction? Whenever A. Guntrum called to mind that sacrificial tenacity of the suffering man, he tended then to shake his fat, smoothly shaven head without any understanding, and the short fringe of hair over his wrinkled neck bristled in all directions. How a young man undoubtedly hungry for life won himself over to renouncing all the delights of his age firmly and coldly so as to construct anew and steel his already half decayed body again with inexorable strength of will through inurement and strong food, that the merchant did not indeed comprehend, but it infused him with a quite uncommon respect. For him, it remained certain that Richard Sell must have thrown a deep look into the mysteries of nature. And the appearance of learnedness which thereby lit up the eyes of the young, gaunt head transported the man feted by him far from the usual commonplaces of existence. In a word, A. Guntrum remained conscious indeed of how his own bank account for the time being showed a few more pages that that of his friend, by which, however, the doubt was for him by no means taken from the world that he might place himself despite these venerable qualities also really on the same step as the owner of the former beehive.

Today was again such a Sunday. A. Guntrum stood in his black frock coat on the steps of the newly built house and pulled on the porcelain handle. And as the tinkling signal spread itself inside, the calm businessman thought, reaching far out, "Yes, if the good peaceful times remain preserved for us, and if the boom climbs onward so nicely, and when my friend has in fact completely recovered his health, and if the mutual pleasure is right, and if he also moreover listens to the advice of experienced people, why not? You could consider it. You are becoming older and have no male heir, and in the end you cannot take your money with you. And in addition, you have also noted already that a certain someone has already frequently had hours long conversations with a certain one over books which describe wild and foreign places. Thus it sometimes begins. And from the wild place, a tame one can be made. Now, as said, you must proceed with deliberation."

With that he sounded anew and took a step back as a shuffling and scraping noise finally approached from within. The green door moved.

"Good day too", Ott Knuth groaned, whose emaciated body was wrapped in a similar frock coat to the great merchant's. And Sophie's father remembered that he must have spotted this piece of clothing already before with Richard Sell himself. Good, good, such a descent flattered the fat man, for it proved that in this house nothing decayed unnecessarily. Yes, even the white handkerchief which the soon-to-be ninety year old wore cleanly about his wrinkled neck found the special approval of the merchant. Collars were in the end just a breath-robbing and sweat-producing invention.

"At home?", the great merchant asked, not enthusing over any circuitous introductions.

"Yes", the former smoker clattered, and rejoicing over the judicious brevity of the visitor, he opened wide his swimming jelly-like eyes spasmodically to add exhaustively, "reading."

"Hm," A. Guntrum acknowledged, "where?"

"Here." The old man crept up to a door painted snow white, and listened a little at the wood; since, however, nothing stirred within, he finally shrugged his shoulders a little reproachfully, and from his toothless mouth it crumbled forth, "Far gone — half a schoolmaster. Yes, and then he wants to go into town to the tot."

There A. Guntrum grasped his stick tighter.

"Again already?", he shook his head, and the fringe of hair rubbed irritatingly over the back of his collar, "why?"

"Don't know", Ott Knuth chewed, and shut his eyes drowsily.

"Now, everyone has their folly," the visitor thought, "perhaps he will yet break the habit." And with that he pounded as considerately as was possible for him against the white door posts, and entered majestically.

It was only a small humble room which received the weighty guest. But the impression that he had rarely seen such a cosy comfortableness anywhere else was strengthened ever anew for the great merchant. God might know from what fisherman's family the young owner had scraped up this old moiré birchwood furniture — certainly for cheap money — and it remained just as inexplicable why the new dark-green rep upholstery lent the venerable pieces such an inviting cosiness. In addition, the walls were surrounded half way around by low bookcases from which the colourful backs of numerous volumes shone forth happily. From the white painted ceiling, a green pennanted electric lamp hung down over the round table, and the inhabitant of that

comfortable space sat right by the window in a comfortable armchair and found himself so engrossed in his
reading that he neither noticed the heavy step of his
guest nor sensed the shadow on his book. Outside a
yacht was gliding past with slack sails over the calm surface of the river, soundless and deserted. Sunday peace
reigned in the still air. From everywhere, gleaming
threads of summer drew threw the autumnal day.

Only, the great merchant did not intend devoting
himself for long to the enjoyment of this humming rest.
He intentionally tapped his bamboo cane on the grey
carpet of Indian manufacture and was secretly delighted
when the rapt man leapt startled from his window. He
had just time yet to discover that the gaunt young man
had likewise put on a well fitting frock coat. And that
was rightly so, for such a piece of clothing is appropriate
in that region for a great manufacturer, so that he also
distinguishes himself outwardly once and for all from
the fishing and farming folk.

"Ah, hello", Richard Sell welcomed his guest, and it
was conspicuous how youthfully and powerfully the
voice of the worthily dressed man uttered it. "Please sit,
Mr Guntrum. It is nice that you do not forget me on
Sunday. What leads you to me?"

That was certainly very plainly and soberly asked,
but the great trader did not resent it. He found it by
contrast very comforting when his protege always
grasped for the essence without any ado.

"Eh," he said, after he had made himself comfortable
on the green sofa, and fidgeted with his fat hand on the
table top — he was apparently a little embarrassed — "I
come because of my last proposal."

The eyes of the other man sparkled sympathetically.

"Ah so," he suggested and pursed his lips into a
gentle smile, "because of the canning factory."

Now A. Guntrum nodded and looked as venerable and benevolent as if he wanted to delight humanity with a great gift.

"So it is, Mr Richard Sell. Just think how comfortable you have it. The fresh wares, the female workforce, finally I myself, I thought — —".

"Now just get to the point", the smokehouse owner cut short all further salutations. "I've told you already that I recognise the advantages. But because I do not intend taking the risk alone, I want to engage myself in it only if you —".

"If I put up half", A. Guntrum completed, who saw himself caught, despondently, and puffed his round cheeks up groaning.

"Yes, nothing else. The negotiations have no point otherwise."

"Lord, how can you be so curt?", the visitor tooted, and shifted to and fro uncomfortably on his green seat. "it is in fact so — I also come out here actually to —".

But the young businessman held fast to his opposite mercilessly. "Do you want thus to disclose your agreement?", he tossed out determinedly.

"Thunderbolts yes, I want to disclose it," the great trader now cried, and wiped the sweat from his bristling fringe of hair with his handkerchief, "what sort of low art it is to transact business. But for my sake, for my sake, if it does not work as it were any other way!"

"No, otherwise I really see no possibility."

"Well good", the other man concluded, exhaling, and sank his handkerchief into his breast pocket. "it is in fact so — you are a terrible daredevil, dear Sell. But that may now be the custom. So this afternoon we will draft the contract with the notary. — And now I have a commission to give you."

The swollen eyelids sank ponderously, and the fat gleaming countenance would have been uncannily like a sleeping man's if the broad mouth had not pointed and smiled sleekly.

"You bring a commission?", his young host asked meanwhile, and became considerably more self-conscious; for it did not escape his sharp mind that it must now concern the affairs of ladies. And since his first rapt dreams, the barely recovered man avoided almost fearfully the realm of these lovely beguilements.

"Eh," A. Guntrum perked up, still dozing, "it is in fact so — a beautiful fat goose has flown to us. And my daughter Sophie suggested, if we iron things out with the notary this afternoon, then we will taste what an effect the poultry has with apple and bread stuffing. The lawyer will be there too."

Now Richard Sell lowered his head, and his previously so considered speech became noticeably less confident.

"Oh, your invitation is very kind," he thanked him waveringly, "but I don't really know whether I can accept your hospitality — —".

"Poppycock", Sophie's father interrupted, and at the same time, he suddenly raised his eyelids, and the bright blue eyes bored inquiringly behind the massive forehead of his friend. "I will also be placing a few bottles of strong red wine on the table. it is in fact so — you are permitted to take a good swallow again now, aren't you?" And after this was confessed by the smokehouse owner taciturnly, A. Guntrum struck the table heavily and rose groaning. "So done", he suggested like someone who had just then removed a ridiculous contradiction from the world.

After some time, however, as he fastened one more fleeting side-glance at the frock coat of his companion, he tossed out as inconspicuously as possible, "It seems to me that you have a visit planned?"

"Yes", the younger man fudged with lowered eyes and began leafing assiduously through his book.

"In town?", A. Guntrum asked interestedly.

"Yes," the other man wrestled out, "it is only a trifle."

"So, so — that is no concern of mine at all either. Private affairs have nothing to do with business. That you must cede to the individual." And after he had clothed this inner disapproval according to his intent as finely and diplomatically as possible, he struck the helmsman powerfully on the shoulder and reminded him once more, "So from tomorrow I am again involved somewhat more with you. The cuckoo knows, A. Guntrum and Richard Sell are slowly merging into each other. Now, we are both finding our own reckoning thereby. Right, my dear man, that remains the essential thing with all friendship? And now do not forget the notary. And we shall enjoy tasting Sophie's goose! Good morning."

***

At the same time as these important negotiations were attended to in Uhlenhus, the kitchen of the foster mother Mrs Christine Braesel echoed with a suppressed three-voiced sobbing. And every time the midwife, who stood in the doorway of the bare, semi-dark hole, let her enraged voice rest somewhat, the shrill wailing rose still stronger and more impressively. A gurgling and nose-blowing, a whimpering and groaning hit against the bare walls so that a cat which sat below the stove crept deterred behind a pair of old brooms, and the top to a boiling kettle danced and trembled in fright.

"Such a thing I have never experienced", the asthmatic organ of the foster mother wheezed, and at the same time the soft sound of a cuffing was awoken in the darkness.

"Oh, but no — but no, Mrs Braesel — won't do again." —

"Yes, won't do again", the midwife rattled fadingly. "And that happens after such an excellent example. "My

Lord in heaven, lollies under the mattresses, and running off to see the circus riders!"

Again the soft sound cracked.

"Oh, please, please, dear Aunt!"

"Quiet! Will you surely stop with the incessant howling? Nothing is happening to you! Or perhaps something is happening to you, you defiant worm?"

"No, nothing is taking place."

"That I also want to think. Great God, if Pastor Köper or even the orphans' councillor, Mr Tredup, learnt anything of these irregularities. It is terrible. Do you know then what consequences could arise for poor, ailing woman me from it? You will say immediately whether you know that!"

A wild clamour shrilled in answer, and the cat also broke out into a piteous whimpering.

"God's mercy on you", the midwife threatened anew, provoked by this racket, and pressed battle-ready again somewhat further into the dark hole. "That is the thanks for my supervision and my good treatment. At Christmas, I cut up my own apron to make a blouse out of it for the blighters which they were permitted to wear alternately on Sundays. Should that not be cried over? The entire town was amazed at my kindheartedness. And now? And now? But I must get to the bottom of this beastliness. Will you tell me on the spot, who of you secretly gave the money for the wicked escapade? Do you want to tell me it now? Or shall I perhaps lock you up again? How is that? Out with it!"

But hardly had the foster mother posed that question which was so justified for an ordered household than the outbreak of childish despair died out suddenly as if by agreement, and a fearful silence occurred. It became so paralysingly calm that you could hear the trembling breaths of the little ones. Mrs Christine Braesel, however, grasped at her chest, and in the darkness, her steady eyes began to flash like those of an owl.

"Eh, look here — eh, look there," she sucked in air rattling, "that is pretty, that is nice. So it is a proper conspiracy. Now just wait, wait, my little moppets. You can sit calmly here, nobody will disturb you. And with an empty stomach, the perverse courage will perhaps reconsider. Wait, wait, I want to see though whether such villainy is at an end."

With a hoarse laugh, she pulled a key of antiquated shape from her pocket, stepped once more into the darkness, and performed with it a few invoking motions to the left and right. And immediately the appalling shrieks of those struck answered the bold woman.

"Wait," Mrs Braesel said with gratification, "I will show you what a good upbringing is. You are not the first who became pious and patient with me. But it is bad that I must sacrifice my health for such tackle. And woe if you now make another sound!"

The key rattled in the door, the last light was extinguished, and the lid of the kettle clattered ghostily up and down like a skeleton blowing in the wind.

***

Someone who sits in darkness cannot measure off the hours hurrying away. Even the striking of the tower clock sounds to them dubious and full of mocking. And only hunger, which stirs and gnaws like an animal that would like to break out, gives those locked away a sure sign.

Closely huddled to one another, like a flurry of escaped partridges, the three boarders of Mrs Christine Braesel crouched on the bench in the kitchen. And although they could not mutually recognise each other with the prevailing darkness, they whispered back and forth quiet remarks in the ear to drive away the fear and the stabbing unease. The three little girls thought their present circumstances woeful, but they had already endured this principal means in the midwife's art of upbringing to often for it to be able to release anything but a dull horror in them. And the fear of what would come when they were first permitted again to look in the bluish red countenance of the foster mother was considerably stronger. Kathrin sat in the middle. She must have been markedly taller than her companions, for she had slung her right arm — ah, a thin, slender arm — about the shoulders of the tiny Grete Kräwt, and the ragged head of the weak creature, who did not want to wash, and whose voice sounded only like a dying breath, rested wearily on her chest.

"I can hear your heart beating", the little one said contentedly.

There was a change in the dark monotony, a mysterious warm music which Mrs Christine Braesel could neither suppress nor forbid. But from the other side, a hard, furious organ growled. It was barely comprehensible how roughly and inconsiderately the stocky Luise Mie could gesture.

"I'm hungry," the heavy-boned girl complained, and at the same time, she gave Kathrin an angry jab with her elbow. "I wished that old sod would be fetched by Satan."

"Ugh", the daughter of the sailor Brodersen responded, and started in fear at the curse. "You must not think of that."

"The best is if you sleep", the weary little being on Kathrin's right side agreed, and slid shivering down into the lap of her friend.

"No, but I want to think of it, I must think of it", the girl on the left hissed. "You are to blame for everything, Kathrin."

"Who? Me? For God's sake not so loud!"

"No, no, please, please," the pitiful Grete Kräwt now pleaded too, and grasped Kathrin's hand, seeking protection, "just think, if Aunt were now listening again at the door."

But her antagonist was not concerned by this objection, instead springing up so that the bench almost lost its balance, and made a bitter blow against the humming kettle with her fist.

"That is all the same to me", she raged. "Kathrin received the money and must pay for it. And she received it from a fellow."

Now the attacked girl freed herself stormily from the clasping arm of her friend. "If you don't shut up, Luise," she burst out, trembling with fear and rage, and moved at the same time over to the stove, "then I will scratch you. Yes, that I will."

"You just try that," the heavy-boned girl laughed, and clawed her right hand into Kathrin's shoulder, "then you will be able to experience something though."

"Luise — Luise," the ill child begged, having collapsed onto the bench, "it is not all so bad. And this evening, Aunt will let us out. She has never locked us in for longer."

"Yes, and meanwhile I am getting sick. I will not endure it any longer. No, what concern of mine is the entire rubbish? I'll tell the old bat, I'll tell her. In the dark, I always get such nasty ideas there. I will die in here. No, I will tell!"

Then Kathrin pushed the kettle to the side, and at once a reddish firelight blazed up in the narrow hole. A few glowing, children's faces, as it were detached from their bodies, hung now in the darkness opposite each other.

"If you tell," Kathrin cried choking, "then I will do something to you."

"Oh, dear God," little Grete Kräwt prayed, "I wish I were dead." And her head struck hard on the bench.

"Eh, nonsense", Luise answered back, obviously afforded fun in proving her strength to both the others. "I would rather let myself get beaten and have something to eat for it. The old negligent woman would also prefer me then. No — no, I will choke here in the smoke."

"Yes, it burns you in the chest", the whisper came from the bench.

It was a wild, desperate look with which Kathrin gazed around in the reddishly blazing darkness. Where was there an escape here? Where a salvation from the long spidery fingers of the foster mother which could burrow so clasping into the lean flesh of these miserable bodies? But suddenly her eyes, sparkling with despair and tears, adhered to a wooden window shutter which was so narrow that daylight could hardly have stolen through. An old rusted iron bolt always closed the dark wooden boards anyway, for Mrs Christine Braesel did not like strange eyes being granted information about the events in her kitchen. You could never really know. Something was boiled and roasted in favourable hours which lent the soul of a pious woman a special uplift. But the neighbours remained too obdurate for such a discovery. And the aroma curling out would perhaps have been able to excite their suspicion and envy. No, no, better was better. And so a bold hand had never ever dared a go at the iron clasp.

Never yet!

But now it set off light-footedly through the space, a little hand pushed and tore at the bolt, and at once the worm-ridden shutters screeched apart.

Ah, light, light poured in. Even if it were only the reflection which painted itself on the barely three feet distant back wall of the next house. A dull smell of rotting potatoes and neglected rubbish piles struck them. No window manifested out there, no sympathetic human countenance appeared, and yet the little criminal, throwing herself far out, stared as if spellbound at the bare grey wall. Over there leant one of those sooty black fire ladders which spent their forgotten existence everywhere in corners and crannies of the little town. A bold grip across the small breadth, and one of the rungs could be easily grasped.

"You," Luise Mie hissed, having comprehended what a mad, crazy idea was springing about in the brain of her companion; and it provoked the mischievous girl to stoke the desperate blaze still higher, "listen, the old woman is rattling the door now. Now I will tell!"

"It is not true", the youngest cried, and plunged likewise to the window.

Only, the horror of the spidery fingers had won the upper hand in Kathrin. She sensed painfully how the sharp nails of the midwife scratched over her neck to tie both the dark-brown pigtails of the culprit firmly about her fist as was her custom. In addition, the vinegary sharp sound of the accusing voice was already boring into her ear, 'Look here, my moppet, you were the one one who wreaked everything?! Just wait, you hideous sprog, now we will have a bit of a discussion with each other.'

And without making certain over whether it was not only hazy schemes which were closing in on her, the provoked and martyred child rushed outside and floundered in the next moment on the posts of the ladder like one of those tightrope walkers whom she had admired the day before. The scaffolding bent and danced back and forth, splinters penetrated into the palms of the girl gliding down, a wild cry shrilled out from the stinking pit, and the phantom swishing to earth vanished in a cloud of dry dust.

In the kitchen of Mrs Braesel, however, that benevolent friend of humanity on whose aims in upbringing such a blatant injustice was being committed, the wooden shutters shut with a powerful blow, and a rough voice commanded with unmistakable menace, "We saw nothing, we know nothing! God have mercy on you if you babble anything. Do you understand me, you daft milksop?"

And then the kettle hummed again, and the lid clattered like a skeleton in the wind.

Meanwhile the foster mother sat on the sofa with good and edifying thoughts in her narrow little room, and before her on the table lay all sorts of packages by whose contents the midwife tended to be delighted on Sundays in particular. There were various edibles which you never suspected of her, and which also served only to invigorate and strengthen Mrs Braesel's body which had been strongly disordered by its noble task. Secretly of course, for, as stated, the foster mother showed a painful consideration for the envy of her fellow man. Thus she now reclined leisurely on the cotton cover of the sofa, and as she examined affectionately through her glasses her inventory of rice, flour, and plums, she ceded herself to amiable thoughts. And she had cause for this peaceful stocktaking. Was not a strong beef stew cooking in there in the locked kitchen, made rightly to support the holiness of Sunday by its enlivening heat? And did not the contentment of the good aunt also have to be appreciably increased by the consideration that there in the adjoining dark hole three young creatures were crouching, whose strength of character was being cemented and considerably raised by the prohibition of even just smelling the stewing meal?

Yes, she simply possessed principles! And in her holiday mood, she was sometimes ambushed by the conviction that she could actually with justice call herself a benefactor of mankind.

Lord!

There was a knock outside.

Startled, the midwife tore the glasses from her smoothly brushed hair and stuffed the edibles quickly under the sofa. She was puffing and wheezing still from the exertion, when her visitor was already entering.

"Ah, is it really you, Mr Sell?", she emitted with a stiff smile, and the blue and red flecks on her countenance began a graceful round dance. "You have certainly received my letter, Mr Sell?", the foster mother continued accusingly, and threw her head back severely. "Yes, I must say, such a viciousness had never happened in my house before. Never before, Mr Sell. I do not want to praise myself, but you know well yourself in what repute I stand. Seriously, I cannot explain the bad spree."

Hereupon she impelled the young man, whose solemn black frock coat also infused Mrs Braesel with a decided respect, into a half split wicker armchair, and it did not escape her tautened eyes how little her visitor felt gratified by the role of judge falling on him. In fact, an expression appeared in the sharply chiseled features of the young man as if he were ashamed by the time wasting which all these silly tricks involved.

"Dear woman," the smokehouse owner began quickly, and played around somewhat impatiently with the pompoms of the tablecloth, "my time is tight. Please, will you explain to me in brief what cause for discontent my ward has give you?"

"Kathrin", the midwife said chastisingly to exclude in advance any misunderstanding, and then she leant back in the corner of the sofa and looked at her visitor, gauging him from the side as if he were also somehow enlisted in the crime. "What? It is perhaps nothing to hide big bags of lollies in your mattress?"

"Follies", the young merchant responded cold-bloodedly, and looked penetratingly at the adjoining kitchen door as if he would prefer to be placed opposite his little ward as quickly as possible.

She had recently been displaying a shy, almost humble being, she did not dare address him outright and often curled up in the corners like a little beaten dog, but her large brown eyes spoke the truth. Fear and esteem for the mighty man who reigned over her destiny from a distance detained her apparently from serving lies up to him. Perhaps the poison had also not yet eaten into her soul at all. If only her parentage had not been, that dismal inheritance!

Richard Sell passed his hand quickly over his forehead as if he intended to wipe away something quite especially nasty, and thus how his hostess girded herself for a new blow escaped him. Yes, quite decisively, now something shattering must follow, something which ran directly contrary to human nature. A half bitter, half mocking smile played about the pursed mouth, and the splendid row of false teeth were bared as if she intended to snap at a fat morsel.

"So, so," she remarked affronted, and rocked her head critically back and forth over such loose notions, "they are follies!? Well good, men do not understand much about a proper upbringing, although I naturally do not reckon you, Mr Sell, among them. All respect, you conceive your duty as guardian right seriously and even let it cost something. As is appropriate."

"Enough", the man in the frock coat interrupted here reluctantly, and pulled more strongly at the tablecloth. "Come to the point finally! What actually has happened here?"

"What has happened here?"

Mrs Braesel rose, rounded her body with dignity, and with an inimitable gesture, she stuck her glasses before her frosty eyes to steer her gaze with a sharp boring into her taken aback audience. The glass sparkled, the false teeth menaced more ravenously, and the fatal smile announced quite distinctly, 'You stand before your judge, worm.'

It became very uncomfortable for Richard Sell. Lightning quick, he ran through in his mind whether he had not sinned against this venerable woman somehow, and at the same time, the knowledge tormented him once again that the life in those rooms must at base be like an everlasting torment. Lord, did you possess the right to lock up innocent creatures in these secret prisons? And were you permitted to still be credited with such an action afterwards by an agitated society as a good deed? And above all, how long would the strange relationship between him and the strange child persist? Sometimes it depressed him extraordinarily though. Anyhow, why was the state actually permitted to presume to produce such responsible ties? Hm, yes — certainly, Kathrin — —

Then he was roughly tossed out of these series of considerations.

"Mr Sell," the midwife spoke weightily, "have you gifted your ward money recently?"

Now the deliberating man was startled and looked up.

"Me? No. — You know, dear woman, that I prefer to hand over the small sums which I consider necessary to you yourself."

"Good, good," the foster mother praised, "that is also the only correct way." But straight afterwards she gazed around her room and shrugged her shoulders ambiguously. "Certainly, then the case becomes still darker. And it may surely be appropriate to count out my own few groschens again thoroughly."

"Yes, but — you do not want to claim perhaps —?"

"Who knows?! If it turns out otherwise, then it would be still worse, for then the sum originates from outside."

"What sort of sum?", the smokehouse owner urged now, honestly appalled.

For although he constantly held that he would be in no way responsible for the behaviour of his ward, the concern about the actions of the little creature never entirely left him. The thought constantly oppressed him that the strange girl could impair or exalt the reputation of his newly constructed house. And after some time of hesitation, he wrestled out darkly, "I did not appear here at your place to hear dark intimations. Tell me please now without further ado what you have to complain about, and whether some claims on me arise from it."

"Claims?" In the wide eye slits of Mrs Braesel, a rapacious light ignited, but she mastered herself, and after she had folded her hands before her chest as if she could thereby defend herself from all this unholiness, she burst out with a hard, inflexible tone, "Think, Mr Sell, the three females yesterday, instead of going to the public baths where I send them every week for the sake of cleanliness, went to Speroni's Circus."

"Well, and?", the young man inquired without fully comprehending the horror apparently.

And the disappointment of not having plunged her guest into despair made the foster mother sink back now powerlessly into her cotton-covered upholstery.

"Well, and?", she repeated in stiff outrage over so much businesslike indifference. "Mr Sell, I ask you, where shall it come to with us if young girls, poor orphans who are taken in from sympathy, look at half naked men and women? Women who sit in tight-fitting clothes on horses and spring through silk hoops?"

Here Richard Sell inquired in his sober and calculating way first of all over where the midwife had learnt all this irreproachably, and whether perhaps a mistake could not exist. Then, however, the blue and red flecks of his hostess sprang into wild circles confusedly. The fury over the seeking of detail robbed her of a part of her cautious deliberation.

"From where do I know it?", she howled suddenly. "I was there myself, I saw these sprogs with my own eyes."

"Ah!", Richard Sell thought and smiled bleakly. But the main question, which offered her a sleepless night and infuriated the widow more, consisted rather in the fathoming of where Kathrin had raised the money for the entrance. For it must originate from Kathrin. She was the liveliest and most enterprising of the house, and the other two had not a human soul in the town who took any interest in them.

When Mrs Christine Braesel had gone so far amidst anguish and laments, her visitor breathed out audibly, and his knitted brows, which lent his gaunt face something reserved and cold, relaxed. And what the young man now shared with the midwife must truly have strengthened her in the view of how far the man who had risen so quickly to affluence was from a truly straight and narrow course.

"Dear woman," he uttered, like someone who did not wish to waste time unnecessarily, "where my ward received the small sum from, we will establish straightaway, for I will ask her. But in addition, I would like to make the following remark to you, I do not consider it proper if you ruin any delight children have, particularly poor and outcast children. Life is short, and who knows whether the memory of the artificial sparkle of the circus does not extinguish much of the bitterness and sorrow in the young souls. Do you understand?"

"No, I do not understand you, not a word", the midwife responded now snappishly, and the skin over her cheekbones stretched startlingly stiff and firm.

"That isn't needed either", the smokehouse owner refuted cold-bloodedly and rose. "For the time being, I am more concerned about something else. I would like to learn from you how Kathrin is doing in school and whether her behaviour has become somewhat more amicable and forthcoming."

Now the midwife swallowed, and pushed her dignified body slowly behind the sofa. It was clear she had to penalise her impervious guest through something. For she was sent to earth for raising children.

"No," she considered, as she lowered her glasses awkwardly into a broad leather case, "the timid and obdurate being has still not been shed by the girl. I don't know the reason for that. Over her attentiveness in school, I need not complain exactly. She writes well, likes listening to stories, and she can almost always be found as she crawls into some corner to read in the book of discoveries which you gifted her for Christmas. It was by the way far too splendidly bound. You must not accustom such children to finery and noblesse, Mr Sell. But as said, the being of your ward is inexplicable to me. I act towards her really like a proper mother. Particularly because you support me in my striving through all sorts of contributions. But can you perhaps get through to the child? No, a proper answer never comes out of her. She is obdurate, remains obdurate, and only from her eyes, which she does not have power over, do I frequently read with my experience a defiance, as if she would like to destroy me and my entire residence. Perhaps that comes from her mother."

"Perhaps," the merchant agreed in disgust, "who can know? And now call Kathrin in."

"Immediately", the midwife assented, rejoicing over the prospect of lending the appropriate verve to the trial.

Stiff and dignified, like a heavily laden ship, she sailed off. Only, she had hardly vanished for a second behind the adjoining kitchen door when the man left behind heard a polyphonic scream of horror shrill from within. It was a shrieking so full of fury, helplessness, and thirst for revenge that the young man, who on the outside always tended to carry an appearance of impenetrable coldness, felt his unguarded heart begin jumping almost up to his throat.

Mercy of God, if the mistreated child had perhaps been harmed?! He saw the little creature lying before himself, bloody and deformed, and at the same time, the knowledge penetrated him quite contradictorily that such an end would at base be no contemptible act, but rather born from an intolerable compulsion and to be expected with reason.

Who bore the blame for it?

Lord — Lord!

He bit his lip, and with long strides, he wandered back and forth in the room. Short breaths passed from him, and for the first time after a long absence, a stabbing pain cut through his back. Then Mrs Christine Braesel also swayed through the kitchen door, and behind her appeared the wildly agitated faces of her fosterlings. But where had the never-failing majesty of the foster mother fled to? A picture of breakdown, she sank down on a chair at the entrance, dangled her arms down powerlessly, and as she spasmodically sought to tame her clattering teeth, she murmured with an unnatural smirk, "Gone — Kathrin is gone."

Behind her, both foster children emitted a long drawn out howl.

"Mrs Braesel, think," Richard Sell cried, sliding away completely from his previously exercised control. "What does that mean? I demand an explanation."

"I know nothing — I know nothing at all. Great heavens, the orphans' councillor!"

Mad voices rose in confusion, oaths and shrill sighs were heard, and yet — and yet — the crazy discovery was not to be shaken, both girls had slept, and when they awoke, Kathrin was gone. Vanished from a firmly locked chamber from which there was only a single way out. The midwife, however, sat on her chair, sent glazed looks around and groaned barely audibly, "I must have a doctor fetched for me — my mother and grandmother also died of a stroke!"

And really, her countenance resembled a garden in which garish red and blue Chinese lanterns had been lit at night. A sparkling, glowing, and flashing emanated from it. And thrown into horror by this uncanny firework, Richard Sell grasped for his hat and plunged aimlessly down the narrow, twisting stairs.

5

Meanwhile Kathrin was rushing through the lanes of the Pomeranian harbour town. She pressed herself along the walls of the houses, and her own shadow, scurrying on her trail, infused her with horror. It was just as tall and black as Mrs Braesel when she had put on her Sunday best. The low rows of windows also glistened in the sunlight and then resembled conspicuously the glasses which her foster mother placed on her nose to uncover hidden misdeeds.

Onward, onward.

The brown plaits fluttered about the young girl's shoulders with the hurried run, and under her shabby grey dress, which she had already long since outgrown, a stocking had slid down and now bared an injured knee. A hefty burning burrowed down there, but the little fugitive was incapable of paying attention to that now. Was it not wonderful to taste the storming cool air? And her heart also hammered so powerfully in her flying breast like never before in her life. The entire town belonged to her, and it just depended on ferreting out a little place, a corner, a loft or a cellar, from where she could not be pulled out anymore. And even if she only enjoyed one or two days of freedom, then she had gotten to know this magnificent gift for once. Afterwards let whatever may happen. Something must finally happen with her. For girls like her were destined some day for other people to take command of them and instruct them on their place in life. No, no, she had no worries at all. Whichever way, it was not important. Just one thing stood firm, she felt hunger, boundless hunger. But in the happy, sunlit town where everyone strode along so peacefully, something would also appear for her in the end. You could after all beg from someone. Yes, if you then just knew how to curtsy and ask right charmingly. Eh, and that she could. Mrs Braesel possessed no idea of how sweetly Kathrin achieved such a thing. For she had never allowed herself to do it in front of the hard-hearted old woman.

But suddenly the child interrupted her course, for a tavern sign showing a dancing white bear in a golden oak wreath turned her thoughts to a quite definite, to a redemptive point. Ah, how good that this occurred to her at the right time. Naturally, in there behind the smoky windows of the 'Dancing Bear', her old friend Bob Swanegel tended to cater to his body's needs. And indeed, as Kathrin recalled, in company with his master, Captain Julius Kohlrausch. For Bob Swanegel always felt obliged to also oversee the meal times of his boss because of the constantly alarmingly increasing voracity of the skipper.

The child straightened up on her toes, clasped onto the iron bars of the window grill and tried to throw a look through the dusty panes into the interior of the sailors' tavern. Aha! Across one of the tables, which in contrast to the others was covered by a clean linen cloth, the now snow-white Neptune's head of the master of the 'Green Herring' rose in fact. And Kathrin noticed from her place of observation with inner delight how Bob Swanegel was just then holding firmly the fork right before the mouth of his master, because a massive piece of fat green eel was about to vanish into it right then. A fierce dispute between teacher and student over the beneficial nature of such fatty nourishment echoed dully and indistinctly outside.

"Muttonhead," Mr Kohlrausch parried, and seized the fork more firmly as he already swallowed the piece in question with his eyes, "such an eel is slithery, and all slithery things are a true salve for gout. Do you not also smear my knee every evening with fat?"

Only, this objection had no effect on the student. Instead he seized the fork from the other side still more firmly, and the eel remained floating like an unresolved question.

"Capt'n," Bob dissented with greater determination, and his blond, shorn head shook back and forth disapprovingly, "why are you not thinking of aspirin and colchicum and quinine? For every bite of this here, a pound of such drugs always results."

"Ugh, the devil", the old mariner was appalled, and let the fork fall in fright back onto the plate. "Boy, you are nasty. How can you spit such a horrible thing at a man right in the middle of eating?"

"But it is healthy", affirmed Bob contentedly, and at the same time, he meant just then himself to see to the elimination of the contentious morsel when he suddenly rubbed his eyes and had to stare uncomprehendingly at the window panes. "Now the thing is right," he stuttered, "there she is."

"Who, Bob?", his boss growled grimly, who despite the interruption had not let off ogling covetously the plate of his companion.

"Well, who? The sprog of Mr Richard Sell. Kathrin Brodersen. I tell you, Captain, there is something not right. For the old box does not usually let her chicks fly out alone. Wait a minute, I must surely catch her." And with that he ran out, and forgot completely that the abstinence of his master was allowed to be subjected to such dangerous tests only in his presence.

After some time, however, Bob returned again and was leading the radiantly delighted Kathrin by the hand. And when he politely pushed a chair up to the table for the young lady — the former ship's boy understood good manners — and after the white-haired Neptune had received a quite unusually charming curtsy, Bob Swanegel did not hesitate any longer in putting an act, glorious and worthy of imitation in his opinion, in the proper light.

"It fits," he uttered full of inner applause, "she has run away from her dragon. On a fire ladder, Capt'n, two stories high", he added admiringly. And so as to also decorate himself with a branch of the full laurel wreath, he also added, "I am to blame for it."

Entranced, the master of the "Green Herring" grinned, not only because he had meanwhile succeeded in choking down unnoticed a part of the beautifully juicy fish, but mainly from inner delight over the trick played on the foster mother. For Mrs Christine Braesel was an old, bluish red piece of tackle who struck children; above all, however, she seemed suspicious to Mr Kohlrausch on account of her profession as midwife, among which he imagined horrid torments against the human race.

"Ran away," he repeated as he stroked his body with delight, "beautiful, then the old witch will surely leap about a bit and get out of breath — very good. But how are you to blame for it, Bob?", he asked after a while enviously, as if he grudged his first minister a little the share in something so beautiful and elevated.

"I gifted her five groschen", Bob Swanegel declared, flattered, and looked dreamily at the ceiling. "With the money, the sprogs then went to the circus. And the entire spectacle resulted from that in the end."

Here the boss of the "Green Herring" stuffed the serviette in his mouth, for a spasm of laughter was shaking him.

"Look," he uttered finally, after he had calmed down a bit, "that I realised. Such old wives should only be fit to ride on broomsticks. And even that only on Walpurgis Night. But what will be of Kathrin now?"

"That is what I was just thinking about," Bob Swanegel declared, whereby he rocked on his chair and closed his eyes for deep deliberation. The white-haired man ducked down reverently at this announcement. He had never ever disturbed the votive of such a collection.

"The best thing surely is that you meanwhile eat a plate of green eel," he whispered, struck by the sight of his apprentice, respectfully to the young lady in the short grey woolen dress, "I can very much recommend it to you."

"Yes", Kathrin accepted condescendingly.

Then the famed fish floated onto the table, you heard nothing but the clattering of Kathrin's fork as well as the anxious groaning of the white-haired guardian for whom the quick disappearance of the meal excited an incomprehensible pain.

"So," Captain Kohlrausch said finally, when Kathrin wiped her mouth, "now only the fish bones are left. What will become of you now, girl?"

At this grave inquiry, the three propped their heads in their hands and their elbows on the table and stared at one another. Oh horrors, it followed that for the first time stubborn head-shaking arose from his listeners against the well-considered plans of Mr Swanegel. Whatever he brought forth, an obstacle stood in its way. A man in a black vest and black frock coat who sometimes coughed quite gently. But the man was not to be pushed aside, and became larger and larger the longer you thought about him. Without him, everything was actually so simple, quite smooth and pleasant. The girl could come with them on the "Green Herring", and she would deal there with the paperwork or rub hare fat into Captain Kohlrausch's swollen knee every evening. An extremely greasy occupation which was at base no longer appropriate for a helmsman-to-be. But no, no, that did not work, the sprog possessed no papers. And then Mr Richard Sell! What would he say to it if you planted the thing on the vessel leased by him?

"No, no, Bob, the piece is no good."

Or, my God, you could perhaps make the young woman with the brown plaits independent? Why should
she not sell stockings in a shop? Or, what would be still
nicer, climb with Mr Guntrum onto one of the high office chairs? But, the devil, for such a piece she was
lacking six or seven years. And then above all things —
the man in the black frock coat. How would Mr Sell like
it if you went thus over his head — —?

"Bob, it comes to nothing", the Captain determined
with boundless disappointment, and black thoughts befell him because even his infallible advisor could have
an empty and flat day.

Thus even the elevated are also sometimes doubted.
And that happened right at the moment when the young
sage, admittedly secretly and furtively, was weighing
something so overwhelming that his mouth remained
open with inordinate astonishment.

Thunderbolts, you could also *marry* the little young
lady! She had sparkling brown plaits in which it flashed
like the dust in a ray of sunlight, and a pair of dreamy
dark eyes. And she was also unflinching. Dammit, if
someone could swish down a fire ladder two storeys
high, the most fastidious demands must not be demanded anymore.

"How old are you actually, Kathrin?" the contemplative man inquired from his meditation a little doubtfully.

"Nine years old", Kathrin responded ingenuously, for
she was now dedicating her entire attention to the remains on the Captain's plate which the latter no longer
dared to consume in the presence of his apprentice.

"So, so." Bob Swanegel scratched behind his ear and
reluctantly shook off the last threads of the torn web of
thoughts. But a regret almost lay in this decisive motion. "Then it comes to nothing", he determined. And
then he announced grimly and full of distinct loathing
the outcome which was clear to everyone, which was
raised now to a decision in the general counsel, "For

nothing further remains but that we take the sprog to Mr Sell."

"Yes", Kathrin sighed deeply, and propped her head in her hand.

A few images swished in quick flight through the little fugitive's consciousness reflecting what she expected out there from the strict, brusque man in the black frock coat. Many in-depth questions which all began with the words how and why, and at the end a serious remonstrance over diligence, modest behaviour, and truthfulness. Yes, yes, she knew all that. And the worst was that you did not like to laugh about it at all. For the few syllables which Mr Sell directed at her always had such an especially memorable ring to them which you did not forget and which stayed with you. He also never reminded her of the good things he had done for her in the way she was accustomed to hearing from Mrs Christine Braesel. Ah, if the man had just a single time appeared a little friendlier, if he had not always wanted to confront her like a schoolmaster with a cane, then, yes, then you would really be attached to him more. But she did not dare, even now in the circle of her allies, the sharp and penetrating sounds of how and why were swirling in her ears.

She sighed.

"Keep quiet, girl", Captain Kohlrausch soothed her self-absorption, and with that he hesitantly threw a coin onto the table for the bill which he had long since flipped over with a furtive shudder. "This evening, we will take you to Uhlenhus. Yes, we will do that. But we will stay together for the day. Right, Bob, it is pleasant when ladies are with us?"

There his companion nodded, and looked as cheerful as if the old white-head had just written an unexpectedly brilliant exam grade.

"So it is", he agreed. "And first of all, we will now all go to the circus. We must see what the old prickly one has to object to with the ponies and short skirts. Do you know what, Capt'n? The old woman was just annoyed because she herself cannot stand anymore on a caparison and spring through silk hoops. So it is and nothing else."

***

In the great room of A. Guntrum, the massive Flemish grandfather clock in the corner struck the ninth hour. It rolled and droned over the white damask tablecloth with the vehemence of an old man who is accustomed to everything listening to his weighty voice. Every conversation had to fall silent before the pertinence of this utterance, and so no further attention could be brought to why Mr Richard Sell fastened such a timid and depressed look at the clock face. Nobody noticed it. Neither A. Guntrum who had risen to make a toast, whereby he now played with his coattails behind his back because of the disturbing noise, nor the intoxicated figure of the lawyer Franz Seiler. No, not even the latter, although nothing usually escaped the soaked giant's roguish eyes, shiny with wine. In addition, the loudly booming man did not once require the assistance of his little pitiful wife, notwithstanding that it was customary that she indicate all less important events to him with her field mouse face.

"Franz, you have poured red wine on your white vest."

"Beautiful, mother."

"Franz, don't kick your serviette about with your feet."

"Eh, God forbid — thank you, dear Amalie."

"Do you want to say something perhaps, Franz?"

"Yes, dearest. Oh, in what glorious colours does the character of such a royal goose not radiate. Can you repay the maidenly bird its dedication to the human race? Your dreams, beloved, wing their way at night on its white feathers. And does not the juicy fullness of its noble flesh penetrate you with an increased feeling of strength? Pass me the wine carafe, beloved."

From that the participants of the binge could have recognised, if they did not know already, that the lawyer Franz Seiler — already in his usual state a powerful orator who enlivened all public meetings — turned into a poet when the gift of Bacchus ignited a sacred fire in his brain.

No, nobody noticed the badly concealed unease of the young smokehouse owner, although this evening feast took place in his honour. And only Sophie Guntrum, who sat opposite him in her softly shimmering blondness, inconspicuously followed his efforts to split the coal-black night behind the windows by a sharp look. Without infusing her guest with suspicion, the incorruptible mind of A. Guntrum's daughter had long since discovered that only the physical shell of the young merchant lingered amongst them, while his spirit was rushing through the night and darkness outside. He was seeking and searching there for something, otherwise he would hardly have looked around furtively so frequently or eluded her conversation, which he consented to at other times, with barely concealed uncertainty. And Sophie Guntrum opened her calm mouth for that discerning smile so peculiar to her. For it had not remained hidden from her with whom the young smokehouse owner had visited towards midday. She had still avoided asking her guest about how his ward was faring, because she knew how shyly the taciturn man tended to eschew such inquiries. But today, opposite his conspicuous unease, she decided to renounce this consideration. The conviction was rooted too clearly in her clear bookkeeper's disposition that the close bond between the sober merchant and that outcast spawn of the sailor Brodersen must have a harmful effect in the long run on the reputation of the young man. And

Sophie accounted coolly for how much the plans and threads which her father was spinning for the future of his business friend were disturbed and confused by the inordinate sense of duty of his partner.

And she herself? No, she did not like to deny it, a sort of jealousy, a feeling of discrimination stirred in her against the strange coupling of the striving, fortunate man with a daughter of misery. Certainly, you could feel sympathy. That you ought to even, for it pertained to good custom. But it decidedly did not behove to get en-meshed all too deeply in such a coexistence. That was bad. Here the usually so surprising worldliness of the upstart was obviously lacking. And she was certainly appointed for a warning, because the lines of their fates ran ever closer together through money, affection, and usefulness. Quite certainly, she had decided, as soon as she could grab hold of her interesting guest after dinner to have a few hints flow across to him about this. But she did not need to wait so long, chance came to her aid. Sophie's father meanwhile, after he had played with his coattails behind his back for a time, had namely thought of something better, and instead of making a long-wind-ed speech, he suddenly burst out short and sharp with the end of his line of thought, "it is in fact so — long live my dear guests, I have no more to say."

"Excellent", Franz Seiler bubbled, merry on wine, and tapped his Amalie tenderly on her shrunken cheeks; "and indeed they shall live quite frequently at A. Guntrum's, delighted by the presence of numerous portly gentlemen from Bordeaux and a few darker, firmly wrapped Cuban women. Oh my queen, life is beautiful indeed!"

"Franz," his wife interrupted him, ashamed over this stormy homage because it was applied by her to herself, "you wanted to share something with Mr Sell."

Straightaway the lawyer held a wineglass in suspense and sought to remember.

"I, my love, I wanted —?"

"Yes, quite certainly," Amalie persisted, as she pointed with her forefinger stiffly at the smokehouse owner, "you wanted to tell him this story from the prison — —".

Now A. Guntrum perked up too. "Prison?", he erupted with his fat voice, and at the same time his heavy eyelids dropped down so that he could observe his sheepish partner all the more inconspicuously under them. "Has Mr Sell perhaps ordered prison work?"

Everyone fell silent for a while. Only the daughter of the house shook gently, for even the mention of that terrible place put her in a bad mood. She also did not doubt for a second that this must all be connected with the unsuitable obligation of her young friend. Always when she thought of it, it gave her a stabbing pain, and she distanced herself inwardly from the pale man opposite her.

Then Richard Sell straightened up. It was a forcible pulling himself together, the effort for which was well noted by Sophie. And the usually so sharp and imperious eyes of the young man did not dare to rise from the white tablecloth as he inquired with constricted voice, "What do I have to do with the prison, Doctor? Please, will you not explain yourself to the company more clearly?"

"Indeed, Franz," Mrs Amalie demanded, and pushed the giant's glass furtively towards herself, "Mr Richard Sell must really know so that no unpleasantness arises for him."

"Unpleasantness", A. Guntrum now boomed, having seemingly sunken into a deep sleep.

Truly, the distastefulness, the timid and concealed thing, it already sat with them at the table, it kept its arm slung about the young man and pressed itself to him as if it belonged to him. The wind also whistled outside, and a short rain shower passed to the nearby river. Hissing and clattering, it drizzled down as if a few shovels full of shot had been tossed across the surface. And at the same moment, the idea jerked up in Richard Sell, although he struggled against it with all his strength, of how terrible it would be if a young child were perhaps wandering through the storm at this hour. No, no, he did not find it comfortable at all today in the circle of feasting people. The calm, the abundance, and the comforts were failing to have an effect on him. He instead calculated unceasingly the moment when it would finally be appropriate for him to hurry home.

He was still deliberating, when that word fell on the richly set table, that word which caught him and spun dark threads about his clear thoughts. It fluttered to him like a black moth, floated right before his eyes and robbed him of the usual outlook. Away with it — away, what at base did he have to do with prison and prisoners? Only, the moth continued fluttering and overshadowed the concerned man's forehead and eyes. Meanwhile the lawyer had lovingly bedded the wine bottle in his arm, and since he was missing his glass, he stroked the label tenderly like a beloved baby.

"A fiery little number", he crooned blissfully, and flashed his eyes greedily at the glass which his Amalie held captive. "Yes, good grief, what is there to be told at large? The woman was just let out of prison last week."

"Kathrin's mother", Sophie Guntrum tossed out in-between, as if an incontestable clarity would be because of her especially. At the same time, she sent a glance straight and implacably over to the young smokehouse owner, and both pairs of steady and hard eyes grasped at one another like contending fists.

The others noticed none of this quiet struggle, for A. Guntrum had still not given up his protective sleep, and the lawyer Franz Seiler was brushing apart his sparse greyish blond hair on his red pate so that his powers of memory could unfold more undisturbed. Yes, he had been her official defence counsel, for which you of course need calculate no honorarium. This just by the way. A damned strapping woman incidentally, this Mrs Brodersen, with moist, melancholic eyes.

"Just like the sprog", the host snored here, and stretched out his knee complacently.

Outside it rattled on the windowpanes, and about the free-standing corners of the house the wind wailed a lamenting sobbing. You could believe a convict were defending themselves in shame and disgrace against evil, vicious tongues and libels. And again Richard Sell sat there with lowered head amidst all these accusations, and as he plucked agitatedly at the edge of the table-cloth, he felt then how the sweat of fear was beading on his forehead. For as foolishly and ridiculously as he also scolded himself, the idea oppressed him incessantly that he would be pushed away silently and cold-bloodedly from his educated rank deep down to be with the rejects of existence. He shivered quietly, and deliberated.

"An end, and end," it screamed in him, "it must not last any longer."

"What will now become of Kathrin then?", Amalie threw in-between with her sorrowful shrew's face, and at the same time, she let her tongue glide between her pursed lips so that it looked as if her image scented fresh bacon.

At that Richard Sell started. The brooding flew away from him, for the fear seized him that the withered other half of the lawyer could possibly already have learnt of the girl's disappearance. That too! Discouraged, his severe eyebrows frowned, and when he now addressed the desiccated woman, his gaunt countenance had won back its old and decided expression.

"Why, what do you know of Kathrin?", he asked hard and curtly, and it sounded no different than if he were asking an employee of his smokehouse, a poor little woman who for a mark a day had to hang countless fish up in the acrid smoke. "What do you know of Kathrin?"

Now the shrew crawled somewhat more into herself, and her lamenting eyes flashed fiercely. She seemed always to fear that she would be struck dead the next moment by a boot jack.

"I only wanted to say," she breathed bleakly, "what if Mrs Brodersen — thus the woman is surely called — now raises claims to her child?"

It was actually a quite harmless and understandable submission which experienced and clever people ought to have expected. And yet the young smokehouse owner noted with his sharpened powers of observation immediately how the others rejoiced and eyeballed each other a little gloatingly, yes, that even A. Guntrum interrupted his magnetic sleep to throw a contented look at his daughter. But that just strengthened him in his tough defiance, for something was towering up unconsciously in his inner being against the idea that his work of upbringing, which he had exercised with circumspection and sober consideration, could now be broken down and extinguished by a wild, yes, depraved person.

"I do not believe at all in any right or claim of Mrs Brodersen," it burst out of him stubbornly, "at a minimum, my consent must surely apply to it."

Meanwhile the lawyer had finally succeeded in stealing the contentious glass from his unsettled, listening wife. Hence the verdict of the massive man formed itself somewhat more mildly and indulgently as he could elicit finally the dark drink from the bottle of red wine.

"Hm, my most worthy man," he swallowed, "that may be arguable. But I would like to provide you with some good advice. Quite for free of course, purely amicably. In my opinion, you would namely be acting quite reasonably if you delivered the worm up on demand as soon as possible to its dear mother."

"But if I would now see a danger to the child in that?"

Here Sophie Guntrum let her arm slide down, and as quietly as the movement heralded itself, Richard Sell caught how the blonde shook her head damningly.

Heavens, he wished at base likewise for a separation as quick and thorough as possible from the office forced on him. Only the urge of the others to influence him, which was so distinctly on show, made him for the time being go astray from his own intent. And something erupted from the reluctant man which he thought hidden in the deepest cabinet of his being.

"Do you mean then," he inquired falteringly of the lawyer, "that the attributes and lapses of the mother must be passed across unconditionally to the little girl, even though the child has escaped her influence over a period of many years? Do you really believe that?"

Franz Seiler set his glass down just then and comfortably followed with his right hand the path which the red drink took through his neck and throat.

"Dear friend," he replied with a blissful sigh, "the appreciation for that may surely be trusted to an old criminologist. I have in fact always observed how the evil-infected blood expresses itself also in the following generations. Those born later can actually do nothing about it at all. Quite simply, the memories of the aberrant urge lives on in them, and they are barred by their ancestry and parents from civil society. Yes, in my experience, the children display almost without exception the same vices, and the better upbringing which the state now and again has forcibly granted to them polishes the innate principle to an extreme. Really, you could be happy if you were now relieved of the worry and the little creature in such a simple way. And if you carry the responsibility for the time being, then it is though open to you to file a submission for the divesting of your guardianship. I would push that through for you."

Again everyone fell silent. You heard unabated in the rising silence the storm crunching with wet boots across the lane, and only A. Guntrum nodded his head a few times in express agreement and uttered meaningfully, "it is in fact so."

***

The hooves of the pony drawing the carriage of the smokehouse owner homewards clopped monotonously through the night. For Richard Sell had purchased an old two-seater at an auction, and his heart swelled more when he was permitted to press into the cushions of the rattly vehicle with great fuss and nodding of his head. It was though no trifle to travel through the world as the owner of a carriage. And when his work coachman let the whip crack, then it seemed to the young owner to swish the command out of the hissing air towards him, "Take it further — take it further."

But today the man returning home leant morosely in the corner of the carriage and listened as the heavy rain-drops splashed on the leather top. And as he half mechanically stared in front of himself at the wet road over which the gliding lantern light scurried, and as he caught the wafting of the rustling bulrushes down there by the river, he searched out there for a trembling ad-olescent shadow which was perhaps right now freezing and bent over following the same path as himself. Only nothing stirred on the drenched paths, no figure inter-rupted the misty loneliness, and soon the hoofbeats were pounding over the wooden connecting bridge, and the first lights of Uhlenhus emerged.

Richard Sell, however, was still grappling with evil thoughts. Whether it were possible, he pondered reluct-antly, that the girl were running to its mother? He shook, for in him the outrage stirred that something which had belonged to him should stray thus into muck and depravation. But it was ridiculous, he rebutted himself, she does not know this Mrs Brodersen at all. On my instructions, even the name of the person was always kept away from her. Whether this was right, incidentally? And whether a stranger was permitted arbitrarily to cut up the ties of nature? Hm, if you were only already out of this uncertain thing.

The carriage stopped. The young man sprang down hurriedly and unlocked the green front door. At the same time, a slight surprise befell him because the light of the pendant lamp was stealing out through the curtains from the window of his living room onto the secluded road. A stray reflection glistened black and golden on the nearby surface of the river. Behind the door someone was droning and laughing. From there Ott Knuth rose, having waited for his boss, from an armchair, and when the ninety year old stood before him bandy-legged, a strangely delighted crackling and clattering ran through the emaciated skeleton.

"Now it has come to that point", the old smoker coughed and rubbed his fleshless hands grinning.

With a short greeting and without paying attention to him, the arrival opened the white door of the living room and then — — he remained standing dumbfounded at the threshold and could not explain at first the image which was offered to him. There opposite him on the green upholstered chairs sat Captain Julius Kohlrausch and his tall apprentice, erect and stiff as if they were frightened of causing a disturbance through a breath or a vigorous movement. And this danger did not actually seem all too distant. For on the sofa under the old-fashioned steel engravings, Kathrin lay outstretched, and her red cheeks as well as her regular breaths exhibited the sound sleep of youth. But hardly had Richard Sell stirred than the Captain was already raising his fat forefinger towards his lips in warning, to straight afterwards whisper very amicably and exhaustingly, "Here we are now, Mr Richard Sell."

"Yes", the man addressed responded, because he could not think of any other proper reply.

The mariner also remained calmly seated in his soft chair, only he pointed meaningfully at his student, whereupon he explained how beautiful it was that Kathrin had torn away from her old dragon. And since she was now sleeping so prettily, which was especially beneficial to little children, in his opinion the affair was dealt with and in order.

"She received the money for the circus from Bob Swanegel incidentally," he noted, still applauding, "he is not asking for it back though."

Then Bob nodded, and looked very modest and restrained. "Eh, God preserve", he assured, although he also made no air to enliven his rigid pose. "I also bought her salve for her scraped knee and rubbed the fat in myself. But the whole thing was thoughtfulness, nothing more."

Once more he nodded and remained sitting coolly in his chair as if the image of both men keeping watch must not be altered in any way. At this moment, the smokehouse owner had meanwhile recovered his composure.

"Listen," he finally pulled himself together, and stepped somewhat further into the room without paying attention to the calming hand gestures of the Captain, "do you think then that Kathrin should stay with me tonight?"

"Yes, where else?", Bob Swanegel responded, and threw a venomous look at the man who had just returned home, while his boss pushed his hand behind his ear uncomprehendingly. "She belongs to you though!"

"To me — yes — admittedly."

Hereupon it remained quiet for a long time between the host and his visitors. And only after Richard Sell had stepped up close to the sofa and convinced himself of the deep sleep of his ward did he seem to have seized on a final decision, for he made a movement like someone who is closing a long lasting sitting and rises. So expressive and definite was the signal that even Captain Kohlrausch, who possessed a fine understanding for pantomime portrayals, could not elude the demand anymore.

"Yes, it is no use then," he uttered regretfully as he gathered himself up snorting from his seat, "then come now, Bob, we will not bother Mr Sell and his daughter any longer. He is certainly also already rejoicing to be alone with her. No, no, Mr Sell," he added in an unsteady way, "you don't need to thank us, it was a delight." And turning to the sofa, he spoke with a note of gentle emotion, "So adieu too, little one. You are now in your father's house."

"That she is", his adjutant confirmed with an unusually powerful intonation, for his sharp powers of observation had surely perceived the deep creases between the eyebrows of Kathrin's guardian. "Here you belong, there is no contradicting that at all. And now come, Captain, we have both done our thing now."

With that he seized his boss under the arm, and pushed him very decisively, as always, out the door.

But the fellow had probably forgotten because of the lack of time to wish good night.

"What is it?", Kathrin stammered, having been startled from her sleep by the hard blow of the front door falling shut or by the shrilling of the bell.

And the child sat up and rubbed her eyes. Right before her, the green pendant lamp was rocking gently, and light and shadow rose and fell cosily over the bookcase and the old birchwood furniture by the walls. A comfortable peace was spinning and dawning here, and even the dark grimacing face of the man in the black frock coat did not trouble the girl slowly coming to her senses, but seemed in his calm and taciturnity to belong to this place of comfort and security. Kathrin carefully brushed her little grey skirt down over her knees, folded her hands on the table, and looked attentively at her protector. The smart thing knew quite exactly that a serious examination must follow now; and Kathrin prepared herself resolutely to stand up to the hearing full of honesty and without hesitating. Only lies must not be given to the brusque gentleman, otherwise he would lose his decided and just composure and could become hard and cruel. That the escapee knew, and she did not make the slightest effort to use the little mischievous arts, which she had picked up with the widow Braesel, here in the clean room. Only, it was made easier for her than she had guessed. The smokehouse owner namely propped himself thoughtfully with both hands on the table, and after he had stroked his forefinger over the furrows of the green rep covering for a while, he wrestled out finally as outcome of his deliberations, "You could not bear it there any longer?"

"No," the child breathed out in relief, "I thought she would strike me dead."

Richard Sell nodded sympathetically. His mien expressed distinctly that he did not completely want to reject out of hand the reasons for the conviction of his ward.

"Are you also speaking the truth, Kathrin?" he asked in anticipation.

Then the black, child's eyes became larger and larger and more serious. "I do not tell lies here with you", she said solemnly.

"Good. But now I want to know whether your foster mother really chastised you so often and so painfully."

'Yes', it wanted to come from Kathrin in vengeance, 'she frequently struck weals over my entire body with a cane.' But wondrously, when the thing remembered how a man was lingering here before her, something like shame rose up against the confession, and she just tilted her head acquiescing, and brushed her arms and shoulders ambiguously as if she were feeling pain. She could admittedly never have devised anything as effective. For the smokehouse owner who comprehended this silent speech strode quickly to her, and instead of rebuking her, he stroked her gently and reassuringly over the now loosened locks of her brown hair.

"Mrs Braesel did not do that by my wishes", he erupted hastily, and it was almost as if he felt obliged to apologise before his ward. And at the same time, he moved a chair to the table and sat now so close to his guest that he could reach her with his hand. He inquired then further with persistence, "Did she give you enough to eat?"

The little girl shook her head, but immediately pursed her mouth disparagingly.

"Oh, I never made much of that," she sought to mollify his dark expression, "I can endure that for a long time."

Now the man threw a quick glance at the gaunt body of his visitor, at the protruding bones of the arms, and at the transparent white skin of her cheeks, and a weird feeling of responsibility arose in him. The neglect of the little one which had been hidden from him with success secretly enraged him, and his rigid sense of justice was already pondering now the possibility that the undaunted midwife's methods of upbringing should not be brought to the attention of the civic authorities.

"It is good," he decided after a while, whereby he was, however, incapable of parting his lowered eyes from the green table covering, "we will not speak anymore of the woman. I will arrange that you do not return there anymore."

What was that?

Hardly had the young man hesitantly uttered the latter than he started, surprised and put out by a quite unaccustomed sound. Was that still the child who usually cowered in his presence always in timid and awestruck obedience? No, the joy, the fierce delight which ran through the slender limbs of the girl must have completely washed away and dissolved the previously so carefully tended respect. With a single leap, the brown haired girl had leapt onto her feet behind the table, unconcerned by whether the wood creaked in all its joints, and now she struck her hands together as if possessed and shook her head in mad delight until her hair whipped her forehead and cheeks stormily.

"Stop", Richard Sell cried in shock.

Only, Kathrin was not to be subdued anymore. Cheering and laughing, the child burst forth from behind the table, the green covering hooked on one of her dress buttons, and without thought of the ruination, the unfettered girl danced up and down the room like a strange being who did not know the rules of custom and decency or whose understanding had suddenly whirled away into the distance. A mad song of battle or defiance shrilled at the same time in high notes through the wild leaps of the girl:

> Good day Mrs widow Braesel,
> Have an umbrella and a blue nose.

That too! With open mouth, appalled and incapable of clear thought, the young man stared at the outrageous theatrics. Only half comprehended ideas took possession of him. He saw as if through a haze the white-covered table at A. Guntrum's and behind it the serious, reproachful faces who prophesied calamity and embarrassment for him.

"It is in fact so", Sophie's father admonished.

And at the same time, a shiver ran through him because in his paralysis he brought himself to tolerate the mad whirl of the strange dance in the quiet space, here where previously a falling scrap of paper had been deemed to be noise and disorder. Could perhaps in this intoxicated whirl the parentage of that undignified female not be revealed irresistibly? Of the woman who had uprooted herself already by inordinate greed for madness and pleasure? Oh, this thought was horribly tormenting. It cut so stabbingly through the brain of the man that his control left him and he suddenly emitted a brutal threat, rough and unruly, a shock to himself.

"Damned sprog," he cried, dark-red, and at the same time, he ran to her and shook the little one, without realising, delicately by her thin arms, "will you surely leave off the hopping about instantly? It is not appropriate in my house, you hear?"

The rough rebuke had not yet faded away when the limbs of the just then so happily excited creature were paralysed as if they were set in cold lead. Torn from all the heavens, the child fell back to earth, and with a nameless expression of remorse, shame, and horror, Kathrin stretched both hands out to the annoyed man. At the same time, a few large tears beaded from her nervously widened eyes. Her trembling lips seemed to want to ask whether she had now forfeited by her incautious behaviour perhaps this place of recovery and peace. Then Richard Sell backed away aghast from the silenced girl, and for a long time both examined each other in complete uncertainty over what they could expect from one another. Only when the splattering noise of the rain penetrated from outside more strongly did Richard Sell pull himself together, and after he had emitted a heavy sigh a few times, like someone who is forced to act against his own clear conscience, he decreed almost worn out, "Come, Kathrin, up in the room next to Knuth's there is a bed, you shall sleep there. And what happens next, that I will leave until tomorrow. Come."

And following a sudden inspiration, he offered his hand to his ward, and after he had drawn her behind himself up the steep, creaking stairs into the darkness, he opened a quite low door, and lit a candle on the red

spruce commode. He paused in the doorway, and followed how the little one, still walking about half in
dream, smoothed and tidied the damp, stiff pillows with
adroit and expert hands. Then he listened attentively.
Next door the old smoker was singing just then in his
sleep, and twanged clearly to himself:

> Rejoice in life because the lamp still glows,
> Pluck the roses before they fade.

***

The next morning at half past five, the grey morning
mist was still sleeping on the steps and in nooks and
crannies when Kathrin sprang down into the brick kitchen in her short, fluttering skirts.

"Good morning," she called freshly to the clattering
frame of the old smoker who crouched sunken down on
a stool next to the stove and stared stupidly into the
empty brass bowl of the coffee mill, "what's wrong?"

"Nothing," the old man chewed, and wiped his red
eyes, "no more beans."

But Kathrin immediately knew a way out.

"Is the merchant Quandt already open?" she called
out and skipped about impatiently.

The old man let his head fall on his chest. It was
meant to indicate a 'yes'. After that he fumbled a coin
from his pocket, placed it firmly on the brass edging of
the stove and murmured something. Anyone who
listened exactly could understand, "Schmidtsch will
provide it."

Schmidtsch was the housekeeper, wife of a fisherman, who tried through washing, sweeping, cooking,
and patching to keep the household of both men in order. Only, Kathrin was already incautiously breaching
the rules of the house on the first morning.

"No," she dissented pertly, as she pounced like a
raven on the money, "I can fetch that too."

The next moment, the bell above the front door rang, and the little girl was running through the gently trickling rain into the first cross lane of Uhlenhus. Above both rows of low, thatched cottages there still lay the soft night cover of smoke and haze. And behind the scraggly vegetable gardens, in which the mocking north wind usually bent and broke everything which tried to shoot up high, something empty, grey, and seething stretched, from which a stranger would have to believe that it was the sky which had sunk heavy and burdensome onto the damp earth. But Kathrin was familiar with the shapeless thing and was not frightened by the enormous bowl full of haze and mist, for she knew that there the bay rested, the tongue of sea which licked with light smacking at the now covered meadows. Soon Mr Sell's ward had reached the end of the lane through the crunching muck of the uncobbled way, and a dreary light behind the window of the last house before the churchyard taught her that the Quandt family must have already begun their daily work. Right, there too the yellow straw mat before the naked figure of the little plaster Moor in the show window had been drawn up, and between a few cigarette cartons, fat flour sacks, shovels, and oilskin jackets, Kathrin spied the spindly figure of Mr Quandt, sitting calmly at his counter, whereby he held his fiery red blaze of hair lowered avidly and blinking over a tattered little book.

Yes, that was Mr Quandt. What man could blame Kathrin when at the sight her naive, beauty seeking heart began pounding, as everything which aspired to adventure and romance in the river-mouth village of Uhlenhus was embodied in this tall fellow with the fiery mane, as well as in his rotund, mercurial wife. You did not need to trouble the older inhabitants at all, even the youngest told half full of pride, half with a certain mocking sympathy, of how you revered in Mr and Mrs Quandt the last remnant of a troupe of actors and

tightrope walkers who many years ago after a barbarous
seizure of their wagon and equipment must have eluded
their admirers quickly by night. But a friendly sun had
still shone on Mr Quandt with this general collapse. An
old, cheery captain in fact, who had always suffered
asthmatic attacks of laughter and shaking cheerfulness
with the very seriously meant songs and duets of the
married couple, paid his thanks as well as his gratitude
for the unforgotten performances of the artists by allot-
ting to the homeless couple the empty wing of his
cottage for a general store. Yes, the risible old gentleman even thrust out to his new residents a small sum
for the business, and desired as compensation until his
parting from the world nothing further than that the
artistic couple give him on Sundays a series of their sad
ballads to their best ability, to which the appreciative
listener had broken out as before into his immoderate
whinnying and bellowing. Now the sea-dog was long
since covered by lawn. But the business of Emanuel
Quandt flourished, for it united for Uhlenhus everything
which was offered elsewhere by theatres, clubs, newspapers, museums, and concert houses. Mr Quandt knew
everything, was familiar with everything, and with his
increasing wealth, he had not even forfeited clambering
anew to the summit of his art as far as the bright peaks
of Wallenstein and Don Carlos, but he also seized the
educated mania of his time in that he amassed all the
old junk reverently as grey treasures of the past. In addition, the many-sided man also possessed the happy
gift of clothing worthless inanities before himself and
others with the golden shimmer of poetry. Had he succeeded, for example, in scraping up an old broken cup
with a painted cannon, or had he even caught an etched
page full of Hebraic characters, you could be certain
that, throwing back his red bush of hair with a bold
elan, he would declare to his customers full of rolling
importance, "You see here, Harbourmaster, this cup.

Napoleon drank out of it during the battle of Leipzig. You can still recognise the hole which he bit out in his fury. — What? What sort of page is that, Mrs Jakobs? You don't know? Hm, they say that it is a page from the prayerbook of Uriel Acosta. A magnificent piece, by the way, which I once saw played in Wolgast, whereby the Jews blew the correct signals on cow horns. — Friederike, give the Harbourmaster's wife three pounds of soft soap!"

Kathrin stepped up to this zealous man at his counter, full of curiosity and awe, and when Emanuel Quandt noticed her, he quickly pushed away the brown coffeepot which he was dreamily slurping from just then, while his spirit had glided thirstily over the pages of the ragged paperback which he had held close before his eyes until now. He was sitting on the board of the counter, dangling his long legs, and when Kathrin stepped over the threshold, the former artist burst out in memory of what he had just read with the strange greeting, "You come late — yet you come! The wide path, Count Isolan, excuses your dallying."*

"Oh eh", Kathrin said in confusion, and looked back over her shoulder in shock to see if some undreamt noble gentleman behind her had thought to honour the museum of Mr Quandt with his visit.

The general store owner, however, twisted his furrowed, smooth-shaven countenance demanding quiet, and the expressive mouth formed into a still more outrageous greeting:

> Thirty regiment's men, the colonels
> Find themselves already together,
> You meet Terzky here, Tiefenbach,
> Colalto, Götz, Maradas, Hinnersam,
> Also the son and father Piccolomini —
> You will greet many an old friend.

---

* [From Schiller's *Wallenstein*, the second part "Die Piccolomini", Act 1, Scene 1.]

Only Gallas is still missing and Altringer.[†]

But here Kathrin, terrified by such a stately as-
sembly, stretched both hands out, and after she had
examined in the light of the bleakly burning pendant
lamp the shelves, yes, even thereupon the herring and
vinegar barrels timidly, to see if behind them a crowd of
strange men had been kept hidden, she cried out to tear
Mr Quandt finally from his frightful dreaming, "A
pound of coffee, Mr Quandt, for a mark."

"Ah so — yes — your loyal servant, my Miss." The red
maned man pondered, climbed down to earth from his
raised seat, and called through the small, curtain-hung
partition door, "Friederike, a young lady wishes for coffee. I believe it is Miss Sell, as she surely is called, if I am
not mistaken. Or do you perhaps possess a second
name? Now, it is no matter. Since when have you been
with your papa?"

Meanwhile, at the loud rolling cry, Mrs Friederike
Quandt had entered in a wafting, half open night jacket,
and as the rotund wife now grasped here and there with
her full arm, sometimes to pull forth a carton, other
times to make the scales ready for use, a cross-examina-
tion was conducted by the artist couple in all honesty
and restraint with the little purchaser, until the naive
Kathrin, who herself attributed some importance to her
existence and hence liked reporting on it, had thus had
wrested from her seemingly even the most insignificant
thing. And then Mr Quandt spoke the words which
would not remain without influence on his new customer in the future, "Hm," he tossed out derisively as he
paced out back and forth with two steps the tiny, fully
packed space, "Mr Sell — an excellent and capable man
by the way, only too serious, don't you think,
Friederike? Too serious! I have censured this often — he
does not like to suffer a song? Well good, my child, if
you are ever urged again to that, here there is nothing

† [From Schiller's *Wallenstein*, loc. cit.]

against this art which is educational and pleasing to the heart, right, Friederike? That I would like to suggest. Visit us as often as you like. And here, my Miss, have a little piece of sugar candy as a gift."

***

Laughing, delighted, and crunching the hard candy with all her strength, Kathrin returned to the smoke-house. In her thankful memory, Mr Quandt still climbed up and down with long strides, that famous man who could bring forth so much wondrous and incompre-hensible stuff. And when the agile thing had already long since set the coffee table with Schmidtsch, the weird necromancy of the red-headed Emanuel still echoed in her persistently. For it had happened thus. Quite certainly. What? Gallas? Altringer? Very weird, they were certainly ghosts with whom the tall man had something to do.

At the same time, the occupied girl did not, however, neglect, despite the opposition of Schmidtsch who shook her ragged head aggrieved, to fish out from the pantry everything which seemed to her somehow suited to increase the cosiness. An old battered sugar can, a proper white porcelain coffeepot of which admittedly the neck had been broken in half, and above all two stately cups with colourful pictures, but unfortunately without saucers. All this was placed reverently and full of suspense on the beautiful blue tablecloth, and soon afterwards Kathrin was herself crouching in solemn si-lence behind these grand pieces, had her hands folded on the table, and waited curiously for what impression her love of domestic creativity, which she had never been permitted to indulge in such measure before, would surely call forth from her protector.

Attention, here he enters!

He was carrying a notebook in his hands, in which he was still calculating while striding, and he only raised his head distractedly when he pushed his chair into place. But then the little girl caught his eye in sudden realisation, as he must doubtlessly have forgotten her, and the unaccustomed gleam of the set up also caused him to stroke his protruding chin a little sheepishly.

"Ah, good morning, it is you of course", he wrestled out in embarrassment while Kathrin made a curtsy to the man as he sat himself down, and at the same time it occurred to him how short the child's skirt was, yes, that it revealed an unmistakeable bareness above the knee.

Hm, what was all this strange surliness. And he engrossed himself quickly in his hot coffee, continued calculating at the same time undisturbed, and only stopped when he had to wonder about the spell-bound silence which had gradually occurred. There was no helping it, now an address must finally follow. Richard Sell raised his short-cropped head and sent to his guest first of all one of his sharp and eyeballing looks.

"Did you sleep well?", he began and made an effort not to look at the threadbare little woollen skirt anymore.

Kathrin pursed her mouth. Slept? That was clear though. How could the clever Mr Sell inquire after such an obvious thing? Hence, she just nodded and swung her legs a little.

"Sit still", her guardian reproved her. And after a while, as he wistfully turned his notebook back and forth, he continued decisively, "You shall thus for the time being, until I find something fitting for you, remain out here with me for a few weeks."

It sparkled in Kathrin's eyes. But the young man caught the flashes and instantly sought to dampen her joy.

"To this end, I must thus today register you with the school teacher Schwarz. And I have to likewise take care of your unpleasant affair in the town. They are utterly time-consuming affairs", he added wrinkling his forehead, and looked at his guest reproachfully. "And now — you can hopefully write and count properly?"

"Oh yes", Kathrin replied in a low voice and let her head hang.

The conversation was taking a very unpleasant turn for her. But her guardian was not to be deterred, he believed far too much that he was on the right path.

"Good," he determined decisively, and at the same time, he had already energetically torn a page from his notebook, "then write my name out for me here."

"Yes, gladly", Kathrin replied. She tore the pencil so fiercely from his hand that it must have attracted his attention.

"Oh, that is fine", she secretly exulted, for she had thrown down on every reachable piece of paper just this name already countless times in Latin and German during bored hours for her enjoyment, yes, even with the finest shading. And when her guardian now bent over her during the test, an open exclamation of satisfaction slipped from him.

"Look now," he uttered in astonishment, "something could perhaps be made of that."

And in his spirit, he saw this girl trained by him already enthroned on an office chair. The devil yes, only Sophie Guntrum wrote approximately as nicely and distinctly. He could not fail but slip the small sheet into his breast pocket with an embarrassed smile. You could perhaps play those credentials perhaps sometime as if by accident into the hands of the young blond lady. Yes, in the thought of the shock of A. Guntrum's daughter, a certain pride almost penetrated Kathrin's guardian.

"That is not bad at all", he thought again, and he moved contentedly somewhat closer to the little one to inquire further with real suspense, "How old are you?"

"Nine", Kathrin tossed out disparagingly, because she was comprehending this ridiculous examination less and less.

"And how old am I?"

"Twenty seven", the little Brodersen noted confidently, for the birthday of her guardian formed a main event of her life.

"Correct. And now multiply both numbers with each other."

"Oh yes." The brown-haired girl lowered her head in shame, led her finger to her lips and began stammering. "That — that I cannot do so quickly."

"So?" Richard Sell suggested very disappointedly, "why not then? That is bad though. What have you managed then in arithmetic?"

Now Kathrin became tearful and began wailing loudly. "I can only count off such a large thing on my fingers."

"Nonsense," her besetter judged grudgingly, "I see you have not learnt well. That is really very unpleasant. — Tell me please, what do you actually know about religion?"

There the bleak face of the examinee became exhilarated.

"Oh," she sputtered out very reflectively, "in the beginning, God created heaven, water and the earth."

"Yes, yes, quite right, but what is dear God?"

Again Kathrin shook her head, perplexed over so much inapt curiosity.

"Dear God is a spirit", she pondered finally.

"And where does he live?"

The little girl opened her eyes wide, but pointed with her finger confidently up above. Straight afterwards, meanwhile, the lower half of her mouth sank in measureless surprise, and she became completely speechless. Dear God, was it all quite alright with her guardian? Or was he perhaps only seeking in jest her opinion over the residence of the heavenly Father?

"Up there?", it namely came from his sharply chiseled mouth, "We don't have any real idea about up there at all. The essential thing remains that He lives in you and me and in Schmidtsch and Ott Knuth, do you understand?"

There the reproved girl shook her brown-locked head energetically, for now she had to finally prove how much better educated she was.

"No," she refused stubbornly, "he does not live in Schmidtsch and Ott Knuth. They are both much too ugly for that."

So!

There stood Richard Sell, the energetic, fortunate up-start, and stared struck, completely thrown from the saddle by that stiff-necked youth whom he had set it in his head that he must teach. Slowly and painfully, the feeling crept up on him of how building up a young soul was infinitely more difficult and required finer arts than erecting a smokehouse, even if you acquired the mater-ial for it so expensively. He stood helplessly, looked confusedly at his ward, skimmed once more, as much as he also resisted it, the much too short woollen skirt, un-til he finally uttered in a low voice, "It will really be best if I take you straightaway to Mr Schwarz. And in the af-ternoon we will go into town and buy you a new dress. You cannot walk about with me like that."

"Nice", Kathrin said very contentedly, as she shook the grey woollen material contemptuously. And yielding to a sudden concern, she added, "And my old things?"

"Ott Knuth can fetch them, but I do not want to see them anymore from now on."

That was something much more liberating for the child than all the endeavours of the clever man over her spiritual enlightenment.

6

The November storms were passing across the bay. They blew the powdery snow up onto the frozen solid covering of ice until it looked as if a giant, wrapped deep in a ragged white fur, was striding across the surface. They broke the stunted fruit trees which creaked and groaned from the frost behind the drowsy cottages, and they blew into the chimneys so that the melody struck out from the flues howling and smoking, "Sweet, dear breeze, how the wind blows!"

It was quite early in the morning.

In the little living room at Mr Sell's, the green pendant lamp was already burning, for outside such bleak snowy twilight reigned that you could recognise neither path nor road. Kathrin, however, lay on her knees in a thick blue woollen cloak, her schoolbag tied over her back, in front of the round white tile stove, and pushed one blocky piece of wood after the other into the firebox. The flames chased out of it wildly and redly jerking, sprang in reflection across the dark floor, and conjured a crimson glaze on the forehead and cheeks of the girl.

The way it was puffing and hissing from the tile stove, it was becoming right comfortable in the little space. And the uniform tick-tock of the clock over the sofa sounded as if time were still cradling itself in morning slumber. Only Kathrin was in a rush. In her soul, the anxiety over whether Schmidtsch would also bring the coffee on time for Mr Sell was stirring, and in addition she was tormented by the fear over whether her own conception of the family of King David could surely stand up before the teacher Schwarz. And hence she threw the iron door shut with a loud blow, brushed off the dust, and was just then intending to rush with her flying brown plaits through the dark hall when the bell rang outside, and straight afterwards there was a quiet and indistinct knocking on the door.

"Come in", the decamping girl hesitated, as she could not comprehend who could be desiring entrance at this early hour and so modestly and furtively.

The door slowly moved as if someone were waiting behind it who did not quickly bring themselves to step from the darkness into the light. And really, when the tall voluptuous female figure finally became visible, an inner urge or an unshakeable bashfulness seemed to hinder the stranger from crossing the threshold as freely and fearlessly as other people and from expressing her desires. The schoolchild also remained standing, led her finger to her mouth in embarrassment, and stared at the unfamiliar visitor with large astonished eyes. And truly, even a being of more mature experience would surely have examined the early guest not without apprehension. There was first of all the clothes of the statuesque woman, which did not agree with each other so well. A conspicuously enormous plush hat framed the brown wavy hair of the infiltrator, and the snow layered on the edge had almost bent a few upstanding feathers. A dark jacket with fur lining enveloped the supple body, but, oh wonders — it even struck Kathrin's attention — the lady's skirt hung ragged at the seams and slit downwards, and bared a pair of formerly elegant patent leather boots which were now cracked and ruptured. The stranger also held an old, bent umbrella in her hand, and her black eyes scurried uncertainly and stealthily around in the corners as if she were seeking someone who could forbid her arrival.

"Yes, what do you want?", Kathrin stuttered in a low voice, for the strange appearance had such strong effect on her from an unfamiliar basis that her voice faded. "Mr Sell is not yet down."

Then the beautiful woman straightened. The assurance of the child over the absence of her guardian must have lent her somewhat more confidence.

"So, so," she burst out quickly and hoarsely, "when does he tend to come down then actually?"

"Oh, that could take another half hour", the little one responded attentively, and at the same time, it seemed to her as if she must not leave the room unguarded.

The stranger, however, shrugged her shoulders, touched with displeasure. And when the light of the lamp now fell on her slender countenance, the girl was shocked over the strangely stiff redness on the woman's cheeks. In her perplexity, she thought her visitor must have put on a mask. Even the black-rimmed eyes infused her with fear.

"I cannot wait so long," the unfamiliar woman said restlessly, and plucked at her perforated gloves, "I must go on the next steamer to Stralsund. It surely moors outside here?"

"Yes", the little one confirmed obligingly, since she would not have disliked seeing the visitor leaving again as quickly as possible.

"And what is your name then?", the uncomfortable oppressor inquired further, and stepped closer to the girl.

Only, the questioned girl backed away shyly.

"I'm Kathrin", she stuttered without thinking, while she was already looking around for whether she could not slip behind the table. The stranger, however, pursed her full lips.

"Kathrin?", she repeated in surprise. "Why are you called that? Are you not called Emma like me?" Again the woman approached the defenceless protector of the residence, and now she stretched her arm out and tried to grasp the child's hand with a quick movement.

Then Kathrin gave an instinctive slap to the groping fingers, and crying out quietly she pushed a chair between her and the stranger. Her heart began pounding wildly, and her mouth was already forming to call out loudly for help. But her guest noticed, tilted her head, and broke out into a weary, almost inaudible laughter.

"You don't like me surely?", she inquired quickly, and at the same time, she bent over the table so that the child now sensed her breath. "You surely aren't pleased by me?"

"No", Kathrin burst out defiantly, although her entire body shook so heftily that her pencil case clattered in her schoolbag. "I must go to school. And anyway," — she added suddenly with up-springing archness, "if you don't go, then you will miss your steamer, it has already moored."

"Ah right." A quiet sigh escaped the reminded woman, she shook herself, and her look remained riveted on the tiny iron safe which was planted in the darkest corner of the room. "Mr Sell surely never comes about this time?"

"No, my father is still dressing."

"So, so, your father", the stranger uttered, and showed her white teeth mockingly. But after thinking for a while, she tore a little card from a ragged muff and placed it on the table. "Do you know something?", she said, shrugging her shoulders, "give that to Mr Sell. But only to him, do you hear, so that he knows who visited him. And inform him that I would have waited if I had not had something to do at court in Stralsund. But I will come again, for my request is urgent. And now adieu, Emma. You need not be afraid of me, no, really not, you stupid sprog."

With that she nodded, brushed the wet from her clothes once more, and before the girl left behind had fully recovered, the strange visitor had already vanished with inaudibly rocking steps into the darkness of the hall.

***

"Goodness, why are you so inattentive today, Kathrin?", the teacher, Mr Schwarz, was shouting an hour later, a herculean fellow with a walrus-moustached, full-moon face, and at the same time he, as was his his habit, struck the cane smashing down onto the top of the school desk. "How can you forget among the tributaries of the Oder the Havel? Put yourself immediately in front of my desk and say thirty times in a row the word 'Havel', understand?"

"Yes, but — —", Kathrin apologised, turning blood-red.

Only, Mr Schwarz let the cane swish through the air, here and there, until he was more like a wildly moved fencer than an educator of adolescent youth, and under his red clumpy nose his massive moustache was bristling violently.

"Will it happen soon?", he commanded in his menacing bass which passed through all the children's limbs. "I know what will do you good. For someone who forgets the Havel with the Oder just doesn't want to remember. Yes, they don't want to."

And Kathrin had to plant herself before the teacher's desk and begin her recital.

That was one of the education methods of Mr Schwarz, which was accepted by both the massive man and his charges especially. Not only because those uninvolved could kill time during the whining so nicely and unendangered, no, the spreader of village education also found in such pauses the wished-for opportunity to think undisturbed about whether eel catching, in which he was a master, should be done with the spear or with the net. Thus the monarch of the school then also now stabbed his yellow cane like a spear into an imagined deep, and he could not be blamed if he found no further time with his difficult preparations to examine the facial features and behaviour of the little malefactor in-depth.

Usually the pedagogue's attention would perhaps have been caught by how the transgressor grasped the seam of her dress pocket almost uninterruptedly, behind which a piece of firm paper crackled treacherously. And as the waters of the Havel poured incessantly from her lips, the little thing rolled constantly and stubbornly in her inner being the same concern which had taken possession of her entire being since that morning.

Havel — Havel — Havel —

Strange, on the card which she kept to herself, the name Emma Brodersen was to be read. How did it actually come about that Kathrin bore the same name? Or was she deceived in that? It was at base not entirely clear, for many people also awarded her the name of Sell. An appellation which she preferred hearing inordinately, since something much more noble and splendid lay distinguished in the name of Mr Sell. She had never thought about it, but the entire thing was in the end right peculiar. Why did her name waver back and forth so oddly? How was she related to Mr Sell? And what could the woman with the fine hat and torn skirt, who likewise called herself Brodersen, have wanted this morning?

No, a thing which tumbled the tributaries of the Oder rushing all over each other surged together in hissing foam and tore the brooding child around in circles.

Havel — Havel — Havel —

"Well, now you know it", the teacher Mr Schwarz determined graciously, and looked desperately at the clock on the wall.

He had meanwhile committed to the net.

***

The midday meal crept solemnly and quietly past in the little living room of Mr Sell. The young owner, who also felt responsible for the outward habits of his charge, had used the good opportunity after Kathrin's

entrance into the small household to banish the old
smoker Ott Knuth during mealtimes forever to the stove
in the kitchen. The child would under no circumstances
learn from the rotten, crumbling ruin of a man the dis-
gusting customs of unmannered dining, and even he
himself, who had long since realised with the fine in-
stinct of the upstart the importance of such forms for
bourgeois society, applied himself with the accustomed
control to any consideration in order to also offer here
the little one a dignified example. It could not thus remain that in their meeting at the table a stiff seriousness
always penetrated which was not free of force and hence
never let a harmless chatter or even a merry jesting be
raised. Mr Sell earnestly annihilated with his ward the
simple dishes which were carried in to them by
Schmidtsch, and the guardian considered it thereby extremely expedient to extend and lovingly supplement by
his own further explanations what the little one might
perhaps have heard in school that morning.

Thus he was also practising today.

She had stuttered something to his question of how
difficult it would be to find your way in the moors and
morasses of the Havel country. And when the young
man wiped his mouth clean, leant back comfortably in
his armchair, and as he closed his eyes a little, he began
sharing and giving to his at first absolutely unwilling
listener his own knowledge of the Brandenburg countryside which he had obtained only arduously through
reading. Ah, to the speaker such an opportunity became
far too comfortable and proud. It was actually splendid
though that there was a needy being for whom his
knowledge could be a blessing. And at the same time,
the lonely man was raised by that enthusing into another world above the grey everyday of his business
days, so that he did not seem at all so abandoned and
deserted anymore. It was really as if green iridescent
soap bubbles in which the world was reflected sparkling

were driven by the wind in through the open window of the sober businessman's room, sparkling more and more mysteriously, more and more luminously until they burst while slowly rising. Thus he salvaged himself today also from the everyday, he conjured the fir-encircled, dark-blue lakes of that region from nothing, reported the praise of a few especially popular princes who dominated here with ladle and walking stick, and described the blessings and grace which penetrated on these waterways far from the sea as far as the massive capital. The rattling of Kathrin's spoon, with which she had previously been eagerly ladling her potato soup, gradually died out. In the child's black eyes, the lively appreciation for the descriptions was painted, and her ardent, adventure-loving soul leapt far ahead of her guide.

"Ah," her enthusiasm wanted to release itself just then into a single irresistible wish, "that is fine. To Berlin, there I would like to go."

Only before those syllables could be formed into something comprehensible, the hidden card crackled again captiously in her pocket, and with a deep sigh, she pushed her hand into the lining to wait in ambush anew for when she could surely finally reveal to her protector the still secretive experience with the stranger.

"Do you have something?", Richard Sell asked, interrupted by her sigh and recalled to the present again.

"No," Kathrin stammered, shying from disturbing the flight of the beautiful images by something ugly, "it just sounds pretty. You note why you learn something quite differently than with the teacher, Mr Schwarz. When I close my eyes, I see it all before me."

"So," Richard Sell nodded, "that is also the aim, so that you do not forget it again."

But inwardly, the unwitting flattery warmed him further pleasantly, and hence he acquired after the end of the meal something over himself which he until then had always avoided. The binding of a habit becoming dear to him was already beginning to influence his being. He remained thoughtfully before the little one, raised his hand indecisively as if he wanted to stroke her curly, brown hair, and instinctively started when he suddenly sensed the touch of the silky tips. Both the thankful look of the girl as well as the scurrying redness of her cheeks confused him, and he immediately rebuked himself because he was engaging himself in things which displayed no proper aim at all.

Yes, what had he intended actually before he plunged himself into this unnecessary embarrassment? With a powerful jerk, he deliberated, buttoned up the blue duffel coat he was wearing today, and as he sent a quick look through the window to the still, sunny, snowy landscape, he threw back triflingly and indifferently, "I am going to Pottwiem to the cooperage. If you want, you can accompany me, Kathrin." But before the child could spring up from behind the table in wild delight over the unheard-of request, the decamping man was dampening her fierce willingness already again by the very definite admonition, "I ask, however, that you brush your coat down as cleanly as possible. Your boots are in order, aren't they? And above all things, wrap yourself in a woollen scarf, you hear?"

"Yes, yes", Kathrin exulted, already sweeping away to collect together her things. And when she swept past the kitchen in which Ott Knuth was holding his winter's sleep, the soup bowl on his knees, she could not abstain from crying in the rapt man's ears full of satisfaction, "You, I am going for a walk with Mr Sell. Just think, with him himself."

And Ott Knuth raised his heavy jelly-like eyes a little, and from the wrinkles of his mouth something stole forth which could have sounded a bit like, "Women — foolishness."

With that his opinion over this unexpected incident was exhausted, and he shook his clattering skeleton weakly again when the doorbell announced with a bright ring the departure of both his house companions.

It was a curious picture, the way Richard Sell strode with his ward now through the blue-breathing winter's day. Not only the slender village street, but also the sea meadows penetrating everywhere slumbered as far as the eye reached under an untouched white covering, and it was so calm that the fine crystal wings on the branches of the trees neither stirred nor detached. The light smoke curled candlestick straight up from the chimneys into the frosty clear haze, and every step, even the next noise, everything was enveloped as if in a soft, impenetrable twilight. High above the sea, a coppery liquid ball rolled along behind thick veils of cloud, and on the snow-covered roof ridges of the little cottages violet lines were already beginning to run like strangely scurrying mice who swirled along in quick pursuit, one on the trail of the other. And both wanderers seemed just as solemn and Sunday-like as the soundless winter hours when they now sought their way measuredly and silently through the deserted, dreamy village street. Not a speck was to be seen on the coats of the two, and even the peering eyes of the fisherwomen encountering them had to confess to being filled with envy, "Looks spick and span. Look at the little girl, how well she walks, always one foot before the other. Yes, yes, Mr Sell knows what is right."

And really, the young man who was so assiduously concerned about his reputation was ambushed during this first communal walk by a pleasant reassurance that the strange child at his side could be quite well suited to the membership of a bourgeois household. As charmingly as the fluffy blue coat nestled about her childish limbs, and as cheerily as the brown plait with the curl of black ribbon over her neck. Even the hulking grey woollen scarf which he had gifted her from his own stores flowed in two graceful ends over her chest, and the young smokehouse owner did not comprehend at all how this item of daily use could suddenly have assumed such a becoming form. For the first time, he noticed that the cloth on its lower tips was displaying broad colourful stripes, and he accepted emphatically that Kathrin had plucked apart that harmless adornment very carefully.

"The thing must possess taste", he thought. "Why not, perhaps something agreeable will develop from it sometime later."

Without suspecting, the sober practical man occupied himself again and ever again with wanting to guide the innate abilities of this little being to a distant future for the better. And when he now let a glance sweep over his companion furtively and unnoticed, he recognised with pleasure her erect gait and how something proud and lofty resided in the slender face of the girl. That pleased him. It fitted well to the calm insularity which he wished to impart to his life and his home. And he did not notice in the slightest that the increased self-confidence of his companion only sprung from the brazen honour of being permitted to stroll with the mightiest man in Uhlenhus so amiably and naturally before the sight of everyone.

Yes, Kathrin was almost perfectly happy during this walk. She only entertained one last desire — that from the low windows to the right and left, a good many witnesses of her charmed existence might be resurrected. And when they arrived near the snowed-in churchyard, she could barely suppress the wondrous idea of how beautiful it would be if the widow Braesel and the orphans' councillor, Tredup, were sitting on the highest of the white crosses so that they could enjoy the splendid procession of the former orphan child quite clearly. That wild desire squeezed her chest more and more strongly until she suddenly forgot everything around her, her measured step, her clean boots and not least the nearness of her taciturn guardian, to break out abruptly into the spontaneous eruption, "Ah, it is so splendid!"

"What?", Richard Sell asked in astonishment, thinking the loud tone obviously unfitting.

"Everything", Kathrin murmured contritely, for the severe look of the man chased her back into her confines. And at the same time, she sensed how the card of the strange woman was moving again crackling in her coat pocket.

Kathrin shook. Good grief, why had she simply forgotten this affair? She had wanted though to wait for a properly suitable moment so that she could then tell Mr Sell about the incident of his early visitor. Strange, and now she did not dare! It even bored the suspicion into her that she must not speak to her protector about the woman in the torn skirt, who was unfortunately called by exactly the same name as herself, until she had spied him in an especially good mood. Better to postpone somewhat. Why rush at all this thing which could perhaps annoy Mr Sell? Anyway, it had been such a weird, gelatinous-eyed woman! If the female had perhaps come now to take her herself somewhere else again? Lord in heaven, Kathrin was one who was pushed here and there every moment. Quite certainly, it would be best perhaps if she kept her mouth shut over the encounter. It could have escaped her. What did she care in the end for the woman in the feather hat? Right now when it was becoming so excellent in the world?! No really, she would take care. She pushed the little slip of paper decisively back into the thick lining of the pocket where it could make no more sound anymore; only, a quite new thought unexpectedly announced itself painfully. But what was that? The man next to her hated nothing so much as dissimulation and lies. Just what would he do if he discovered such a misappropriation on her?! — Lord, Lord! — In silent torment, the child pressed her lips together, and the more she was oppressed by the first temptation in her life, the more fiercely she threw her head back and the more darkly and reluctantly her black eyes flashed.

Meanwhile the wanderers had paced out the wide undifferentiated expanse of snow, and the little village of Pottwiem appeared, where the wooden clog makers and the coopers lived. The lusty knocking of mallets sounded from left and right, and before a light blue painted cottage Richard Sell commanded his ward to wait outside there for quarter of an hour because he had to submit an order in the interior of the workplace.

"You can walk up and down here calmly", the young merchant directed. And already on the brick threshold, he turned his sharp head back once more and added warningly, "It is not necessary either that you begin a conversation with a Pottwiem resident. The people are very curious."

With that the slender figure turned into the hallway, and straight afterwards, the triple beat of the mallets was interrupted as if by command. Kathrin, however, stood obediently before the entrance, held her hands lowered in her coat pockets, and instinctively turned the hidden card again thoughtlessly between her fingers. Then she jerked back suddenly from the piece of paper as if it had caught fire in her pocket, and to switch to other thoughts she began strenuously examining the outer shape of the cooper's home. Soon it seemed to her as if the white snow crystals were sparkling and shimmering across the blue walls like countless stars on a light winter's sky. And immediately after that, her curiosity sprang again to something else, to the yellow perennials there in the low frame of the open window. Look, they were trembling lightly in the wind, and the girl thought she could catch their dry rustling. Golden and luminous, the flower heads peered out from the blackness of the room, and Kathrin's lively power of imagination feigned to her how pretty it would be if you could pocket such a full bush. She approached half unconsciously, peered into the dim room, and when she saw nobody, she began smelling the flowers wistfully. Then she paused, started, and struggled against the wish which had suddenly shot up burningly in her. She did not know either why she submitted to it all of a sudden. But if you could have offered Mr Sell now such a long-stemmed flower or even fastened it in his buttonhole, it would have to certainly agree amiably with him and bring a beautiful thanks from him. Truly, she would have so liked to gift a person something for once. And now indeed to the quiet man who did not receive anything dear from anyone. If the cooperage people possessed one stem more or less, they would not notice at all. It was anyhow ugly and coarse that they fostered something in there for which another yearned so. How did such dirty people arrive on wooden clogs after all? A fierce antagonism towards the owners of the pot of asters crept into the soul of the brooding girl, and it drove the blood fitfully and hotly into her cheeks. And before she had properly considered it, her fingers were already bending the quivering twig, and the next moment she sprang back with a stormily pounding heart as far as the village street. A fierce urge impelled her to make certain in all directions that nobody had overseen her deed. If anyone had observed the child at it, they would not have recognised her. The whites of her eyes protruded nervously and guiltily during her blinking here and there, and the proudly raised head stooped as if it were seeking a hiding-place. Strange, the flower in her hand had also abruptly lost all its brilliance and shimmer, yes, it looked actually quite dry and commonplace. And in the first surprise, Kathrin tried to shove the yellow piece of gold under her coat. She was still occupied with tearing open a few buttons of her overcoat when unexpectedly behind her back just that voice was heard from which she fled.

Richard Sell had hurried out elastically over the brick threshold, and the snow had muffled his steps. Thus it occurred that he could almost place his hand completely unnoticed on the girl's shoulder to summon her for the walk home. But Kathrin sank almost to her knees. The flower stretched far from her, her back bent in fright, she remained as if the ground did not want to let go of her; and she trembled so strongly that the young man came sympathetically to the idea that the long lingering in the open air must have driven a chill into the child's limbs.

"Are you cold, Kathrin?"

"Yes, yes."

"Well, we will have a cup of warm coffee here in the village tavern", the smokehouse owner reassured his ward, since he rebuked himself because he had so completely neglected to think of the tender constitution of the little one. "Just come along, you will get a piece of cake too", he added hurriedly. And when she did not stir, but still stretched the yellow plant motionless before herself, he inquired in astonishment, "How did you come upon the aster?"

There it was. Kathrin felt at the same moment an ungovernable pain in her neck, and for a scurrying second she thought of tossing the ill-fated flower away from herself to then run away never to be seen again. But that formed just a trick of the senses without result, for her mouth was capable despite all that of conjuring up an innocent smile, and her voice sounded, in spite of the numbing fear which constricted her throat, fawning and fresh when she strove to chase out an answer with great effort, "The aster?" she emitted, as her dark eyes adhered avidly to the open window frame, "it — the woman gifted it to me."

Praise God, there it was out. Now come what may. But Richard Sell was already striding next to her; she must surely have pressed the flower with gentle force into his hand, for he fastened the yellow flower really as she had hoped in the buttonhole of his coat, and it looked very nice.

"The woman?", he repeated subsequently. "Hm, is she in the room then?"

Kathrin nodded animatedly. "Yes," she continued to fantasise breathlessly, "she was just fetching a wiping cloth."

"Aha. Well, thank you", the young man praised her, warmed pleasantly by the modest gift; and as he moved closer to the side of the girl, he could not contain himself from tossing out once more as if unintended, "Why did you not keep the woman's gift yourself, dear child?"

Then Kathrin's eyes flashed. She turned her head vigorously to look back, but thank heavens, the cooperage was already becoming indistinct behind a snowy haze. Just a few steps, and they were wandering over the bridge of a ditch, and a snow-covered alder bush towered protectively before the little malefactor and the place of her misdemeanour. "Why did you not keep the woman's gift yourself, dear child?" Hastily she sucked in the enlivening air of the expanse before, still shuddering from the weird rushing in her veins, she could collect herself for an answer, "I wanted so much to make a gift of it for you."

And she spoke the truth. This wish alone had led the vigorous little being, and it was not her fault that with her, quite unforeseen already, concepts and new ideas were arising over what was right and wrong or forbidden and allowed. The man next to her and the life in the ordered household had generated all that. Had she become happier as a result? Kathrin did not know. But as Richard Sell placed his arm paternally and as it were in play about the shoulders of his companion, the child crept burdened up next to him, and even the gleam of the yellow flower in the buttonhole of the feared man was incapable of attenuating the heavy hammering of her whipped up heart.

The day was already fading, and blue shadows were swelling up from all sides when they finally arrived in the village tavern which lay a good stretch from Pottwiem. Soon they were sitting behind a brown coffeepot, and the smokehouse owner saw with quiet sympathy how the hot drink and the coarse cake strengthened and calmed the child who had been agitated by the wandering. She crouched with propped up arms, and her eyes hung thoughtlessly on his own. Her eyelids quivered again and again when her look skimmed over the stolen flower. In her inner being, she was not clear at all yet. Then a cheerful tinkling sounded behind their chairs. The landlord had, in order to offer his guests an amusement, wound up the music box, and at once a simple folk ballad jingled and rattled forth from the turning metal disk, a song which the girl had often sung with her fellow students at school without especial appreciation. But now the blood streamed into her fine slender face, and her entire body began shaking again as if she were hearing the voice of a ghost.

> Always practice devotion and honesty
> Right to your cool grave.

The song slowly purred out. But every word of the text which the child instinctively spoke to herself tore like a sharp thorn in her young breast. She straightened up full of horror, and in the endeavour to also throw the last secrecy from herself, Kathrin suddenly drew out the card she had so carefully guarded until now and tossed it onto the table before her companion as if he had already been long since informed of everything.

"There!"

"What is that?"

The smokehouse owner grasped the card uncomprehendingly. But he had hardly read the name inscribed on it than he turned dark-red and straight afterwards conspicuously pale again. And as the young man, shaken as if by disgust, crushed the card in his fist, the words flew in scared-up haste back and forth between the two. Clinging to the table, the child emitted everything it knew, and her tumbling voice betrayed frequently how clearly it loathed in the strange woman who bore the same name a possible enemy of her calm and her happiness.

"Her skirt was completely torn below", she underlined ever anew with especially derisive emphasis.

"Let that be — let that be."

Richard Sell had buried his head in his hands, for in his usually so ordered thought, it was burrowing and whirling in confusion. But strangely, not a single time did the fury rise in him that he had been brought into such bad society by the stray child, and not for a second did the desire stir to push the little being away from himself once and for all, to eradicate in this way fundamentally and forever the stain which he already saw with seething rage spreading on the clean floors of his house. Wonderful — who would have thought? — There the brooding man sat and tortured his brain for how he could preserve untouched from the danger of corruption his possession, the pretty neat child with the brown plaits and the expressive eyes. Yes, that was it. This knowledge twitched back and forth constantly before his closed eyes; contact with the dissolute woman must be avoided, whatever it took. But oh God, she was the mother! And had the lawyer not assured him just a few weeks ago that the kindred blood could not be dammed or suppressed? Was it not actually a madness when he wanted to dislodge such a natural urge singly and alone by a painstaking education? No — all the same — his indomitable, conceited will, which had paved a path through life for him until now, just this rebelled defiantly against the tyranny of incomprehensible and blindly raging nature. He wanted to see whether you could overturn its work so simply. And hence, as he incessantly pounded arduously against his forehead, he returned ever anew to the question which seemed to contain more than any other the greatest distress.

"She wants to come again then?"

"Yes, when she is finished with the court."

"Right, that too!" And Richard Sell pressed further apprehensively, for now the climax was approaching, which he must not evade, "Has she told you nothing further about yourself? What was being held against her in Stralsund, and above all things, who she is?"

There lay so much badly concealed unease in the behaviour of her guardian, such an unusual forsaking of his cool measuredness, that Kathrin forgot her own suffering. She slowly and timidly raised her hand towards her protector. And see there, the man grasps the slender fingers and squeezes them hard and firmly in his own. A bond was concluded over the coarse oak table between the two, a solidarity was announced without hesitation and without diffidence, yes, the eyes firmly anchored in each other, they mutually vowed loyalty and holding out against a malicious world gone mad which wanted to chase them apart.

Richard Sell seized the girl's arm higher and higher.

"Did she really not impart to you who she is?"

"Not a word", Kathrin responded, listening attentively, whereby she brushed her hair from her forehead bashfully. And she cautiously added, "I thought you would perhaps have told me that."

"Me?" The smokehouse owner pulled himself together and tried to force a disparaging smile. "But no — it does not matter at all. We will keep the woman at bay. For see, Kathrin, please," he suddenly closed with his old conclusiveness, "that is a person who has taken something from other people. Do you understand? And such a person is not counted among decent people. Do you not think so too?"

Kathrin nodded apprehensively, for she dared not speak.

A while later, they both strode home hand in hand. The night had drawn in, and the snowstorm was groaning its cruel lament across the sea.

***

Since that time, Kathrin displayed a great tendency for thinking to herself. She could frequently prop her head in her hands in the midst of her schoolwork to stare at nothing. But there she saw things and connections, on the bare wall such strange images wafted up and down that she occasionally spoke her thoughts aloud to herself, although she almost always started fiercely when she heard her own voice. At such a moment, it could happen that her unconscious words escaped in this way, "Now we have already been waiting four weeks for her", and another time, "Whether she has died perhaps?"

"Who surely?", Ott Knuth breathed hoarsely, as he lay, enveloped in thick blankets, hunched up on the sofa and shivered to himself like a sick cat.

The old man had for some while already not been able to tolerate even the slightest hint which somehow referred to ending or stopping, and his own inability to still grasp numerical values properly offered him a pure and blissful happiness. It was actually also quite magnificent when you could suddenly again consider yourself a twenty year old in this way, from no other basis than because all other numbers had charitably vanished from memory.

The old smoker tried to turn his bound head from the back of his place of rest. It had seemed to him as if someone here had spoken of death and dying. Ugh, the devil, who was behaving here so boundlessly stupid and mean? There had been a time especially when you still felt young and strong!

"Stupidity — who is dying here?", the little clump of human residue wheezed, and he struck his needle thin fingers weakly against the crocheted blanket.

Then Kathrin came to and bent her head assiduously over the open map.

"Oh, I was just thinking", she apologised.

"But it isn't true," the smoker growled irritably, "it has not been for a long time."

And Kathrin nodded hastily and responded sighing, "Yes, yes, I believe it myself."

Another time, however, she was clearer. It was on an evening shortly before Christmas. Richard Sell was reclining in his green upholstered chair, smoking his cigar comfortably, and observing full of interest how adroitly the sparkling knitting needles moved in Kathrin's hands. The child was working on massive black woollen socks, and it increased the satisfaction of the observer because he knew that this warming item was intended for himself. The little one had circuitously taken his measurements just a few days before. It was actually wonderful when he recalled how attentively the girl had knelt before him so that she made sure from his boot of whether the socks would sit widely enough and comfortably. Now she was working under the green-shaded lamp, and blue and violet lights glided over the hurrying needles. The steel rods tapped against each other furtively and pleasantly.

There — quite unexpectedly — the child suddenly interrupted her occupation, and as she let the sock fall into her lap, she directed her dark eyes firmly and unflinchingly at the resting man before the bright window curtains. Then she said quietly, but yet as if it were just the end of a long chain of thoughts, "The day before yesterday, I had my birthday."

What was that?

The smokehouse owner bent forward in astonishment and looked searchingly at his charge. His cheeks slowly coloured, and his calculating eyes were penetrated by the understanding that this harmless remark contained not only the accusal of an unappreciated girl, but was also the precursor to those dangerous discoveries which he liked so much to keep distant from himself and his house. Whether you could prevent any longer the desire for clarity which resided in every awakening being? He assumed an indifferent air, and although the unease oppressed him heavily, he tossed out seemingly heedlessly, "Truly, it is so. You were born on the 19th December. You are now ten years old, Kathrin."

The girl nodded, but did not lift up her sock again, instead continuing with the equally unavoidable look, "Where was I born actually?"

Now the man of the house moved his chair uncomfortably, and the desire crept up on him to finish this disturbing hearing through severity and brusque behaviour. Nevertheless, he still wrestled out, "It was in town."

"Yes, I know that", Kathrin agreed thoughtfully, and it was as if she were shaking at a gate in her spirit though which she would like to stride as it were. "How comes it though," she continued speaking groping, and a conspicuous unease twitched over her countenance at the same time, "that I am called Brodersen?"

"Why?" Then Richard Sell sprang up noisily, pushed his chair back, and began looking for old notebooks on the bookshelf above the commode. It was probably very important, and it concurred well that his head was now submerged completely in the shadows. "That is so", he emitted during his rummaging curtly and monosyllabically. "Anyhow, where are the wage books? No proper order is being kept here again."

With that he threw a few volumes from the shelf, murmured something indignant and left the room quickly and as if affronted. — — —

Only, the curtain of Kathrin's existence had now been rolled up once more, and the little one's agile power of imagination equipped her life's stage with all sorts of mad and strange decorations. She looked everywhere for mysterious fellow actors. And see there, that one from whom she strove at first to catch a meaningful cue, he made it especially easy for her.

On the last morning before Christmas namely, on the first school-free blessed day, the little Brodersen had left her bed very early and was now peering in the grey of morning through a crack in the front door. Outside the snowflakes were whirling in slanted flight across the river, and the wind was driving fine white powder up as far as the dark hallway. Then a light whistle was emitted in the proximity of the house, and as the path was over-shadowed, a thickly wrapped figure pushed itself along, dragging a felled fir tree on a tiny sled behind itself. With a strong swing, the fir flew from the shoulder of the bristly visitor, and only after the man toddling in had placed his burden in the kitchen carefully in a corner did he raise the fur cap drawn low over his fore-head and release at the same time the thick woollen scarf from over his neck and mouth.

"Good morning too", wished Bob Swanegel, who had in the intervening time shot up so inordinately tall that his short-cropped head towered far up into the blackened flue. "There is the thing", he said mutedly, for he placed no worth on being heard by those unbidden. "Since it should be so cheap, I have fetched it from the agricultural school up there. I had to wait at five o'clock in the morning with the superintendent. But for that it also only cost forty pfennigs."

"Beautiful," Kathrin said, and she plucked a little embarrassedly at her skirt, "I can only give you the money

bit by bit though. Mr Sell knows nothing at all of the entire purchase in fact. For he has never had such a tree."

"Never," Bob Swanegel suggested coolly, and lifted
his nose up somewhat more haughtily, "that I surely
thought to myself. Mr Sell is an old grump, such a
proper misanthrope with whom cherries are not good to
eat. Take care, young thing, you will yet be made quite
mute with him."

But Kathrin stamped her foot irritably.

"That he is not", she cried upset. "For such as you or
myself, we do not understand Mr Sell at all. Do you
know what he is?"

"Well, what then?", the former ship's boy inquired
very reflectively.

Here Kathrin assumed a solemn air.

"Now, I believe he is a wise man. Such a thing as
King Solomon from the Bible." She spoke it quite seriously and timidly, but this explanation also exercised
only a very slight impression on her admirer.

"For all I care," he said, shrugging his shoulders, "he
has always had something Jewish about him. He is possessed over the scraping together of money. But tell
me," he diverted when he noticed how Kathrin was
turning with displeasure to the stove, "how will you obtain the candles and paper chains for the tree? For such
things belong with it."

Then the girl turned back hastily to him and as she
began twisting one of the buttons on his fleece jacket,
she revealed to him with lowered eyes that she had calculated on Bob Swanegel standing helpfully at her side
for this necessary purchase from Mr Emanuel Quandt.

"Ah, so you think that?", Bob smiled nobly. "Well
yes, if you don't spend your pocket money on sweets
then I can surely join in on that unworried. Well, then
hurry up, sprog."

Kathrin promised to, but while she was still putting
on her blue woollen coat, which was held for her by Bob

in an attack of chivalry, she hesitated once more, and as she examined him in a strangely inquiring way, it came out slowly and reflectively, "Hey, I will ask you something afterwards."

"Afterwards?" The tall boy bent his head forward, scratched behind his ear, and even his cold-blooded disposition seemed to be agitated by the strangeness of the approach. "Just afterwards?", he repeated, dumbfounded, and his large self-confident eyes opened wider and wider.

But Kathrin nodded definitely. "You will still have some time for me?"

The former ship's boy could in no way resist such a mysterious request despite all his innate noblesse and worldliness.

"Well yes," he hesitated, "I am planning with Kohlrausch a quite corrupt thing. Women affairs. But if it must be! Who knows what sort of stupidity you have concocted", he added for reassurance. "And now put your cap over your ears, for outside we have an easterly, and it is blowing outrageously."

The purchase passed without further fuss in the Uhlenhus shop, and only when Mr Emanuel Quandt showed his customers a few pages of a two hundred year old calendar and brought to Miss Sell's attention that in the new year apart from a famine a collision of planets had been prophesied, the girl listened up blinking at the name Sell, and it almost seemed as if something long suppressed wanted to wrestle its way out of her. But a look at her tall companion who was impatiently rubbing his right foot on his left — for he still had not yet given up this distinctive habit — made her fall silent anew. Soon they found themselves again in the kitchen, and when they were crouching opposite each other under the flue on two stools, Kathrin suddenly interrupted the cutting out of the green and red chains to let scissors and paper fall into her lap with a deep sigh. Then she asked short and sharp, "Since when have you known me, Bob?"

For this introduction, however, the experienced youth had not been ready. Why did the worm wash such long faded things out anew? Hm, that must mean something though?! And he raised his haughty nose suspiciously, and parried the first blow with the very indifferently presented remark, "Is that all? Yes, it may already be a few years ago."

Kathrin moved closer, so close that the knees of the young people almost touched, and Bob Swanegel felt how his great confidence suffered a considerable loss before this child. At the same time it fumed and hissed so hot and confusedly under the sloping roof of the stove that the thoughts of the young sailor were incapable anymore of marching so well in lockstep. After a while, within which they both observed each other silently, Kathrin started again, "Bob, I remember something. It was so funny, and you should tell me the truth about it. Did we not meet first on a small ship?"

"Of course," the beset man responded, for he considered this information to be harmless, "it was on the 'Green Herring'."

"Where?", the little one continued inquiring.

"Lord, worm, what is all that about? In the North Sea of course. The water was making quite a spectacle at the time. And when we pulled you out of the water in the grey of morning, then — then —".

But here the young sage broke off in shock, drew his pipe out, and tapped with its bowl, enraged over his own talkativeness, on the brass edge of the stove. The depressing feeling tormented him grievously that he had revealed something here which had most likely been kept quiet from the curious thing until now. But in addition, he was furious also over the absurdness of such a secrecy. It was actually terribly nice because the sprog had not given the yellow puddle the honour of drowning in it. No, really. An old blowhard, this Mr Sell. Why the devil should you not clarify for the kid with the black eyes how you had also in the end been enlisted with gruel and rice for his revival? And when Kathrin picked up his last statement urgently, he made an especially rumbling blow against the blackened tiles, and in defiance of the child's guardian, his previous caution broke down.

No, right now!

Graphically and with inner self-satisfaction, Bob Swanegel hence began explaining to his tense listener that unusual event of how she had been spat at the time by the raging sea onto the little ship. There it rose before the horrified girl. The howling water, the seething mist, the grey bundle which was only arduously pried from the stiff arms of the man, the red-checked warm bed, and above all the circumstances and grievances which it caused before you could pour a few spoons of hot gruel behind the numbed worm's clenched teeth.

"No," Bob concluded, as he leant back nobly and lost in dream, "you would not believe, thing, what an ugly sprog you were. Such pockmarks were on your face, as large as a thumbnail. And when you were touched, then you began whining. It sounded like someone had stepped on a cat's tail. And even Julius Kohlrausch got headaches from it despite his deafness. Well, let that be. Afterwards I dressed you in decent clothes in Amsterdam, for the others did not know about such ladies' things, and after that it became somewhat better with you."

Oh, it provided Bob Swanegel a strange enjoyment when he could wrest these images from the past. He folded his hands devoutly on his chest and smacked his lips with delight. Kathrin, however, did not let a word escape. Bent far forward so that he almost felt her breath, she stared at him, and over her black eyes, an abrupt sparkle and brightness passed unrelentingly. The dark kitchen had long since sank away before her, the tiled stove along with the flue had for some time been transformed into a slender ship, and her trembling shoulders were being clasped by the two icy arms of a man so that the air passed from her and she threatened to suffocate.

"Why are you looking at me like that?", her companion inquired finally, taken aback.

Then she stirred, and tried dreamily to shake off the arms squeezing her. But she did not succeed. The breath-taking clasp remained.

"So he hauled me through the sea?", she breathed, trembling.

"Who?", Bob Swanegel suggested protractedly. "I see! Yes, of course, what was great about that? He was not responsible for his actions. The principal thing remains that I gave you a decent slap on the back so that we could then get something warm into you."

Kathrin brushed the hair from her forehead. "And then Mr Sell brought me here with him?", she inquired further.

"Well yes," her friend replied, moved his hand disparagingly and rose noisily, "that he could also do. He was paid a hundred guilders from the consulate for you. You were yet a quite fine income for him. And now, girl," he reproved her, and looked very injured and irritated, "now don't roll up here like a piece of chewing tobacco, but give me your hand quite sensibly. Who knows whether we will not also have to take leave of each other for a long time. There is in fact something in the air, for something bad and very changeable is going on with Julius Kohlrausch. Well, if the thing cannot be held back, then you will hear of it. And now adieu." He slowly fumbled for something under his fleece jacket and pushed the little packet casually into her hand. "Here," he said with his usual indifference, "there is something for Christmas for a certain person. It is very

163

expensive and is properly packed in cotton wool. Pink cotton wool! For without such stuff it is squeezed and is not so excellent. And now do not peek in the wrapper beforehand so that the great surprise is lost. For you are very curious! — Morning."

He pulled the fur cap over his ears, wrapped the scarf about his neck, and without grudging his little friend another look, he vanished with his collected dignity into the dark hallway.

Kathrin remained alone. She was strangely depressed and apprehensive of mind as she now turned the little brown packet irresolutely back and forth between her fingers. The next moment, however, she had torn it open, opened the cover of the now revealed cardboard box, and now — she froze. Embedded in pink cotton wool lay a tiny silver heart. And when she drew it out with delicate fingers, there finely engraved stood the name "Kathrin" inscribed on it. No, that there was such a glorious thing. A brilliance and glimmer radiated from the piece of jewellery, and the kitchen was at once as bright as if the sun had gone up under the flue. For a long moment, the delighted girl forgot everything which had been before. She saw just the treasures of the earth sparkling before herself, and a vague notion swept over her that she must have been imparted with the power to bring other people to offer her sparkling treasures on full shovels. Bob Swanegel was such a fellow for example. Oh, and that produced at base a precious feeling, almost as if you were drinking hot mulled wine. And yet, how did it happen that she was abruptly and against her will torn from these glittering dreams of power and wealth? From the adjoining room, she suddenly heard a firm step, and at the same time, her inner ear divined how a chair was being moved to the table. It was nine o'clock and consequently the time had come when Mr Sell wished to take his warm glass of milk. For even if he did not speak about it, the man of the house still nursed

damage to his chest which he had suffered through being in the sea for a long time after a ship's misfortune.

There Kathrin stood in the middle of the kitchen, her
hand closed slowly about the silver heart until it was
completely covered, and from the soft hissing of the
wood under the kettle, the dull noise swelled up in
waves crashing against each other. She felt anew the
painful pressure against her shoulders, and she sank
into the strangely numbing and yet gladdening thoughts
of obliteration and close rescue.

Ah, what was more beautiful now? The silver heart
or the new life which he in there had gifted her?

Who could know? Who could work it out?

7

On the day of the blessed birth of the Lord, however, things happened which raked up anew the clear course of Kathrin's lifestream until it looked as if a pot full of tar had been poured over it from one side. It drew heavy and dark across the surface, and yet blue and green and silver coloured streaks formed in its further course, quite destined to entice the eyes with deceptive hope. Indeed the day began wondrously and auspiciously, for Kathrin received a gift on it, a cerebral gift which had such a captivating, exciting and enormous effect on her, so that her startled disposition was completely thrown off the rails by it. Yes, over the new thing she even forgot the little silver heart, although she already wore it secretly on a red woollen string on her chest.

It was in the little backroom of Mr Emanuel Quandt's store in which the adolescent received that decisive jolt. She had run there very early to request a few little sheets of golden tinsel from the red-maned artist who actually only traded in soap and lubricating oil out of condescension. For it was needed to thereby lend a few worm-eaten walnuts a fairy tale shimmer. In the shop, meanwhile, the rotund Mrs Quandt was reigning in her eternally fluttering night dress, while her husband was in the mysterious room prising wistfully from his violin the solemn tune, "Silent Night — Holy Night". His admirer crouched patiently on a stool before him and waited until the music's spirits which floated about the red-head would have engaged their round dance.

But suddenly Mr Quandt waved his bow several times through the air, and then tapped with its tip demandingly on the tabletop.

"How goes it with your father, my dear young lady?", he began finally with patronising benevolence. "Does he celebrate the feast like other Christian men? He has not in fact bought the slightest thing from me yet."

"Oh," the little one apologised and looked at her lap, struck by the justified reproach, "Mr Sell has so much to do. But — but —," and she abruptly pulled together all her powers of resolve, "he is surely also not my father at all?"

"So?", Mr Quandt murmured forlornly as he turned his violin inquiringly and held the instrument attentively to his ear, "do you know that so exactly?"

"Me?"

There it was. Kathrin faltered and stared avidly at the unsuspecting chatterer, that fantasist who at base loved to illuminate the fates of others with grotesque lanterns for his own exhilaration. The former comic actor also found himself alone with his astonished and deeply agitated audience, and it would have been a pity to break off straight after the first scene again such a performance which, as he noticed, began amidst trembling suspense. He ought to attempt a few dancing steps before the invisible prompt's box. It was none other than his innate, outrageously suppressed passion for gambling which forced him to it. It also did no harm.

"Now," he said obliviously, and plucked a few chords from the gut strings, "there are secrets which have not been aired for a long time. But expert eyes penetrate them. You save something up because you dare not uncover it out of shame or some other considerations. But later you then step forth and endow a great fortune in your testament. And then the next of kin learns finally with whom they have been dwelling for so long, and the tears swell, the heart wallows in blessedness."

When he had emitted this in a solemnly hushed way, Mr Emanuel Quandt again drew a few strokes with the bow over his violin, and his red bush of hair bristled in delight when he noticed how his listener had followed him half soullessly. Her knees embraced by both arms, she sat there, and her raised eyes discovered between the oilskin jackets, gumboots and sharply smelling onion sacks hanging from the ceiling vague black shadows which passed around her head and made her dizzy. What actually lurked behind the words of the, by her idolatrously revered, Mr Quandt, she did not know how to decipher. Her fairy tale loving soul, however, cheered up because some miracle must be at play with her. Confusing voices muttered to her, "Richard Sell — lifesaver — the next of kin — testament — the great fortune." And the longer she listened to these tones, the more intimately she was convinced of their truth.

"Yes," she finally began, and rose proudly, for she felt how important she became at this moment, "Mr Sell is very kind-hearted to me. Recently he even gifted me his own scarf."

"You see — you see," Mr Quandt threw in fawningly, "there we have it. Such a thing cannot be denied. I can always count on my conjectures. But of course, that must all remain a secret. The half-darkness always has the most pleasant and enchanting thing about it." And he laid the bow diagonally across his mouth and whispered insistently, "For God's sake, no hints, and especially no mention of my person. Yes, none, otherwise perhaps a resentment will arise, and his last will can possibly change. Not a word — I have said nothing."

With that he straightened up, threw his red bushy head back spiritedly, and to reinforce his warning, he let it roll pithily from his lips, "Ah, perhaps while we hope — misfortune has already met us! So think of glitter — and silence, my Miss."

With the last words, the artist, rapt in himself, filled an envelope full of golden tinsel for his customer, then he lowered his head in farewell and opened a side door chivalrously for the little one.

"Many thanks," Kathrin stuttered, "many, many thanks!"

It seemed to her as if an old conjuror had just then in his cave delivered her a massive clump of gold, and she would be too weak to carry the metal.

***

Meanwhile, however, the black rats were already gnawing the white floor on which the dreamy girl had previously walked. The planks creaked discordantly, and a poisonous, yellow dust penetrated through the cracks.

Precisely at the same time as Kathrin was floating away to the heaven which the oilskins, gumboots and onion sacks no longer blocked, the porcelain bell tolled before the clean house in which she found residence, and straight afterwards the daughter of the firm A. Guntrum stepped into the living room of the young smokehouse owner. Yet before Miss Sophie offered a "Good day", she let her shiny eyes sweep attentively through the room, and it seemed not undesirable to her to meet the young owner alone. In her hand she bore a large envelope to which the entire interest of her host was immediately directed. She came, as she expressed it without fuss in her fresh, truth loving way, to bring in the name of her rheumatism-afflicted father a demand for his business partner to complete. Soon she was sitting on the green sofa, carefully stroking the bent corners of the envelope smooth and explaining at the same time to her serious listener how A. Guntrum had not been very edified by the renewed payment to his associate at all.

"You must not resent him," she sought to apologise for her progenitor, when she noticed how her opposite wrinkled his brow woundedly, "he is now often heavily tormented by his ailment, and you know he is always irritated when he must for some reason expend more capital than the estimate allowed him to hope. Now you will admit yourself," she continued calmly, "how the building of your canning factory was not only delayed, but also demanded significantly more than we all could have guessed."

"The materials have just become more expensive", Richard Sell tossed in-between irritatedly from his arm-chair, whereby he regarded the daughter of the friendly firm entirely like a businessman with whom he had a difference of opinion to fight out. "Above all things, we had estimated the sheet metal deliveries too low."

"Quite right," Sophie Guntrum agreed immediately with her clear insight, "it is because of that. I have just argued this with my father too. And you see," she added somewhat more warmly, as she buttoned on her becoming velvet jacket which her host had forgotten to take from her, "I have finally succeeded in totally fulfilling your wish. Here are the forty thousand marks, and I hope that the sum will be the dearest Christmas surprise for you."

"Well yes," Richard Sell returned a little frostily in rising, "although I did not fear for a moment that your father wanted perhaps to escape the commitment received." With that he took the envelope, and intended locking it in the iron safe.

"Do you not want to count it first?", Sophie Guntrum smiled fleetingly.

Only, the smokehouse owner shrugged his shoulders in the negative.

"That is not necessary with you," he demurred, "since I would not like to lose your respect though, I will gladly make up in your presence for anything missing."

Then they bent over the table, the envelope was opened, and it ensued, as both knew and presumed, that the notes agreed down to the last penny.

"It is unpleasant," the blond young lady suggested incidentally, "that the money must lie so uselessly with you because of the holiday."

And Richard Sell, who was already rattling with the keys whilst turned away, responded that he could never calculate in advance whether the master mason and the suppliers would not wish to be satisfied on the quiet.

The iron door was locked, and with that the business part was dealt with.

Now the blond young lady could dispense a few incidental inquiries. Meanwhile she remained seated, and by the manner in which she awkwardly played with the buttons of her fine leather gloves or blew gently into the fur of her muff, the man of the house realised that she must be pursuing some special intention. For A. Guntrum's daughter tended never to expend her time without a definite goal. And really, hardly had she inquired sympathetically after the health of her friend than she drew out a tiny white carton to place it modestly and humbly on the arm of the sofa. But how astonished Richard Sell was when she declared at the same time, "This is a little Christmas gift for your ward, dear friend. And since I can imagine that a bachelor, like you, does not pay especial attention to such things, I did not want the poor thing to go completely without this evening. I have sought out a red hair bow," she continued more animatedly, and about her fine lips played a trace of pity and kindheartedness, "and I am convinced the little lover of finery will share my taste."

"Seriously?", the young merchant cried in extreme surprise, and Sophie Guntrum noticed with a smile how completely he was thrown into confusion, "that is really extraordinarily good of you, Sophie."

Never had he called her so out of hand by her first name. Yes, in his joyful excitement, he surely barely noticed how he had grasped the hand of his visitor to shake the delicate fingers powerfully.

"I would really not have expected that you would re-member the child so lovingly", he burst out in a rush.

"Why not?", the young lady responded even more definitely, although she was still smiling, "she is a right pretty, clever, and obedient creature."

"Right? Don't you think so too?", Richard Sell inser-ted contentedly, and it became much easier for him with this conversation than he would have ever guessed.

"Yes," his guest continued reflectively, while blowing assiduously into the muff again, "you will certainly not believe it, dear friend, but I have been occupying myself recently really quite often with your household, and how you could best arrange everything here. And you see, just today I would be in the position of submitting a suggestion to you which would order here once and for all the uncertain circumstances under which you must doubtlessly suffer inwardly and outwardly."

"Me?", the merchant asked, now standing upright at the table, suddenly again suspicious, and he attempted to unravel her secret intentions.

His visitor, however, opened her clever blue eyes fully towards him, and in fact there was not only active sympathy but also something like concern to be read in them. She inducted him clearly and vividly into her plans.

"You must realise rightly," she spoke quickly, and a proper warmth lay in her words, "how it irritates me fre-quently when our acquaintances here and there judge uncomprehendingly your interaction with Kathrin."

"What?" There it was again, this interference which the upstart hated to death. Furrowing his brow, he ven-ted himself, "What have strangers got to worry about something so natural?"

"Well, your behaviour can actually be deemed to be not so natural in the eyes of those uninvolved," the blonde parried his reproach coolly, "you must always consider, my dear friend, that not everyone is as capable as I am of recognising the real nobility of your actions."

"Oh, please, please," Richard Sell dissented with forced cheerfulness, although secretly the annoyance was gnawing at him, "it is only missing for you to call me a saint. And at the same time, you know quite well," he continued hastily, "how only consciousness of duty or, if you want, also the desire for a little equalisation and equity is leading me."

Sophie Guntrum nodded gently like someone who just hears a long recognised error advocated with passion. Then a trace of knowing better glided over her lips, that expression for which the smokehouse owner had been peering anxiously the entire time, because it was always betrayed anew in the attitude of the girl how much she had founded her entire life on order and reason. The devil too — the young man balled his fists furtively — he strove actually for the same things, only he did not want to do without the adventure, the extraordinary, through which he had risen to his heights. And in defiance against this bourgeois leveling, he shoved his hand straight into the hedge of nettles.

"It is thought then," he said bitterly, "that it's strange or unfitting or improper that I presume to want to raise this little being in my vicinity, all the more when she has the misfortune of being an outcast girl. Do you not also find no excuse for me at all?"

"Oh, but yes." Sophie Guntrum placed her muff to the side and folded her hands on the table. "You could for example have become very fond of the little orphan."

When she suggested this, their eyes caught each other's, and Richard Sell could not prevent an abrupt heat passing over his forehead. The feeling that the tender germ which had rested unrecognised and hidden until then in darkness should be destroyed by the garish light of day tormented him inescapably. His guest, however, increased the unending embarrassment as she continued without timidity and always with the same force of will, "Such a guardianship would be appropriate if a housewife reigned here with you. As long as this is not the case, I cannot hide from you that you are doing the child are wrong which is certainly not intended by you. For a girl at this age can only be guided by a woman's hand."

There it was finally spoken, clothed in sober, hard to contradict rules of life, what had run back and forth for so long already between both of them as calculation, as numbers and sometimes also as possibility and as something desirable. Only that the band stretched taut this time to tearing, and a single awkward movement, a grasp too hard or firm would have to burst the long lasting attachment. But, the indelicacy and the hidden force which was hidden in the admonition of a justifiably believing woman, they affronted the man so bent on his freedom. And in the effort of avoiding the path which had been appointed to him once more, he wandered restlessly up and down the room until he finally decided on the question of what Sophie's implied consisted then.

The blonde did not stir for a short while, she was also entangled by the darkness which did not want to clear between them. But then, mastering herself, she smoothed her forehead, and now she unfolded before her listener cleverly and maturely that goal which she thought so desirable for him. Already with the first sentences, the smokehouse owner interrupted his lively gait, crossed his arms over his chest, and threw his head back strongly as he always did when he wanted to raise an objection.

"What?" he paused, and twisted his dry mouth defiantly, "Kathrin should go to those two old eccentric spinsters?" And he smiled a little disparagingly.

A. Guntrum's daughter, however, pulled her plumply fitting velvet jacket right and grasped her muff as if to part.

"You forget," she countered very decisively, "that both Miss Müsebecks are relatives of our house, yes, that I just hope for the present that the ladies could decide for this reason on acceptance of the little one."

The smokehouse owner could still not master his ill-humoured cheerfulness. He stepped somewhat closer to the table and stretched both hands out sideways as a sign that he felt that image of the future to be half incomprehensible and half hilarious.

"How did you just," he repeated shaking his head, "come upon these two comical old women? The one, as far as I recall, writes poems for the little local papers. They may be very nice," he added, "I understand nothing of it, and the other, as I have often heard from you, gives music lessons in the so-called noble houses. Also certainly very meritorious, only I just do not comprehend — you must really not be angry with me — why the right place for Kathrin should just be with the ladies Müsebeck?"

He would almost have broken out once more into his curt derogatory laugh when Sophie Guntrum rose quickly and responded calmly, "I did not come here to argue with you. I just thought that a businessman like you would himself entertain the wish to discover a decent and excellent way out of an indefensible state. But you must of course consider my suggestion carefully first. And when you have made a decision, then I will always be ready to help you in carrying it out. It is also obvious that I would look out more often where appropriate for the child. And now, my dear friend," — here she offered the smokehouse owner her hand measuredly and obligingly — "commit to the feast with your household right joyfully and healthily, and do not forget entirely your friends in the town. No, please, you need not accompany me, I know your house thoroughly, for I saw it rise stone by stone. And now give Kathrin my hearty regards, and tell her that I mean well with her. Until we see each other soon again, dear friend."

She strode out with her erect gait, followed by the bowing host; soon her hurrying figure was darkening the window, and some time later Richard Sell was still sitting in the green armchair and shaking his head fiercely.

Eh God preserve, those were pedantries. A man who was accustomed only to following his own opinions never engaged in such things.

Eh God preserve!

***

Yes, the fir had blazed.

The rats were gnawing inaudibly under the floor beams so that everything must collapse, the green tree and the candles and the trust and the beginning tenderness. But for this short evening hour, festive shimmer radiated in the small room, flickering and wistful as never before in the lonely house.

Astonished, speechless, Richard Sell had sat before the twitching wax candles to listen incredulously to the fine, wavering little voice which was heard there under paper chains and the fragrant branches.

"Silent night — holy night," it thus sounded.

No different than everywhere else in the sparsely strewn cottages all around, and yet trembling and penetrated by an especially hopeful bliss, for the little girl, who had dared here with the gathering of all her courage to step singing under the fir, in her mood wove a search, a stretching out of her hands lost in dream towards the most mysterious thing there was on earth, towards belonging and towards the blessing of a certain protection for growth and prosperity. All that resided unrealised in the thin, quietly muffled voice. At the same time too, confused apparitions of silver hearts and red hair bands fluttered through her excited soul, only, this strange tension increased still more the deep impression which she exercised on her listeners. For Ott Knuth also crouched waxen and motionless in his corner of the sofa, and the flames of the candles breathed over his dying, wrinkled face with an unnatural glow of redness and health.

The song finally died away mutely and modestly. Then Richard Sell pulled himself up out of his rapture.

With a quick grasp, he went to his wallet, and then he fetched out without thinking a hundred mark note, unfolded it, and stretched the paper out towards the staring girl wordlessly and insistently. For in his view, money formed still the highest thing which a mortal could obtain, and the greatness of the sum should show the child how much his mind was exhilarated and gripped by the unaccustomed impression of this light-filled evening. By the fragrant branches, by the colourful curling chains, by the massive socks which spread as a gift on his knees, and not the least by the memorable song and above all things by her presence, which he suddenly likened to a lively stream which breaks skipping and humming through a dark forest. Ott Knuth also seemed agreed with the contribution, for life came into him, he doddered a little with his head and wheezed, astonished over the unexpected generosity of his successor, nothing but the one word, "Look."

What this approval, however, implied to the flabbergasted disbelief of Kathrin, who could not convince herself of the reality of what she held in her hands. In her childish mind, it was a charter, a document which made her independent from hardship and the exigency of existence. Numerous laughing kobolds crackled for her on the blue note, and the enraptured girl thought more overpoweringly still than that inexhaustible treasure the irrevocable certainty that such a princely gift could only emanate from someone quite close, a next of kin.

And then it crashed in again over her, without re-straint, the wild sacrifice to the moment. With an intoxicated cry, filled by thankfulness and overflowing yearning, she threw herself at the seated man, and be-fore he could even distinguish what she was planning, she had bent down already to cover his hand with stormy kisses.

Whom could it amaze that the strangest feeling streamed into the brain of the lonely man, who until now had always remained alone with himself and his scraped together money, when he felt the ardent, tender child's lips so burning and devotedly on his skin? Oh, it was a precious feeling though to suddenly form the central point of a family, and to be permitted to sit en-throned on this green armchair venerated like a god, to be able to look down from there, self-doubting and helpless, on the enraptured, kneeling and stammering creature. Overwhelmed by joy, sense of well-being, and confusion, Richard Sell, the youthful father of the house, threw a hasty look to Ott Knuth, but he was crouching, quietly trembling in his corner and keeping his eyes closed half asleep. Then the scent of all the fest-ive things which fluttered about him befogged the already half-shaken senses of the cool calculating man. And in the consciousness of undertaking something both scandalous and very charming, he bent down and kissed the little one gently on her forehead.

Kathrin did not stir. She lay enraptured in a dream full of dancing hearts and whirling butterfly wings, and she only twitched sometimes as if she were a candle and the flame were seeking to part from the white body.
— — — —

Star-filled night, now you look into the darkened room and listen and hold your breath. Inside in the iron money safe, the blue notes crackle and curl together as if in fear and uncertainty and, on the back of a chair, the old tousled raven of the master of the house crouches and sighs in heavy dream, "Thief — thief!"

Then the night nods grimly, for it does not stray in its resolve, and breathes on the windowpanes so that wild frost patterns grow on them. As a result it becomes still darker in the locked room.

The tired bird buries its head shivering under its feathers. — — — — —

***

Yes, it was an ambiguous and significant evening. Captain Julius Kohlrausch and his apprentice noticed that also, for they were both sitting in the loft which the gouty man had been renting from the widow Plonnies for years, and they were occupied with the most difficult thing which there is in the existence of men — with the choice of bride. Before them a massive carp was steaming, made sweet and sour, and because Mrs Plonnies knew what an important part in the great decision fell to the first spokesman of the Captain, she had placed an enormous piece before Bob Swanegel and now busied herself persistently with guiding the streams of sweet ginger sauce onto the plate of the haughty advisor. In general, however, she acted quite quietly at the same time, for first of all two front teeth were unpleasantly missing from the swollen face of the fifty year old, and then her power of conversation, especially in moments of excitement, suffered under a fatal stuttering which increased in proportion the more this innately calm nature felt strange looks directed at herself. And now the misfortune, or even the unshakeable cold-bloodedness of her renter wanted not only that the widow Plonnies be stared at constantly today by a pair of totally unfamiliar eyes, but that those seeing implements that were hostile to her also examined everything in-depth, yes, penetrated with stabbing police-like sharpness at what played out at her table, at her body, and overall at the entire room. Julius Kohlrausch had in fact invited to this dinner also the other candidate to which his undecided wishes applied. And now this old spinster, Miss Wiedemann, who ran a little public library and also apparently possessed a few very solid savings books, was sitting stiffly and erect at her table, and her black stabbing eyes and the stipulating look of the corners of her gaunt mouth betrayed distinctly what an evaluating yardstick the adversary placed on the housekeeping arts of the widow.

'Just wait,' Mrs Plonnies thought irritatedly, as she grudged the disturber of her calm a decidedly unfriendly look, 'you may well know about dust-covered musty books, you old, gaunt telephone pole! But does such a trifle perhaps offset the feminine virtues? And in your savings books perhaps, is there the recipe for how to make ginger sauce or rub hare fat into swollen knees? No — don't put on airs — for that requires lovingness. And did not Julius Kohlrausch only recently express with the rubbing that I was like a quite natural hot-water bottle? No, Alma Wiedemann, I could feel sorry for you. But it is unpleasant that he invited the old tackle. Why? — why? — why? —"

"With all regard," the gouty Captain suddenly interrupted that series of thoughts decisively, and at the same time he stepped on the foot of his advisor irritably under the table, for he was justifiably annoyed that Bob Swanegel was losing himself more and more devotedly in the sweet and sour carp, although the boy had actually been commissioned to assess the dispositions of both potential brides strictly and impartially against each other, "with all regard, my dear Mrs Plonnies," the oppressed Captain composed himself, "where have you scraped up this fine ginger sauce? It seems to me that you keep a full larder."

The fat woman nodded eagerly. "Of course — that I do", she tried to reply. Only, through the gap of the two missing front teeth, just a hissing came out at first, and the fatal stutter merged disruptively into her good intentions.

"You have surely caught a cold?", Alma Wiedemann inquired sympathetically, without even altering her stiff pose in the slightest. "Do you often suffer from it? Perhaps I may offer you my silk shawl. I always carry such a one with me in my handbag."

Here the white-haired bride solicitor knitted his ragged eyebrows and gave his shield bearer a heavy kick under the table again, as a sign that Bob might pay attention to the chided defect. The former ship's boy, however, continued slurping assiduously and only blinked his eyes casually to indicate he placed little weight at base on that well-known little aberration of the widow.

"I just wanted to laugh", the landlady burst out, turning coppery red, and her bosom heaved. "I l—l—like to laugh."

"Truly," the bride solicitor now murmured, and leant back comfortably, "whoever has a full larder can laugh too. There must be long sides of bacon hanging in there, and pots of lard should be inside. And then a cross bar must be present from which soft and hard sausages hang down. And a glass dome with Swiss cheese should be found in there."

"But above all things salted meat", his apprentice stipulated. "It must be stuck in large earthen pots, and a plate with a stone on it must close it up. It is arranged thus with you, Mrs Plonnies?"

Now the widow nodded enthusiastically, having lost her breath. "I have only recently had three large field stones arrive", she assured triumphantly, and at the same time, she forked up the carp's head, which she had prudently spared as the prized piece of the dish, and bedded it delicately on the beloved man's plate.

"What did you have arrive?", the hard-of-hearing man inquired, bending over the tasty morsel, forgetting for a moment that he was aiming to conceal his malady from the brides as much as possible.

"Field stones", the learned Alma Wiedemann declared, shrugging her shoulders, and at the same time, she furrowed her brow into a few long creases and adjusted her glasses as she always observed when she recommended a new book to her customers. "A larder is naturally very pleasant," she pontificated and placed the forefinger of her right hand vertically before herself on the table, "only what use is it when sufficient imagination for its use is lacking?"

Julius Kohlrausch had only scantily comprehended this last sentence.

"What is lacking?", he uttered, dumbfounded, and looked like a lost child over to his assistant.

Bob Swanegel, however, waved his hand casually.

"What do you think?", he inquired, unmoved, as Mrs Plonnies opened wide her round, aquamarine eyes, "What do you think?", the former ship's boy asked once more.

"God," Alma Wiedemann replied, and pursed her narrow lips a little contemptuously, "I consider it shameful that they serve up the old traditional dishes here always. Hence I have borrowed for myself the famed cookbook of Henriette Davidis."

"Aha", Bob Swanegel tossed in enigmatically.

"A magnificent work. You learn from it dishes which really make the heart rejoice. Twelve different sorts of plum pudding, alternating with red wine and rum; and only now the pastries. You would not believe at all how a fine taste is provided for there. Of the Strasbourg goose liver pie, I will not speak, for it is well-known. But have the company already heard of a cold hare pie, of quail, fieldfare, mock turtle, or even of eel and salmon pie?"

"Not possible," Captain Kohlrausch smacked his lips enchantedly and, again irresolute to the highest degree, "have you learnt all that and can prepare it all? Bob, my boy, what do you say to that?"

Here the widow Plonnies, since she fancied her game was lost, had a hefty spasm of choking, and the counsel had to pat her on the back.

"What do I say to that?", he tossed in drily during this activity. "I say, Miss Alma Wiedemann, that every unnatural thing possible can be muddled into such pies. And what do you do when two pages of the cookbook are stuck together, and the fat from the eel is running into the cold bowl?"

"Ugh", the marriage-ready man snorted, and pushed his plate away appalled.

You did not know whether a fishbone had gotten into his throat or what else he was shaken so strongly by. In any case, with the powerful shove, a part of the beautiful brown sauce had flowed onto the lapel of his veteran frock coat, and the solemnness of his accoutrement had thereby suffered an irreparable harm. Both the other participants of the feast sat around the kingpin aghast. Then the widow Plonnies had a brightening thought.

"Oh, that does not matter", she stuttered helpfully, for a suspicion whispered to her that her renter would never risk the decisive word in his befouled state. "In the cupboard of my tax collector there still hang a few men's clothes. All in mothballs, for I don't like parting from them out of attachment. But for you, my dear Captain..." She struck her protruding chest out reassuringly.

Bob Swanegel rose.

"Well, then come along, Mr Kohlrausch," he suggested benevolently, and winked craftily in the direction of the large landlady, "the wardrobe of the late Mr Plonnies can be of much use to you. Particularly as I am now going to the Kiel Helmsman's' School and cannot support you anymore with my taste. And now excuse us for a few minutes, dear Miss, but the change is necessary."

The yellow spruce wardrobe in the small bedroom of the widow opened shortly afterwards and contributed in fact a frock coat which, after it had been turned back and forth expertly by Bob Swanegel, could be skimmed over the shoulders of the marriage-ready man by his student without much fuss. Mrs Plonnies, however, became quite emotional over it.

"No," she stuttered, "how beautiful."

"Yes, it fits like a glove", Bob confirmed, as he brushed smooth a few creases on the back of his boss.

"Merely the revolting mothball smell", the newly dressed man sniffled once more critically.

"It is healthy", his counsel refuted decisively. "Everything which smells bad is healthy. For example, our tar as well. The principal thing is how precisely you fit into the clothes of the late Mr Plonnies."

"True, that is wonderful," the Captain said reflectively, "don't you think so too, Mrs Plonnies?"

"Yes, I have thought so for a long time already", the widow breathed.

Now the counsel tapped the shoulder of his charge encouragingly, "Well, then make a note of what," he suggested compassionately, "we find now to be nice amongst us."

At that the white-headed man sighed heavily and miserably a few times, like someone whom a bitter medicine has been offered to, then he bent his tousled head still further into the dark wardrobe and addressed with the exertion of all his courage a pair of black trousers which were hanging there quietly and respectably, "Mrs Plonnies", the mariner murmured brokenly. "After New Year's Bob Swanegel is going away. Otherwise I would never have submitted to such things late in life. He has always been like a dear son to me."

"Ah yes," the landlady swallowed, and pulled a handkerchief out, "he is a loyal man."

"But that is a quite unnecessary detour," the former ship's boy adjudged with displeasure, "it leads to nothing, make it quick, please."

Anxiously the bride solicitor wiped the sweat from his forehead. "Devil, you will have your preliminaries", he got excited, and shook the trouser legs furiously. "But there is no helping it anymore — what do you think about Easter, Mrs Plonnies?"

"I am always ready", the chosen one whispered with a thrill.

Her breast was heaving, and at the same time her cheeks were puffed up astonishingly wide. The suddenness of the proposal had done it to her. It was in fact too much for a delicate nature. The quiet trouser legs there in the wardrobe, to which so many significant memories were attached for her, the broad back of her Julius, who was still looking strenuously into the dark cavity as if in there the future for him was written, but especially the haughty face of the counsel, they all began swaying about her quietly. And since in addition something floated into her mind of kissing the bride and engagement ring — utterly exciting things — she would perhaps have really been overcome by a faint if a tinkling music had not at once merged into this confusing mood.

"Listen!", she heard the sober voice of Bob Swanegel say. "Alma Wiedemann has wound up the music box out of boredom. She is getting impatient."

At mention of that name, however, the Captain suddenly spun around, incensed, and cried out affrontedly, "What does the old cookbook know about such difficult affairs? Right, Mrs Plonnies, the more often you do it, the more magnificent it becomes. But now come. We must give her a signal."

With that the mariner, already very relieved, offered his future wife his arm, and thus the happy couple, followed by the trusty man who was rejoicing over so much sophistication, moved again into the adjoining room.

"A weighty couple", Bob thought approvingly when he noted the dangerous creaking of the floorboards. "Everything about them is round and upholstered, and they will not hurt one another. I am merely curious as to what the thin, spectacled spider will say."

But this inquisitiveness of the young worldly-wise man would not be staunched. When the rival namely grasped the meaningful procession in its significance, she was overcome by the courage which characterised her in general. She energetically shifted herself to be somewhat more stiffly erect and twisted the corners of her mouth into a truly sneering line.

"Entirely as if she were brewing vinegar", Bob thought.

Admittedly too, the power of opposition of the brave spinster found its limits. And indeed in the moment when the covertly betrothed couple, spurred to it by Bob, and to divert a little of their emotional stress, began a steady dance to the sounds of the music box. No, such a trampling was decidedly too plebeian. Alma Wiedemann rose contemptuously, and experienced before her departure the satisfaction at least of seeing the landlord, Mr Tredup, swirl into the room like a great black fly with wafting coat-tails to inquire anxiously as to whether a misfortune had not perhaps taken place.

Yes, it was a really harmonious evening. For Mr Tredup also received in the general fraternisation his share in the sweet and sour carp, as well as a marzipan heart with an aiming cupid, and only Bob Swanegel sometimes sent a look out the window into the darkness, and at the same time, he said to himself now and then, half touched and half defiantly, "Pity that everything finds an end — and you also leave something behind."

***

At the same hour, the moon bows down its pale, frozen watchman's face to the river and the long rows of Uhlenhus. But whenever it also presses its round head forward, grey scraps of cloud are wound ever anew about its eyes, as if you would have cause down below to make the office of the ancient night watchman difficult. It grasps for its spear, but nobody recognises the fleeting flashes; it toots warningly on its horn, but no man hears the rusty sound. The Christmas punch on the coast is good and strong, and keeps all senses shrouded.

There — there — the watcher excitedly tears apart a thick wall of cloud, and in desperation pushes his dog towards the body. The toothless animal barks furiously. But dear God, the great distance! And, since time immemorial, such strange sounds are only caught by children and dreamers.

And rightly, Kathrin starts under the sloping wall of her loft room, and grasps under her pillow. There lies the neatly smoothed out blue note which she has received from the dear, kingly Mr Sell. And on her chest, the tiny silver heart gleams in the moonlight. Ah, how glorious it is to be so richly endowed. But that is just a minor matter. The most peculiar thing remains that you have received a caress for the first time. Such a thing scares off sleep and glows through all thoughts like a strange magical potion. Hence she must also constantly stroke her own forehead and cannot comprehend at all why her locks should all of a sudden have been so distinguished. No, it had been too wondrous, this feeling of security and calm in those arms which had once carried her across the sea. If you just knew how to show your appreciation for it. For you must now do that, doubly and triply, so that the dear protector, who was surely actually her father, notices it.

There — from far off, a hoarse barking sounds. And does not a scraping and crunching also register from the first floor repeatedly?

Kathrin straightened up.

From time to time, a creaking arose, and now and then something tumbles and flutters against the door.

"That must be the raven", Kathrin thinks. "Will it have knocked over its water bowl perhaps?" Here something was possibly occurring by which you could serve Mr Sell, for the raven was his oldest friend.

Without further consideration, Kathrin springs from the bed, and runs bare-footed and in her nightshirt down the dark steps. The breeze wafts frostily about her limbs. But she keeps the blue note, from which she does not like to part, unchanged in her right hand. Now she has reached the lower landing.

Mercy, what mad, frenzied images emerge before her eyes down there? Is she dreaming or has she not rubbed the sleep sufficiently from her eyes? It is quite impossible that the front door should be half ajar so that the starry night can sparkle in? Four blurred shadows escape noiselessly through the gap, and last of all follows something wrapped up, something which the little one discovers with her appalled look has its head hidden under a thick headscarf and wears its skirts pinned up high.

Then the eavesdropper makes an inadvertent movement, and a whistling breath betrays her.

Quick as thought, the shrouded woman turns — for it is a woman — steps menacingly closer, and two flashing eyes stare up at the child.

"Are you there again already, accursed sprog? What are you creeping about here for?" With that a fist flies up to the landing, and a pair of cold fingers rustle against the paper which is still mechanically clasped by the little one. "What are you bringing there? — So, so, that is right!"

A fierce tear steals her possession from the speech-less girl, and at the same time she receives a blow against the head that knocks her tumbling over the steps.

"Woe, if you open your mouth, then your life is history", the stumbling girl hears from a hot voice. "It would be nice if you plunged me into misfortune right now. That is still amiss, you sprog."

Then a mocking, sickly laugh, and straight after-wards it is paralysingly and ghastly still. Only a broad piece of night sky forces itself fearfully and coldly breathing through the somewhat wider space in the doorway.

***

Kathrin had screamed so loudly that it shrilled through every corner of the house. Collapsed in a heap, senseless, exposed, she lay on the stairs, and an unre-cognised pain maimed her breast. Not because something gruesome had happened here, and that through theft and violence all the laws of order had been overthrown and her own carefully guarded treasure had been stolen, the desolate girl did not scream and clam-our so boundlessly for that reason, but rather because an inexplicable premonition was biting at her like a furi-ous dog, a premonition that her own innocent person would somehow be enmeshed in this indescribable crime.

"The woman," she murmured numbly and half madly to herself, "the woman —", and she grasped her forehead, shook herself until she heard her teeth chat-tering, and screamed anew.

Then a beam of light glided over her from above. And when she turned her battered head up hesitantly, she fi-nally recognised the man for whom she alone wailed.

That man who bore in himself all protection, all justice, and all order on earth for his little venerator. In one hand the scantily clad man held a wavering candle, from the other gleamed the cold light of a defensive arm. Again holiness and protection emanated from him, and the stretched-out girl felt a new lifestream running in her veins, for his presence covered her shivering limbs as though with a warming cloak.

"Kathrin, what's wrong?", the man swaying down called with wavering voice.

Not for a moment did he bear witness to himself that a naked girl was writhing before him, defencelessly exposed to his shocked look which was struggling for comprehension; no, he simply gathered up the broken, impotent shape and pressed it to himself as the fear shook him that something gruesome and inexorable had crept into his house and wanted to struggle with him for his most precious possession. The candle, which he placed on one of the steps, painted encircling rings about the two lonely people in the deep night.

"Kathrin, what's wrong?", he said once more, as if by his call the fleeing senses of the little one could be guided back.

Only the foundering girl slid ever more unresistingly down into a smoking hole.

"The woman," she murmured wearily and bristling, "she took my money."

"What? — for God's sake — was someone down there in the room?"

But the slack body, as much as it was also constantly caressed and warmed, just started once more, and then exhaled its consciousness with a relieved sigh.

Then the tormented man, struck by a new suspicion, let his burden glide onto the steps and sprang with a few wild leaps down into the room where he thought his relaxation, his comfort was resident. At the entrance, however, he had to clasp the door posts. The flickering light which he held high above his head disclosed to him unpityingly the horrific, the numbing reason why such a wild lament had shrilled through his house. No piece of furniture appeared to have moved, everything stood peacefully in its place. Only the opening of the tiny safe hung there, thrown far back on buckled hinges, while scraps of burst iron pieces covered the floor. Struck by a lightning bolt, numb and yet torn away only by a single thought, the smokehouse owner, the fortunate merchant who considered it his task and a part of human blessedness to gather up boldly and ruthlessly the money of the earth, stormed to his disturbed treasure chamber and grasped, for confirmation of the pillaged body as it were, into the yawning vault.

Empty. He had known it.

The silent, thoughtless confusion suddenly drained away from the robbed man. While he still felt the cold metal between his fingers, a furious, unfamiliar desire for revenge and retaliation shot into his affronted brain. His clear mind, accustomed to work, began flying and connecting up icily sharp. One thing stood unshakeably before his soul. The forty colourful notes which greedy hands had stolen from him, they prescribed collapse for his existence. The trust between him and the stingy A. Guntrum was uprooted by the crime. Derision and contempt must meet him from this side. And finally it would certainly happen, that which he had evaded for so long, that the firm would take his freedom and his hopes for compensation. Now the great merchant's daughter would coolly and rationally buy his future, for, to the son-in-law of the action, you calculated those items certainly grudgingly as a part of the dowry. All that ran into him from the cold iron which he still held tightly clasped. But suddenly the stream changed, and his old hasty energy sprang up in him.

Retrieve that which was so dear to him, track it, pursue it, it cried in him. Had not the naked child rambled about a woman?

Almighty! He hesitated, shattered by the horrifying thing which lurked behind this word.

At the threshold of the door lay Kathrin. She had crept as far as there tiredly and weakly, had crept after him like a dog that seeks its master. Now she sent him a mad, lamenting look. Only the smokehouse owner was seized by loathing. The thing there had certainly enticed the unclean and coarse thing into his home, she was the rope on which the depravation groped along as far as him — as far as him, who wanted to rise from poverty and abjectness. Yes, the people of the ledgers were proved right, the child of disgrace must go before he was completely sunk. A blindness befell him. He did not see anymore the beggingly wrung hands of his charge, her stirring nakedness, her languishing look. With a rough sound of contempt, he pushed her away from himself with his foot, and stormed away past her to the sparkling estates of a betrayed humanity.

SECOND BOOK

I

Spring light danced through the window. The young woman shifted in the green chair behind the panes, and since she found herself entirely alone, she exhaled and stretched cosily in the beginning, foreboding warmth. She looked around uneasily to see if she was also not caught by anybody in her unaccustomed effort, and then she propped her arm on the arm of the chair and smiled raptly to herself. As if she were eavesdropping on a secret. At the same time, the regular ticking of the round wall clock vanished for her, and she also did not notice how the raven had fluttered onto the cabinet to earnestly follow the moving of the hands. How could she have submitted to the thought that a conversation was being tended to up there? For all that, her mind was still too much entangled by the things of the earth, she did not hear the like. And at the same time, they were both talking quite freely and easily about the mistress herself.

'Tick — tock', the clock creaked.

'That you have already said often', the raven suggested and lowered its head attentively, from which a single
feather protruded. 'Do you not also keep, however, what
you prattle to yourself in the course of time?'

'Oh yes,' the old work grumbled, 'you surely mean I
possess a dusty memory? God preserve, I have a blurred
sound of most who have passed. Tick — tock. But my actual thing is the present. I am its secretary, you
understand? Its clerk.'

'Well, and of the future then,' the black bird urged
tensely, 'you know nothing at all?'

The clock cleared its throat. 'That would be taken
wrongly,' it suggested, 'I must not go ahead. And anyhow — who divines the future?'

'I divine it', the raven nodded gently. 'It is a thing peculiar to me. You know surely that previously I was
Odin's bird, and something has remained to me from
that.'

'Really?, the work creaked, and gave out a sharp
note. 'You should give it a test straightaway. I am always
so curious over how what I inscribe in the moment de-
velops further. It is like that with all secretaries.'

'What do you want to know?', the raven inquired
yawning.

'See, down there,' the clock whispered, 'there the
blond woman has been sitting now for eight years. I remember quite distinctly the hour when she entered. It
was a few weeks after the great mischief which was per-
petrated here amongst us on the old money locker.'

'Yes, yes,' the offspring of Odin's messenger blinked,
'since that piece of mischief, the feather has protruded
from the tuft. That is all atoned for too. Death and ruin
lie in-between. But what more?'

'It has proceeded here in the house right uniformly
and regularly', it spoke under the clock face. 'The first
thing the young woman did, having hardly crossed the

threshold, consisted of locking a great number of shares and bonds in tidy files in the recovered hidden safe. Do you still remember?'

'Certainly, and then she made a list of them, and she brought a large grey account book with her, in which on the first page was: A. Guntrum's Successor. And below: Richard and Sophie Sell.'

'I don't need you for that,' the work grumbled, 'all that I did with them. And I may just draw my coils somewhat tighter, then the old images and events purr anew through my memory. So let us see then. How was it? Ah yes, the grey book. They sat together many an evening and rejoiced over what they noted on the white pages. He walked up and down then, hands behind his back, and quoted the numbers exactly which she wrote down. If he ever took up a newspaper or wanted to read a good book, then she admonished him constantly not to forget the principal thing. Thus the items became more and more enormous and fatter, particularly since old Guntrum was committed to a wheelchair, and had had to cede his business grumbling and muttering to his daughter's husband. "It is in fact so" — he said at the handover. But whatever the truth is, I must confess of the housewife, she goes to the most imaginable trouble to look after her husband and arrange everything as he wishes it. She even forgets, as hard as it is on her, herself and her own pleasure. There is sometimes something like an unrecognised unease over her as to whether she is transgressing perhaps against old habits of her husband. Occasionally she is even assaulted by a distant foreboding, as if despite all the prosperity and wealth, despite all the order and tidiness, something were still missing in these rooms. Or as if perhaps something had gone away from them which had previously resided here. And then she looks about hastily and searching, and strains her poor cool head to bursting to find the thing unknown to her. Has it never occurred to you, blackcoat, how she behaved particularly fitfully when Kathrin was out here to visit?'

'I have eyes in my head', the old bird croaked, affronted, as it drew its right leg under its feathers. 'Kathrin's laughter and her cheerfulness always remain attached to the furniture as well as the walls. And that is something foreign which the merchant's daughter does not feel up to. Kathrin is anyway a charming woman. The good little women with whom she lives, the two Miss Müsebecks, were meant to have an affect on her heart and disposition according to the will of Mr Richard Sell. And that has also happened. Do you not seemingly notice with the fine child how much the silly spinsters afflict her with the poets and the Bible, with languages, song and dance? Hehe, but look in her eyes, they gleam as darkly and ambiguously as my own.'

'Simply,' the clock coughed anxiously, 'hence we are also, that is, Richard Sell and I, tormented by the idea that the fine, supple, attentive young woman could despite all the arts of upbringing be enslaved by the corrupt blood.'

'Always this delusion of inheritance,' the raven croaked very reflectively, 'also such overrated hocus-pocus. You should convince yourself rather that there are remedies against it.'

'Yes, we are very frightened of it', the clock continued evenly and in deep thought, as it straightened its larger arm a little, for it was about to strike half past. 'Hence the young woman has also succeeded in limiting the interaction with Mr Sell's ward to only the most necessary. More and more rarely do I see her appear here, and even then Mrs Sophie only lets her come when the smokehouse owner finds himself in the offices in town. Whether that is right?'

'A stupidity', the old bird judged sneeringly, and scratched behind its ear. 'Jealous and envious women always behave foolishly. Otherwise the clever accountant would have to bring to mind that this pretty girl is the mature man's past, his adventure, his poetry, the will o' the wisp which romps along ghostly over the boring field of his path. Such a sparkling thing makes you commonplace and ordinary, in a word, a kitchen light. Do you understand that?'

Only the work was just then striking, and afterwards it sang and hummed for quite a while its usual melody. Through this activity it seemed to be completely occupied, and in the dusty brain-casing it rumbled so much that the old one became nervous and everything discussed slipped away from her. Only the beginning of the conversation had entrenched itself thereby, as tended to happen with aged people. It stubbornly perked up, 'Here though someone was wanting to prophesy the future? Right, I am surely not deceived? How will it be then, when Mrs Sophie brings something chubby faced, rosy, lustily flouncing as a new business contribution to the firm? For we now have — after eight years — certain prospect of that? I really believe a great change will eventuate.'

At that the secretary of time cleared its throat haughtily as if it had itself created the event which it only recorded. Many historians find themselves in such error. The black bird, however, stood taciturnly on one leg and rolled its eyes mysteriously.

'Do you really want to know?', it croaked finally awakening from its dream.

'Of course! — What do you see?'

'I see threads tearing', the black one murmured mutedly. 'Without sense or reason, the end again swallows the beginning, the night the light, the earth its flower.'

'That is too elevated for me,' the clock grumbled indignantly, 'you are speaking like in Odin's days. Can you not express yourself in a more understandable way as behoves towards a dignified, industrious lady?'

'God,' the tousled bird croaked snappishly, 'I could also say that I scent black painted pine wood and the strong aroma of falling leaves. It is nothing unusual, only the people do not want to comprehend how they derive benefit from it.'

Only, the clock began rattling and purring dreadfully. Its officious soul bristled fiercely against the absurd and quite aimless conclusion of the plan which it had guided so neatly for years.

'Stop', it cried angrily. 'Look, you are one of the newer ones who hate all order and any calm running down. Truly, they should chase all the forward-looking ones out of town and family, for what else do they bring but fear and shock? Away with you, I have already considered it unfitting for a long time that you constantly step about on my head thus.'

It stirred powerfully, let its coils purr, and magnified its chastising jangle thus until the raven winged its way down half numbed to the money locker. The clock, however, collected itself — tick tock — tick tock — and tried to fathom circuitously why the fate which it had accompanied with earnest solemnity for eight years should arrive at such an absurd result.

Why should it not also run backwards for once like its newfangled sisters? Tick tock — tick tock.

Twice an invisible, a busy set of scissors had snipped. Threads were cut as a result, threads which just then wanted to disappear still stubbornly into the human fabric. At first an almost nameless creature was met by it. It had been always called just "the woman", and even the newspapers, which reported at the time over a burglary and the following flight in a tiny yacht, employed only speculations over the person of the ringleader. For the winter storm had buried vessel and inhabitants, and the deeps did not spit their loot out again.

'From sympathy', Richard Sell thought, and in his inner being arose a pressing conflict over whether the spotlessness of a certain name and the peace of a childly cheerful soul would be compensated for too highly or too lowly by his likewise sunken money. Indeed, as he had to consider to his own advantage, the calculating man had long since found himself in the clean over it. And since also on the opposite side similar considerations were given, one day the decent, fat A. Guntrum could tap himself on the greasy knee contentedly in his office to utter with closed eyes in the presence of both main parties involved his view that the matter was in fact so. At first, the circumstances were clear and well-ordered. And such outcomes were always forged most profitably when each of the rivals found his advantage with the other.

In this way, he had himself founded almost thirty years ago his alliance of hearts and his business, and it was right pleasant that the matter now repeated itself so happily and conveniently. The forty thousand marks had to be written off admittedly, but for that a constant thankfulness would be attached to the love from the male side. That was something his dear future son-in-law would never be permitted to forget. The matter would in fact be so.

As A. Guntrum was expressing all this in the style of a business letter, twiddling cosily over his knee, with hooded eyes, a sunbeam had glided through the curtain-less office window. It illuminated Sophie's light blond head and forced the smokehouse owner to lose himself for a while thinking of the future in the golden abundance of light. And he found that the calm blue eyes which looked at him, large and open, contained not only the assurance of unconditional attention, but there also resided in them the wish which he had never read in them before so explicitly. Then he quickly stretched his hand out to the pale girl, and had sealed her fate according to his habit with a hasty decision. After that, they walked as on the first day through the bare, dim storerooms, but now hand in hand, and both strengthened by the consciousness of a common possession.

Tick tock — it was all regular and in order.

The engagement had not yet run its course when the scissors snapped anew. But this time they met a thin, completely frayed and unreeled, woollen thread which had marred the young fabric for a long time. Ott Knuth, the ninety year old, was placed in the black painted coffin and, in the glow of candles, he moved his wrinkled head sometimes as if he wondered why he must occupy such an unexpected and uncomfortable place. The raven fluttered about uneasily over the waxen human figure, and then Ott Knuth was buried.

The house opened to new inhabitants, and one day the church bells rang. The smokehouse women of Uhlenhus pressed into Mr Emanuel Quandt's shop and listened curiously to the wondrous information of the storeowner-artist that the bride had looked in her white silk dress exactly like Philippine Welser*. Kathrin was meant to speak the wreath poem. But at the last moment, the bride had forbade her this honour, and even as the couple knelt before the altar, the newly married woman was incapable of withstanding a certain apprehensiveness whenever she was met from a distance by that pair of black, peering eyes. In her own home, however, she began extinguishing the traces of Kathrin's presence. She did not even like to hear the name of the child, and it threw a shadow on Sophie's regularly flowing day every time she learnt the smokehouse owner had again called on the old Müsebeck sisters. She finally managed to make these dutiful visits less frequent and shorter. Richard Sell began putting into writing what he had to share with his charge, and he himself hardly noticed how he let many a thing flow into this writing which had no reference to his guardianship at all and at

---

* [Phillipine Welser (1527–1580) was wife of Ferdinand II, Archduke of Austria.]

base only served to alleviate an uncommunicative disposition. Kathrin hid the large yellow sheets in a
disused sewing box, and with progressing age, she sat
frequently day-dreaming over the pieces of writing, for
both her custodians had long since disclosed to her her
true parentage. That shocking knowledge, however, only
had the result that the adolescent became more and
more insistently attached from a distance to her protector, yes, that she even did not accept the instructions
of the old ladies before she had obtained the express
agreement of her guardian. Thus the girl manufactured
half craftily and half from actual need a dependency
which proved stronger than the cold rejection of the
young wife out in Uhlenhus. Apart from that, however,
many a happy light played in those years of young maid-
enhood over the slender blossoming girl, and both Miss
Müsebecks soon told everyone in town about how their
finely weighed art of upbringing had performed a true
miracle on their student.

You would not believe at all, suggested Miss Helene
Müsebeck, the poet of the local paper, who limped
through life fat and pug-nosed on a stick, what nevertheless exercised a secret driving force in such a child of
the people. That she developed grace in dancing and
comprehended both languages and history easily, God
yes, that was not surprising with a fine and observant
system of teaching. But the quick-witted incursion of
the pretty girl into the garden of poetry, whose rosy
gates had admittedly been opened by an expert hand,
remained extremely conspicuous and commendable.

This favourable advantage was certainly added to not
a little by the circumstance that Kathrin tended to listen
with a lost smile and seemingly in great suspense to the
poems which the poetess read aloud asthmatically and
with mournful voice. And unforgotten to the slender
student remained the enchanting impression aimed at
her when the lyricist of the local paper completed that

famed verse one evening which dealt secretly with the sorrows of her just as round and likewise pug-nosed twin sister. The music teacher Miss Hildegard Müse-beck was namely beset by the adversity of frequently falling in love with the stately fathers and uncles of her female students, and this misfortune then almost regu-larly awoke lamenting notes on the harp of the sister dedicated to the god Apollo. Who could even evade the stirring softness of those closing verses which read:

> Savage fugitive, do you hear
> The last that I have to signal to you,
> Do not disturb either my blessed rest
> In the grave, ah, in the grave.

Both sisters cried fiercely when this was recited, and their listener sank into a respectful silence.

The interaction and instruction from another side, which likewise considered itself authorised to an ex-pression of opinion over the transformation of the brown-locked head, was not viewed quite so agreeably. Every quarter namely, Bob Swanegel called in on the boarding house, and both Miss Müsebecks were soon in agreement that a young man who gave such indifferent opinions about himself, although he was only the helmsman on a ship on the American route, must quite decidedly have an enormous inheritance to expect from somewhere. Otherwise such a confidence would be not only completely incomprehensible, but would some-times also have a quite affronting effect. Bob's knowledge of people and the world had, admittedly ac-cording to his view, been deepened considerably by the interaction with the passengers on his steamer. And when he sat with Kathrin in her little room to survey quite clearly and unconcerned her people, then his haughty features often seemed to assume a directly af-fronted stamp as soon as his friend conversed about her comprehensive plan of study.

"Why English and French?", he tossed out coldly, "why dance and song? Mr Sell is an upstart, what they also call a parvenu. Do you want perhaps to be a stewardess on a steamer, or should you leap about in a circus? For that you are much too thin. Anyhow, it is now gradually getting serious. It can't always remain thus. And a person, particularly a female, must prepare for the future."

When Kathrin did not then understand these dark intimations, but, clapping her hands, broke out into a silvery laugh, then the helmsman to America shook his short-cropped head with still more displeasure, to now declare without consideration that the poetry of Miss Helene Müsebeck was "nonsense" which twisted the heads of young people because they taught them utterly fanciful things about love.

"Beware of it, thing," he advised, full of contempt, "for you are now coming to that age. Love is good, but it must not spring over the fence, but must always think of the bowl and the table. There you can take Julius Kohlrausch as your model. He has one who tends him, and also yells everything he wants to know in his ear. Almost as comprehensibly as I do. Well, and what do you think surely? Recently he asked me whether the former Mrs Plonnies did not have the neck of a swan. That comes gradually when people become dependent on each other. Everything else is harmful. And now, thing, when I return, then — then —". Bob searched for words, was irritated, and finally concluded grumpily that he was losing his courage before the astonished eyes of the girl, "Then I will argue with the old women over what a young maiden of your years needs to know. For it is time, and long waiting does no good."

Tick tock — the clock was incapable of thinking of anything further.

***

It had turned into spring.

Refreshing scents from the nearby sea wafted through the open window into Kathrin's little room and made the curtains sway back and forth gently. Stalk bearing swallows shot to and fro in the blue air and distracted by their happy chirping the attentiveness of the young woman from her large yellow pages which she had spread out before herself on her sewing table. Behind her, Miss Helene Müsebeck reclined on a very comfortable brown velvet sofa, and tapped with her rubber-tipped stick on the carpet, demanding attention. The poetess entertained namely the conviction that she would embrace most happily in this tidy, young girl's room that mood which had such a beneficial effect on the outpouring of a poetic disposition. But in addition, she wished to learn what the mysterious, and so extraordinarily interesting to her, Mr Richard Sell had written over the participation of his ward in an excursion of the students' association Ottonia. For since the dance lesson, a few Ottonians had consorted in the boarding house, extremely distinguished young men, sons of country squires who squeezed monocles to their eyes and prepared for government careers. In her poetry the lyricist advocated indeed noble-mindedly for equal rights for all, but for her acquaintances she could not hold back her secret admiration for the proud nobility.

"Well, how does your foster father comport himself with regard to our suggestion?", Miss Helene inquired finally, short of breath, since Kathrin remained with interlocked hands silent over her reading. "We induct him indeed into our plans only out of respect and esteem, but the views of such a serious man always contain something stimulating and advantageous."

The struggle for air and the strangely singing note which the old spinster emitted through her nose at the same time distracted her boarder from her own, rapt line of thought. A peculiarly ready-to-serve gleam came into Kathrin's eyes when she now turned back to the bulky poetess, as she perceived her rubber-tipped stick and the fleshy, bloodless hand. Then the fine dark-cheeked head rose, and listened. From one of the back rooms, a shrill piano playing had penetrated, for there Miss Hildegard Müsebeck was just then instructing one of her students in the belabouring of the field of keys. An arduous and sorrowful work. When Kathrin, who was bound by the example and admonitions of her guardian closely to life, and hence pondered just as frequently as he over how you could most safely obtain respectability and prestige; when the blossoming girl again recalled the squalidness of her educators, whose ardent thirst for beauty and poetically transfigured worldview were too often disappointed by the raw facts, she was then seized by a quiet pity for the two unnoticed creatures still wheezing along behind the wagon of fortune. Hence it came that the clever thing constantly treated the twin sisters with a tender consideration which was celebrated by the pair of sisters on the other hand as the latest discharge of their own spiritual impact full of thankfulness and delight.

"Dear Aunt Helene," Kathrin said now attentively, "I will gladly read aloud to you my foster father's letter."

Then the poetess nodded genteelly. She wanted to indicate thereby that curiosity did not plague her, but that the urge of her profession to fathom the secrets of the human soul was constantly alive in her.

"Yes, do that, my child," she agreed, wheezing, and impatiently traced with her stick the flowers on the carpet, "educators and writers like very much to hear what wise men think about the joys of youth. So what does your foster father write over the planned excursion?"

Now Kathrin stroked the page smooth and threw a quick glance to the window of the house opposite, where one of the Ottonians had occupied himself for some time in trying out his green velvet cap, swung her chair around with a strong swing so that she turned her back to the observer, and began reading in a low voice. It sounded as if she were searching between the lines for a deeper sense only comprehensible to her.

Dear Kathrin!

I have received your weekly dispatch. It is all in order. But I would like to ask of you that you exert yourself diligently further, despite your dislike, in natural history. It is necessary that a person knows with what creatures and under what conditions they live.

"You see", the poetess added sighing, for the knowledge of nature seemed for her herself to be far too sober and unpoetic an exercise.

But Kathrin smiled willingly and continued.

With respect to your excursion, I will have no objections to it. The ladies Müsebeck will have examined everything, and I thank them for the courtesy in informing me especially about it.

He is really very polite," Miss Helene blushed, "he reminds me always of the merchant that Gustav Freytag describes so splendidly."*

Here Kathrin also nodded seriously, for any praise which paid tribute to her guardian was regarded by her as something self-evident. The man who reigned self-willed and arbitrarily over her life up to now had remained completely spared from the lust for knowledge of people and things which usually stirred in her.

She lowered her head and continued her reading with her bright voice, seemingly untouched, although she arrived right now at the place in the letter which had just before caught her attentiveness in the extreme. Really, something was there which excited her constant brooding over past and present again in a painful way,

---

* [The figure Anton Wohlfart from Freytag's *Soll und Haben* (*Debit and Credit*).]

so much that a red wave of agitation ran over the seemingly uninvolved girl's cheeks.

There it was written.

> I need not tell you, Kathrin, that I expect from you in the society of these young, and hence by rights mischievous students that restraint and modesty which remains fitting to our circle alone. I like it when someone desires for everything which is somehow achievable by them, only we must at the same time never deny to ourselves the memory of our origins, because we thereby easily become ridiculous and untrue. I will not touch on these uncertain circumstances further and would also like never to be forced to speak of them with you. But since you are now stepping out into life more and more, and you bear responsibility not only for yourself, but a part must also be passed to me, I believe you must draw a visible line. I think you will understand me and also that which I do not express, and will act accordingly. And now, my child, I give you my hearty regards and wish you every joy in the planned excursion. Richard Sell.

"And below there is a postscript", the girl added, breathing out, "The ladies Müsebeck will have certainly expressed to you their wish that your absence must be concluded before curfew."

"Hm," the poetess stuttered on her brown sofa, confused by this wealth of openness as she tapped about helplessly on the carpet with her stick, "certainly, that would be all taken to heart. But — —".

She faltered. In the tenderly-strung disposition, a half-unrecognised aversion arose towards the unsparing hint as to what a low position her charge had begun her life path from, and her kind and sickly heart pounded heftily and breath-takingly as she thought of the fears which the calculating man out there in Uhlenhus associated with the origins of his ward. For this leapt out of the lines more distinctly than anything else for Miss Helene Müsebeck.

The clever guardian suspected the stirrings of the blood. His trust in the moderating effects of a loving education did not seem unshakeable. And the large poetess, who gauged life only from the side when she was enthralled in her rhymes, distinctly read from the words written by the distant man the fear that one day the roguish whore's head of Kathrin's mother could stare from the lovely features of their joint charge. And had not the father of this delicate little one been a drinker? A dissipated man who had choked all his better intents in intoxication and unconsciousness? Horrific! Quietly shivering and struggling arduously against her difficulty with breathing, the washed-up spinster sent a doubtful look over to her boarder, and at this moment, she furtively disapproved of her, because the young girl was moving her slender foot, surrounded by a half-open patent leather shoe, imperceptibly to and fro, unsuspecting and lost far away in her thoughts. Shall perhaps a conscious craving for admiration be present in this delicate, compliant creature?

"My God," the poetess thought in a fluster, "perhaps Mr Richard Sell in Uhlenhus did not in vain let so many anxious warnings infuse his writing. Is it not actually terrible when half dead spirits circle around a young life?"

But straight afterwards, sympathy prevailed with the kind-hearted woman, and her sky-blue eyes became overcast with a moist veil. Thus it occurred that the heftily breathing woman overlooked how Kathrin quickly rose to listen to the rolling of a vehicle which was rattling past under the window.

"Whom are you greeting there?", the spinster asked a little distrustfully and curious at the same time.

"Oh, it is only the general practitioner, Kruse", the girl responded, shaded with a quite rosy breath from the the deep flexing. "But think, Aunt Helene," Kathrin added thoughtfully, "he is using the smokehouse's sulky. Mr Sell will not have fallen sick perhaps?"

The little one thought of nothing else. The figure of her guardian, who defended and constrained her so much, overshadowed enormously all the phenomena which could usually penetrate into her circle.

Then the poetess listened curiously and with understanding, and as she busily drew all sorts of incomprehensible figures on the carpet with her stick, she tossed out soothingly, "Oh, it will surely have its reasons. And now we will think about how we will dress you for this excursion. Both airy and modest."

***

The barrel-organ rolled and tinkled a dance, the fresh, supple limbs rocked in large circles to the rhythm, and the delicate ribbons rushed swirling through the spring air as they initialled their shadows scurrying on the golden green meadows. From the nearby walls of the grove which surrounded the clearing in the cool glory of spring, a bright cheer or a young laugh was sometimes thrown back echo-like, for this budding humanity was amusing itself here outside in an ancient game whose charms progressive big cities knew only from antique pictures and hence greeted with smiles. But the forest meadow as well as the youth of the little university had preserved the memory of the joy of past races, and the harmlessness and the charm of the round dance refreshed their life powers.

Only a single elder had been invited by the green-capped mob of Ottonians to their forest celebration. But then this older girl also stood in a special relationship to the corps, for Miss Magda Heinse had had to shovel her life's happiness into the green caps. And hence the Otto-

nian's felt nobly obliged to constantly enlist the kind ingenuous creature, over whose lips no angry word had
ever flowed, in their escapades. In place of another. And
this was simply a quite strange tale.

Ten or twelve years before namely, when Magda —
today surely a thirty year old — was still in her blossom,
there it had come to an engagement between her and
one of the Ottonians who had taken quarters in the captain's cottage of her father. A proper student's love full
of youthful stupidity and unshakeable idealism. The
young bliss had easily ignored all sorts of hindrances
which peaked for others in the noble clan of the young
country squire and above all in the so mixed education
of the promised one. Only, one beautiful evening, with
wine, all that difference was alluded to by an honest and
just as heedless comrade both kind-heartedly and reck-
lessly, and the last word in this dispute unfortunately
had to be spoken between the excited men by pistols.
There Magda's love had fallen, and he now rested under
a mound which was not only planted with the most
beautiful flowers by her and the mourning corps, but
under which also the human sensual happiness of a
poor, simple and love-strong creature ossified for ever.
Admittedly the brimming heart, which believed itself
bound by an eternal loyalty, stopped hoping and wish-
ing for itself. For soon it followed that the lonely girl
believed she owed the corps a part of that care and
servility which she had dedicated to her vanished lover.
And since the young fellows also showed a chivalrous
regard for her, one day the golden green corps ribbon
was conferred on her by a deputation, a sign like no
other woman of the little town had ever received. Since
then Magda Heinse was vested with the position of sis-
terly assistant advisor to the Ottonians. Her clear
insight into all the practical things of life was highly esteemed, but also many a young man crept to her when
pained by that place under his chest through which the

calamitous shot had penetrated the fallen man. And the gentle mind and the gentle hand brushed away many a thing.

The barrel-organ sounded, the supple limbs rocked, and the ribbons swirled through the blue air. Much swelling joy in existence revealed itself there, many a ravishing, girlish movement climbed unconsciously to perfection of form when the arms bent and the limbs tautened powerfully. And some of these muses' sons knew already that in the movement alone full beauty was capable of expressing itself. But most were agreed that in Miss Kathrin Sell or Miss Brodersen — the devil knew what she was actually called — such a special grace of gliding and flexing, of fleeing and pausing was displayed that she steered the admiring glances to herself more than all the others. And then this oblivious wantonness, this boyish naughtiness when she felt provoked to exercise some bedevilment.

Right, there her ribbons again flew across the circle until they lost themselves in the trembling spring foliage of the forest. Should you chase after her? It perhaps deserved a nice thanks. But dammit, already a bright and a dark shadow were storming after her, and with some envy the one left behind confessed how the neighbour of the little one, the heavily rich commoner of the society, who also induced her invitation, was not shamed from obliging attentiveness. Quick as thought, the couple had vanished between the thin beeches of the immediate forest. You instinctively looked for Magda Heinse, the soother, the pacifier; only, this good spirit of youth also remained invisible. Then the ribbons swirled anew, and the game continued.

Each leaning on the trunk of a brown beech tree, thus the student and the girl stood opposite each other. Her breath flew and, from the wild race, her heart pounded loudly and distinctly so that they both had to laugh. Between them, unreachably high, the lost ribbon swayed on a green branch, and the loop rocked gently as if it were secretly mocking that there were so many things on earth which were tossed away heedlessly by people, and after which they then sent out their wishes passionately.

"Lord," the student Martin Gerloff began after a while, without giving the ribbon even the slightest attention, "how out of breath you are!"

"Oh, it isn't going much better with you either", Kathrin suggested airily, as she let her dark eyes rest on the broad, stocky figure of the youth.

"But why could you not allow me the pleasure of doing you a favour?", her opposite persisted, whereby he clutched a little awkwardly backwards onto the slender beech. "Why actually must you race so wildly after me?"

Kathrin brushed a strand of her golden brown hair back.

"I don't know either," she confessed finally, "what it is that excites me so in overtaking you. But it is glorious though to be able to measure your powers for once. Isn't it? Particularly when you must almost always sit still."

"Certainly," her companion confirmed in an honest tone which held the mean between devotion and sympathy, "you sit a lot in that little room. And you are constantly studying."

Then a cheeky gleam passed over the features of the delicate girl, but at the same time she knitted her dark brows frowning.

"And you," she tossed out drily, "are observing me from your window all the time! The Müsebeck sisters don't like tolerating that at all."

"For heaven's sake," murmured the unspoiled muse's son, who could not confess though how the little room opposite his in the lonely street had appeared in his mind for a long time to be a paradise in which a bright angel had been caught for his edification, "for heaven's sake — I have admittedly — that is, only quite by accident — it would though be extremely unpleasant for me — really distressing to the heart," he added ingenuously, "if you perhaps gave me some grief on account of my being your neighbour, dear gracious young lady."

Again the girl puckered her forehead. But at the same time, a hidden sorrow twitched about her lips.

"So you must not call me," she said curtly, "my foster father does not desire that."

"Your foster father?", the student stammered with an instinctive bow, wanting to show some love to Kathrin, "he must be, from what I hear, an extremely industrious man."

"Yes, that he is," Kathrin beamed suddenly in relief, for at the invoked figure of the smokehouse owner, she had returned abruptly to her trusted, certain ground. And now she threw a thankful and warm look at her listener. "Mr Richard Sell knows everything and can do everything."

"So, so", Martin Gerloff rasped in a low voice.

The ribbon danced in the wind above them, a rustling went through the beech branches, and a bright ray of sunlight wreathed down the trunk of the tree opposite Kathrin's hair. There it collected and formed a golden cap. The black eyes gleamed contradictorily under the heavenly adornment, and her neighbour's breath faltered anew. But this time from fright. At the same time, a cuckoo called quite close by, and a large, sparkling green beetle whirled heavily humming before the eyes of the blinded boy. There was so much that was confusing all around which was implanted frighteningly in Martin Gerloff, and robbed him of his senses and speech. He just felt timidly that this moment was beautiful like resurrection and death. And at the same time, he was moreover a strong fellow, a son of the farmland who was brought up to obtain through industry and wealthy means an esteemed position in the service of the state. Over there from the meadow, the bright calls of the playing youths sounded. No, no, this sweet and yet tormenting silence must be interrupted, otherwise the meaningful moment would flow past unused and perhaps foolishly. But what? What?

Meanwhile the girl had stretched comfortably in the warming sunlight, now she was leaning on the beech and closing her eyes a little acquiescently. That lent him courage.

"How old is your foster father actually?", he burst out impulsively, for some distant unease had broken over him. "He gives yet the impression of a stately man."

How old? Kathrin did not stir, only her black eyes unveiled themselves again, and she gave an impression of extreme astonishment. It had never occurred to her to think about the age of her guardian, for he seemed to her to be both quite young and quite old at the same time.

"Let me see now," she spoke from the depths of her thoughts, and began gently bending the fingers of her right hand one after the other as if counting, "Mr Sell is, I believe, 35 years old."

"So, so," Martin Gerloff responded, ashamed and a little disappointed, "so still a young man."

"Yes? You think so?", Kathrin asked in astonishment.

But then she shook her head, and peered attentively at the distant figures in the meadow which moved small and shadowily as if behind a trembling gauze curtain. Her companion caught how she twitched her shoulders as if she had given up leaping for the ribbon swaying above her and now considered that it signalled a return to their companions.

"No," Martin Gerloff considered lightning quick, although it seemed uncanny to him that he so quickly found a saving means for extending this shimmering fairy tale in the solitude of the forest, "no, the slender, exceptional and fine being must not leave me now. If we mix with the others, then the everyday will return, then the silvery bells will not ring again which I now hear tolling throughout the entire forest. Throughout. And it is so pleasant when you possess something for yourself alone."

The student did not ponder any further, for what he at base hoped and wished was for him covered by an indifferent darkness. The pleasing moment sufficed for him, as for youth in general. Quickly resolved, he gathered up a green mossy stone and tossed it weightily against the branch which had caught the ribbon. The branch shook heftily, but threw the red and white loop down so that Kathrin could grasp it adroitly with her right hand. She stood for a moment swaying on her tiptoes triumphantly there. Then both broke out into a joyful laughter, the self-consciousness vanished more and more between them as a result of this bold stroke, they became better friends than before.

"That was good", Kathrin praised quite happily, and looked at him contentedly. "You aim brilliantly. And now we need not return having not achieved anything. Shall we not go?"

Only, after the confident throw, a great part of his awe before the strange girl really had drained away.

"Already?", he deplored, and twinkled his sweet-tempered eyes persuasively.

"Yes, what do you want to do then actually?", Kathrin inquired with surprise.

"Look", the student pointed hesitantly, and stretched his arm out uncertainly towards the thick wood. "The forest is putting forth fresh foliage, every leaf shimmers as though plated with silver."

"True," the girl concurred animatedly, having now turned likewise in the indicated direction, "you would think you could seemingly hear the awakening."

"In fact, you'd believe that. And nobody is on the forest paths to notice."

"Yes, it all lies almost fearfully alone. And then — how this light blue mist creeps on the ground."

"Oh, it means you well", the Ottonian argued un- thinkingly.

Without a further word of understanding, the young people strode at once next to each other, merged into the light haze of the broad, beech and acacia edged path, and looked around sometimes furtively at how far they had already distanced themselves from the dimming meadow. But just this separation from the dying voices of the barrel-organ and the indecipherable calls of the playing youths seemed especially delightful to them. Their hearts again began racing more quickly, and sometimes they looked back furtively and blushing, like violators of order who surely know how little their beha- viour would be supported.

They they arrived at a half decayed bridge made of rotten fir trunks, under which a black miry water flowed along lazily. The crossing was bordered to the left and right by two moss-covered, low brick walls, and after the wanderers had gazed down into the sad course for a while, bent close next to each other, Martin Gerloff sat on the wall, but not before he had carefully spread his handkerchief on the free space next to him so that his companion would not, should she perhaps dignify him with her proximity, besmirch her pretty blue dress.

And really, Kathrin sat down hesitantly next to him. Her senses, her cleverness, and her caution were already enmeshed by the unaccustomedness, the adven- turousness which was dancing past her in such a life- awakening and at the same time so obscuring way. Like the blue mist which rose silvery soft from the ground to reshape everything familiar and known for so long in playful ways. The world looked different today from how it usually looked.

A chill breathed from the moist coolness of the young foliage. Stirred by it, the limbs of the secluded pair shivered sensitively, and they moved closer to each other than before.

It was a long thoughtful look with which the student gauged the fine countenance next to himself, but the slender, delicate being sat so coolly and strangely at his side that he suppressed quite unhappily and with anger at himself the turmoil governing him and turned back, murmuring something incomprehensible, to the dreary water.

"An accursedly melancholic ditch," he said without thinking — "cocytus*."

Kathrin pondered, then she turned around likewise, and at the right time the poetry lessons of Miss Helene Müsebeck occurred to her. "Ah yes," she recalled indifferently, "the underworld."

Her arm brushed against the student at the same time, and the excited young man immediately thought he felt the seething and twitching of a fierce blood.

Now the fence which he had erected around her collapsed completely.

"But that does not apply to you", a trembling ardent voice shook from him, a voice which he no longer considered to be his own, and at the same time his eyes rested with an open expression of boundless adoration on her dark face which stood still with shock and yet as though drawn to his own. "What have you to do with the underworld? — You are life — beautiful, sunny, covetable life. You do not know at all how wondrously pretty you are."

Kathrin emitted a choked cry, only, she did not otherwise stir. She neither sprang down from the wall, which was still open to her, nor did she create a space between herself and her so strangely altered companion; her dark look just adhered half appalled and full of strained expectation to the disturbed features of the stu-

---

* [River of the underworld in Greek mythology – souls that refused to be ferried by Charon were doomed to wander its banks.]

dent. Quite exactly, sharply and certainly, the question stabbed through her mind, why surely was he raising his right hand? Did he want to embrace her? And then? — What was that surely? — Oh — What was that surely which you must not tolerate, and which you would like to become acquainted with though? And why can you straighten the blue dress on your freezing body so distinctly, and even the ironed pleats in your lap, although an enormous change must the next moment burst apart your existence up to now? What will surely become visible behind it? Something beautiful? Or something terrible? You are only curious — irresistibly curious.

The forest mist rolled past gently fuming and veiled both figures deeper and deeper in unreality. And the seducer, this ingenuous, considerate seducer who would not commit any evil to the beloved at any price, who would perhaps like to dedicate his life a thousand times jubilantly to her, ah, he is driven by a dull power which he cannot withstand, which is there because it certainly grows up from the moist spring soil, just like all these reinvigorated, budding shrubs about him.

Once more he wants to resist, to tell her of his life on the mundane paternal estate where he grew up without a mother, a late birth amidst his brothers on whom no attention was really paid because he was always a child amongst men, wants to tell her of his loneliness in the town, which is not dislodged by restless work either, because — yes, because you simply feel such a painfully inexplicable desire. He would have liked to have stammered out all that, as a safeguard, or perhaps also to obtain her sympathy. But the urging and sprouting in the fresh greenery, the numbing haze about his forehead, they wiped away all realisations, and drew him into their compulsive weaving.

Trembling, as if imploring leniency, he stretches his hands out, encloses the motionless head of the girl, bends over her half-open eyes in which the astonished question still swims, "whether the future hides something beautiful, magnificent, sparkling behind all that?" And then both shivering and glowing creatures warm themselves in hasty, unthinking kisses.

Above the waters of the underworld, life celebrates its very own festival, the young beech trees shook, conscious of their strength, as if they too felt more fiercely the circulation of their sap, and through the dense forest it rustled like a mysterious secret.

But ah, the green silence obtains a voice, and through the budding bushes a pair of eyes stare which slowly fill with tears. Not very far at all from the couple who seek to solve the deepest puzzle of existence in an impatient urge, Maria Heinse, the old fiancee of a dead man, sits on a hidden, circular stone bench in the midst of the overgrown wilderness, and her twitching mouth expresses full of sadness and pity what years and earthly sorrow teach all disillusioned people, "Ah, you poor children, will you also be able to remain together? For the world always penetrates between beginning and hope. And every way is crossed by many side paths on which you are so easily lost. And then worst of all, behind the joy, fear and remorse always stride. Will you deal with them when they overtake you? How I would like to help you, you poor children!"

***

Senseless, in a daydream, the couple wander through the endless clearings of the forest. On rails reflecting the sun, a train on the narrow gauge railway travels past them. Strange faces emerge blurred behind the narrow carriage windows — the dreaming pair do not see and do not notice even the enormous rumbling and steaming of the vanishing train. But see — what sort of figures were those which wafted towards the striding pair from out of the blue haze? In blissful pride over his boldness, Martin Gerloff thought he saw loud flag-waving heralds storming towards him, exulting and cheering, "You are not alone anymore, fortune strides by your side, and you have conquered her. — What will come of it? Petty bourgeois questions at such a moment. Of that you do not think. Be jubilant, you young heart."

And his soul and his mouth really are singing an old drinking song which, however, strangely knows no other word than, "Kathrin — Kathrin". Thus it occurred that he did not notice how stiffly and uncertainly the captured girl followed his path, yes, how the fine countenance was overshadowed by a ghostly pallor, and how an erratic, flickering fire burned in the black eyes. Vague projections also swayed out of the mist towards her. But see there, they were loud acquaintances, and the closer they swept towards her, the more fiercely shame and despair burrowed into her. And from time to time she threw her head to the side and peered wildly around to see whether you could escape this ghostly pressure somewhere. Then a tall rascal rushed up before her in dark-blue sailor's uniform and with a haughty and superior face. He threw his hand up as if he wanted to tear her away from the other, but abruptly drew his fist back again as if it were not respectable to touch her.

"Look, girl," he said coldly, "so you are doing well. Something bad lies in you which will send you down once more. And you really believe that I will shake your hand? God forbid, don't lie to yourself, thing. Such as you are on every corner."

Oh, how contemptuous it sounded, how painfully it dug into her writhing heart. But another voice tore her last self-esteem much more unbearably to the ground. A voice which sounded hard and gruff, and before which you did not like to shut your ears, as vehemently as the frightened girl also sought to hide from the tidily brushed, black frock coat.

"I guessed it, Kathrin. Through upbringing and teaching, I wanted to turn it around. I have expended much effort and money on it. But you have rewarded me badly."

Oh, leaping away, vanishing, creeping into the darkness in the middle of the bright day. Only, how strange, right across the forest path which opened onto the approaching main road, something fat and ponderous was limping along, a rubber-tipped stick propped in the soft ground, and a choked, short-breathed organ lamented full of anguish and exaggeratedly, "My poor, sweet child, have I not always referred to the power of passion? It batters the weak and sinful with its club as though they were clay, and throws them onto the rubbish heap. God in heaven, how dirty you are. I would like to straighten you up, really, very much — but you know my white hand is so squeamish about dust and uncleanliness. Shame — shame!"

Then Kathrin wanted to cry out, "None of that concerns me at all — I was just so terribly curious and will soon forget this stupid absurdity." — Only before she arrived at full consciousness, a vehicle rattled along the main road, and at the same time she felt how her companion was gently stroking her arm. She pulled back reluctantly.

"What is it?"

The student had paused. "Kathrin — young lady," he stuttered, for he did not know how he should address her, "do you not see the man in the carriage? He has already waved over to us several times. Is it to you?"

Only now did the dreamer awaken to full reality. Before the figure who was waving over there in the sunny dust of the country road hard and angularly, those shadows scattered which had risen up before her until now, and an enormous fear shook her every limb. At the same time, however, the concern about the very familiar man there in the carriage swept everything which concerned her away like dry leaves. What did this encounter mean? Had he come after her? Or had a misfortune met the house in Uhlenhus? For Richard Sell did not tend to interrupt business trips at any price. He calculated every minute according to its monetary value.

Without begrudging her companion any further words or even offering him the slightest explanation, Kathrin gathered herself up and whirled senselessly through the middle of the unpathed wood towards the country road. Now a leap across the ditch — and she stood with whistling breath before the wheels.

Mr Sell did not ask her from where she came, he did not greet her either, but just bent down hastily and entirely preoccupied to her. He looked unbelievably wrecked and aged. Only, he seemed dominated by the one thought, by that one which suffused him, detaching from himself to call it out somewhere into the world.

"I have a dead person in the house", he said grimly, and it twitched angrily about his clenched mouth. "A little child. And my wife is gravely ill."

With that he grasped the whip, sat down again on his seat, and as he struck fiercely at the animal, the carriage rolled away creaking and rattling.

Kathrin followed him. She held both hands tightly interlocked in each other and sucked fast with her eyes unchangeably to the black figure in the fuming cloud of dust. Where he was leading her, she did not know.

***

It was turning gently dark when Kathrin arrived before the house in Uhlenhus. She had needed such a long time for the short way, for she set step before step, and she wandered at the same time imperceptibly through years of her adolescence. She had quickly said goodbye to the student, and at the same time shaken her head uncomprehendingly as if she did not grasp at all why she was involved with this person and what he had to do with her. Back here in her home town, someone had died. An incidental, nameless being. But it was a thing which concerned Mr Richard Sell, and that must suffice for the stranger. Sometimes during her way, she paused and laughed shrilly and defiantly, quite similar to how she had heard shortly before from her foster father. Then she got angry with herself and made bitter reproaches that she could hang her thoughts on something absurd and unimportant while at the home of the smokehouse owner, to whom she belonged, heavy sorrow and misfortune had moved in. But most frequently of all, she balled her little fists because she had not behaved according to her own standards as her guardian and everyone who meant well with her desired. Filled with hate, she struck in spirit at the power by which she had just been urged onto a wrong way, against which she at base bristled against vehemently.

"Ugh," she grumbled bitterly to herself, and struck her fist against her forehead, "I wish I was dead. But first I must see what has happened with us."

It was turning gently dark when she entered through the green rep covered door of the smokehouse. The bell was covered with a cloth so that it only gave out a ghostly soft note. And when the girl whom nobody had called crossed over the threshold of the living room, she saw there how her guardian was pacing out the narrow space restlessly from one corner to the other. He had bedded his hands behind his rumpled frock coat; he seemed hardly to notice that the hoarse voice of his father-in-law could be heard from a wheelchair right next to the table and was speaking to itself in a very dignified and expressful way, "it is in fact so — such a thing cannot be altered."

"Hello", Kathrin greeted them timidly.

Then the smokehouse owner interrupted his wandering and turned his hollowed-out, sharp face to her. The shrunken eyes burned still as though in an ungovernable accusation. He did not seem to comprehend why fortune had left him.

"What do you want?" he asked curtly.

"I would like to help here", Kathrin replied timidly, for she was shy before the second witness to her presence.

The smokehouse owner stroked his bald-shaved head, and turned pondering to the closed door of the adjoining room. Through the curtained glass panes, a vague light shimmered.

"You?", he asked after a pause, as if he had not calculated at all on this offer.

From the wheelchair, however, a reluctant scratching arose, the swollen eyes of A. Guntrum opened, and the fringe of hair at the back bristled over his fat neck.

"Nonsense", the lame man parried, since he shared his loathing towards this unwelcome money swallower with his daughter. Yes, he even considered the claims of the questionable foundling to the common grief to be cheeky and impertinent. Anyhow, Sophie did not like to suffer the black-haired sprog. The female had also already become too tall. Where should that all lead? "Nonsense", he coughed once more and struck his fist on the table. "We have a doctor here, and that suffices. In addition, I have brought along an expensive nurse. Money is no object to me at all. Everything else is nonsense, for in a few days, little Sophie will be healthy again."

"Yes, that she will", the smokehouse owner emitted in suppressed fury, and swept diagonally through the air with his balled right hand as if he wanted to knock away something.

"And we need peace here too", the fat man added from his wheelchair with an intent that could not be misjudged.

Yet Kathrin hesitated in the doorway which she had not left up to now; she directed her eyes insistently and demandingly at the man in the black frock coat, for whatever opinion anyone else uttered flew past her. In this house, she was accustomed to receiving her orders only from a single place.

Then a hoarse cry penetrated from the curtained adjoining door. The three people were rooted in shock, each firmly to their place and listening intently.

"Cold — cold", an exhausted voice whimpered from within.

Straight afterwards, a different female spoke in-between to utter something about a hot-water bottle in considered and admonishing tones. All with a confidence as if this instrument represented the infallible means against every adversity of humanity.

Kathrin did not ponder any longer. "Quick," she started, "hot water."

With that she was already plunging down the dark corridor to the kitchen and moving the iron pots around. Just as she was bending to pull out from a corner the pottery vessels which the eternally rattling Ott Knuth had used against the chill shaking though him, a hard hand tapped on her back. And when she stood up, Richard Sell was standing before her. He did not look at her, but stared doggedly into the fire and smoke of the open hearth.

"You shall stay here," he ordered in a business-like way, "I desire it, for — for —". And it passed vehemently out of him, "I need someone now. And now quick."

Without a further word, he turned away, and strode with his crunching boots back to the room. And yet it would have been worth lingering a moment longer. For the abandoned girl stretched up to her full height now, shook herself as if tossing off all sorts of strange things from herself, and then she stretched her body and threw both arms up. It was as if she were taking ownership of this hearth and this kitchen after a long time.

"Thank God", she murmured.

2

The summer had moved into the countryside with warmth and the scent of flowers. Long, glittering golden threads hung on the trees and, before the open door of the shop of Mr Emanuel Quandt, the learned bullfinch of the artist trader sat in its birdcage and incessantly whistled for the pleasure of those passing by the first beats of "Good health, comrades, on the horse, on the horse"*. To the great anguish of the former tenor, the bird had not arrived any further in its classical education, only, for the schoolchildren of Uhlenhus, this extraordinary achievement sufficed perfectly so that boys and girls usually encamped in a narrow half circle about the window and the bench standing before it, to call attention occasionally by a prod in the ribs to an especially successful attempt.

"Look, Dörth, that is a fine one!"

"Have heard it all, Mr Quandt says the bird can read music!"

"Oh, what a weird bird."

Even today, such an enthusiastic crowd of children was again clustered about the mysterious cage to the not in any way small pride of thin Mr Quandt, although on this golden morning, the sky-blue painted bench before the window was densely occupied too. Here in fact, three friends had taken their seats next to the former artist. Three friends who had appeared to pull in authentic news over affairs quite specific to Uhlenhus. And Mr Quandt stretched his improbably long legs still somewhat longer from himself when he noticed how devotedly and unconditionally his news was listened to.

---

* [From Schiller's *Wallenstein*, the first part "Wallensteins Lager", Scene 11. Put to music by Christian Jakob Zahn (1797).]

The red-maned man held delicately between the two fingers of his right hand a long-stemmed clay pipe which no man wanted to buy off him anymore, and he puffed comfortably on his dampened tobacco. The stuff was crackling so terribly that even Captain Julius Kohlrausch, who reclined next to him, secretly described that semi-luxury as "stinky seaweed".

It was really somewhat close on the sky-blue bench. For his wife, the former Mrs Plonnies, was enthroned next to the Captain, and she was occupying herself at the moment stubbornly with preserving her grey silk dress from being crushed. On the arm of the bench, however, rode Bob Swanegel in a brand-new sailor's uniform, and the golden stripes on his sleeves as well as the band about his cap proved that Bob must have moved on again considerably in his bourgeois position.

"Yes", Julius Kohlrausch repeated unhurriedly, and drummed his fingers on his tautened body meaningfully. "I have presented the 'Green Herring' to him now once and for all. He has his certificate now, and he need only pay me a small lease sum every year."

"Be quiet, sweetie," his wife interrupted here, and lifted her swollen hand as a sign to the white-headed man that he be silent from now on, "Mr Quandt knows all that. It just concerns now whether Mr Sell will let our Bob operate for him. And whether that cannot be agreed contractually with him straightaway."

"Yes, contractually, my sweetie", the portly Captain enthused, and licked his lips as if after a tasty meal.

Bob Swanegel, however, rode on his arm somewhat more energetically, and threw out decisively in-between, "Certainly to be certain. You must not entrust so much goodness in such great merchants. But I will suit him for the service."

"Yes, do that, my boy", Julius Kohlrausch praised, and looked admiringly at the resolute helmsman, whereby he was already enjoying in anticipation the blissful feeling of how much his gifted student would have the edge on the rich Mr Sell during the negotiations about to commence. "You can always rock him a little."

"Rock", Mrs Gertrude agreed, and she nodded her greasily gleaming face approvingly, for she felt a maternal affection towards Bob because she entertained the firm conviction that she had the counsellor alone to thank for her radiant happiness.

"Yes, that is all very beautiful," Bob said finally, as he stood up and, according to his habit, buried his hands in his pockets, "but the principal thing remains whether I now meet Mr Sell in the right mood. How stands it with him, Mr Quandt?"

"God," the trader replied, and cautiously turned the long clay pipe between his fingers, "I have already noted of the master that, since the blessed parting of the wife and the little child, he keeps himself very much in the house. Miss Kathrin keeps house like before, and in the evenings you can almost always see them both in the ground floor room sitting under the green lamp where a heap of books always lies between them." The artist shrugged his shoulders. "I am also in favour of education," he rocked his red-bushy head, "and have, I believe, proved this in my animated life. But a bit of the schoolmaster has been lost in Mr Sell. And then — he is no longer up for a proper conversation. For since the bereavement, he hardly still opens his mouth. He also finds himself travelling a lot. Otherwise he would certainly place more weight on the gossip which circulates here about him and the little girl."

Now Bob Swanegel threw an especially dark look at the artist, a look in which was distinctly written, "You are an ass."

"What sort of stupid stuff is that?", he asked haughtily, and shook his fist menacingly in his pocket.

"But let Mr Quandt tell," Mrs Gertrud Kohlrausch said curiously, "he knows how to word things so nicely."

"Yes, but it is nonsense", Bob maintained stubbornly.

"Good health, comrades, on the horse, on the horse", the bullfinch piped here mildly in-between and puffed up its red breast.

"Dear heavens," Mr Quandt took up the interrupted thread again, "the view of the helmsman Mr Swanegel concurs at base with my own, if he also occasionally likes to express it in a somewhat dry, seaman-like way. I am of course far above such gossip and do not tolerate it in any way in my shop. But the bourgeois people in Uhlenhus, my venerable customers, have lagged behind in it somewhat. It cannot be denied that most find it unsuitable that Mr Sell does not take a proper housekeeper into his house, but rather lives with the pretty Miss under one roof. A few, however, whisper much worse still."

"That is smut", Bob burst out furiously, and stamped on the hard-trodden ground.

But he meant thereby not the behaviour of the smokehouse owner, but the stupidity and low manner of thinking of the Uhlenhus fisherfolk towards their benefactor. Mr Quandt, however, drew in his legs, for he feared being trodden on, then he kowtowed obligingly.

"Entirely my view", he soothed, and raised his pipe up carefully so that it would not be broken by the ever closer moving Mrs Kohlrausch. "And in addition, people don't know what I know. No, no, they have no idea of it, for otherwise you would judge the entire matter exceedingly differently."

"Then be so good as to tell what you know", the helmsman grumbled brusquely, stepped up to the shopkeeper, and made an air to seize him by the coat lapels.

Mr Quandt meanwhile pulled back quickly before this attack until he almost pushed the birdcage from the window latch with his mane, for he feared with justice that his eminence before the village youth could suffer harm.

"I beg," he collected himself, "I beg — what do you wish for, helmsman Mr Swanegel? It really only concerns a loving and joyful incident to which I wanted to point sincerely. You must namely know," he continued with greater emphasis, although he sought to utter everything further in a mysterious whispering tone, "a young man also comes to the house sometimes. From the green caps. An Ottonian. The student, Mr Gerloff, extremely fine and prosperous family. The father is chairman of our county council."

"What?", Bob Swanegel cried in loud indignation, although his sunburnt cheeks paled noticeably, "what does the learned man want there?"

Captain Kohlrausch, however, suddenly whistled loudly and apprehensively to himself, and his wife gathered her grey silk dress quite closely to herself to then almost fall on the chest of the storyteller in suspense.

"Is something developing there?", the Captain's wife breathed excitedly. Her blinking little eyes sank at the same time seemingly into the folds of fat surrounding them. And her desire to learn if possible something about a future betrothal had climbed so high that she almost forgot how much such news must pain her Bob. The experienced woman entertained no illusions over the true feelings of this haughty and know-it-all fellow, yes, she had often secretly shaken her enormous head over whether the foster child of Mr Sell, who had to learn so absurdly much, would also be a fitting companion for a man sweeping across the sea. "Is something developing there?", she nonetheless encouraged the thin shopkeeper once more, and pressed her fullness dangerously close to his chest.

Bob Swanegel had meanwhile regained his composure. He clenched his teeth, and since nobody could hear his heart pounding, he tossed out in a contemptuous tone, "Tattle!"

"Now, now," Mr Quandt turned with the air of a man from whom nothing can remain hidden of the workings of the inconsequential world of men about him, "why shouldn't there be something in it? She is a pretty little woman with patent leather shoes and an education, and — just among us — Mr Sell is, as you know, a striver. The County Council chairman," he suddenly sprang back what had been previously mentioned, "to whom would it not flatter to enter into such prosperous and influential circles through certain family ties? Moreover," he played as his strongest trump card in retrospect, "the young gentleman, the green cap, the Ottonian, always takes flowers along. Quite few at first, a couple of loose roses or carnations, but it is becoming more and more. Should you not draw a quite definite conclusion from that?"

Here the artist straightened up to his full height, and passed his hand unburdening and in quiet triumph through his red bush of hair. Only, how it hit him when the helmsman, for whom the last threads of patience were tearing, stepped up quite close to him to blast in his face with open contempt, "How much does the soft soap cost in your store?"

"What? What? Soft — —? Do you perhaps want to insinuate — —?"

"That you are an old washerwoman", Bob nodded with twitching lips. And before the sky-blue bench could recover from its shock, he turned away, and strode decisively to the smokehouse.

"Bob, my boy", Captain Kohlrausch called after him warningly.

Only, the admonished man just shook his short-cropped head defiantly and self-confidently. A minute later he was already pulling strongly on the bell pull without being able to desist in this important episode from himself riveting a peering look at the brass letter-box sparkling in the sunlight. And rightly, under the receptacle, a brand-new sign had been attached with the inscription, "The main office is found in the town."

"He is becoming ever grander", the man adjudged, shrugging his shoulders.

At the same time as the covers of her fate were being aired so intrusively before Mr Emanuel Quandt's store, Kathrin was sitting, occupied with her sewing, in the large armchair before the window, and Martin Gerloff, having taken his place close next to her, must have discovered with astonishment how the slender fingers of the girl stabbed around a large man's handkerchief in whose corner she was affixing a red monogram. Indeed, she occasionally bent her dark countenance at the same time over a bunch of blood-red roses which he had just set down before her on the sewing table, but the obvious pleasure of the girl in the strong scent was incapable though of dislodging the question which arose again and again in the student over why the beautiful creature placed herself and her dexterity so unconditionally in the service of this older and taciturn man. For the handkerchief certainly belonged to the smokehouse owner. Again and again, the Ottonian had to gaze at the white linen. Kathrin also occasionally riveted a fleeting side-glance under her lowered lids at her visitor, and again she felt a quiet discomfort over the furtiveness which reigned between them. How could it just happen? Was it not something quite strange that, since the student had introduced himself so respectably into the house of the smokehouse owner, as if by agreement, that first stormy rapprochement of the two young persons was never mentioned? The childlike forgetting on the brick wall over the dank water was extinguished, swept away as if the black stream had carried it away with itself into the darkness and irreality.

"Cocytus", it occurred to the thoughtful girl again as she whipped her foot vigorously, for she was annoyed at base over the deception and cowardice which was expressed in this considerate denial. Mr Richard Sell would never have brought himself to do such a thing. He was sombre, brusque and decisive, but ah — she stretched cosily — it gave so much confidence to be permitted to live next to such a merciless seeker of the truth. And she also wanted to gather up something of this courage for herself. It was the best means against all the faltering and uncertainty which she saw with horror breaking ever anew into her harmless existence. Her foster father never spoke anything he did not mean. He never suggested anything which did not really live in him. Where might he have stopped at the moment perhaps? For Mr Sell had made a journey, and the girl did not know when she might expect him back. She instinctively examined her surroundings for whether the pleasant room was also completely ready for his reception. At the same time, the assiduous girl almost forgot her companion entirely, and now started as if caught when the warm voice of the student suddenly became audible close before her. For a moment, her heart skipped a beat.

"My God", it overcame her, "there he is again. Whether it will now always remain so, and whether he will really lead me out of this house someday?" And she nestled deeper in the massive armchair as if she wanted to maintain her place with all her strength.

"Miss Kathrin," Martin Gerloff began more firmly than usual, and at the same time, he shook off from himself a little the bashfulness which tormented him always opposite the chosen one, "something difficult is always saved for last. And it really does not come easily to me to say this to you. I must in fact take leave of you for a longer time."

There Kathrin opened her black eyes wide, and let her sewing fall into her lap. She did not know herself whether she should rejoice or grieve over the Ottonian's revelation.

"Why then?", she just asked quickly.

The Ottonian moved in his chair, and his beardless, adoring face sought the floor self-consciously.

"Yes, you see," he stammered, "in the last few months, I have not pursued my studies as they really should be. My attention was occupied too much with other things for that. Absolutely", he added yet, and his look clambered timidly up to the seated girl. "But now it is about making up, and I want to attempt that for a few weeks in the calm and solitude of our estate."

When he spoke thus, filled by an emotion which the young man, dominated entirely by one wish, could only hide a little, Kathrin, listening attentively, was seized by pity. She was accustomed to dispensing to all the poor, careless and unconcerned over whether something also remained to herself. And she had already often been re- buked earnestly by the shocked smokehouse owner because of this disconcerting prodigality. She also suffered under it unrecognised today, yes, she was ashamed because the kind fellow who adhered so poignantly to her, should move away unconsoled and without a ray of hope from here. And hence she threw out hurriedly, "That is really a pity, Mr Gerloff."

"Pity?", the student caught her regret tensely.

Kathrin smelt her flowers again. "Yes, because with you our only visitor is moving away", she explained honestly. "You know how isolated we live here, and I have always rejoiced that my foster father also seems to find delight in your acquaintance. You are in any case one of the few whom he has asked to come again."

At this she certainly fell silent, in that the request of the smokehouse owner remained always inexplicable, yes, she had already often endeavoured in vain to interpret the puzzling behaviour of the usually unsociable man. "His knowledge and his modesty appeal perhaps to Mr Sell", she secretly thought. Only, her friendliness had sufficed to draw her visitor up from his chair. Doubting, he approached the sewing table, and as the girl again sank entirely into her sewing, Martin Gerloff asked with a forced restraint which was meant to sound cheerful and ingenuous, "Well, and you yourself, Miss Kathrin? Will you notice sometimes the empty place here in the house?"

Then Kathrin plied her needle still more assiduously than before. Only after a while did it sound from under the lowered head, "But certainly, Mr Gerloff. It is so nice for me to have someone to chat with more often."

"Is that it?", the student asked both unbelievingly and at the same time avidly.

"Yes," Kathrin said, alarmed by his trembling voice, and because the image of the rotten bridge in the grove suddenly appeared before her again, "the uniform chatter with the fishermen out here, as you can imagine, does not excite much. My foster father also does not desire much association with them."

"And you of course follow Mr Sell's opinions most strictly?", the Ottonian inquired.

"Of course", Kathrin responded, and puckered her forehead.

Now it went silent between them. Something leaden sank down and pressed on both their souls. The visitor stood motionless before the sewing table and drew all sorts of figures on the top with his forefinger. That stubborn silence distinctly indicated to him how it was high time he left. And yet he did not find the manner in which to part. Kathrin was also becoming uneasy. Her breathing was going quickly and irregularly, and her sharp mind sought urgently for a way out so as to shatter this burdensome and pressing silence. Right, there she had discovered something.

"What does your residence in the country actually look like?", she inquired suddenly so as to attempt something against the paralysing silence.

Martin Gerloff shrugged his shoulders, but he did not lift his head.

"It has in the middle two massive, square towers," he reported indifferently, "and to the left and right wide side wings. From the terrace you can look through the park to a river which flows through the middle of the forest."

"That is a castle", Kathrin said in astonishment, and looked at him; in her black eyes, the sparks of longing and desire flickered abruptly, "a real castle."

"It is called that by our farmers", the student calmly agreed. "There are halls within in which four to five hundred people could comfortably sit at table. Large, empty rooms with reflecting, parquet floors and old family pictures on the walls."

"And what do you use these enormous rooms for?", Kathrin asked.

In her captured imagination, she saw a whirl of golden sparkling uniforms and low-necked silk dresses floating in dance across the gleaming surfaces. Diamond crowns beamed and the light tinkle of spurs sounded. That infatuated the abandoned creature, who dreamt only from a distance of the joys of the world.

"These rooms," Martin Gerloff explained, as he raised his head attentively and inquiringly, "are only opened when a marriage is organised in our family. They have not served us anymore for a long time," he added blushing, "for I am the last on whom they wait."

They both looked at each other, steadily and questioningly. It was as if each wanted to fathom in the other the most hidden things. At the same time, they heard the creaking of the high wing doors which were pushed back before the halls of the castle. Still they struggled mutely with one another, then the doorbell tinkled in a hefty pull, and straight afterwards a tall sailor stepped into the room. A haughty, self-confident face gazed down at the shocked pair, to examine at the same time the small space as far as the most hidden corner as if it were his sacred right to exercise an oversight here.

"Hello", the entering man then uttered very cold-bloodedly, and pulled his cap from his head, all with the expression of an official who entertains distrust towards various things catching his eye.

With Kathrin, however, the joy of reunion prevailed. She sprang up wildly so that needle and scissors fell clattering, and if the presence of the alien student had not hindered her, she would according to her habit have liked most of all to have flown about the neck of the loyal protector from her youth. So instead she sprang to him and caressed his chest obliviously and lovingly.

"Lord, Bob", she beamed, and at the same time, she leant against him and tried to touch his smoothly shaven chin with her outstretched finger; she desisted though and laughed loudly over her assault. "Lord, Bob, that is fine though. How do you come to be here?"

"Funny question", the helmsman dismissed it curtly, without turning his stiff and challenging look for even a second from Martin Gerloff. "I come from Rio, that is quite simple. And I did not ride here, but floated over the great soup bowl. What are you asking such stupid things for? But I believe you have a visitor", he added coolly, for it seemed fitting to him to inspect the claims of the unnecessary intruder immediately for their legitimacy.

Now a telltale redness shot over the girl's cheeks, a redness which was noted by Bob Swanegel at once with displeasure.

"Well then?", he demanded drily, like someone who pounds on his irrevocable rights of possession.

Then the bashful Kathrin pulled herself together. "This is the student, Mr Martin Gerloff, a friend of our house."

"Ah", Bob said, pulled up a chair and sat, without waiting for an invitation, importantly and broad-legged in the middle of the room.

But here the higher culture and finer manners of an intellectually labouring man showed themselves. Before the dangerous tension which already reigned between the adversaries could assume alarming forms, the student stepped up to the new guest and politely offered the seated man his hand. This welcome was admittedly only replied to by Mr Swanegel quite casually by the stretching out of a single finger.

"Alright", Bob said dismissively.

Only, he listened up when he now heard from Martin Gerloff that his person had long been familiar to the student through in-depth descriptions and how much the young man rejoiced to finally meet for once the rescuer of their common lady friend. All that sounded good-natured and respectful, but the former ship's boy nevertheless knitted his bushy brows above his stub nose reprovingly and performed a dismissive gesture with his right hand.

"That is old hat," he remarked disparagingly, "you should not tie such things to anyone's nose, but preserve them in silence and secrecy. In addition", he burst out excitedly, "you in the country understand nothing about us. When such a grey bundle floats by, then you just fish it up. Sometimes it is a dead dog and sometimes something else. As the case may be."

Kathrin had not been prepared for so much rudeness. She slowly began to be ashamed of her old friend, yes, her own upbringing rebelled decisively against his impudent manner. Hence she tapped assertively on the top of the sewing table as if she wanted to bring the defiant man to his senses.

"You have not had a good day today, Bob," she bridled with flashing eyes, although her mouth sought still to smile engagingly, "what shall Mr Gerloff think of you?"

"I do not want to impose on Mr Gerloff", the helmsman explained calmly, but sent a chastising look to the blood-red roses. "Apart from that, you are mistaken, thing, it is going magnificently for me, and I am very cheerful." — The student, however, grasped for his green cap, and bowed gently.

"I see," he spoke measuredly, although his broad face was completely blanched, "the company certainly have all sorts of intimate things to share, which a stranger would disturb."

"Oh, absolutely not", Kathrin cried hastily.

Bob Swanegel, however, nodded as if the learned man had spoken a sensible word for the first time.

"And since my steamer goes anyhow in a few minutes to the town," the decamping man concluded tactfully, and offered the girl his cold hand, "I ask you not to resent me for my quick withdrawal. Keep well, Miss Kathrin."

"You too," the girl wished him heartily, for it pained her that the good boy could be affronted, "and you will certainly write to my father sometime", she added in conscious defiance towards her overseer.

Yet as she spoke it, she would not have thought of the possibility of such an admission. And she immediately rued her intimation when she saw how the student started as if hit by lightning. But then she placed herself by the window and waved after the man striding away with Mr Sell's handkerchief. Her patient guest, however, waited quite a while. When the girl, however, did not alter her averted position at the window, he scraped his feet a little and considered it expedient to recall his piqued companion to himself by the following address,

"Now, when he has sailed off, you could haul down the signal flags, thing."

According to Mr Swanegel's view, this should have represented a right smug bit of wit. But to his astonishment, the chosen remark did not entice the slightest smile from Kathrin, no, she rather shrugged her shoulders disparagingly and stared rigidly through the narrow panes out at the river.

Then Bob decided to let off a heavier gun. For it seemed high time really to come clean with this strange and yet a little aggravating matter.

"Hey," he thus said grandly, "I have in fact now leased from Julius Kohlrausch the 'Green Herring'." At this revelation, the speaker stretched his legs out, and leant back importantly, since he believed he could lay claim to some admiration as a made man.

And really, the girl in the bright summer top forgot the inclemencies which the friend from her youth inflicted on her, and although she held fast with one hand to the window latch, she turned though animatedly and excitedly around to him. The flattered Bob noticed with delight how her dark eyes radiated with joy.

"Aha, she bites", the worldly-wise seafarer judged.

"Ah how nice for you," Kathrin cried with delight, "there you are becoming independent, Bob."

The seated man nodded leisurely. "Agreed, thing. If he offers me decent conditions, then I will conclude a contract with Mr Richard Sell. And then — then the other thing will follow so slowly afterwards."

So weightily and considered was the last bit spoken, and it was accompanied in addition by such a strange twinkling of the eyes, that Kathrin instinctively fell silent in extreme suspense. Straight afterwards, however, it forced her to pull away and burst out impulsively, "Bob, do you perhaps want to marry?"

Mr Swanegel scraped his feet again and straightened up stiff as a post on his chair. In addition, he opened his haughty blue eyes wide to embrace his clueless opposite half menacingly and half imploringly.

"It will surely amount to such a thing", he wrestled out finally in a quite measured way. "It comes down entirely to whether you haven't perhaps put twisted ideas in your head."

Then Kathrin, who had certainly not understood the last allusion, folded her hands almost sorrowfully, and in open pain at losing that one whose possession she had deemed up to then as something self-evident, she burst out fretfully, "Ah, what a pity, Bob, what a pity!"

"Pity?" The usually so self-confident suitor could not regard such an exclamation as the hoped for agreement at all. Dark red and very confused, he suddenly rose, and for the first time in his life, he was seized by the conviction that the existence of utterly blurred ambiguities was confirmed. He looked around helplessly. There should — thunderbolts — what did it all mean? He could not possibly kneel before the immature thing? Or should such female hearts really have some other place than the rational consideration to provide respectably? No, here he could not obtain a place to anchor at all, the entire thing was monstrously embarrassing.

"It is okay," he stammered finally, whereby he again begrudged the blood-red roses on the sewing table a bitterly angry look, "I see already, I must reach an agreement with Mr Sell over all that. When does the great merchant come home then?", he added ironically.

Kathrin breathed quicker. The close quarters with the old friend from her youth seemed today far too pressing and strange.

"Hopefully I may expect him this evening," the girl responded like someone who sees someone long gone approaching from a distance.

"Hopefully?", Bob growled incomprehensibly to himself. This word also seemed suspicious to the distrustful man. He hurriedly turned his cap in his hands, and at the same time, he had to recall the stupid phrases of Mr Quandt. No, in this house everything was quite crazy and out of place. It was high time that it was thoroughly straightened up here. And for that he was, praise God, the right man.

"Well then, I will return," he said graciously, "and then we will see whether something can be made of the business. Adieu, thing," he added shaking his head, and offered Kathrin his hand benevolently, "by the way, you do not need to signal from the window after me, that is all extravagant and superfluous stuff, you hear?"

Kathrin's foster father returned earlier than she had guessed. The afternoon sun was still rolling as a red, glowing ball on the tips of the beeches of the nearby grove, and shimmered in long, crimson paths on the silver expanses of water of the gulf, paths which intruded deep and jagged into the reed-surrounded green meadows. The cosy little living room was also filled by the red light, and when Kathrin now, as she assiduously carried in the coffee cups, saw the gaunt figure of the smokehouse owner sitting wearily and thoughtfully behind the round table, a little bowed and sunken in thought, the lively spirit of the girl felt with astonishment how completely the return of the taciturn man had altered the accustomed surrounds. No, it was not only the magical, almost bloody glow which was suddenly flowing down onto the bright birch furniture, rather the certainty strengthened in her that now something was fulfilled and rich and lively which yet a few hours before had lain dead and useless. But next to that, the torment of this hard silence befell her anew. It provoked her irresistibly to tear at the veils which the taciturn man pulled around himself. She wanted to ask, to inquire, to participate in this fate which seemed to her enormously rich in substance and dispensing blessings, and yet she did not dare to press demandingly or even discerningly into his closed-up mental world. She would just have really liked to fathom something. This curiosity strode after her and frequently grasped for her with pointed fingers. Even when the blossoming girl was then occupied with completely different and everyday things. An urge which was inexplicable to her forced her constantly to wonder whether the shadow of the blond woman who carried his name still swept ineradicably through his brooding, or whether the bitterness of his short talk resulted from the grief over the loss of the child which had been barely born then had fluttered away again. Thus it occurred that she occasionally, with downcast eyes, since she at base feared her own undertaking, mixed the name of the vanished into her conversation without, however, achieving anything else than that the smokehouse owner raised his hand forbiddingly, and the look in his eyes became still cooler and more accusatory.

Today, however, Richard Sell seemed to be burdened by an adversity lying closer to him. Without thanks, he enjoyed the strong, aromatic coffee, then he pushed away heedlessly the cigar box which Kathrin had set down attentively before him, rose and finally leant turned inward against the small round stove. For the first time since the girl had known him, that very thing slipped away from him for which he surely lacked the strength or the attentiveness at the moment to hide in himself any longer.

"No, it cannot continue", he spoke to himself judgmentally.

The heart of Kathrin, who was just taking the tray, pounded. It seemed priceless, yes, a great preference, that her foster father wanted to inform her somewhat of his troubles and worries, and be it also only because he needed a human ear which listened to him at that moment. Like that, just like that he had shared with his wife who had previously reigned here in this place. And to Kathrin it had always been as if it were certainly the most difficult thing on earth to stand up to these calculations and numbers and business affairs which constantly went through his brain. Now he was speaking to her. Quite unintentionally. Certainly, he barely noticed her. Before she was ready to ask what he meant, she grasped already that you must not bring his attention to the accidental audience, if you did not want to run the danger of having the man fall back into his obdurate unapproachability.

"No, it does not work any longer with the old, half childish man," Richard Sell repeated sombrely, and it twitched through the girl that he must be alluding to his father-in-law Guntrum, "this ridiculous stinginess could be fatal to me. Despite my instructions, he has left two of our largest steam-powered trawlers uninsured. And I just learnt in Stettin that both ships have not returned. Bad — bad — a great loss."

He stroked his hand over his forehead, woke up, and looked around in astonishment. The sound of his own voice seemed to have awaken him. He shook his head weakly over his indulgence, and yet it seemed to Kathrin as if the man striding out had added yet, "And just today."

Then the door closed behind him, and Kathrin sprang to the window. She saw the smokehouse owner striding along the embankment slowly and ponderously, with eyes which sought the ground unerringly. Kathrin opened the panes silently to send a peering look after the man moving into the distance. The figure became smaller and smaller, sank into the red haze, and gradually faded away on the stone wall which protruded like a pointed tongue into the sea. What was he seeking there? For the eternally busy merchant tended neither to undertake strolls nor begrudge himself a relaxation in any way. Kathrin did not think any further. It seemed to her as if it were allowed to her today to dedicate her company to the lonely man more than previously. Without even untying the little black apron or protecting her hair from the sea wind, she ran resolutely after the man who was disappearing into the evening shadows. Soon she had reached the mole, only, on the ungainly stones the foam of a wave was hissing up here and there, but otherwise the wall was empty, and of the man she sought there was no trace to be seen. Exhaling, Kathrin let her eyes sweep about. Black and red streaks flowed strangely together on the surface rocking under the evening wind, boats leaning askew swept with their yellow sails across the blue wavy hills, and thick swarms of seagulls lay like massive snowflakes on the restless field. When Kathrin turned around once, the scattered houses and trees of Uhlenhus had come together as if on a tightly drawn rope and stretched their contours up blackly and sharply against the violet evening sky they were embedded in. Right at the end of the narrow mole, the little grey-painted lighthouse rose low and bowed, and blocked the view of the girl striding out. But the girl knew that on the other side of the tower there was a perhaps metre-wide platform which protruded out openly over the sea, unprotected by grating or balusters. The searching girl turned supply around the curves of the iron building, for an inner voice betrayed to her that this must be the place where the man, turned away from the world and embittered, thought himself alone with his thoughts. What memories might it well be which held him firmly so?

Yet one quiet leap — and right — a dark figure, which until then had leant motionless against the iron curve, was startled by the approaching shadow, and a pair of absent male eyes returned reluctantly to the present. The lonely man shook his head reproachfully and disturbed, but then he moved to the side to offer the girl a safe place.

"What does this mean?", he scolded dismissively, "why are you running after me?"

Kathrin held fast with both hands to the cold wall, and she first had to overcome a shudder before the burrowing and boiling sea, before she could bring forth with half-closed eyes, "I wanted to look for you."

"That isn't necessary", Richard Sell cut her words off, unmoved. But straight afterwards, he murmured something, and the anxious girl, who still did not dare shake an eyelid, heard how he almost added in astonishment, "In any case you also belong here. Fifteen years ago we both found ourselves likewise quite alone between the waves."

There Kathrin tore her eyes open, and despite the dizziness which enveloped her, she turned glowing hot.

"It is the day and hour when the 'Heron' sank, and all the beautiful and precious things which it carried with it", her foster father continued speaking haltingly. "I have never forgotten the day."

A strange shaking lay in the man's voice, a wavering and lamenting the such as Kathrin would have never considered believable with this unemotional man. The girl opened her eyes wide in shock to take in the image of the transformed man in his surprising indulgence. Only, see there, the smokehouse owner stood as sombrely and self-confidently as ever right by her side, and it surely only signified a deception of her excited disposition when she feigned to herself that her foster father fastened a hate-filled, hostile look at the menacing water below himself. Suddenly she sensed how he held her arm clasped. It was a firm, ungentle grasp by which he sought to protect her from foundering on the wet surface. She wanted fiercely to ask something which already shook on her tongue, only, the novel, incomprehensible nature of her position confused her completely. A single illuminating ray shot incessantly through her churned up senses, a ray which she could not banish again. Did not the truth now finally announce itself to her? Was it possible that the man next to her thought more of people and things which had belonged to him on the sunken ship, and stronger than those vanished people who had shared his work-filled life with him recently? How could that be? The flushed up imagination of the hot-blooded girl abruptly called to life distant, blurry images trembling in the uncertain light of the past. Had she not sometimes heard mutterings of it? A very young, blond woman was supposed to have resided on the sunken sailing ship? This one then? Was it for her sake the taciturn man strode when possible on the anniversary filled with hate along the inhospitable shore to shake his fist in impotent accusal against the rapacious sea? Ah, if it were so though! An unnameable reassurance befell the young creature. She did not herself know why, but it seemed so comfortable to her that the memory of the daughter of A. Guntrum should only signify something incidental, something overshadowed in the life of the lonely man by a greater sorrow. Her unacknowledged aversion towards the sober businesswoman unexpectedly received thereby a tangible excuse.

"Take care," the sharp voice of her companion struck through the flying swarms of thoughts of the rapt girl, and at the same time, she felt how painfully tight her arm was clasped, "why are you quivering back and forth like a reed?"

"Is it good that I did not go under as well at the time?", Kathrin said instead of an answer, completely senseless.

She felt how the man shook her arm more roughly as if he wanted to call her back to consciousness, but then it forced itself quickly over his lips, "Yes, it is good, something remains though. Come, Kathrin, we will go home. You look bad, my child, and it is not a suitable place for you here. Quick."

He turned, and strode ahead of her. Kathrin followed as though in a dream.

***

On the evening of the same day, however, that thing happened which convinced Kathrin to her joy still more strongly of the fading of those shadows which had surrounded the smokehouse up to then. They had just completed their silent evening meal, and the man of the house was now reclining on the green sofa and following the supple movements of his companion who was taking away the traces of the meal without a sound. At the same time, she was smiling furtively to herself. Whether the man probably noticed how a greater luxury than ever before surrounded him in his domesticity since the death of his wife? For it was Kathrin's pride to present to her foster father, without making it intrude on his consciousness, quite gradually the grand pieces of his household for daily use. Thus he had already been dining for a long time on the brilliant damask tablecloths which had formed an almost never used inherited treasure of Sophie Guntrum. Heavy knives and forks from the silver cabinet were used and, for some time, Kathrin had to the horror of the maid even begun to make up all sorts of select dishes from the cookbook. Certainly, Richard Sell did not betray by any sign any knowledge of her beginning to. He thought of his business plans as before, which admittedly were permitted to claim an infinitely greater importance, and seemed not especially to sense the change around him. But it provoked the young creature in his proximity all the more to continue the quiet burrowing against the past. Sometimes she shocked herself over her own intentions. Something malicious lay in them, and at the same time, the hasty bustle again to do her closest good. And as often as she also sought to decipher her desire, she just as frequently had to confess to herself that it was at base only about ordering and executing everything better than those hands which had previously worked here.

"I did not like to suffer her," she thought, shrugging her shoulders; and made confident by the experience on the mole, she added, breathing out, "She just did not belong here at all."

But today it would become still more distinct.

The girl had opened the window, and the mild summer air floated from the river into the small space. Outside in the deep darkness, it rustled sometimes busily in the leaves of the scattered, massive lime trees before the house, and a large dark moth tumbled swirling about the pendant lamp. It was very still and cosy in the narrow room. Richard Sell had just then inquired of his companion who had called on him in his absence, and when Kathrin mentioned last of all the visit of Martin Gerloff and of the helmsman Bob Swanegel, the merchant had only found an indifferent, "Good — good". But now the smokehouse owner rose, strode to the tiny safe, and after he had unlocked it, he threw a few account books on the table and began, standing as per his custom, following the rows of numbers with his finger. Kathrin stood by the window and looked at him. God alone might know why it so tormented her that the old regular emptiness spread out again. Perhaps it was also a suddenly worked up effrontery which could not bear to see her own person again judged to be the usual insignificance. Anyway, had this calculating and comparing not been a favourite activity of the dead woman? Suddenly the indecisive girl stood next to her foster father, and as she became quite cold with fright, she heard how she defiantly burst out, "Can I not help you with that? I can count and write very well."

The man's finger immediately stopped gliding down the long rows. Shaking his head, he measured the young creature who was urging herself so unexpectedly into his work. And at once, a weak, almost grudging smile passed about his narrow mouth. He energetically shut the book and tapped Kathrin kindly and instructively on the cheek.

"It is nothing," he said decisively, "I do not think it is good for women. It does not bring you anything good."

He slowly strode to the window, and drew in long-ingly the warm air which was streaming in. Then he sent a quick look through the room, and like someone who is afraid of something pursuing them, he forced himself wearily to say, "It is quite hot and sticky here, I want to sit on the bench before the house for a bit. You can come with me, Kathrin. And bring something to drink!"

Before she could even respond, he was already strid-ing out the door, and so he probably did not catch anymore how the girl, who remained completely daun-ted by the table, emitted a quiet, irrepressible cry of joy. In her receptive mood, the youthful idea surely dawned that the pressing solitude on this earth would finally have an end, and the small place which she demanded would also be recognised by another person. She ran ex-citedly into the kitchen, with the intention this time of seeking something quite especially refreshing and un-usual for the weary and thirsty man out there. —

The lime tree stood bright and silvery before the house in the full moonlight and threw its shadows over the bench and table so that they were submerged in darkness. Kathrin, when she stepped over the threshold with a tray and was herself struck by the vague shim-mer, had to peer out more closely first before she recognised the motionless outline of her foster father. But the smokehouse owner seemed to have immediately noticed her own figure which was captured by the greenish light, for in the darkness something stirred, and a voice, which was obviously forcing itself to cheer-fulness, commanded her to step closer quickly.

"What are you bringing, my child?", the invisible man called out, "it smells so good!"

"Oh, just a trifle which I have picked up for you", Kathrin smiled.

She hastily placed the plate full of strawberries before him and set a bottle of Moselle on the table at the same time. Richard Sell followed her actions in disbelief, for he was incapable of explaining why such a prodigality. should have been induced in his usually so frugal household today of all days. To his mind, this almost signified a feast.

"I believe you want to spoil me, little one", he said in the end good-naturedly as he moved to the side.

But at the same time it occurred to him how homely and comfortable that rest in the tepid summer night felt to him. And he figured out himself that he was begrudging himself the time for such a relaxation without care for the first time to his knowledge. Why had the desire for it never crept up on him before? Was he perhaps getting old, and was the need for rest already establishing itself? Disconcerted, he suddenly counted up his years. Also an occupation which he had considered very superfluous. And as he lowered his head in resignation, he established that he had already passed his thirty sixth. Really a difficult truth — the years had escaped soundlessly behind him. And the thought seared painfully through the man concerned of how he had stood by the same river a long time ago in radiant sunlight to journey for distant silvery isles. Strange, what had remained of that? The journey had been shrouded in grey and mist, and he found himself alone again.

Something rattled before him. Kathrin had filled both glasses and was now holding his out to him. He recognised only the little hand which wavered a little.

"No, praise God," the smokehouse owner said, awakening, "not alone."

Yet someone was present who was trying to help him. It was actually not right that he accepted all this as something self-evident.

"Sit down, Kathrin", he said once more.

The girl gathered up her dress, and wedged herself into the bench, but yet so that some distance remained between them. Then the man raised his glass, thought for a while, and spoke quickly like someone who wishes to put something difficult behind him hurriedly, "You take good care of me, Kathrin, you take great pains. I believe I have not yet thanked you once for it."

Kathrin had also grasped her glass, for she thought it was the custom that the flutes must clink together. Only, under the effect of what she had just heard, she paused motionless. It seemed to her as if the dark earth were suddenly illuminated. Her heart pounded in fright, for she had never guessed that a word of praise from a human mouth could resound so tremblingly in another being.

"Oh, that is nothing", she stuttered in shame, because she did not know anything else to say.

The smokehouse owner, however, who had meanwhile emptied his glass and not guessed at what was struggling and surging next to him, propped his head in his hand, and when he saw her hands resting crossed on the table, he suddenly good-naturedly bedded the fingers of his right hand over hers. He had finally found what he had been searching for already for a long time.

"You are really a dear child to me," he said aloud and without hesitation, for his soul was not frightened of the eavesdropping night, "you give me much joy, and hence I would not like anything alien to stand between us. You should from now on likewise address me as Richard. It should have happened long ago, and I do not know actually why it never occurred to me, Kathrin. I just have little time for such things."

He squeezed her resting hands once more in affirmation, and was astonished in silence over how strangely the entire arm of his companion gave way under his touch. Then he decided to make it easy for her.

"You will get accustomed to it," he hence diverted with a curt smile, "for we will not part in the next few months."

"Part?", Kathrin repeated, finally emerging from the whirl of confusion, and her voice sounded so restrained and uncomprehending that a longer lingering over this matter became unpleasant for Richard Sell.

"That will come", he suggested and looked attentively into the pale mist which was drawing over the river. "Every time wants to have its rights. Why not yours?" And almost inaudibly, he added, "There are no fixed possessions on earth. I have had to learn that."

The words were still dying away, and before his anxiously searching companion was able to pierce the veil of what she had just heard, two conspicuous figures then pushed into the stream of moonlight. Nestled closely together, a pair of black silhouettes, the wizened figure of Mr Emanuel Quandt as well as the round corporeality of his wife were gliding along in the incredible flood. The black couple had merged into each other quite closely. It looked as if a long slender spoon were protruding from a fat-bellied soup tureen. And the spoon swayed a little, bowed, and declaimed through the darkness, "A glorious evening, Mr and Miss Sell. Magical, quite magical. You are surely also enjoying this precious hour of dream? Yes, yes. — 'Oh you look, dreary moonlight, for the last time on my pain.'* I wish the company an easy rest!"

The shadow play vanished, the grey shapes danced on the river more animatedly and strove in crowds to-wards the awakening stars.

---

* [From Goethe's *Faust*.]

3

Since that day, a proper bond of friendship arose for the two in the smokehouse. The serving and cowering which almost always adhered to Kathrin in the presence of her protector began imperceptibly to vanish under the greater attentiveness which the smokehouse owner bestowed on her, and the sputtering cheerfulness of her wild and ardent temperament stirred occasionally. The quiet Richard Sell could sometimes not orient himself in all the leaping and exulting, between laughing and singing, through the music and teasing. At such moments of astonishment, he then confessed that his household was peopled unexpectedly by many personalities absolutely different from each other. Without noticing it, he thereby became himself livelier, and began now and then interesting himself in other things than ships' courses, high seas fisheries, and soldered tins. And he could have used this diversion at just about that time. For his days, which he mostly spent in the town, were filled up by hidden and open annoyance with his father-in-law, who, robbed of free movement by his wheelchair, fell more and more unresistingly into a childish old age. In addition, the smokehouse owner had to tell himself that A. Guntrum despite all his weakness and demoralisation used the last residue of his acumen to sweep a malicious recalcitrance against his partner, because he gradually hated him surely as a no longer dispensable guardian. But the younger man was especially injured by the way in which the lamed man mixed the words and views of his late daughter into their disputes with every suitable or offbeat opportunity, and Richard Sell did not think himself deceived that a derisive smirk always ran over the bloated face

whenever the invalid succeeded in thoroughly tormenting his listener by such eternal hints. The old man
seemed to consider him in excess to be the destroyer of
his child, and this consciousness was sometimes barely
withstood.

It was on a morning in late July. The smokehouse
owner had just steered his little carriage, which he still
drove himself, before a shed of the strung-out work
buildings, and as he now strode through the storerooms
through which he had once strolled hand-in-hand with
A. Guntrum's daughter, dreaming of the future, he tried
to recall the melody of one of Schubert's little songs
which he had caught off his foster daughter the previous
evening. He spontaneously forgot the enormous rolls of
ships' ropes, and the oilskins and instruments which
towered around him in heaps. Really, he had experienced a quite odd surprise the previous evening. And
the cheerful incident also continued working today act-
ively and stimulatingly on the serious man. After the
joint evening supper, he had found himself alone in the
little room for a period. He had already not been accustomed to that anymore for a long time. Suddenly a
quiet, pleasant music swirled and plucked in the hall.
And now even a subdued female voice merged into it. In
the most overt surprise, Richard Sell had opened the
door, and now the man averse to all joking had to learn
that a proper serenade had been brought to him. Out
there, drenched brightly in the electrical ceiling light
which the red bushy mane almost butted against, the
fire-ladder figure of Mr Emanuel Quandt towered, who
at the moment of recognition was playing his violin with
quite special passion, and right next to him remained
Kathrin, a colourfully ribboned mandolin hung over her
shoulder, from which she enticed all sorts of sonorous
chords. As mad as the effect this prank also had in the
eyes of the sober man, the clinging folk ballad also en-
deared itself to his mood, and it did him good that the

girl had certainly only learnt the difficult art of accompaniment to offer him a gratifying change more often. With her fine sense of rhythm she must surely have guessed that the man who was becoming insensible in the empty silence of his house yearned frequently for a relieving sequence of notes. How embarrassed and uncertain Kathrin stood in the hall before him, and how questioningly her dark eyes were courting his applause. Richard Sell nodded in passing now contentedly to himself, since he recalled how his agreement signified the last law for the boisterous being. Thus it had to be in a well-ordered household. And his first question had also been the previous evening over the circumstance of when and to what end his foster child had undertaken these difficult exercises.

There Kathrin had plucked with a furtive smile at the ribbons hanging down from her instrument; the shopkeeper-artist, however, pushed past at this moment, and took over the answer, thirsty for applause.

"Good evening, great merchant", he greeted the master of the house with a deep bow — for his rage for titles devised ever newer honours for the wealthy man of Uhlenhus — and at the same time, he tapped with the bow on the back side of the violin as if he had a waiting orchestra for which to command a pause. "Miss Kathrin has only been studying for six weeks with me. But she possesses talent, Mr Sell, stage blood, which only the gifted directors demand. When she sat thus with me in my back room, then my own past awoke under all the debris. Enticing and frightening, Mr Sell. A soprano-coloured contralto with a full middle pitch. We must still polish a few glottals."

Thus Emanuel Quandt spoke, tapped again on the back of his violin as a sign that the orchestra had feted enough, and the exultant song began anew in the hall.

Richard Sell whistled gently, he felt that youth had sent him a messenger.

Through his backwards directed thoughts, his steps echoed dully from the white walls of the storeroom. Suddenly he paused. Through the rectangular window in the sidewall, he saw the bloated face of his father-in-law, and the wooden frame concluded right under the missing collar. But who was the lady who sat in a simple grey summer dress and with a little blue straw hat right next to the wheelchair of the invalid? The smokehouse owner did not remember ever having seen those calm, honest features under the wavy brown, lightly greyed hair. And his quickly awoken distrust ran aground on considering why A. Guntrum, who was occupied only with his suffering or still more with the loathing of his overseer, tolerated this company next to him so without contradiction. Yes, it even seemed to the hesitating man on renewed examination as if those malicious lights, which tended only to ignite sinisterly in the struggle against him, were glittering in the half squinting eyes of the invalid during the conversation. Had the old man perhaps sought out a confederate?

Determined to tear up this web too, Richard Sell stepped into the blue wallpapered partition which A. Guntrum called his office, and immediately, as if he had been expected for a long time already, the strange lady rose to nod her head towards him in greeting. A pair of large submissive, female eyes looked at him timidly, and in her uncertain expression as well as the derisive smirk of the lame man, the sharp reader of human nature recognised on the spot that some unpleasant discovery was in store for him.

"It is in fact so," his father-in-law chewed, his speech having become quite incomprehensible, and made a motion of introduction with his crooked right hand, "this is Miss Magda Heinse, daughter of Captain Christian Heinse. A very good man, has bought a lot from me. And the young lady herself is the Ottonian's bride. They call her thus here", A. Guntrum murmured, twinkling

257

his eyes, for he could feel in the anxiety of his guest that his words and his thoughts did not want to march in step once again. But then the bloated face enlivened once more, and with fat derision, he added, "She wants to tell something. A nice little piece, a thing of novels. But what did Sophie always say? Nothing good is in there. And Sophie knew her people."

After this long prelude, the old man clapped his eyes shut, vanished somewhat deeper into his coat lapels, and acted as if he were asleep. The good old girl, however, drew her veil up, and the great embarrassment which surrounded her chased a dark redness over her cheeks.

"Oh God, Mr Sell," she groped forwards, "I would certainly not have allowed myself to seek you out, because one can hear from all sides how busy you are. But you can believe me, I am only driven by the intention to help and to advise, and the wish to divert young people from stupidity."

As the stranger talked so insistently, the smokehouse owner knitted his dark eyebrows, and his face looked as sober and indifferent as always. But inwardly he did not doubt for a moment that this visit must be in connection with Kathrin. And before he asked the young woman to take a seat, he skimmed the old man in the wheelchair with a discontented look. The presence of the vexatious witness seemed superfluous and demeaning to him. A. Guntrum, however, as if he had somehow read in a mysterious way somewhere in the air the wishes of his partner, shook his massive head appeasingly so that the fringe on his neck bristled all the more, and let out in a loud snore, 'It's nothing, I am asleep — quite fast asleep.'

Meanwhile both the others had sat down before and behind the desk, and Richard Sell collected himself now for the declaration that he was now ready to examine the request of his visitor. Then such a timid, bashful look struck the calmly seated man from the eyes of the old girl. Half whispering and with hands clasped, she began, "Mr Sell, you may really be convinced that — God, how do I express myself? — the most hearty friendship for the foolish youth induces me quite alone to my perhaps disconcerting step. And perhaps also the sympathy with the disappointment which usually follows such high-flown plans."

"Sympathy?", the smokehouse owner picked up; in the curt word resided already a quiet repudiation.

"That does not apply to any member of your house," Magda Heinse stuttered, taken aback by the cold tone, "that is perhaps also — it is not kept apart so difficultly — but I would like to explain to you first why I take the liberty at all. You see, your foster father called me the Ottonian's bride before. I know they describe me thus here. Certainly that which underlies the name consists only of a great, certainly undeserved confidence which the young people show me. And there now one of them recently came to me with a right deep sorrow and at the same time in open helplessness. You might smile over it if someone did not feel sorry for the confused youth. You know the young man also. He is Martin Gerloff."

"Certainly", the smokehouse owner threw in here, and grasped quickly for the edge of the desk. The affair suddenly seemed very serious to him, and yet he could not prevent his brow knitting hostilely. Something distant began resisting in him. "What does the young man desire?", he inquired tensely, although he knew quite exactly what it could only be about.

"He has a yet unfinished, enthusiastic nature," the gentle voice said, imploring leniency, "he is one of those whose will has been dominated all too long by others, and who consequently disesteems himself often and rates himself lowly."

"Yes, but why should that interest me?", Richard Sell asked severely.

From the wheelchair came a hoarse chuckle, and the smokehouse owner noticed how the supposedly sleeping man licked his lips smugly. This strengthened him in the intention of bringing the conversation to an end as quickly as possible.

"I notice, my young lady," he hence began quite firmly and without further consideration, "you want to indicate to me openly that your friend has been seized by an affection for my foster daughter. This would not be inexplicable at all with the age of the them both. But with the unfinishedness of your protege mentioned by you yourself, you need not really take such roseate fantasies all too seriously. At least I don't like to make up my mind about it."

He rose slowly, with a bow, like someone who is finally breaking off a business conversation. But strangely, at the same time something old and long forgotten awoke in him. A strange reluctance burrowed in his throat, a reluctance which directed itself against both those persons besetting him here so bourgeois-like.

But the Ottonian's bride did not follow his example. Quite taken by her task, she remained instead seated in her chair, and now stretched her hand out animatedly towards him.

"No, it is not that alone, Mr Sell, for which I have sought you out."

"Yes, what else is there then?"

Now there was a nod from the wheelchair, as if the sleeping confederate wanted to infuse her with courage, and with her good and bashful smile, Magda Heinse continued, "Dear Mr Sell, I only turn to you so that we can mollify and displace this student's enthusiasm without fuss and especially without anguish for the children. But for that you must know what is contained here in the letter of my young friend. Think — it is actually half touching — the brooding defiant head is completely convinced that there is no blessedness for him anymore without the girl. God yes, over that you might smile," she added good-naturedly, when she noticed how the merchant bit his lip painfully touched, "and of course, my protege is also jealous."

"What, that too?", Richard Sell cried now, honestly indignant.

"Yes certainly, Mr Sell. Without such frothing, such early passions simply do not come apart. Remarkably, however, Martin Gerloff directs his suspicion against a helmsman of her acquaintance. An odd arrangement, is it not?"

From the wheelchair came that liverish cough again, quite as if the invalid had heard a lovely, lulling melody. The smokehouse owner, however, sat erect in his chair and did not stir anymore. The knowledge crept up on him disturbingly that behind his back, perhaps intentionally hidden from him, events had played out which had escaped his oversight. And the powerless role to which he was condemned enraged him inwardly. Thus he only caught half obscured how his visitor told of fierce disagreements which had broken out between the student and his father because of the son's affection which was decisively disapproved of by the manor owner. And he was only startled to full attention again when the last words of the Ottonian's bride struck his ear. Here finally came something tangible, something business-like which desired a resolute decision. And the smokehouse owner straightened up, clear of mind and with a certain bitterness. What was demanded of him there? This green fellow wrote to ask if his confidante would like to report to him something of the origin of Kathrin Brodersen so that he could reassure his father over this point? Aha, there the wind whistled. Quite right, quite right, all upstanding people would look to that first. And a derisive satisfaction penetrated the affronted man quite contradictorily.

"Dear Miss," he endeavoured to put forth politely, although the icy sharpness streamed out under his speech, "here we have come to an end in my opinion. I will of course speak with Kathrin to induce her to cut off this childish dalliance at the root. For since nothing proceeds in my house of which I am not informed in the most detailed way, I believe you can be assured now that the imaginative young gentleman has not been offered from our side the slightest foothold for this romantic whimsy."

The merchant had brought this out with confident conviction, quite penetrated by the thought that his Uhlenhus home was immune to every reproach, to every suspicion, from no other reason than because he himself stood before it with his pure bourgeois mind to fend off every tarnish, yes, the slightest speck of dust from the guarded region.

Then he faltered. The gentle eyes of the Ottonian's bride remained fastened so delicately and uprightly on him. Moreover, an unexpected silence arose, only interrupted by the sawing breaths of A. Guntrum. A stabbing shock seized him and ate at the most tender point of his pride. Was his certainty perhaps not so firmly grounded as he thought? Did deception and betrayal also reside in his midst? Was the feeling of pleasure which he carried around with him growing on rotten soil? Just then he wanted despite his wavering to impatiently push open the door to certainty, already he was pounding with his signet ring loudly and demandingly on the table, when from the lips of his guest was wrestled that thing which he strove to snatch from her to his calamity.

"Mr Sell," the bashful voice reminded, "here you find yourself mistaken. In growing up, such a thronging together is certainly never to be taken entirely seriously. But I must in defence of my friend appear as a witness for him. My own eyes can confirm for you that at the time of the student excursion between the young pair it came on a secluded path to all those stormy tendernesses which certainly have effect for a long time in such untouched hearts."

Here Richard Sell rose. He did not know himself how he left his seat.

"Good", he said and forced himself to an unnatural smile. "I will now seek to learn the details. I thank you, dear young lady, heartily for your sympathetic endeavours. And I can promise you only that light will be brought to the matter. On that you can rely." And as he threw a note down on a sheet of paper as per his habit, his sober mind forced from him yet, "I assume that our discussion will remain strictly between us."

Affirming and again a little overawed, Miss Magda Heinse nodded, and prepared without further objection to depart; only to her own surprise, the sunken sleeper in the wheelchair took over her representation quite un-bidden.

"Quite among us", the crabby organ murmured. "Of course, it is in fact so! But Sophie knew her people. Adieu, Miss Heinse, come back right soon."

***

"Are you going away already?", the invalid asked his son-in-law half an hour later, since he had been secretly observing the man busy at the desk from under his swollen eyelids. Now he discovered in the rustling of the paper how the younger man was pushing together wearily a number of letters to leave them like something burdensome for a later answer. A. Guntrum had not seen that with his partner before. This remissness could cost money. And yet the lame man was offered through the uneasy behaviour of his partner an indescribable pleasure. "You want to go already?"

"Yes", Richard Sell said, thinking to himself.

"You certainly have something important to do out there?"

"Yes."

"Is there nothing more to work on here?"

"No", the other man responded, shrugging his shoulders, at which he was already rising. "I have set my remarks on each letter, the bookkeeper can draft them."

"So, so," the fat man in the wheelchair cracked, and folded his swollen fingers across his body complacently, "so it is certainly important." With head pushed forward, he followed the steps of the departing man and was delighted over his ability at guessing when he saw the lightly bowed figure of the smokehouse owner driving his little carriage straight afterwards along the road by the river. "Going to Uhlenhus," he slurred at the same time, enthused, "wants surely to look a bit into the bad household. That is healthy for him though. Eh, eh, if Sophie had lived to see it!"

With that he clapped his heavy eyelids shut, and sank completely into the salaciousness of painting out all sorts of adversity for his son-in-law. —

***

Bright sunlight floated over the vegetable and potato beds of the small garden which Richard Sell had laid out behind his house. Originally the piece of land had been a stubbly waste, and only a few cherry and pear trees had shot up wildly and untended from the sharp-edged sedge. For Ott Knuth, the former owner, had only seen the place as a site where, crouching on a pile of sand, you could let the clattering bones roast in the sun. The thrifty sense of the current owner, however, did not like to tolerate anything which yielded him no profit, and so not only the well-tended kitchen plantings but also thickly knotted currant bushes and gooseberry hedges were also gradually won from the tousling sea wind. In irregular growth, they fenced in the place as prickly walls, and Kathrin lay in their sparse shade at this hour on a strip of grass and, a little tired and bleary, she

looked in the streaming fervour at a large plate of dark,
sour cherries which she had just plucked from one of
the trees. She pulled her bare arm snugly under her
head, for the light, pink-flowered batik top which she
wore was only fitted with short sleeves. And now she
also stretched her foot out freely and easily because she
could not be spied on here by any human eye. Mr Sell
only returned to his home in the afternoon, and much
time still remained therefore to make all the preparations for his late meal. She blinked contentedly at her
fruits, and heavily entangled in her summery dream,
she could not deny grasping a triple bunch of the red
spheres to let them rock back and forth playfully over
her head.

Then she nibbled one of the cherries quickly, and
rested a while quite motionless and almost without
breath. Over her lay a silvery-blue sky, under it millions
of spidery fine golden rays shot, also a quiet, indefinable
hum, and that feeling specific to youth of belonging in-
divisibly and importantly to the mighty universe. But,
all of a sudden the look of the recumbent girl did not
fasten to anything anymore. The golden air circled and
dazzled, the gooseberry hedges grew up, the hanging
berries sent out diamond flashes, and the firm ground
began imperceptibly rocking. Kathrin smiled incredulously, but then her contrariness fell silent, and she
submitted to it.

> Can you guess who springs from the cherry tree
> And sweeps together sailing leaves?
> Dear, young, ripening child,
> It is I — the wind,
> You have placed yourself right at my feet
> So that my secret pours into your ears.
> Listen how it whispers, how it swings dancing
>   about you,
> You smooth, supple girl, you,
> I nestle up to you and steal your calm.

Then there is no hiding, there no error helps,
You cannot chase the wind from there,
I am a voice of air and light,
I form only the sound which breaks from deep
 within you,
I sing you yourself, your secret law,
I fish for your soul with silvery net,
I climb shafts in your wishes,
Let candles waver in buoyant night
And mutter something was and something per-
 haps never happened,
I kiss you, Kathrin, and we sing a song.

***

No, do not kiss me, you have already done it once
On the red bridge made of brick
In the grove.
Under us the stream drew its course,
The black of our shadows washed away from
 there.
Yes, I proffer lips to you, and you are alien to me.
Don't you know why my blood surges so,
What my being listens for urgently
Far above you away in the sunlight.
Strange, but where is the grove now?
Are we then in a castle?
And rider and horse
All yours?
Just see the carvings
On the cabinets,
And the sparkling silver on oak chests.
And all that you want to gift to me?
Ah, I would like surely on silk shoes
To float over the polished floors,
Whirling and quick,
Past the golden pictures on the wall,
But, God, is it not just now

Kathrin

Mr Sell calling?
Or was it Mr Quandt?
Or even funny Bob?
Here, take your roses, and I thank you too,
But why are you vanishing like a hazy smoke?
Yes, the helmsman is surely a bit rough,
But that is just his custom now.
His eyes, sharp and bright,
Look down haughtily on everything,
Calls me nothing but dumb thing.
No, Bob, leave it, there it calls already again,
And this time it really is Mr Sell.
There I must be quick,
Scurry once more through kitchen and cellar.
Before I can explain it properly,
It is becoming lighter and brighter in the house.
There he enters — hello, hello!
Could I smooth the sombre demeanour
Which vanishes at once in the moonlit night.
Do you just know how I like to serve you.
I say now "Richard", yet only Mr Quandt hears it
Playing his violin next to me.
How our music penetrates through the house!
Am I myself the one who sings with beating
heart?

***

Remain lying, you young, ripening child,
I am Mr Sell or I am the wind,
Stroking over you coaxingly and warm,
Taking you tenderly in my arms,
I am your father and I am not,
I am a shape made of air and light,
I extinguish with my cool deluge
Your blazing fervour,
I am your torment and I am your discipline,
I am the one who scares you up

From the flowing dream,
I am on the red cherry tree
The distant fruit
For which the human hand stretches hesitantly.
Dream yet a little while, you happy child,
I am Mr Sell and I am the wind!

**

Across the soft sandy path by the river, there was a crunching like that of wheels sinking in. A horse snorted, and the harness was shaken back and forth. Kathrin surely heard it, she wanted to gather herself up, only, she just smiled and sank back again. From the crimson hollow in which she rested, she found no way out. Were not a pair of doors hastily opened in the house and closed again? That might be or then again it might not. The bang reported itself to her, but it merged immediately again into the humming air. Now there was a rattling at the garden gate, heavy steps awoke a dull sound on the earth; only, Kathrin shook her head dismissively and continued smiling. She just clasped the plate with the cherries, groping uncertainly with her right hand as if she had to protect them.

Now the smokehouse owner stood before her.

He had probably envisaged along the way how the girl might receive him. He was convinced that a furtive, guilty smile would play about the red lips like that which he had often noted in the unfinished child, particularly when you had reproached her for small errors. This gentle, captivating trait had already disturbed him at the time, for he thought of how an inner urge forced him along irresistibly on such occasions to think of the belonging of his charge to a debauched and undignified family. But that had gradually been wiped away. Until today. Yes, until today. For on the way home under the motionless brooding sky, he had been mobbed by an entire hell of stabbing and venomous thoughts. Like a swarm of glittering hornets, they circled about his head and could be dislodged neither by blows of the whip nor by curses. The most horrible thing of all was that images were following the irritated man, images as accursedly luscious, ardent and yearning as had never desired entry into his sober working existence. As much as he might want to bristle at this unaccustomed early return home, might want to fulminate reflectively and mockingly over good-for-nothing childish tricks, might want to give himself for comfort the assurance that he was the man to force back everything which perhaps defied order and convention unsparingly into customs and above all into a good respectable bourgeois state — it was of no use, fantasies which he had not recognised before, and which infused him with an unnameable unease were fluttering through all the self-evident things. Did he then even know what he was doing? Why must nothing remain to him from this ridiculous absurdity but the tenderly lascivious nestling of two lovers? He saw things before himself which he barely guessed at, but had certainly never considered noteworthy. Dark shadows of the grove opened up before him, he heard the velvety noise of kisses, and between fury and breathlessness, he saw two figures striving to each other, figures who had nothing more in common with the surrounding humanity, but rather dozed in a white glow.

Yes, hell had erupted behind him, bleated its mocking laugh in his swishing ears, and as he cracked the whip to escape them, the black figures threw glowing balls of fire at the bowed figure in the driving seat. The shots exploded before him and behind him, and from their haze it smouldered out, "You see, the white glittering thing is Kathrin — your Kathrin — the daughter of a drunkard and a whore. A being which you wanted to raise well. Well, how about that, clever Mr Sell?"

"Childish tricks", he cried out in rage, and again he struck at the gaunt horse heavily.

But hardly had Richard Sell paced out the red hall which lay in such cool dimness, hardly had he let a searching look sweep through the tidy little living room — whereby it occurred to him, despite his tension, how many colourful bunches of flowers illuminated everywhere on the table and windowsill, and what a caring comfort spread out here — than he felt to his own annoyance how the outrage he had brought along and a part of his severity with regards to the conventional sank down to a sober extent. He had come out, had abandoned his day's work, to form a fair judgment. But to that belonged certainly that he also let the image and the opinion towards his ward affect him. He shook his head. Strange, she was actually an independent being who could choose another path with her future, and this possible expression of will seemed so incomprehensible to the smokehouse owner who was accustomed to winding up all those belonging to him like clockwork. Sighing and still in fury over having imposed such a burdensome torment on himself, he began loudly calling for the one he sought. He finally reached her in the garden. There she lay in the half shade of the gooseberry hedge stretched out next to the heaped up cherries, herself like a glowing fruit which had slid down gently and without harm from the tree of existence. And despite the deep stupefaction by which the sleeper was embraced, the man gazing down thought he perceived how a happy greeting for him was now also to be read in the lovely features. That shocked him, that he had not expected. He was raising his foot reluctantly so that he could awake her by a quick touch when he hesitated anew, for he would have brushed by a hair with his dirtied sole the bare arm of the recumbent girl. He remained incredulous and knitted his brows. But at the same time, he balled his fist, for he did not know why suddenly something stirred which was not far distant from fright and shame. His discerning eyes betrayed to him what he until now had left entirely out of his calculations. There before him — that he felt all of a sudden quite strongly — that was no child anymore. Before him a young woman was unveiled in all the frisson of blossoming and ripening. And when she just stretched a little, then an inexplicable, numbing shock seared through him, the man who wanted to step before her as judge.

No, no, it was certainly not the hour in which he could execute his undertaking. For the worst thing of all consisted in that, as he surveyed her with such conflicting emotions, at the same time an agreeable pride in the rare beauty which he hid here in his house trickled through him. This possession which breathed so cosily and healthily, her dark head bedded on her white arm, that was not to be grudged him, and it was already affirmed by him. No, this was not the hour of reckoning and clarity. Later!

With a long lost look, he tore himself away, and hardly had he closed the garden gate behind himself than the merchant shook himself as if he had to put himself in order. Something else — to use up the time which he was wasting out here. With strong steps, bareheaded as he was, and in his fine grey suit, he took himself into one of the smokehouses, opened the round door on the beehive-shaped structure, and stepped into the flames and smoke. Close by the entrance, surrounded by the sparking haze which had to cause a fit of coughing for anyone not accustomed to it, a slouched woman sat on a basket and cleaned a large fork-shaped spear with which you took the dried fish from their poles. The woman had a creased, sooty countenance, and during her work she looked sometimes at the red wood fire, monitoring it. At the same time, it dripped gently from her eyes and streamed down her cheeks as the flames played over them. Usually such a trifle would not have occurred to Richard Sell, but today he remained standing next to the workwoman and slapped her encouragingly on the shoulder.

"What is it, Mertens", he asked sympathetically. "Can the eyes not endure it anymore? You are crying!"

The woman lowered her head still lower, and cleaned more assiduously.

"No, Mr Sell, I am not crying", she responded drily. "That is no use. I am merely thinking."

"Well, over what then, Mertens? You are usually such a diligent woman."

The seated woman nodded, and now rubbed the crunching sandpaper so fiercely that a singing note arose.

"That surely, Mr Sell," she coughed in-between, "but that is all no use. I am forty five years old, and he is almost fifteen years younger. He does not come home at all anymore and roams around."

The woman continued cleaning, and now the smokehouse owner also fastened a thoughtful look on the wearily burning flames. Dark balls ran back and forth there like rolling cherries. And it must surely have been the choking smoke which constricted the man's voice now.

"Yes, Mertens," he said to himself, "that you would not have had to consider before. Years separate. Well, keep your chin up, I will speak with him."

"No, Mr Sell," the dry voice asked from the wavering glow, "don't do that. It is no use anymore. And then — it is so ashaming too."

Between the two in the beehive it went still. But when the smokehouse owner opened the low door after a while, he saw how the bright drops were still running down onto the iron fork.

***

Richard Sell continued his wandering through his facilities. Only after he had convinced himself everywhere of the regular course of the operations, received in-depth reports from the overseers, yes, even examined carefully the equipment of a fishing cutter soon to set off to sea, did the owner, soothed and sobered by these business worries, return to his home. Already on the path by the river, he saw Kathrin standing in the doorway of the house. With her elevated right hand, she was holding firmly onto the closed green wing-door, while her other arm carefully embraced the plate of cherries. It was clear that the girl could have just then torn herself away from her healthy slumber. This was evidenced not only by a few cherry leaves which had strayed into her hair, but above all by her cheeks which were brightly reddened by the deep rest. She also must have already learnt of the unusual presence of the gentleman of the house. And she was really behaving thus, for Kathrin had examined with astonishment the doors of the house standing open, and the hat of her foster father, which she had found in the green living room, gave her the certainty she still doubted. Now she stood expectantly in the dark recess, and the joyful light of her eyes announced to the approaching man her unabashed gratification over his premature return home. It signified almost a gifted day, the interruption of the silence and the possibility of cheering the serious man up or snaring something from him which could serve for her instruction. She bent forward further and further, and followed each of his steps. He had still not reached the lime tree by the front fence when she sprang towards him, forgetting herself. And then she straightaway raised the plate, offered him suddenly in her ebullience the red spheres and called quite happily, "The largest which I have plucked up to now. Guess, please, whom they are for."

The smokehouse owner started a little when he heard the familiar address. His eyes also opened wide at the sight of her, for the blossoming creature with the bare arms and blazing cheeks beset him in the first moment as something alien and unusual for which he could not find the right note so quickly. He became more uncertain and more bashful than he would ever have expected. Thus, torn along with her liveliness, he could not prevent really stroking the stems of the offered fruit with his right hand, examining them. The next moment, he certainly collected himself and calmly pushed the plate back.

"Not now, Kathrin," he declined in his usual strict manner, "I came to discuss something with you."

"Yes?", the girl cried in suspense, and her entire being expressed a flattered gratification.

She endeavoured thankfully to caress his arm as if she had to reward him for a great preference. And again it seemed to her foster father as if he stood now on the point of crudely wronging this obliging child and as if everything he had heard about her sprung up from an incomprehensible calumny. No, it was almost not possible that her open, helpful being should already know small, lurking secrets which in his view contradicted all the teachings which he had planted in her.

"No, not in the house," he ordered as he strode ahead, "the housekeeper need not hear us. We will sit in the arbour in the garden."

Kathrin followed willingly, the plate still in her hand, but on the path around the house, all the possibilities which could now be imminent for her flew through her mind lightning quick. Only, she found herself cradled in such unconditional confidence by the trust with which she had been dignified by her educator in the recent past that she also waited now for his revelations with pounding heart, but at the same time also in fearless craving. She would not have wanted for all the world to miss an appointment with such a revered advisor. Oh, it was glorious though that she lived as the only one on earth whom Mr Sell, the mighty man from Uhlenhus, sometimes revealed himself to quite trustingly. She followed him excitedly, and at the same time, she threw a half glance in passing at the abandoned place of her rest. Truly, there she had woven together in her mind terribly stupid stuff. Mr Sell had also appeared in those webs. And her blood faltered for a short while when she considered whether such strange things really would have befallen them if even only in a hazy realm.

She blushed fiercely and pressed the plate closer to herself. In the narrow, vine-covered arbour at the end of the garden, a pleasant, green dimness reigned. Soon they were both sitting opposite each other at the rough wooden table. But even now the man was incapable of breaking his reserved silence. Kathrin felt constantly how he strove to decipher something hidden in her countenance. This constant searching, however, infused her gradually with a fearful disconcertedness. And so it happened that, to escape the insistent examination, she grasped at the plate of cherries for her salvation. She pushed the fruit towards him anxiously. Only, Richard Sell shook his head this time too. But then, after a difficult decision, he used his old method of setting his adversary at a disadvantage by dispensing with a lead-in as well as by unsparing attack.

"Kathrin," he erupted thus suddenly with his drilling look, "did it come to a pledge between you and the student Gerloff during the excursion in the grove? Why do I know nothing of it?"

At this moment, the green shadows placed themselves corpse-like over the still smiling features of the girl, and the plate in her hand clattered back and forth perceptibly. The experience on the brick wall, which the light-blooded creature had thought with the forgetfulness of youth to have long since sunken behind the backs of the mountains, reared up before her and struck with a club crashing into the middle of the wooden tabletop. The plate was shattered by it, the cherries sprayed red blood, and the breeze tossed the unsettled girl suddenly into dependency and compulsion again.

"Oh, that was nothing," she stuttered like a child caught in a misdeed, and the dark eyes turned helplessly in their surrounding whites, "I — I — I haven't thought anymore of it at all."

In her disoriented shame, she thought she had thereby found a sufficient extenuating cause. Perhaps she would just as well have stammered out, "I will not do it again," but the next question of her guardian already taught her that she could not escape the firm grip of the smokehouse owner. He sat steadfastly opposite her, and only a harsh twitching about the corners of his mouth announced his own distaste for the hearing being held by him.

"Have you formed an affection for him then?", he asked further, as if he had to write down her answers in minutes.

Then Kathrin sent him an imploring look, but after she had skimmed him anxiously, she immediately lowered her head, and began rubbing her hands assiduously between her knees.

"Sit still," Richard Sell rebuked her impatiently, "I hope you have understood my question."

Now the oppressed girl would have liked most of all to relieve herself by a stream of tears. Only, that too she did not dare. The strong power which reigned over her drew her rejoinder on the contrary violently out of her.

"I like him a lot", she heard herself reply with a strangely guilt-ridden voice, and yet a quiet defiance was mixed unrecognised in it. It did not direct itself against the one whom she submitted to without will, but against that submissive admirer who put her in such a nasty position by his stupid passion. "Like him a lot," she repeated, "but nothing more."

"And you are also otherwise tying no continuing intentions to your acquaintanceship with the young man?", Richard Sell inquired, infuriated with himself because he had been forced to undertake such an unseemly digging up of childish secrets. "You are not pursuing any further plans?"

"Further?" Kathrin brushed her confused hair from her forehead, and as she strove to penetrate the roof of leaves to escape at least fleetingly the well-known look of the man, she whispered, seemingly relieved to be able to make an immediate decision, "No — quite certainly not — of that there is nothing to think about at all."

"And why not?", the smokehouse owner inquired quickly, the accursed images of the grove emerging in him abruptly again. He saw the white shadows striving towards each other and, in a complete reversal, he believed himself embraced by these bare arms. That appalled him, it was repulsive to him. In impotent fury against the mad urge, he rattled the table. "And why not?"

No, he surely did not see how fiercely the blood shot into the cheeks of his companion. He possessed certainly too little understanding for the finer stirrings of such an awakening soul, otherwise he would have definitely have spared the so visibly struggling girl more, not leafed in her as if in a book. And yet it struck through him vehemently, yes, it robbed him of a greater part of his confidence, when now the reply came almost incomprehensibly, "Why do I not think of Martin Gerloff? Because I feel well here, and because you are so good to me."

That was thus it! Opposite this simplicity, the judge, who had appeared to pass sentence, suffered a loss of his clever restraint for a moment. He moved back and forth uncomfortably, just endeavoured to avoid the look of the girl patiently sitting next to him. And then he thought he had also discovered already a new objection.

"Then I am just surprised," he tossed out bitterly, "that with such an attitude you allowed the stupid fellow so many freedoms. Are you not ashamed?"

Finally it was out. It did him fairly well to have injured her, for he revenged himself thereby for all the disorderly things which had found entrance to the house through the foolishness of this actually alien creature. Only, he would not enjoy the advantage of his triumph for long. For see there, at his reproach, Kathrin did not respond with a word. Weary, weak, crushed, she sat before him, had folded her hands gently on the table, and sent him now from her dark eyes just a single pleading look. It spoke more distinctly than the most adroit rebuttal could. It also announced to the oppressor how he was contending here with a woman who was surely subject to other laws than he himself.

"It is okay", the merchant finished, happy to have at least achieved a temporary conclusion.

In cool exposition, he hence reported to the girl waiting there motionlessly those tidings which he had learnt in the office of A. Guntrum that day, and concluded in a business-like way, "I will thus have pure wine poured into the young man by Miss Magda Heinse. From you, however, I must desire that the contact now broken off is not taken up again. Have you understood me?"

"Yes", Kathrin replied patiently. And after a long hesitation, she wrestled out what especially oppressed her heart, "Are you angry?"

The smokehouse owner rose, he did not look at her, and said in walking away, "No, but it was wrong. I myself have climbed up from small beginnings and must keep my house aloof from bad aspersions. And anyone who belongs to me must direct themselves accordingly."

With firm steps, he strode out of the garden. The girl, however, sat for a long time yet at the table, held her hands firmly clasped together, and followed the golden circles which were turning on the rough tabletop. But she breathed much easier, for the pressing secret had been found by him, and his happy disposition suggested the whorls on the table only danced such a buoyant reel for that reason.

Hour after hour elapsed.

4

After lunch, Richard Sell had again travelled into the town, which usually only happened very rarely. But today he indicated to his companion that he had something important to deal with there, and Kathrin noticed how he hid a letter in his breast pocket, which he had drafted beforehand on the top of his old birch bureau. Hastily, almost without farewell, he sprang onto his carriage as if he could not leave the village and his house, and the girl gazing after him, behind himself at all fast enough, and soon the rolling of the wheels had died away on the other side of the bridge into the soft sand along the riverbank. Kathrin gazed for a while yet at the distant towers of the town which were floating in the blue half-light, then she turned back cheerfully to the house and began arranging everything for the return of her foster father. She was even singing. She felt so unburdened since the only stone had been cleared from the way which could, as she thought, block her free stay in this peaceful little house. No pitying voice muttered to her that she would be pulled out onto a sea during the present day, a sea wilder and more murderous than the waters by which she had been tossed about already in her tender youth. And this time no swimmer would carry her through the destroying flood, no, the same hand which once guarded her golden life was destined to thrust the unresisting girl into the depths.

Only, she still guessed none of that.

The yellow sphere drew its course seethingly over the tips of the grove, and the heavy heat danced over the glimmering river and struck breath-taking waves in the stagnant air. Everything longed for a refreshment, and Kathrin, after she had set the table for the evening, also stood at the open window and waited for the house to enliven again. A few irregular sounds from the village clock floated across through the haze. It was striking six. The drowsy tones had not yet faded away when down on the river the red bushy head of Mr Emanuel Quandt appeared. The artist-shopkeeper sat rigidly erect at the helm of a boat floating past and was holding fishing bags and angling gear between his knees while an adolescent boy diligently moved the oars. In the midst of his dreamy tranquillity, he noticed, however, his mandolin student, and he immediately shot up despite the alarming rocking of the little boat, rounded his hands to form a funnel before his mouth and imitated a foghorn quite admirably in dire notes.

"Miss Kathrin," he cried, "little Kathrin — singing siren, will you accompany me? Or if you wish, I will land over on the beach of Rumin; you will plunge yourself into the flood, and I will fetch you out again later. Now, Miss Brodersen — Miss Sell, beautiful child, what do you think?"

The glassy heat made the suggestion of the singer, who was already making his dinghy glide over to the harbour steps, very enticing. Kathrin threw a quick look behind herself at the white covered table; but since it seemed to her that her time would stretch completely to the nearby excursion, she did not consider for long, and shortly afterwards she was springing adroitly down the stone steps of the embankment, from where she was lifted chivalrously by Mr Quandt into his little boat. Soon the oars were slapping anew, and the light breeze began playing with the girl's dark hair.

"You look thoughtful," the constantly curious shopkeeper began, and at the same time he let his fat, bushy-browed eyes rest as emphatically on the girl sitting opposite him as if there were no contradicting his worldly experience, "perhaps a significant discussion has been had with the mighty great merchant? In fact I saw you sitting with him in the arbour."

"That surely," Kathrin hesitated, turning her head ad letting her right hand splash in the water, "but Mr Sell is always so kind to me."

"That he is," Mr Quandt confirmed avidly, and made his rod perform a humble bow, "who would be permitted to argue that? If someone in my presence were guilty of such a slander, then I would reprimand him, roughly reprimand. For you know, Miss Kathrin, the people in a small place are curious and are constantly endeavouring to find something out."

As the shopkeeper brought this out, he rocked his red mop weightily and struck meaningfully at the fishing bags between his knees. It was unmistakable that he was seeking to arouse the attention of his companion. And really, the girl turned to him now and began searching for a while tensely in his beardless, prophet's countenance. Only, soon after she was shrugging her shoulders uncomprehendingly. She did not grasp his meaning at all, and something just dawned indistinctly before her that her fate still rocked in uncertainty, and that she had not yet up to this moment found any proper ground under her feet. But that whimsy only beset her for a moment. When the water played anew coolly about her fingers, the old confidence flew to her again that Mr Sell was indeed there. And Mr Sell had the power and the will to make everything good for her. Quite certainly.

Thus she went out into the bay, and the long line of the village began unfurling before them. A refreshing wind wafted across the wide expanse, and with dignity, with a beautiful movement, the artist threw his line into the water. Mr Quandt followed the dancing of the red cork with import, as he did everything, and when no twelve pound pike showed an affection for approaching the bait of such a significant man, the shopkeeper moved his hand derisively and damningly and considered it advisable to turn back once more to his mysterious intimations.

"Yes, your foster father, my dear child, is an energetic and imposing phenomenon."

The girl nodded.

"He is a well-read and learned man", Mr Quandt said.

Again Kathrin agreed heartily.

"He is surely also a pleasant and arresting man?", Mr Quandt asked insistently, as he let his rod bow low again. "A nature which with closer contact possesses something captivating and enmeshing, am I not right?"

Now his companion became attentive and looked at him in astonishment. She almost forgot as a result to give a sign of agreement.

"Well then," the artist spoke convincingly to the cork springing about, "this opinion is held for miles around. And as far as I am concerned, I constantly advocate the maxim — on that you can rely, Miss Brodersen — Miss Sell — that you must always trust in the very best of your fellow citizens, as long as the opposite is not demonstrated. Ha," Mr Quandt interrupted himself with a dramatic shout, "the cork sinks, something has bitten. My deep placement has stood the test this time too."

The oar beat of the boat boy was interrupted, and his right foot propped up in a beautiful arch, Mr Quandt pulled with both hands. It was almost to be regretted that no photograph could capture this effective image. But to the evident outrage of the angler, he only conveyed a bundle of rotten seaweed above the surface.

"Ugh," Mr Quandt cried, screwing his nose up, "and how it smells! Please, excuse me, my young lady, but you know, 'Ah! perhaps while hoping thus mischance e'en now hath stricken us'*."

He tossed the bundle in a wide arc into the calm sea. At the same time, however, the keel was already crunching on soft sand, and the happy fisher turned around in surprise.

"Ah, Rumin already?", he regretted. "How time flies with a beautiful one! I note this by the way daily in conversing with my wife. Now then, Miss Kathrin," he bowed with an inviting movement as he pointed to the yellow strip as if the land all around were subservient to him, "refresh yourself now in the discussed way, and in an ample half hour, I will be delighted to fetch you again. Our conversation has offered me a real pleasure. Please, your hand — so, and now leap out. Good evening."

The boat slowly floated on a red path away from there, and Kathrin stood on the secluded beach, let a handkerchief flutter and waved her farewell after the vanishing boat. In the end she had convinced herself that both the boatmen had distanced themselves sufficiently. She scurried hurriedly now to the wooden shed which was erected for such purposes on the deserted tongue of land, and a few minutes later, a white streak was merging into the glittering sparks of the waves on the beach. Ah, that cooled all the spirits of life, it made them fresh and amenable. And in long strokes the liber-

---

* [From Schiller's "The Lay of the Bell" (Das Lied von der Glocke) – translation by Thomas Arnold.]

ated girl romped about under the glowing evening sky and in the foam gently melting away. From a distance, you could have mistaken the cap-adorned head for a seal searching for prey. And really, she strove likewise to catch something flashing past even if it only consisted of the capturing of old memories. As she threw her arms powerfully, she envisaged how she had once been hauled many gray days ago for many hours through a howling wasteland of water. Now she herself was master of the element, felt confident and strong, and it shot through her mind as to whether her rescuer could also surely render a similar service today. And at the same time, she exulted and felt with all its might the precious gift of life which had been obtained for her at the time by a young fellow. Oh, it was so pleasant to always think of it, and to carry around with yourself everywhere you were found the resolve to provide an everlasting thankfulness to the donor of this beautiful existence. Every wave was his head which she caressed trustingly to whisper to him that she would never again hurt him like today, and from which she wanted hear that all was forgiven and forgotten.

Then the black dinghy was nearing back there; a fine, thin stick waved above it, and Kathrin divined that it was high time to return to the shed.

"See, dear Miss," Mr Quandt suggested soon afterwards to her when they already found themselves again on the way home, and at the same time, he fetched from the fishing bag with an aggrieved, yet forgiving air a tiny perch as long as a finger, "this is the yield today from my efforts. Don't laugh, Jochen," he reprimanded suddenly the boat boy who was twisting his broad mouth into a grin, "my theory of deep placement must only gradually acquire some force, like every new discovery. And moreover, I have cause to believe that this gloriously pictured fish is a very rare subspecies of its race."

***

The smokehouse owner was sitting peacefully once more on this hot summer evening along with his child, both almost timidly endeavouring not to invoke by any intimation that conversation which they had had in the arbour. And as they lingered in the evening-lit room over a cool drink, the master of the house sought by all sorts of description from his business or by apt description of people of his acquaintance to banish that silence which had up to then kept Kathrin's cheerfulness so victoriously at bay. And Kathrin sat opposite him, she looked at him, and she gave the impression as if she sucked in every word as something vitally important. An elevated joy in receptiveness must have been at work in her today, for only thus could Richard Sell explain the urge which activated him to gradually abandon the close at hand to reveal to his listener things which he had never touched on before. Plans for the future. He did not know himself how he arrived there and whether he had firmly believed in them in his innermost being up to now, but suddenly he was speaking of how he now wanted to use a part of his means for beautiful journeys that he yearned for, to range through distant cities, the blue seas, and the white mountains of this old earth whose soil he had burrowed through until now only for pfennigs and talers. And Kathrin's heart pounded harder because she thought she heard in her delighted listening that he did not see himself alone and solitary on these trips. Why else did he so frequently mix into his talk the description "we"? And from what cause did the so strangely torn away man say that only with such a survey was the education of young people complete? He could not mean himself. Indeed, whether he was young or old, the girl was never able to guess. She did not concern herself over that either. Only, if there was in her view a creature for which nothing could be polished anymore, then it was this all-knowing and all-capable man. And quite won over, delighted and trusting, she thrust her right hand out over the table in thanks to him, even if still hesitantly and irresolutely, and she experienced the joy of her protector bedding his own fingers firmly and strongly in hers.

Thus they sat for a time and did not notice that the feared silence had already broken in again. But suddenly the man of the house knitted his heavy eyebrows and pulled his hand back hastily. The pulse which was pounding animatedly in the joints embraced by him had tapped warningly on his conscience, and he rose impulsively to distance himself from her and sit down to rest in the high armchair by the window.

Outside it was becoming dimmer, the shadows of the grove were already pushing darkly and jaggedly across the river, and the pennants on the masts of the boats were fluttering before the evening wind skimming past.

Only, the need not to succumb to the silence, which was filled for him so often by thinking and heavy brooding, seemed to dominate the man in the armchair completely. He began abruptly to determine from Kathrin the events which had occurred in his absence, he learnt of her little concerns about the house and heard finally something about her excursion to the beach at Rumin.

There he faltered. The girl still stood at the table, occupied with the clearing away of the dishes, and could not explain his unexpected silence. No, he himself also shuddered and placed his hand over his eyes as if damming something back. Almighty, there it neared him again, what had never commanded a place before in his sober life. And now he sat here between fear and horror and saw white limbs cutting through the water, and the distaste before his unfamiliar lust shook him, and he could not tame it, and grasped with both hands for the scurrying shadows. He shook himself furiously and groaned loudly and painfully.

"Are you unwell?", he heard Kathrin's bright voice questioning.

The unsuspecting voice itself confused him as it whipped him further along the precipitous path.

"No, just tired," he responded after a while, forcing himself with all his might, "I will go to bed."

But when he said it, it cried then in his ear, 'Kathrin — Kathrin Brodersen, the daughter of the fallen and defiled. She possesses an innate power against which you are incapable of anything. Do you want to wait until her flickering fire consumes you and your house? She must go away — she must go away! Lord, why have you brought the flames here?'

"Will you go to bed so early?", Kathrin deplored, suddenly standing next to him and now stroking lightly his shoulder. "I had already put the hurricane lamp out in the arbour and want to see for once whether it isn't cooler there."

Without waiting for an answer, she ran out and hurried now smiling over to the place where she had dreamt so turbidly in the morning.

"He is certainly still cross with me," she thought meditatively, "if I could get him out of it though."

Through the branches of the cherry tree there was a rustling, and from the bright moonlight a pair of silvery threads fell through the leaves.

> Remain lying there, young, ripening child,
> I am Mr Sell or I am the wind.

She was standing in the recess of the vine leaf arbour when outside by the fence a firm, self-confident step resounded. Listening up, she recognised the tall figure of Bob Swanegel; despite the falling evening, she saw the shimmering of the golden braid on his sleeve lapel, yes, she perceived how the man wandering past stroked the posts of the fence with his finger.

"What will he want out here so late?", she thought,
shaking her head, whereby she instinctively drew back
into the shadows of the arbour; for without being aware
of it, she held a grudge against the friend of her youth
because he had interrupted the rare celebration of this
still evening.

She heard him striding through the open front door,
a strong pounding announced itself, and now the arrival
must have surely already found himself opposite the
smokehouse owner.

From the village clock, a few drowsy strikes wafted
over, and after them the bells struck disorderly several
more times. Already nine o'clock? So late? Nothing
small would certainly have led the new skipper of the
"Green Herring" here. A restless curiosity was growing
in the listening girl. Cautiously, so that her step did not
crunch on the gravel, Kathrin crept along the slender
path of the garden. And when she had arrived near the
house, she ducked down so as not to betray her figure
before the open windows. Quietly and bent over, she
huddled onto the green bench and leant her dark head
on the wall.

She did not need to wait long, for the voices inside
became hard and loud, voices which were deciding her
fate. —

"Yes," Bob Swanegel said, sitting at the round table
opposite the smokehouse owner, "over the contract we
are now agreed."

The merchant nodded measuredly. He was happy
that he had been torn from madness and shame to a
realm familiar to him by a good calculator who reminded him of his youth. He blessed him secretly for it.
And yet he observed his old businesslike manner when
he replied coolly, "You raise greater demands than your
predecessor. But I do not want to give you any difficulties."

Bob Swanegel lifted his nose. "You also surely know why", he countered cold-bloodedly.

"That I do not understand," Richard Sell said, straightened up, and the pride of the rich man over the small man opposite him obtained power over him, "what do you mean by that?"

Now Bob's eyes took on a steely gleam, and as he leant firmly on the back of his chair and stretched his feet before himself, he looked entirely like a mariner who held the wheel firmly in his hands.

"I mean," he responded with blunt openness, "you think perhaps that what benefit I get from the 'Green Herring' will benefit in the end another."

"Whom?", Richard Sell asked darkly as he looked stiffly at him.

"Kathrin."

"Aha", the smokehouse owner murmured through clenched teeth.

"Yes, aha", Bob repeated in relief, for he thought the most difficult part had been dealt with in a very quick and smooth way. The main thing was out, and now he observed bright-eyed how the wealthy Mr Sell, of whom the gossip Emanuel Quandt told such strange stories, would surely react. For on that much depended. See now, the trader throws his fists across the table as if he wanted to demand something back which had been robbed from him, and the self-assured suitor did not understand how at the same time in these hands thrown forward, a movement was pronounced, wild and desperate, as if someone were striving to toss a burning bundle from themself, 'There — there take it, I can not hold it anymore — perhaps it will torment you less — just quick — just quick.' But the tortured man said aloud quite reflectively, "I knew it."

"Well, then it is okay," Mr Swanegel determined calmly, "for the things lie somewhat in order, and I wanted to ask — —".

"Further, what do you want?"

"Whether you have anything against it?", Bob concluded his suit to some extent astonished over the heated tone of the smokehouse owner, for he was convinced to the utmost that the things really lay very much in order.

He raised his finger to his nose momentously, and then held it stiffly before his know-it-all face, because he wavered yet as to whether he could not perhaps add additional recommendations for himself, "I'm much more than you were ages ago, and whether my head is not just as apt as yours for business, that remains to be seen. Julius Kohlrausch affirms it. And what A. Guntrum has been for you, R. Sell can become for me in the future. In any case, I have the 'Green Herring' and am healthy, and you had nothing at all in contrast but a problem in the chest."

The opinionated fellow did not actually want to dissemble this talk, for it was convincing and clear, but the dwelling on his own person could in the end be spared somewhat. Hence, he lowered his stiff finger again, and after he had pushed it comfortably between the buttons of his vest, he asked with a polite bow, for it seemed expedient to him to also express some manners, "Well, so Mr Sell, are we in agreement here?"

'Yes, yes,' it screamed in the man who rose, deliberating, 'take her — and then go far away across the sea so that calm and decency and good reputation returns here again, as soon as her image has sunken behind the roaring of the sea. I will not keep her, I abandon her to you, gladly, far too gladly!'

The smokehouse owner slowly strode with his bent, brooding head to the round stove, and when the coolness of the tiles on which he leant penetrated his body, his clear consciousness was shocked over what he had brought forth from himself entirely in contradiction to the will prevailing over him. Craftily and calculating, as if it issued from a cleverly weighed plan.

"Your proposal does not surprise me, dear friend," he began, struggling against himself, and at the same time, he attempted to show his guest a half encouraging smile, "I was prepared for it."

"Really?", Bob shot out in-between, having been inclined to consider all this just to be the social prelude to his entrance into the family circle, "Really?"

"Admittedly," the smokehouse owner continued leisurely from his place, although every syllable ate venomously at his throat, and although a fierce loathing was rising up in him towards an enterprise which he thought to be more and more inexplicable and undignified, "and all up I do have many objections towards your intentions."

"Alright," Bob smiled contentedly, and waved away with his hand as if he acknowledged every flattery, but wished to ignore them from good breeding, "what else?"

"I consider it just to be my duty to indicate to you those qualms which could perhaps discourage some."

"Discourage?", Bob repeated very precisely and perked an ear, but immediately added resolutely, "If she is otherwise decent, I am not discouraged by anything."

"That we will see," the merchant cried bitterly, and now for the first time, he threw a disparaging look at the young, self-assured man; straight afterwards, however, he composed himself — "or I should perhaps say all the better", he continued more collectedly. "Are you clear over whom Kathrin's parents were?"

Now Mr Swanegel acted as if he did not notice how his opposite was clasping the stove from behind. The tile stove seemingly shook.

"Eh yes," he laughed heartily, and now stuck both forefingers in his vest pockets, "there would not have been much good in them. What concern of Kathrin's is that? I say if she is otherwise right in her gait, then I whistle that away. And to everything else which anyone else says still."

"What is said?", Richard Sell inquired hoarsely, and suddenly he could not endure the large-eyed look of the younger man which was directed at him.

One thing stood firm, the man over there was tormented by no scruples. The mariner had made an honest decision and was acting according to it, while he, the upstart who had enriched himself with so much knowledge and money, crept a devious path. His heart pounded to bursting with fury and shame, and at the same time, he opened and shut his cold hands mechanically, for he was consumed by a mad meanness to have taken from him neither by this crude fellow nor by anyone else what was dear to him.

"What is said?", he rounded on his guest once more gruffly.

Only, the seated man looked over to him steadfastly.

"What for?", he countered simply, and pulled his vest taut, "a man has his decency, Mr Sell."

And when the smokehouse owner turned dark red, because he comprehended against whom this intimation could have been coined, Bob lifted his right leg a little, and drew with it a straight line as if he could thereby extinguish all irrational gossip.

"That is blah — blah," he said, "I know my people." At the same time, he directed his haughty eyes somewhat more sharply at the smokehouse owner, and stroked his smooth chin assiduously. "Soft soap and herrings gossip. And now, Mr Sell," he demanded suddenly and in earnest, and rubbed more strongly at his chin, "why should I be discouraged by Kathrin's parents? They are dead, and the dead do not return."

"Perhaps though", the man by the stove spoke more to himself.

"What?"

The web of lies suddenly ripped apart before the struggling man, but only so that his old fever for the truth covered him with a still darker fervour.

"We do not know whether such dead do not return in their children", he murmured sombrely to himself, and at the same time he flipped his hand and threw it forward as if he had to fend off an old enemy. "Kathrin's father was a drunkard and her mother someone who sold herself for money and broke into other's cashboxes. Who can know whether all the terrible things are held fast in the grave, or will not secretly continue living? I have taken great troubles to bury them forever, for I have gradually become fond of the child — very fond. And yet, doubt has often disturbed my best hours. Once," it reluctantly crept out of him, "when reproaches were made to me by my wife because of the sympathy I showed the girl, I even spoke with a famed doctor in the town about it, and the man said to me — he said that we all haul around with us without exception our ancestors. Only a loving upbringing in youth sometimes gives the long threads a different colour. And look, it oppresses me directly as to whether I have not frequently erred in that. For when I too was bristling against it with all my might, I was often horrified by the little one and her family. Now I have accustomed myself to our living together, for the fresh, charming being of the child does me well, and I do not keep an eye on Kathrin anymore. But will you be capable of the same?"

He again knitted his sombre eyebrows cagily, clasped the stove anew, and let his look rest on the dark floor. Thus it happened that he was almost startled when Bob now quickly straightened up to his full height and broke out into a free and unabashed laughter.

"Well then, all that's true," he finally calmed down and did not take it so badly not to tap the smokehouse owner a little patronisingly on the shoulder, "that comes from when you engage with professors. You must have a tic for that, Mr Sell. But I don't think it is any good. Such a man has twisted some rope in his four walls and now believes the world must run along it. Sometimes it may tally, and much fuss will be then be made about it by the spectacled men. Of that which does not tally, we of course get to learn nothing. Look, Mr Sell," he said very insistently, and expanded his broad chest, "if merely the professors have something against it, then I laugh about it. For Kathrin and I belong certainly to the cases which do not tally. And why? Well, because I have trust in her, and because I already want to twist my own rope on which she will run along. Then rely on that, Mr Sell."

It was so confident, ingenuous, and openly spoken that the man by the stove sensed a burning envy because he was not himself filled by a similar simplicity. The man there before him stretched his hands out, ever closer and more insistently in order to drag the girl away from him, the girl who now at the moment of parting seemed indispensable to him. The man there, the accursed fellow, created clarity with one word, while he, the rich man, the distinguished man, was torn here and there by the greatest reluctance. What new excuse should he now devise? He did not want to miss his living property and balked yet from it as if before a consuming fire. He yearned to break the petty prejudice and listened nevertheless to the people's talk. And the worst thing of all, the people were right. His age — and he was her father, the man who raised her — the mother a thief, and his age — and at the same time the mad desire to grasp the white shadow, and the mad lust to feel this frisson more and more — and his age — and his bourgeois position — —

He did not get any further. From the darkness which surrounded the space outside softly and eerily, a white face arose before the window. A pair of arms propped themselves weakly on the back of the bench as if only thus could a support be offered to the exhausted body. Then a weary step shuffled along the hall, and straight afterwards both men saw how the girl over whom they had contended for so long appeared in the doorway. She offered neither of them a greeting, but groped with her hand for the light switch. It became bright.

"What is wrong, Kathrin?", Richard Sell cried, beside himself, when he perceived the ghostly pallor of his charge.

For the first time in her life, his child paid no attention to his loud address. Without raising her head, she swayed ponderously to the friend from her youth, who followed the strange procession shaking his head. There she slung both her arms about his neck, and bedded her head as if to rest on his chest.

"Well then," Bob cried after a pause of astonishment, although it seemed quite wondrous to him, "then we have come thus far."

Only, nobody answered him. The smokehouse owner held fast clasping the stove, and stared soundlessly at the white floor. He thought he was lingering again with Kathrin on the back wall of the little lighthouse, and beneath them the ravenous waters were surging.

This was Kathrin's engagement.

5

"What is it with the little girl?", Captain Julius Kohlrausch inquired, and he interrupted for a while the slurping of his watery gruel, the only meagre breakfast which was allowed to him daily by the former Mrs Plonnies for the avoidance of further weight gain. A nasty brew, particularly if you imagined in your yearning spirit what delicacies gleaming with fat Mrs Gertrud Kohlrausch was otherwise capable of producing. "What is it with the dark-haired hen?", the white-haired man inquired once more, and tapped disapprovingly with his spoon on his plate. "The departure of the 'Green Herring' shall be postponed for her sake, Bob?"

"Merely for another eight days", the advisor apologised quite against his habit and a little bashfully. "You know though, Captain, women! They get something of the like in the limbs."

"What? Did you say limbs!", the Captain repeated in suspense, and at the same time, because the eyes of his better half were resting on him, he decided to choke down the contents of a further spoonful, "beautiful, they get it in the limbs. But with differences", he explained proudly, for he thought that his dearest, who was just now tailoring a massive shirt for him by the window, had only arrived in full possession of her virtues after his proposal of marriage. "Gertrud," he asked, made thereby braver, "just a little caraway seed. I cannot tolerate so much water at once."

"Do you see," Mrs Kohlrausch noted punitively, although she did not rise at all too hastily to produce what was desired by her husband, "you cannot tolerate this beautiful healthy soup. And then you wonder constantly over how our daughter-in-law's happiness has travelled into her limbs."

"Eh, wife," the hard-of-hearing man defended himself, "did you say limbs? Hence I do not need to put the sprog in bed straightaway. With us at least, it was not so. You shall see, it comes from much reading of books, which he required of her."

"Quiet", Gertrud countered determinedly, and flung a sideways glance from her eyes that were surrounded by peaceful pockets of fat to her professed son, who was sitting in his shirtsleeves before the old roll-top desk from her first marriage and drafting a document in large letters there. "It is just a long love."

"Well yes", Julius Kohlrausch grunted to himself, "you surely said love, wife? But that someone falls ill from it straightaway is also such a modern thing. How will she just get on when children come?"

"Kohlrausch," Gertrud became enraged, and stabbed at the shirt, "you are speaking of an engaged couple!"

"Eh wife, I was just thinking," the Captain sank back under her censure, "but in Bob's place, I would pay attention that she acquires a stronger pair of shoes. Fiancees who lie in bed are a very awkward matter."

Now Bob pushed his papers together noisily, and in consciousness of representing the implicit guardian of these childish people, he closed off the debate with a very distinct stamp of the foot. It sounded monstrously distinguished when he was ready to explain from pure sympathy that certain people could not at all begin to understand the finer things of love. Besides that, the doctor had established that the constantly recurring fever of his fiancee had its source in bathing in the sea right on the day of her engagement. In a week, however, the critical day or something similar was expected, and then the little one would shake everything off and spring about like a wet cat. After this actually superfluous explanation, Bob defiantly threw his head back and raised his document up with great ceremony.

"What is that?", the Captain asked, full of reverence.

The helmsman looked very condescending.

"Oh, nothing," he once more lavished a teaching on them, "I have heard it is now the custom to make gifts to the ill, and so I have just now written over to the funny thing the little house which I bought for us in the harbour from my savings. It has in it brand-new things, with upholstery, curtains and drapes, so that you don't know where you should smoke your pipe of tobacco. But she will already find everything," he added reassuringly, as he brushed down his jacket and let the document fall into his breast pocket, "afterwards I want to specify everything as it must be. Well, and now", he stumbled backwards, and nodded graciously in parting, "I want to inspect how the little one is bearing up today. It could be scary for her otherwise. And such a thing is harmful with an engagement."

"Yes," Mrs Gertrud Kohlrausch said, and brought the shirt up to her eyes, "that is love."

***

The smokehouse owner had never known so many visitors to Uhlenhus as now, where the old clock on the lower floor again began whimpering and groaning to count the minutes of a young life.

'Better — worse — fever — chill — earth — heaven — consciousness — daze — better — worse.'

The hard ticking of the mechanism striving hurriedly to an entirely determined day could be heard up in the little loft room under whose slanting beams Kathrin lay stretched out on her pillows.

"White as snow", the poetess Helene Müsebeck described the sight of her former boarder, for the asthmatic spinster had not been refused the undertaking of a great part of the care of her favourite.

Now she sat day in, day out in a wicker armchair before the enormous bed, and she drew in her emotion and wistfulness all sorts of invisible verses on the floor with her rubber-tipped cane when she had to perceive how unchangeably the countenance of the ill bride-to-be was played about by a smile.

"Dear God," Miss Helene wrote then, unsettled, and her watery eyes shimmered lustrously, "it could actually be her most beautiful time — naturally without this incomprehensible ordeal — but to be quite open, I did

envisage the future of the little creature in a fundamentally different way. Ah, the miracle does not let itself be
hailed, and the counts and dukes unfortunately also do
not. But that it must in fact be a herring fisherman — I
would not have gauged Mr Sell so simply, although this
prudent man will have his reasons."

And then she pressed her hand to her aching heart,
smiled at the recumbent girl stiffly, and trembled before
the rising knowledge of how easily all plans could flutter
away into a void.

But the doctor in charge from the town engaged himself in nothing more than that in going away he always
rubbed his wine-drinker's nose with extreme vigour and
entrusted to the door of the loft room as if it were an important secret, "Rest — rest."

Thus it happened that most visitors were already dis-
patched before the house, and when they wanted to
make closer inquiries, they had to take themselves to Mr
Emanuel Quandt, whose business in this period in-
cluded quite select outsiders. Even A. Guntrum had
himself pushed out to him once in his wheelchair, because to the fat dockyard supplier the ever curter and
ill-disposed tidings of his son-in-law did not suffice at
all for a lasting enjoyment. The chair stopped before the
green bench, and Mr Quandt stuck his red bushy mane
out the window.

"Good morning," the artist called, flattered, and
passed his hand through his hair, "how can I help you?"

"Well?", the curious man slurred, "how's it going?"

"You must not give up hope", Mr Quandt wrestled
out glumly, but it sounded like a death notice being declaimed.

"So bad?", A. Guntrum sucked in greedily, and his
neck fringe bristled delightedly.

"You have to wish for the best," Mr Quandt proffered
his cautious dose of sympathy, "she is indeed a young,

strong creature. If only the suffering did not have such a mysterious seat!"

"Just so — just so." A. Guntrum turned his swollen hands about each other. Then he groaned animatedly. "Cold water works sometimes like pure poison. Did you not know, my son-in-law also fetched his trouble through that? Cold water saps your energy very quickly."

He wrung his hands more avidly, his eyelids dropped, and he had himself pushed away, full of satisfaction.

It was quite remarkable how without physically appearing before her, all these odd visitors who had so surprisingly discovered their deep sympathy for the invalid swirled through the blazing door of the fever to up close before Kathrin's bed. She heard the creaking of A. Guntrum's wheelchair, she perceived the fat drinker's voice of the lawyer Seiler, before whom she had previously always crept away timidly because he had something to do with the court, the black fly-like figure of the orphans' councillor, Tredup, buzzed up and down before her in bad hours and threw walnut-sized lollies at her forehead, and one evening she cried out aloud, for the midwife Braesel had appeared before her in her grey dress, and with her wobbling belly and her bluish-violet apoplectic countenance. And the old lady expanded her black umbrella over the outstretched girl so that she suddenly lay in darkness and horror.

But how peculiar, when she opened her eyes after a few minutes of foundering, bright sunlight was radiating then through the window and, next to the poetess Helene Müsebeck, Bob Swanegel sat broad-leggedly before the bed and speaking as loud and unconcerned as if he had something to shout into the ears of his skipper Julius Kohlrausch. The ghosts rolled away before it, and Kathrin was able to sit up to her astonishment to offer her hand to the faithful protector from her youth, weakly and with a helpless smile.

"Is it you, Bob?", she whispered. "Ah, how good!" She stretched her arms out to him seeking help.

"Well then", her fiancé, having already waited a few hours shaking his head, now cried out triumphantly, and his superiority over his fellow man expressed itself in perfectly stormy way. "Have you finally come to your senses, thing? How can you merely prattle such stupid stuff and mix me up with that old tackle of a midwife? And why are you constantly making up stories about an umbrella? Is it perhaps raining in here?", he inquired, as he examined the ceiling beams critically. "Or do you perhaps want to have a new one? At the merchant Heimann's there is a blue silk one with a red edging. I will gift it to you, thing. Be quite still."

At such an outburst, the poetess tended to admonish the all-too-loud man to be calmer. But before Bob could just as politely as decisively present the idea that every sparing would now be superfluous, since everything was, praise God, finally in better order, Kathrin nodded to him in agreement, and as she stroked his chest according to her old custom, she whispered, to the great surprise of the poetess always, one request which Miss Helene Müsebeck could at most explain as arising from the unclear disposition of the feverish girl.

"When are we having our engagement, Bob? — Quick — quick."

"Unheard of," the asthmatic nurse thought, and she looked at her cane helplessly, "Unheard of for a bride-to-be!"

Only, Mr Swanegel's triumph and his people-despising pride swelled up like a sail in a full wind.

"You are right, thing, why only a lot of fuss when you are of one mind? It presses on the health. And the 'Green Herring' cannot wait so long either. You are quite right, I will speak a serious word with the doctor and Mr Sell. And here," he added to give still stronger evidence of his agreement, and at the same time, he pulled the long saved-up document from his breast pocket, "here you have something which not every beloved receives." He looked arrogantly at Miss Müsebeck. "A house," he declared to her over his shoulder, "with upholstered furniture, carpets and curtains. I don't need people, we can have our engagement when we want. Right, thing?"

But Kathrin was staring into the sun. Then she shivered softly, and it fell trembling from her lips, "Hold her fast, Bob, she wants to break into the safe."

"Eh, God preserve," the master of the 'Green Herring' fell silent, "I have my few groschen in the bank. You can rest easy over that."

And then Kathrin sank back, murmured something, and the umbrella of widow Braesel turned anew over her.

"Rest — rest", the doctor confided to the door on striding out, and the 'critical' day moved ever closer.

In the evening hours, however, when the nightlight already flickered in its glass and, in place of Miss Helene Müsebeck, who had gone down the stairs groaning and puffing, a taciturn nurse sat on the sofa behind the table, then Kathrin received that visit which merged most wondrously into her dream life. Soundless, without the floorboards creaking or the door hinges betraying a perceptible noise, the tall figure of the smokehouse owner appeared, stooping already under the doorway, and as he leant for a long, long time by the stove, he maintained always his bowed pose. He did not inquire after her state of health, at least the recumbent girl could not recall that the silence and the darkness had been interrupted at any time in his presence by a word. And only sometimes did it seem to the scared girl, who observed the dark figure on the bright background tensely from under closed eyelids, as if he were secretly counting her breaths. Thus he stood for hours until he wedded himself with the advancing moonlight. When Kathrin then, penetrated by her old shyness and fear before the man, opened her eyes, then the place where he had just loomed was usually empty. And only the light danced in its glassy frame, and her heart beat quicker against the light bed covers. At such moments, the girl sighed heavily and pressed the pillows to the side as if she wanted to rise from her bed. And the taciturn sister rose, murmured something, and tucked the restless girl back in with gentle force.

In the lower rooms, however, which were now filled by a yawning bleakness by day as well as by evening, the unnatural calm of the forlorn man was transformed into its opposite. Half the night long, he paced out the narrow space uninterrupted. Then he shook his head uncomprehendingly, as if he did not understand why he was boarded up in this solitude, to straight afterwards strike in derisive despair with his fist against the steel safe in the corner as he wandered past. There was a clinking echo, and Richard Sell started, and was amazed at his pointless act. Yes, the Quandt couple, who undertook on these hot days their nocturnal promenades as persistently as ever, frequently lingered outside in the dark shadows unnoticed to follow avidly and pruriently the bustling of the rich man of Uhlenhus.

"Look, Quandt," it then whispered out of the night, "how he clasps the stove and shakes at it. Whether that is despair over Kathrin's death? For the poor girl is dying. The house brings misfortune to young women."

"It could also be his bad conscience," the artist instructed with a frisson of delight over the dramatic thrill, "who knows what he taunts himself with, and how confusedly the threads of fate are entangled. Yes, yes, my dearest, we will always recall the verdict of the poet, 'But the greatest of evils is guilt.'*"

---

* [From Schiller's "The Lay of the Bell" (Das Lied von der Glocke) – translation by

The closer the "critical" day drew, the more erratic the activity which befell the rich man of Uhlenhus. He was dominated by his old error that you can guide the actions of fate by calculating, planning ahead, and by reckless work, making provision according to his own strict will. At sunrise, the little carriage was already rolling to the town, and the little nag heard above itself the unaccustomed noise of a fiercely swung whip. Richard Sell travelled constantly, before he sought out his offices, to the house of Doctor Pogge, resolved every morning anew to elicit from this not very expansive, healing artist a binding answer. Yes, he was tormented by the confused idea that for a greater sum of money, for heaps of taler pieces, he could command an immediate healing from the learned man. But when he then stood in the bare, badly smelling room before the bald-headed, glasses-adorned figure in the yellow dressing gown, then he harvested nothing but the very laid-back prescription, "Rest — rest —".

When the smokehouse owner returned afterwards to his work, agitated and irritated over this meagre news, he revenged himself on his helplessness by discarding the present facts as if no resistance were to be thought of at all. One day he surprised his father-in-law by inviting Kathrin's husband-to-be first thing in the morning behind his desk to reveal to the blond rascal that the capital for the purchase of the 'Green Herring' lay ready for him, and the lease must herewith come to an end for the previous proprietor.

"Eh, eh," the fat belly in his wheelchair remarked here, having bent forward to not lose a single word, "noble, noble, that I will accept. Yes, anyone who has it, they can achieve something."

But the smokehouse owner just threw the invalid a cold, antagonistic look.

Thomas Arnold.]

"It is a part of the dowry which I have set aside for Kathrin", he said with the full intention of having a dispute with the other man, and his inner unease abated a little when he noticed the beaming of the usually so unemotional skipper, and since he caught at the same time the snappish response of his father-in-law.

"Look," A. Guntrum murmured, and wrung his swollen hands, "a part. You truly cannot do more for a family member."

"That I also want to herewith signify", Richard Sell persisted resolutely, whereby he was already pushing a filled-out document over the table to his opposite. "Put that in order as quickly as possible."

Only, this time it was assured that the neck fringe of Sophie's father did not need to bristle over so much vulgarity. For Mr Swanegel did not read over the writing at all, but whistled quietly and contentedly to himself.

"I can put it in order straightaway", he countered, winking slyly, and at the same time, he was already flinging open the window, leading his fingers to his mouth, and letting a shrill whistle sound. Oh wonders, at the same moment, the white Neptune's head of his former master also rose before the opening. "He has in fact accompanied me here, because he constantly talks himself into believing I could be outsmarted in such an accounts' office. And now the gentlemen will hear themselves straightaway how Julius Kohlrausch conceives the gratifying tidings."

"That is nice," it groaned from the wheelchair, "the more visitors the better."

Only, as Bob's confederate sat down in an old leather chair amidst many bows, there followed to the extreme refreshment of A. Guntrum that the decision of his son-in-law should also be confounded this time in an extremely odd way. The Captain in fact shook his head sheepishly after Bob had shouted the most important things in his ear, wiped the cold sweat from his forehead with his red cloth, and declared finally in a low voice, "that won't work, the writing has a hook."

"Why won't it?", Richard Sell inquired, restraining himself; and despite the his father-in-law's clearing his throat, he added, "Is the price perhaps not high enough for you?"

"That surely," the old Captain murmured despondently, "a nice little sum. But it won't work — it won't work nevertheless, for it jars."

"For whom? — What?", the fat man slurred in his wheelchair delightedly.

Meanwhile the white locks of the man oppressed from all sides had become as damp as if he had been going for a walk in the rain.

"It jars with a great document for which I have already paid a law twister", he burst out finally with a groan, for he was convinced that he was at fault now for a heavy judicial infraction. "You don't live forever, although my wife and I find ourselves in a good way. But you must know where it is going. And there we have," he finally tossed the pressing secret from himself, "written everything over to Bob. It was both her will and mine. For we have no children, and Bob will receive whatever. So," he concluded, completely dejected by his revelation, and rose puffing, "I do not have any more to say, and I must now get a bit of fresh air."

With that he bowed timidly to all sides, even grudged his student a similar courtesy, and retreated as quickly as possible to the bench before the building, since he did not in any way feel confident anymore on this ground. But hardly had he removed himself than A. Guntrum, after his initial victory, which he had just celebrated by a delighted drumming on his swollen torso, experienced a sorrow and a loss which remained with him right to his end in agonising memory. Yes, to the impotent man it seemed as if he had to listen as his own coffin was shut up with crunching nails.

The smokehouse owner had meditated for quite a while over what was last heard. Both his companions observed in silence how he pushed the papers on the desk back and forth restlessly, for his downcast eyes seemed, directed backwards, occupied with a different picture. But now he suddenly opened his dark coat, and brought out with serious resolve and yet precipitately and not entirely with confidence, "That of course alters my plans. But you will not always journey to sea, dear Bob. And since you look as if you would also take an interest in business matters, it would be nice for me if you now and then instructed yourself about our business a little."

"Listen," Bob called enthusiastically, and thrust out his forefinger before himself as if he perceived a welcome ship's signal, "partner of A. Guntrum. It would be a quite decent thing."

From the wheelchair, however, a fat clump gathered itself up arduously, the eyelids opened, and the lustreless fish-eyes protruded from their hollows.

"That I need not allow to be tended," a hoarse, barely comprehensible voice whimpered between lack of air and fury, "strange mob — vagrant folk! As long as I live, I have to agree with it."

He shouted the last so that the walls echoed the shrill despair. But then that heave hit him which tossed him back deep into the planed bottom of his coffin. For the first time in the long period of their interaction, the man whom he had once taken in to gift, as he intended, his fortune, released himself from his usual consideration, and it sounded cruelly across, "For your lifetime, nothing will change here. Over what happens later, I owe no account."

There the eyelids of the paralysed man clapped shut by themselves, and as a discordant gurgle poured out of him, his fat hands groped disorderly and seeking a hold in the air. "My property," he wheezed, "my property."

"Gently, gently", Bob suggested sympathetically.

***

One day something miraculous happened in the patient's room. Once again little Doctor Pogge stood with his back towards the room outside the door and talked insistently with all sorts of Latin expressions to the brown wood. But this time the exhausted poetess, Helene Müsebeck, struck through by a dull intimation, determined that the tiny healing artist had even forgotten to take off his top-hat. And suddenly she saw him shrug his shoulders several times heftily, at which he shuffled down the stairs without any further ado until you heard him knocking on the door of Mr Richard Sell's living room.

It was still very early in the morning, and the smokehouse owner had just received the sympathetic visit of Mr Emanuel Quandt. Bob Swanegel had also long since appeared to finally learn of the always hoped-for turn for the better.

"Well yes," Doctor Pogge murmured at a penetrating look from the smokehouse owner who seemed to clasp onto the soul of the doctor, "well yes," he murmured amidst shrugs of his shoulders, as he pushed his top-hat back with his cane, "I have nothing against it if the family gathers around the patient."

The man of the house discoloured, and Bob suddenly began flailing his hands in the air.

"Doctor," the horror spoke from Richard Sell, "you don't want to say — —". It occurred to him that the little fellow had once before issued a similar permission in this house.

The doctor, however, looked like a schoolboy who just remained seated and did not dare to share his grades with his relatives.

"I have nothing against it", he parried, took off his glasses, and cleaned them convulsively.

"Will you not stay here?", Bob cried.

The little man shook. "No," he cried irritably, "good morning."

"But do you give any advice", Mr Quandt declaimed, and acted as if he wanted too plant himself before the door.

"Rest — rest", Doctor Pogge wheezed. So as not to fall out of his habit, he pressed past the tall figure, and was already running past the open window at a slight trot the next minute.

The patient's room slowly filled up. Mr Quandt had also considered it necessary to climb up with them, but he remained standing considerately behind the half ajar door. Inside lay Kathrin motionless on her bed. Her slender countenance was again spun about with that mysterious smile which you could not explain. A solemn pallor covered her, she looked transparent like a wilting, white rose. Dream figures which she sought to decipher with glittering eyes seemed to float above her. She had pushed her finely rounded arms under her brown hair, and it seemed to the smokehouse owner, who was leaning on the stove, as if she still rested under the cherry tree in the sunlight and covered by that sweet ripeness which had disarmed him. In the glass on the commode, the night light, which someone had forgotten to extinguish, was just dying out and, through its polished curves, it threw a trembling half circle onto the wall. The stillness fell fearfully deeper and deeper onto the silent people until Richard Sell started in shock because he did not know whether he had himself been the one who had clapped their hands so loudly. All eyes were directed at the disturber of the peace, and reluctantly, uncomprehendingly, the smokehouse owner responded to the reproachful looks. Once more he placed his hand over his forehead, holding back, but suddenly it climbed up screaming and raging in him. What did the alien people want here? It all belonged to him, the room and the bed, and she who lay in it. He had hauled her through the sea and sacrificed his body for her. Reluctantly and without any idea of why it happened. But they had always been together, had shared at the start the meagre groschen, had grown together, and had always found each other again. As if life were a watery waste, and they clasped each other still, body to body. And now that should stop? It had already been ended by an absurdity, by vanity and foolish rules. And now the last thing was coming and extinguishing the rest? That beautiful sight which belonged to him alone? Again his hands resounded together and met the reproach of the others anew.

"Kiss me, Bob", Kathrin said unexpectedly.

The smokehouse owner listened up and held his breath.

"Quick, quick, take me away, they are frightened of me."

Then Richard Sell struck his hands against each other for the third time, composed himself, and plunged as though chased out of the narrow room.

Where had his dignity and measuredness disappeared to? A trembling, discouraged man who had lost his footing and who looked around now confusedly in the world because he did not understand why he had until now wandered over a desolate, sunburnt field, and yet had not been alone. —

He had hurried bare-headed into the open air, and stared down over the worm-ridden jetty into the river. His powers of perception lay so hammered down that the lonely man was unable to explain the light morning shadows which covered the river and meadows in a coolly still way. Indisposed, he sought to ignore the calling of the larks, although they climbed high into the still empty sky right before him, for this mourning man, who did not want to concede his loss, was closing off his chest hard and hatefully to all the sounds of the day.

Under him the black water of the river mouth curled, but the man looking down cursed it, for like that, just like that, Kathrin had frequently glided past him dancing, cheerfully and playfully. A swallow sailed in slanting flight towards his head until it settled down smoothly on one of the entrance posts of the garden. The sombre man meanwhile did not rejoice in the charming view. For there, right there, his girl had always awaited him, just that her hair gleamed more silkily and gleaming than the feathers of the bird. The world knew only a loss, and he had to suffer it, had to taste it doubly because not only an insane fate, but he himself had determined it so. He struck his hands together anew, and this time he was not ashamed before the ship's boys working nearby, who observed their master with shaking heads.

Thus Bob Swanegel met him, placing himself wordlessly next to him, but at the same time also throwing a demanding glance at him as if the most sacred duty of the rich man consisted in immediately entrusting to the younger man words of comfort or a way out. The smokehouse owner waved him away indifferently with his hand. Then he turned, and to escape the presence of the other man, he strode aimlessly and with lowered head to the only crossroads of the village. He barely noticed surely that his companion remained at his side, so naturally, as if they had both been forged together today in the fervour of sorrow.

"Eh, it will work out still — it will work out yet," Bob murmured in a morbid attempt, "Mr Quandt says — and Miss Müsebeck says — and I myself had an uncle who — —".

The man from Uhlenhus examined the speaker, shrugged his shoulders again dismissively, and hurried on towards his unknown goal. Bob did not leave him, he held himself close by his side.

Over the tips of the cemetery, here and there already gleaming with the blue flecks of the sea, the red tower of the village church loomed towards them, and the golden numbers of the clock sparkled up there in the sunlight. No sound stirred inside, and the white-ribbed portal arch enclosed a dark chasm of loneliness and silence. And yet both wanderers remained standing, yes, in the pale faces an indecisive question announced itself. Here wavered two men who were not accustomed to praying. The self-important nature of the one, because it had arrived by drilling contemplation at the separation of the highest being of all from the things of mankind; the other because he considered himself without profound consideration to be the master of his own fate, yes, deemed it entirely to be indecent to trouble dear God with all sorts of human rubbish. His pride also had not known for many years with the best of wills how he actually stood with the august Lord.

They were two such men who had now been ambushed suddenly by fear and a wild neediness for help, and who hence lingered for a long time doubting under the Gothic arch as if someone must stride out there to show them the right way. Only, nobody approached. Only the village clock rolled above — time elapsed — time elapsed — and the insistent unease reared up in them more strongly.

Then they did it quickly and fitfully, as if they were mutually ashamed for one another. Perhaps they also only stepped into the empty space to escape the sweltering heat which was already moistening their foreheads. The men sat next to each other on the last pew, felt searchingly for the bare walls, and deciphered the colourful play of the light dancing in through the stained glass windows. They let their glance glide timidly right back into the depths to the crucifix on the altar, only, the crucified man hung calm and unmoved, and no visible revelation wanted to show itself.

But — but — from the human breast the miracle of salvation swirled up as ever.

The smokehouse owner abruptly seized the arm of his companion. He seemed to have found something important.

"You are fond of her?", he murmured suddenly with an urgency so that anyone else certainly would have been startled by the erupting voice.

The mariner had surely indulged in similar thoughts, for he nodded his round head without his usual superiority, and said quite simply, "I am very fond of her. Since we fished her out at the time, I have always thought she belonged to you. And hence it has also remained thus." He nodded in reinforcement once more, and as if there were no being shy here, he moved closer to his comrade, and asked now just as urgently and honestly, "And you, Mr Sell?"

The smokehouse owner stared straight ahead at the unmoving silver cross and at the darkness which spread out behind it. Then he liberated himself arduously and hesitantly, "I have nothing else."

"That I thought", Bob said earnestly.

They both did not look to the left or right anymore, sat for a long while yet and waited. But then the smokehouse owner sighed as if after vain endeavours, patted his young companion on the shoulder, and strode hurriedly, without looking around even once, out down the long aisle. Outside blinding light, the dancing shadows of trees, and the white cross which tilted over the site of those transported from all earthly woe. But here both men suddenly grasped for each others hands, and pressed them roughly and weightily as if they had only just then discovered the right feeling for one another.

***

Shortly before midnight, to the not insignificant horror of the Quandt couple strolling along the jetty, a massive yellow and violet fish stretched its snout out of the water, and the shopkeeper later lifted his hand invoking heaven that this fin bearer had swum around three times lightning quick in a circle, whereby a wondrous white flower had rocked above its head. Just as how also, at the same minute, Kathrin had straightened up on her pillows, propped herself up on her arm, and after she had gotten used to the moonlight falling in, she had asked the unfamiliar woman who sat behind the table on the sofa, quite loudly and understandably, even if highly disconcerted, "Who are you?"

"I am the sister, dear child", the nurse replied hopefully as she rose.

"And he?", Kathrin inquired after a while, her arm stretching out towards the dark figure before the stove.

"I am your foster father", it resounded from the dimness.

Again a pause.

Then she spoke from her bed still groping a little, but yet like a stranger who crosses the threshold of their home again after an unending odyssey, "And I am Kathrin. But what sort of funny stuff I have dreamt! Where is then for example the umbrella of Mrs Braesel here over my bed?"

"She clapped it together and took it with her", the smokehouse owner replied, still not daring to breathe, and now cautiously stepping up to the recumbent girl. He bent over her, stroked her hair from her forehead, and placed his hand for assurance on her cool arm. "But you have been gifted to us again, my dear, blessed child", he pushed back his emotion and the infinite feeling of happiness wistfully into himself. "And now sleep, in the morning we will talk more."

"Yes," Kathrin followed, and curled up comfortably, "how tired I am. That certainly comes from such funny things running through my head. Just think, I imagined Bob had — —".

"Let it be, let it be", the smokehouse owner parried.

Meanwhile the white creature in the pillows had thrown a quick look at one of the fingers of her left hand, and saw there a sparkle released from a slender golden ring which she wore, and it sprang towards her staring eyes.

"Ah so", she murmured smitten.

And incapable of orienting herself, she sank anew into the arms of the man who let her glide softly onto her pillows.

That happened upstairs.

In the green room of the lower floor, however, the light blazed up soon afterwards, and Mr Emanuel Quandt, who had been thrown off by the appearance of the phantasmal fish considered by itself, was brought almost completely to his senses calmly by the strange actions of the smokehouse owner whom he espied of course from outside.

What did that signify? In there the rich man of Uhlenhus strolled up and down with powerful strides, nodded trustingly at the pictures on the wall, stroked the tall armchair in which Kathrin had usually purred like a kitten, and finally lifted carefully a ball of wool from a sewing basket to throw the ball up playfully. Now the artist-shopkeeper lost his breath, and shook his red bushy mane in confusion. Here something did not agree. He had previously heard whispers of how especially sober natures can suddenly lose the reins of control over themselves by an excess of horror. Could Mr Sell perhaps — —? For by God, the sympathetic man from Uhlenhus was not deceived that the man there inside was even singing. He sang with a loud voice that song of Schubert's which Mr Quandt had once practised secretly and arduously with Kathrin. Was this not extremely suspicious, particularly when you brought to mind that at the same hour up in the little loft room the pretty child was dying? This in fact was definite, the poor being was fluttering away today into the night and mist. Mr Quandt possessed almost a right to desiring such an exit. And nevertheless the foster father, the gardener of that flower wilting so prematurely, was enjoying himself so madly? For now he was kneeling in there on the sofa and observing with the most active interest two of the pictures hanging there. The one — Mr Quandt knew it well — portrayed the blond wife of the smokehouse owner during her engagement. But Mr Sell shook his head as if he did not recognise the familiar features, and bent over hastily to the second photograph, from which he removed a layer of dust softly with his handkerchief. This picture showed him in a cheap groschen get up as he lingered before the cracked door of the beehive with Kathrin, who was still a quite small child. And the artwork had been produced by Mr Quandt single-handedly many gray days ago. But how avidly the rich man cleaned the glass, and how happily and brightly he smiled at the faded outlines! The shopkeeper had never seen a similar cheerfulness spread from these incommunicative features. And hence it was quite natural that the tall figure began trembling and that he conveyed the bleak news to his wife through all sorts of mimicking signs as she waited separately a short distance away, "Woe to us, the lovely child has passed away. From the tower heavily and apprehensively, the bells toll — death knell."

***

The supposed dead fiancee, however, lived, yes, she plunged wildly and fiercely into the arms of existence as if she had to tear a treasure withheld from her from the quivering breast of everything happening. In a few days, she was again scurrying about the house and made the greatest effort to wipe away the traces of her illness as something unattractive. The cherry tree had to give away its last fruit, the ball of wool danced again in its sewing basket, and when the smokehouse owner sat at the table opposite her for the first time, his silver cutlery sparkled in the old gleam of celebration. The master of the house sensed just one difference, although he sometimes deceived himself, the old days with his accustomed might and her acquiescent servility had been reversed. The cheerful and lively creature constantly kept her eyes lowered; she dared not raise her eyes to him in his presence, and avoided entirely letting some earnest conversation develop. Instead she merged almost deliberately into the conversation at every fitting opportunity the name of her fiancé, yes, she seemed to summon the distant man anxiously whenever her foster father wished to do her good with an especially kind and encouraging word. And many of these opportunities were found. For as the smokehouse owner had worried about her inconspicuously and in a concealed way for an age, he now endeavoured to spread his his gifts loudly and in ample fullness before her. Sometimes he asked her to travel into town with Miss Müsebeck to carefully select her outfit. And it hardly corresponded to his habits when he inquired after such excursions expressly of the girl sitting opposite him whether she had not been all too sparing of his money. That he did not want at all. Sometimes he described to her again in-depth how he had a nurseryman wrest the wild garden behind Bob's newly purchased cottage from its state of neglect, so that Kathrin would not miss the flowers and raising of vegetables which she had become so fond of. Yes, one day he traveled himself to the agricultural academy, and had a row of young cherry trees from the tree nursery transplanted at great cost into the new garden. For all this proof of his fierce benevolence, the recipient indeed thanked him hastily and confusedly, yes, she occasionally offered him her hand hesitantly across the table; only, her dark eyes at the same time did not want to free themselves from under her eyelashes, and straight afterwards, she lapsed again into her strange urging after the definite appointment of the public betrothal. The poetess Helene Müsebeck upheld rightly that the child of the smokehouse owner was one of those fiancees who sought to disown their entire previous existence as quickly as possible.

"Bob wants to make yet another journey before our engagement," she apologised when she once again brought up her wish, with a contradictory smile, "he is becoming impatient."

The smokehouse owner remained silent for a while, and gazed around the friendly room as if he feared that all this could suddenly sink away before him. But then he composed himself, and pulled a note out from his breast pocket.

"Here, my child," he finally replied calmly, "here you have the list of guests which we want to see at our place. I have only written down such as I assume take a real interest in you. And next Sunday they may come to the engagement party."

Kathrin placed the paper before herself, and did not lift her eyes from the white page.

"Shall it also be put in the newspaper?", she asked after a pause.

The smokehouse owner smiled over her thoroughness, then he nodded, and promised to bring about the announcement that very day in town in both papers. Now a stone seemed to have fallen from Kathrin's heart. She breathed out in relief, and only after a long pause did she ask unexpectedly of the man already on the point of leaving, "You promised that four weeks later our wedding will take place, and Bob wants to take me to sea then. I am already rejoicing over that. But what — what will you do in the meantime?"

"Oh," Richard Sell said airily, and gazed out at the little carriage which would take him to the business offices of A. Guntrum, "I will have it much better than you. I will expedite my journey straight afterwards."

"Ah," Kathrin hesitated with concern, and remained sitting at the table, "the journey which we worked out together? To the mountains and to the blue seas?"

The smokehouse owner nodded to her in parting.

"The doctor suggests I need a distraction. I have always wished for it, and just not possessed the proper recklessness for it. But now, since so much is changing here, I don't want to put it off any longer."

"Yes, yes, do that", Kathrin wanted to agree animatedly, but she did not bring it to a loud exclamation, instead suddenly sinking assiduously into the reading of the page lying before her.

Only when the carriage was rolling away from there did her chest relax, and she crumpled the piece of paper heedlessly between her fingers.

***

Kathrin and her foster father were travelling through the countryside. The smokehouse owner had an order to hand over in the village in which the cooperage was, and he thought the trip in the fresh air would do the recovering girl well. He also usually used any opportunity to shake up the girl who was sunk in such an incommunicative shyness. For he thought it quite intolerable that the chasm between them should deepen yet after their separation. For her sake, he did not hound her today, he was also not stingy with his time, but let the little carriage roll slowly along the deep, shady forest roads which ran up close around the gulf. Through the trunks they both saw white, lively flowers nodding in the blue fields, for the wind was fresh, and above them under the green roof they sometimes heard the hammering of the woodpecker, and they rejoiced when a cloud of brown butterflies made their restless chase in a fleck of sunlight. They sat close next to one another, and Richard

Sell looked at his companion frequently, and sought to fathom why he felt today so boundlessly calm and pre-occupied, as if his life had finally found a safe conclusion. He shook his head uncomprehendingly, and told her more about thousands of plans which he enter-tained for the future. He did not guess that he could conceive nothing stronger to tear apart the self-con-sciousness which now always veiled the girl completely, and to draw the avidly listening creature for a while again entirely into that spell in which she had always strolled as if fascinated and enthralled. Both seemed to know nothing more important than the future of Mr Richard Sell, and the longer the vehicle creaked along the shadowy way, the lighter and brighter the man painted one of his golden pictures, and the more promptly and enthralled the other acquiesced. At the same time, it was just strange that both these people of the present let their approaching separation completely fall from their minds, and thus acted as if the few weeks which remained to them still represented an immeasur-able eternity.

"You know," Mr Richard Sell said, "I recently studied the building plan again which you had to draw up for me in winter. But now I will have it executed. We obtain thereby an enormous hall on the lower floor in which you can see yourself with guests more often. And also your room in the upper space will be made airy and healthy by the inclusion of the partition. I am quite shocked at how tiny the window bay is. That must of course become large and double-sided."

"Really!" Kathrin called out delightedly and was quite stirred, "then I will be able to see the bay."

"Yes," the smokehouse owner continued planning, "and I will also wallpaper the old, smoky, lower room and fit it out with bright wicker furniture as is fitting for a young girl's room."

A thankful radiance glided over Kathrin's dark countenance. She grasped wistfully for the reins which the
smokehouse owner handed over to her willingly, and as
she now adroitly guided the little carriage, she basked
comfortably in the future splendour. Then she prodded
him timidly.

"Are the blinds or the shutters not forgotten too?",
she asked avidly.

And when the smokehouse owner could not think,
she explained to him, gazing out always strictly at the
green path, that it would not be advisable if Mr Quandt
and the other people of Uhlenhus were able to spy in
unhindered at any time into the interior of the small
green room.

"You are in this way never entirely alone", she added
as a convincing reason.

"You are right, my child", it occurred to Richard Sell,
and he cracked the whip. "Write that on the plan for me
today."

Thus they arranged their house, and did not notice
that it was built of sunbeams and could be dislodged by
the first wind.

When they steered out into the open fields, and the
sun now threw her garish cloak about them both, it became apparent to the smokehouse owner how a tender
redness was beginning to shimmer finally on the countenance of his child. Then he could not contain himself
from stroking her cheek paternally despite her astonishment.

"Praise God," he determined exhaling, "you will soon
become the old you, you are looking pretty and healthy
again."

The eyes of the girl immediately lowered, she lost the
reins from her hand, and it lasted some time before the
laughing man had brought the leather straps back into
order. But already in the distance, the first cottages of
the village they were aiming for were already appearing,

the little bridge behind the alder scrub was crossed, and soon after they had reached the dusty haze of the country road between the cottages, the smokehouse owner sprang down from his vehicle to pursue his business. Kathrin slowly steered the sweating nag meanwhile through the long lane, nodded to the schoolchildren drawing past her, and reflected her image in the quick silvery glass bells of the little front garden. Suddenly, however, she faltered. By one of the low hanging straw roofs, a long escaped memory returned to her. Quick heat seized her, straight afterwards she again turned pale, and brought the carriage to a violent standstill. With a quick grasp, she tied the reins to the grill before the front seat, and then she also swung down from her seat, hesitated a while yet before the low entrance, and finally vanished quickly into the dark hall. When she appeared again the smokehouse owner had already taken his place on the little carriage. Now, bending down, he offered her his hand, and helped her climb up.

"What sort of acquaintance have you made there?", Richard Sell asked curiously as they step by step put the country road burning in bright sunlight behind them.

Kathrin plucked at the reins from the side.

"Oh," she conceded truthfully, "I already knew the woman from earlier."

"Right, we were here once before."

"Yes, it was a long time ago", the girl said, turning inwardly to herself, and grasping at the bushes of alder scrub, for they were again crossing the rotten bridge.

From here the main road began, and the merchant swung the whip and set his steed in a quicker trot. But as he examined the long lines of the forest towering towards them, he pondered over why he all of a sudden carried the self-consciousness as a burden with himself again, and why his young companion remained so completely sunken in herself next to him. She barely stirred, and gazed constantly at the fields flooded with light which carried their yellow ripeness down to the edge of the sea. Hot and torrid, they finally arrived at the arched entrance of the old divine grove. But here, in the coolness and shade, the foster father's old addiction befell him of tolerating nothing unsaid and no secret next to himself. More amicably and imploringly than it ever lay in his manner, he thus turned to the taciturn girl, and look, he surely did not realise that he was stroking the hair from her forehead at the same time encouragingly.

"Kathrin," he urged coaxingly, and with a voice which was filled by a peculiar apprehensiveness, "you are sitting there so upset, my dear child. Did something annoying happen to you perhaps in the cooper's house? And can I not put it in order?"

Then a wild, flashing look met him suddenly so that he was startled. At the same time, however, an ashen pallor drew over the pretty face, the lips opened and moved, a difficult resistance yet, and then it had conquered her, and she tossed her secret at him half with bashful smile and half as if shaken by a close fear.

"I had taken something from the woman once", she said severely.

"What? You?" The smokehouse owner started as if a shot had struck him just then.

"It was only a flower," Kathrin continued, "a ridiculous childish tale. But I could not endure it, and have given the woman, who was quite astonished, money today."

"What? What?", her foster father stammered, unable to express himself.

Kathrin, however, from whom the shyness had drained away, struck her hands before her face and groaned loudly.

"It is so horrid, taking something," it poured from between her fingers, "honest people are horrified by it, and they do not like to tolerate such creatures in their vicinity."

"Kathrin!"

"And with right," the devastated girl collapsed next to him, "such a thing shall be innate."

A fierce, uninhibited sobbing shook her breast, she curled up, pressed her hands between her knees, and her long cowered and humbled life unburdened itself in streaming tears. And Richard Sell? The educator and in-fallible judge? He sat next to her, and cold horror seized him — a cold horror before his own half understood propositions. And at the same time a wondrous feeling of pride awoke in him, because by living with him a plant which had been rooted in bad earth could develop into such a white, untouched flower. Thrown to and fro between pity and the furious urge of related things, he forgot himself, his house, his dignity, the judging of the people of Uhlenhus, and to rescue her from the fall, he slung his arms around the sobbing girl, and drew her up strongly. But what happened then? Why did he stare as if entranced at the white countenance and stroke her hair incessantly from her temples? And why at the rap-prochement did the long fostered shyness suddenly sink in wild transition from the outcast girl, from the des-pised daughter of debauched parents, so that, as if in defiance, yes, as a last salvation, she threw her arms clasping about the neck of the man next to her?

The reins of the vehicle dragged on the forest floor, the reins of reason dragged next to them, and for a short span, both struggling people rested breast to breast, erased from this earth, in a world-enraptured liberation, exposed and divested of all hindrances, robbed of their names and their origins, and nothing was left of them but the concepts of man and woman. When the red mouth rose close before his own, Richard Sell was tossed out for the second time as a castaway and into the howling storm on the sea of the limitless. Salvation and annihilation danced up and down before him, and again he held the same body in his arms and struggled like a desperate man against submerging in the greedy deluge. The white head with the closed eyes moved ever closer, the dying mouth whispered incomprehensible requests to him, and all around was wavering desolation, and the waves began spewing down words on him, threatening in uniform noises. His age — foster father — bride-to-be — a mad aching lust — and the shame, the shame of the sober man before the inexplicable wildness.

But when he caught the words, he suddenly re-won the lost earth, he landed with his charge, groaned deeply, and let his burden sink down onto the seat next to him. Neither dared anymore to fasten a look on the other. Like two strangers who inflict on each other a harm that can never be made good again, they split the narrow space between themselves, and the dark shadow of the beech forest ran like black men before them, countless coffin bearers leading the sombre procession to its final goal.

6

From then on, the smokehouse owner was barely seen in his house. Resolute and serious, just as he attacked everything, he completed the last preparations for his journey, and it required long and difficult discussions before it could be made comprehensible to the lame man in the wheelchair that from now on an old clerk with extended authority would step into the place of the distant man for a few months.

"Look," A. Guntrum remarked overly sweetly and pressed his swollen eyelids shut, "it is all about wedding trips now. Before, when Sophie lived, it wasn't the fashion. But I am not coming to the happy engagement feast — yes, yes, it is a great shame — but I am sending my wheelchair to be repaired right on that day. It is in fact so."

The bride-to-be also knew no more urgent concern than to now prepare and put into working order everything her foster father needed for his journey. She often lingered for hours before the simple leather suitcase to which she had lent a heightened polish through her adroitness, and she seemed to accompany in her thoughts the flight of the piece of luggage through the world. But she knew almost distressingly to arrange it so that a stranger almost always participated in the joint meals, and both Miss Müsebecks radiated in pride and satisfaction because they were now invited so often to the home of the smokehouse owner.

"The little one feels surely that we take the place of a mother for her", the poetess declared on such an occasion to her accomplished sister as both old spinsters collected together all their threads at home for a higher ornamentation. "If I could only comprehend rightly why our bride-to-be makes such an erratic, feverish impression. Pay attention, the farewell from Uhlenhus is difficult for her. Ah yes," she whispered, and directed her ever teary eyes clairvoyantly at the ceiling, "Mr Sell is a man who makes a deep impression on everyone. You will understand me best if you hear the six-liner which I recently put to paper for the parting bride-to-be:

You are going, you lovely child, and youth follows,
You seek the young fellow and you leave the man,
And what you possess in beauty and virtue
Yet belongs to the mature man.
From his hands you have arisen pure —
The old man's gift carries you to the young man."

"Ah yes", both sisters cried, touched, and grasped each others' hands.

But neither the toilsome ladies knew at all how richly in fact the gift of the old was carried to the young man, and how critically they were taken up there in most cases. Kathrin spent her free time namely, whenever she could make it possible, in the house of Captain Julius Kohlrausch, as if she had a true fear of lingering any longer alone and unprotected in her old home. And the weighty Gertrud reported again and again how promising and touching it was that Bob's future wife emphasised her belongingness to the more intimate family so distinctly.

"You see, Julius," she was wont to infuse her view to her husband together with the watery gruel so loathsome to him, "that is love. She already counts herself with body and soul as one of us."

"Yes, wife", suggested the white-haired man for whom it was not begrudged to let a part of the meal disappear unnoticed. "But she is proud. Why else does she reproach us with all possible things, Mr Sell does it so, or Mr Sell thinks differently about that?"

"Eh, that just proves", the former Mrs Plonnies suggested, and clattered assiduously at her window seat with her knitting needles, "that she likes to duck under his firm hand."

The Captain, however, turned his plate in a circle, and shook his head of white locks.

"Beautiful," he grumbled, "but it is uncomfortable. I smoke pipes, and she recently brought me a carton of cigars and said Mr Sell uses just such. And when Bob

Swanegel, because he has been lumbering about day after day on his ship, takes a little pinch of sleep on our sofa here after eating, she is amazed over it and says Mr Sell never sleeps in the afternoon. What concern of ours is Mr Sell? We are not marrying Mr Sell! In the end the sprog is longing that we put on a black frock coat and all hang in a chimney. Ugh, the devil!"

Even the unconcerned Bob had a strange experience about this time. He arrived at a realisation which caused him for the first time to move away with his own important person a little bit from the centre of the world, to observe himself afterwards quite thoughtfully in a mirror. That he never usually did, for he knew himself exactly.

It was just two days from the engagement celebration. A bright afternoon lay over the little town, tame doves strutted across the secluded street, and the single storey houses devoted themselves to a peaceful slumber. On the slanting footpath of the lower harbour street, two figures met. They only noticed each other when they were barely a step apart.

"Ho, Kathrin," Bob cried delightedly, and doffed his blue cap, "where are you wanting to go, girl?"

"To you", Kathrin awoke, and offered him her hand.

"That is right", Mr Swanegel approved contentedly, whereby he intentionally blocked her way though. "What are you doing in the boring box out there where no fly stirs?"

The girl fell silent, and brushed her foot across the tufts of grass which sprouted up between the cracks of the footpath. Now the helmsman blinked craftily at the brown ribbed door of the cottage before which they were lingering just then, and set his right foot leisurely on the first step.

"Do you also know where we are here?", he asked cheerfully.

Kathrin raised her head, and a quick recognition surged into her eyes.

"Yes," she replied with a smile, "that is your house."

"Our house", Mr Swanegel corrected good-naturedly. And suddenly he thrust his arm under hers, struggled a little, but then shoved every scruple decisively to the side. "Come," he said patronisingly, and yet at the same time very contentedly, "I want to show you our stuff please. Why should you wait so long for it? You will see that I have arranged everything very cosily."

"Yes, but —", the bride-to-be hesitated.

"Eh, dumb thing, nobody can object to it. And if it suits me, then I would like to see please who is able to remonstrate with me. Come, thing."

More excited than he wanted to confess, the new homeowner was already opening the door, a shrill chiming was heard, and from the dark hallway, the smell of fresh paint and new wallpaper struck the timidly entering girl. The bride-to-be remained standing irresolutely in the dimness.

"Can you not make some light, Bob?", she inquired softly.

The master of the "Green Herring", however, shut the door behind himself so that it became blacker for a moment, and as he seized her by the hand, he laughed happily.

"No fear," he declared confidently, "we don't have electric light here, we don't need it either. When we first live here, we will place a little kerosene lamp on the cabinet. That is much cosier and recalls much more our ship. And now pay attention, I will open the first door."

A long sunbeam flooded onto the floor, and Bob pushed his apprehensive companion, who strangely did not give up her bristling, powerfully into the bright room.

"There look", Mr Swanegel said proudly, and planted himself with his legs apart.

Kathrin emitted a cry of surprise. Yes, here a barely surmised wonder really revealed itself. She found herself in the green room of Uhlenhus. The old room was imitated right down to the most insignificant trifles. The birch furniture with the green rep covering stood before her, the green pennanted lamp hung over the table ("gas", Bob explained smugly), the tall armchair was resplendent by the window, yes, even the round white tile stove was not missing from the place due to it. And the girl stared quite numbly at the fully occupied bookcase which drew around the walls exactly like in her old home.

"You possess a library too, Bob?", she stuttered, completely stunned.

"Eh yes," Mr Swanegel replied a little flippantly. "I had brought a few such old tomes with me from the maritime school, and have now stocked up from an antiquary. You are accustomed to the fare, and know how to kill time with them when I am away. Well, what do you say to the treat?"

Kathrin's heart had been warmed. She squeezed her fiancé's hand thankfully, her full disposition sought for words to unburden herself, but strangely, as she struggled with the expression, her look swept still spying through the room which lay in a bright shimmer.

"Well," Bob finally wondered loftily, "is something still missing?"

"No, no, Bob, it is all wonderfully nice. You have made a great effort, you are a good man."

"Well, it works", the groom-to-be suggested flattered. After a while, however, he became attentive. "What are you seeking for still?", he urged impatiently.

Then Kathrin gave up her endeavours, shrugged guiltily, and lowered her eyes.

"I don't know," she confessed, and folded her hands wearily, "I really don't know."

Mr Swanegel tapped her lightly on the cheek and was very contented because he could instruct her superiorly, "It is clear though, you miss the life, you silly thing. That can of course only come when we both keep house here."

"Yes, so it will be", Kathrin accepted in a low voice.

They wandered onward.

It was a sparkling clean, comfortable nest, and Kathrin's attention was attracted in particular to how decorative carpets lay spread everywhere, yes, that even the stairs were covered by slender runners.

"They are from Mr Sell," her guide explained indifferently, "the man does not like to suffer a hard step."

The girl shook her head vigorously.

"Because it disturbs his thinking", she defended the distant man, and withdrew her hand from the helmsman.

"He thinks too much," Mr Swanegel determined, shrugging his shoulders, "better to leave that behind, Kathrin, it leaves you gaunt."

The bride-to-be fell silent, knitted her eyebrows, and since she had come out the back door into the garden, she drew in air alleviatingly. Then she let her eyes sweep around in delight. The fire walls of the houses which surrounded the narrow quadrangle were clambered over up to the eaves by green, long-leaved vines so that the entirety seemed like an enormous arbour. Long rows of tall-stemmed roses raised into the unmoving air their dark-red, white and yellow heads and sent out waves of sweet scent. Countless butterflies fluttered up and down here merrily, and across the square of blue sky, a flock of tame pigeons made circles in the sunlight. In the middle of the short-cropped lawn, however, a white bench had been placed which extended a proper invitation to rest and tranquillity, and Bob drew down onto this his companion who was lost in admiration.

"Dear, how is it?", he sought once more to reap his deserved applause.

And when the confused girl stroked his cheek, like she practised as a child, something overcame the bold fellow which he usually considered to be far below his dignity. But here between the closed-off walls, on his own ground, and in the elation of finally obtained possession, he suddenly slung his arm about the delicate figure and raised the girl's lowered chin up forcibly.

"Well?", he inquired, as if it made a good jest.

Only, Kathrin began trembling, and fended off his unaccustomed tenderness.

"Leave it, Bob", she bristled, and looked anxiously at the sky-high green walls.

"Leave it?" The master of the "Green Herring" became indignant, and immediately moved away from his companion. Why did the thing need to act so prudishly? "Dear," he said, between admiration and superiority, "you surely think it hurts?" He laughed a little bashfully. "Well," he added with a look at her sad face, "it is for all that quite right to me that you find such jests alien."

But hardly had he uttered this than a fright seized him which he could not explain, and the mysterious thing which adheres to every woman threw the worldly wise fellow into a whirlpool of uncertainty and distrust. What the devil did that mean? The little one next to him whom he had not wanted to affront, grasped the arm of the bench and stared at him, white and distraught, as if she had not understood him. Certainly, the infallible advisor convinced himself of just that. For behind the forehead of his bride-to-be, a chain of thoughts rushed past, a crowd of black ghost horses which struck her self-respect and all her arduously preserved peace with steely hooves into rubble. She was sitting there with a contradictory smile and twisted mouth, and through her memory swished at first quite distantly and indistinctly the adventure on the red brick wall in the grove, how she had lain numbed and curious in the arms of an inexperienced and ridiculous boy. Only, those were just shadows which swayed and faded like the dim reflection of the leaves on the forest floor. From the childish embrace, the steady repose suddenly came to a secure stop. She heard herself sobbing, she perceived the creaking of wheels, and she did not know anymore whether she was not also stammering now, despite the extreme danger of discovery, the same senseless requests as on the vehicle from which the reins had fallen. No, that she could not bear, she was namelessly afraid of it. Without an explanation, just yielding to the one urge to stay what she was, she threw herself suddenly at the chest of the bewildered helmsman, senselessly, hounded, all her limbs shaking, and clasped tightly there. Meanwhile Bob Swanegel did not understand her stormy vehemence. He slowly bent down to her, gazed for a long time into her transformed countenance, and thoughtfully shook his head.

"What lies behind it?", he thought bashfully. "Pay attention, there are secrets here."

Truly, he brooded. Much later, when his bride-to-be had already long since said goodbye, he still sat with crossed legs on the white bench, and struggled stubbornly against the disconsolate feeling that there could possibly be on earth tricks and wiles and all sorts of hidden things whose secrets would not unveil themselves to a fine connoisseur at the first blow.

"Trifles," he said grimly to himself, and struck his fist against his knee angrily, "female poppycock."

But the defiance sounded for his circumstances quite uncertain, and entirely filled by the event which had befallen him, the tall fellow finally sprang up grumbling, and ran as quickly as possible to the home of his old master. You had to have about yourself once again a few people of whom you divined from the first syllables what they wanted to express with an entire sentence.

"No, no," Bob fretted as he crossed the street with weighty steps, "she has got that from the incommunicative potentate of Uhlenhus. Who knows what sort of weird tales he has bunged into her. I will have to be very attentive there."

In short leaps, he set off up the twisting stairs, for he did not like to waste any time, and he arrived right before the door of his friends as the couple inside were fighting out their dispute over the great influence of the smokehouse owner on his foster child.

That was bedevilled indeed! The first thing which struck the man pausing for breath before the door was the name of Mr Richard Sell. The arrival indeed felt ashamed, but he could not control himself, he bent down and eavesdropped. He gradually turned dark-red from the effort, his eyes began flashing, and through the short-cropped hair from which he had torn his cap, the sweat was surging. Mr Sell, and again and again Mr Sell. The devil, it was right, the little one hung like a barnacle to the accursed black coat. Even the harmless old man in there found something disturbing in it. But how, if it was not to be disposed of at all? If more lay behind it than his friends guessed? Must you really throw the gossip of Mr Emanuel Quandt to the winds as unalloyed stupidity? And could you ignore so simply the strange behaviour of Kathrin who had made him beside himself just then?

"Mr Sell," it came anew from behind the door, "Mr Sell."

The knee of the eavesdropping man began trembling peculiarly, and in extreme concern, Bob Swanegel swung himself onto the banister to glide down inaudibly on the winding wood. It was a stunt he had frequently performed as a boy, but for the man who arrived at the hall in this manner, all the desire for youthful jests seemed to have vanished. He rubbed his forehead with balled fist, meanwhile nothing seemed to appear advisable to the man who was beginning to sway himself. The straight path on which he marched was dancing up and down before him and forcing him to run around in circles wheezing.

"Lord," Bob murmured quite shaken while he sat down on one of the lowest steps of the stairs, "I thought too little of that. But Kathrin and Mr Sell, they must have known it though. Does someone perhaps run here into his misfortune? That is not at all possible though! I have already bought the house."

In a dull stupor, he remained sitting, and stared, shaking his head, at the colourful glass squares at the top of the front door. Blue and red and green poured into each other here, and contradiction strayed for the first time just as madly into the life of this self-confident fellow. No, the seated man could not fight that out with himself alone any longer. And as he pulled himself up resolutely by the banister, the best in him suddenly stirred, his rough manly forthrightness.

"The most decent thing will surely be if I ask the man while there is still time", he tossed all the fruitless qualms behind himself. "In such things you do not lie, no, that he will not do. He must realise that it all happens only for the security of us all."

With that Bob Swanegel put his cap on and strode, turned inwardly to himself, down the bright street to the river. He strolled heedlessly past his own ship which was anchored to the wharf, and he did not recognise it, for he had lost the pride in his possession.

On that morning, the Uhlenhus harbour echoed with the busy life. The high-seas boats of Mr Sell had come in, and now the brown sails rattled down, the hatches opened to lead silvery blue rivers of scales into the appointed baskets, the fishermen clambered onto shore, pulled off their swollen gumboots, greeted their wives, and squabbling and haggling, the smell of fish, and the reek of tobacco filled the air. Only where the businessman stood in the thick mob did a calm island always form. There the caps were doffed, and the curt words of recognition from the mouth of the rich man who understood their handiwork so fundamentally pleased the seafarer often more than the notes he had already received which were issued immediately after the concluded trade.

"Thank you too, Mr Sell. Eh yes, the trip was good. Just the Albatross drew in much water so devilishly. And there I wanted to ask you please whether the applying of pitch at your cost —?"

"Yes, Lietzow, I will add that to my own."

"Beautiful, Mr Sell, then all would be in order."

The whirl of voices surged onwards, the blue scales sparkled in the sun, the banknotes lost themselves in calloused hands, and from afar the sea shimmered about the land which it had enriched.

The smokehouse owner had gradually surveyed the flouncing harvest. His instructions were received, and now he stood and counted the carts which were setting off to the smokehouses. As the last of his whistling youths was pushing past him, he pulled out his watch and, with his measured greetings, he parted from the mob which immediately made a louder racket. In the middle of the way which was meant to lead him to his home, he suddenly deliberated. It occurred to him that his residence lay in solitude because he was expected by nobody. The happy voice which usually greeted him had fallen silent, for Kathrin had again fluttered into town as she had unlearnt entirely after that carriage journey the dwelling in the old places. Depressed, the smokehouse owner lowered his head, and the eternal unease which tormented him since he had showed such a distorted image of himself to his child drove him away, as if often now did, from the area of the village and steered his steps quite undesignedly to the beach and the enormous stone blocks which had lain in wait for dance

and storm since the infancy of the world. Standing water glittered here between the massive stones, barely
finger-long fish scurried thickly across the sunlit, yel-
low-furrowed sand. And tall bulrushes, out of which
brown velvety bulbs swayed, hemmed the homely place.

Richard Sell sat down wearily on one of the round,
white blocks, but threw another look behind himself to
see whether the unaccustomed break could be perceived
from the village. Only, just a single dark male figure was
moving hesitantly and seemingly aimlessly across the
meadows, and the lonely man turned away soon from it
indifferently and drank in thirstily the blue distance.
Nobody, hardly he himself, heard how he called for an
answer across the expanse. He wanted to know why an
individual, when he possesses his living and hence does
not transgress the laws, considers himself perfect and fit
for educating other, less fortunate creatures and forming them according to his will. He reached out to the
invisible shores so that information would waft over to
him from there, information over whether it was at all
advisable to split the living at the outset into good and
evil, since every mortal carries heaven and hell within
themselves and strays through both realms according to
accident and opportunity. How could teachers and
priests exist, when they found themselves directly on
the dark path which nobody was spared? How did they
then look their students and faithful in the eye? Did
they not have to always snatch at an excuse just like he
did when in his mind's eye Kathrin stood with her questioning eyes before him and he sought to excuse his
desolate caress, his rebelling desire for the one committed to his protection? What lies remained for him there
still? One only, the expression of his supposed father-
hood, the emphasising of his sober years, his age, which
had been invoked by the tender child on that decisive
carriage journey surely also for protection and mercy.
Sombre and obdurate, the man who sat so cold-

bloodedly in judgement over himself knitted his brows, and a derisive laugh twitched about his lips when he brought to mind what threadbare hopes the phantom of his bourgeois status clung to. The girl who enslaved his thoughts, the child who was a woman, who aroused his long drowsy senses daily, hourly to mad turmoil; she had to believe in his disinterested chasteness, while he though was consumed by predatory wishes. This pious simplemindedness was his salvation, for he did not possess the courage of truth. That was it, that was it! In indignation towards himself, the rich man threw himself down and shook both arms, emitting curses, at the hot stone. He did not possess the courage of truth. The bustling merchant had heaped up money on money, had built a ladder from the good opinions of people, a ladder on which he had climbed up rung by rung, and now he feared plunging back from his height by a wild and outrageous action into the gossiping mob. Yes, he heard them already screaming and threatening with their fists, A. Guntrum and Mr Quandt, the orphans' councillor, Tredup, the widow Braesel and the lawyer, Franz Seiler; he saw all of them point with their fingers at the educator who molested his foster daughter, whom he had given duplicitously to another, and whose young, supple limbs he embraced as if he must not allow them to any other.

A chain rattled, and the dreamer started and came to his senses. From the mouth of the river, close by his side, a cutter was just then making out to sea. At the front on the bow, the name of the ship was illuminated on a blue background. It was called "Richard Sell". And the vessel which made its course so confidently and majestically bore a valuable cargo, the fruit of work-filled years, the result of arduous planing and accomplishments, to a distant coast. The sail flew up, the course of the ship became more determined, and the rudder followed the hard pressure of a man's fist. The very one, however, whose will guided the planks from his stone furtively, he straightened up slowly, and the cramp had wondrously drained away from his limbs. That out there, that was he himself. A vessel which had things to carry and hid highly important work in itself. The ship could likewise not deviate to the left or right, but was destined to reach its goal on its prescribed course. The smokehouse owner shook himself vigorously, and now he had won over himself to sway his cap with a gesture of greeting to the departing cutter. He thought he had refound himself again.

Then a black shadow pushed up next to his own. And before the taken aback man was aware of being tracked down in his solitude, a pair of long legs were already dangling down over the block, and a familiar figure was sitting next to him, wide-legged and self-assured, as if it had been called here by an urgent invitation. Only, the smokehouse owner was not in the mood for politeness, for a suspicion whispered to him that the day in court had not reached its end.

"What do you want here?", he called out vehemently.

Bob Swanegel shrugged his shoulders, and now the smokehouse owner also recognised how pale and overstressed the fellow's countenance looked.

"Mr Sell," the unbidden companion began, without engaging in any triviality and, at the same time, staring defiantly at the wavering surface of the water as if he could push it aside with a thrust of his arm, "I'm having qualms. And I cannot toil with qualms. On account of Kathrin. How is that? Do you give her to me gladly and sincerely?"

There the flaming pit opened which the rich man of Uhlenhus had thought was only visible to himself. The poisonous fire shot out and blinded the eyes of the man gazing down. But, at the same time, he was tamed by the philistine hope that his often exacted sobriety, the decency and good sense, and whatever all the means of the petty bourgeois existence were called, could be thrown as a bridge over the glowing abyss so that all who dithered here could get across unendangered.

"What sort of unseemly expressions are those?", he wrestled out violently, and nobody, not even Bob Swanegel, discerned how something broke into pieces in him. "I think I am a man of my word. Why have doubts suddenly arisen in you?"

"Because Kathrin does not gladly go to me", Bob Swanegel said coolly.

"Not gladly?", the smokehouse owner cried between shock and secret longing.

His emaciated figure stood on the smooth stone, now he had to prop himself on his stick to retain his posture. But then the superiority of the older man was exercised, for as the merchant propped himself on the shoulder of the seated man, he mastered himself as far as to be able to toss out without particular trouble, "Those are girlish moods, dear friend. Why shouldn't she be glad to go?"

Now the helmsman shook the hand weakly from his shoulder.

"Because she is too much attached to you", it poured roughly and accusingly from him.

"She is attached to me?" The stick of the smokehouse owner trembled a little, it seemed to become brighter over sea and land, and at the same time, a deep calm came over the exhausted man, for he had achieved what he had yearned for. As if for comfort, he spoke to himself, "I want to believe it. The child has received many a good thing from me, and her thankfulness stirs. But, dear friend, that is the fate of parents and educators, they must sacrifice to youth what cannot in the long run be bound to the old."

Bob Swanegel raised his short-cropped head in surprise. The man there before him spoke so earnestly and solemnly that no deception could be thought of.

"So your opinion is to that effect?", he cried out, exhaling.

And when the merchant once more nodded in confirmation, for it offered him pain to reveal still more of himself, the fellow sprang quickly to his feet and grasped for the hand of his companion, gushing.

"That I think too," it burst out unfettered from the now happily convinced man, "you are actually much older, Mr Sell, than you look. You know so much and have raised up all of Uhlenhus so that they can only have respect for you. Truly, it almost does me well by itself. And there it must not amaze you at all when the little one is likewise so full of esteem. But in the end only like and like belong together, and you cannot live from esteem alone. Right, Mr Sell, am I right?"

"You are right", the man questioned responded.

He was still standing, gazing over the shining sea and, at the same time, he smiled forcibly, because the young man next to him did not guess at all how injurious the effect of his joy was. And it was again the taciturn, inwardly turned Mr Sell who struck the other man roughly on the shoulder to add severely, "The consensus is with you, and such should not be fought against."

"Quite certainly," Bob cried enthusiastically, "that is also my opinion."

***

The children of Uhlenhus thronged in thick mobs before the windows of the smokehouse owner's home.

"Look," they brought to each other's mutual attention, "Kathrin is getting engaged."

"Yes, and here by the wharf lies the 'Green Herring'. With colourful pennants right up the mast."

"Did you not know that? Captain Kohlrausch guided it here himself."

"That has to mean something."

"Eh surely, they say Mr Sell and the bride were once pulled up onto the boat."

"Such a fine engagement there has never been here before. Now the two old ladies in the black silk are reciting a proper poem."

"But they cannot continue, for the tears are running over their cheeks."

It really happened thus. Although the poem had already been made long before, and had been carefully memorised by both the Müsebeck sisters, now, when Kathrin's old friends stood before the bride in her simple white summer dress, now, when they caught her half anxious, half admiring smile, the arduously honed rhymes led a strange dance before them, and both were only capable still of bringing forth the closing verse several times amidst streaming tears.

"We're letting you go so reluctantly,
Farewell, my child, farewell, Kathrin."

"Oh, it is unbearable", the former Mrs Plonnies moaned, whereby she wanted to indicate that she could not withstand the power of the poetry any longer.

"Wife," Captain Kohlrausch soothed her, as he tapped his wife smugly on her fat arm which threatened to burst the surrounds of the grey silk, "wife, the old mademoiselles understand their thing. The morsel remained stuck in my throat with shock. But pay attention, this is only the prelude, and now comes the cheerful bit."

"Loyal servants, my ladies," the orphans' councillor, Mr Tredup, whispered from behind the table, having occupied himself greedily during the recital with the cleaning up of a plate full of currant cake, for his fly-like nature did not allow the red fruit to have any peace, "loyal servants", he whispered now, bowed humbly, and waved his black coat-wings. "Your voices are gloriously suited to the church choir. Particularly the plaintive tone which you have goes to everyone's heart. But I did not want to say this," he deviated as he bent down again demanding forbearance from the entire company, "the honourable assignment has come to me in fact — that is, it arises as it were from my own aptitude — to talk about something very beautiful and charming. Hehe, I mean of course our bride."

Here the orphans' councillor stroked his pointed iron-grey hair stiffly from his skull so that it looked as if a great fly were stretching its antennae, and he hopped onto his other foot. Kathrin, however, who sat between her tail-coat adorned bridegroom and her motionless foster father, discoloured a little, for she was thinking of the time when her fate had been extremely dependent on this being addicted to sweet things. Fortunately, Bob Swanegel noticed her movement, and since this entire celebration seemed to him to be an exercise in courage during which you had to offer resistance resolutely and defiantly to the ribaldry of others, he squeezed her hand powerfully, and whispered quite loudly, "Stay calm, thing, it is all stupidities. It will go away."

Now the orphans' councillor tilted his head on an angle, and stared greedily at the currant cake.

"My ladies and gentlemen," he purred through his nose, "I have had many children, I can say hundreds. When they were not recalled prematurely by heaven, they have all fulfilled their place in life respectfully, for the town and its officials feel an active sympathy for the development of our dear little ones."

"What clumsiness", Mr Emanuel Quandt interrupted here, only it was not meant to represent a criticism of the speaker, but only happened because the coat wing of the orphans' councillor had struck his eye.

"Excuse me", Mr Tredup continued abjectly. "I am very excited and moved, for it has never been begrudged to me to sit at such an ample and tasty table with one of our charges. Particularly at such a pleasant opportunity.

Truly, here you see the hand of God. For the beautiful and lovely bride has surely administered the pound that we gave her and gloriously — gloriously — —." Mr Tredup emitted an anxious hum, and faltered as if he had remained stuck to the red jelly coating of the cake.

"Wife, is he missing something?", Captain Kohlrausch inquired stiff with fright, "does he perhaps want a glass of water?"

"No, not water," the great fly whirled up, "my ladies and gentlemen, I wanted to ask you in contrast to grasp your glasses for the happiness of our loved foster child."

"Cheers", the Captain roared in relief, and grasped his carafe full of wine, and Mr Quandt considered it advised to pull forth the violin, hidden until then behind his seat, to make a sort of fanfare with it.

The glasses clinked together brightly, and even the shopkeeper-artist had joined in it and also confided to his neighbour, Miss Müsebeck, that Mr Tredup was not indeed an entirely logical orator, but for all that a man of deep feeling.

"Anyhow," he whispered excitedly to his dinner partner, "we find ourselves here in a house of fortune. Just see, my dear Miss, how a serious, peaceful gleam plays about the head of Mr Richard Sell. He does not indeed speak much with the bride, for he does not want perhaps to take her from her future husband, but you should really believe a proper father would have achieved the goal of all his wishes today. Right, quite like the poet said so aptly:

> And the father, with cheerful look,
> From his home's far-seeing roof,
> Reckons o'er his flourishing stock. *

And in fact, Mr Emanuel Quandt did not stray all too much when he described the emotions of his host. In his black frock coat, the smokehouse owner sat next to the

---

* [From Schiller's "The Lay of the Bell" (Das Lied von der Glocke) – translation by Thomas Arnold.]

bride, still and smiling, as if he belonged only a little in this circle, and if the observer had taken note more precisely, he would have discovered that the gaze of the rich man of Uhlenhus lost itself across the round table out into a luminous distance, and how his lightly moving lips were not murmuring words of blessing but numbers. Yes, so it happened. After Richard Sell believed he had ironed out himself and his years, suddenly the reigning idol of his youth waved to him from a distance again and painted before him beguiling images of wealth, might, and honours. Quite certainly, the upstart now thought to know that there back in the hazy dusk the golden treasure lurked for him, the treasure which was attainable by him alone on earth, and that he had been designated to fetch the blessing from there for the few to whom his heart adhered. A wondering and muttering passed through the company when something occasionally fell from the smokehouse owner's lips about his future works and efforts.

"What sort of man he is," the poetess Miss Helene Müsebeck rasped, "how he plans everything, and how inexhaustible is his joy in acquisition!"

Then a despatch messenger stepped into the small circle, and handed a telegram over to the master of the house. At first this scene was little heeded, because they were altogether convinced that it only concerned congratulations on the ceremony taking place just then. The merchant also tore open the form heedlessly. But hardly had he thrown a look into it than the light which had played about his severe features incessantly up to then strengthened. He assiduously smoothed out the paper to then lower it carefully into his breast pocket.

"What is that about?", Kathrin asked, being unable to control herself.

The smokehouse owner looked with gleaming eyes into the distance.

"The alliance with the shipping company in Stettin which I proposed is moving close to its realisation", he answered quietly so that only his neighbour could understand him. "The gentlemen are desiring a new negotiation, and I will hence be travelling tomorrow early in the morning."

The bride moved uneasily.

"And me?", she whispered after a pause.

"You?"

"Will you not be at our wedding?"

"That I don't know, my child," he responded calmly, "if it cannot be, then I will provide for us better."

Kathrin looked down concernedly before herself, she wanted to give a quick answer, and moved her plate impatiently, only, before she could get her bearings, the bridegroom rose to the great surprise of the guests and pulled out two narrow boards from under the table, which he had kept hidden there up to then. He stood broad-legged and confident of victory in his brand new tailcoat.

"I am not one for giving talks much," he shared with those listening, "and my old principal Julius Kohlrausch isn't either. In a nutshell, my former master has donated both these things for the bow of the 'Green Herring'. What do you read here?"

"Kathrin", the company called as if from one mouth, for in thick golden letters, the name hung resplendent on a dark-red enamelled field.

"Yes," Bob concluded momentously, "thus shall my ship be called from now on. Of those present here, only Mr Sell knows what sort of background the name has. And it involves only the pair of us. So, I have no more to say."

With that he sat down, placed both boards tenderly on his knees, and every response of the bride-to-be was drowned in the loud applause of the listeners.

What followed afterwards, Kathrin could not concentrate on clearly anymore. Had Mr Sell dissolved the table? Or had the suggestion been made by the artist-shopkeeper to go for a stroll in the garden for a bit? The memory of it had escaped her, for suddenly the girl meditating to herself alone was again tormented by the idea that this house full of people was actually quite empty. And although she held fast by the hand to Bob Swanegel, her anxious looks began anew to seek for some familiar hold. But that lasted for only a passing minute. Straight afterwards, she saw herself strolling with her fiancé in the middle of a chattering crowd over the narrow garden paths; she noticed how her foster father strode ahead of them as he waved cheerfully to the children on the street or lingered here and there to explain to his guests this or that plant. She skimmed past the cherry tree under which she had recently been beset by such a confusing dream, and although Bob spoke loudly to her, she nevertheless brooded avidly over what role Mr Sell actually played in this happy shadow-dance. But she could not find it, the humming chatter around her blotted out everything. She sat with both Müsebeck sisters in the narrow, shady vine arbour, and yet she did not pay attention to the many inquiring questions of the curious little women, rather she had to recall the hour in which her foster father prepared an end to her fleeting friendship with the student Martin Gerloff through a few serious and indignant words. Where might the good boy be dwelling now? It occurred to the thoughtful girl that the strictly uttered wish of the man had sufficed to make the image of the young enthusiast dissolve into a haze. So it had always been. Yes, you must obey here in this house. But soon afterwards, she was hurrying across the red floor of the hall to deliver an order, and she was not at all surprised when she was detained here by Mr Emanuel Quandt, who, deliberating and tossing back the fluttering scarf about his collar, muttered to her furtively, "Now, Miss Brodersen — Miss Sell — do you still remember whom we serenaded here?"

"Yes, I remember", the bride-to-be smiled.

Strangely, the house which she had thought to be empty was nevertheless peopled by several figures. The familiar figures all wore a black frock coat, and they had hard chiseled faces which gazed away far over her, while they tossed out curtly and gruffly the same thing which Mr Quandt had already desired to know, "Do you remember?"

Kathrin nodded.

"Do you remember how we returned together on the little carriage from Pottwiem? That was the last."

"Yes, I remember", Kathrin trembled, lost.

Then the guests turned again about her, a punch bowl was carried out onto the table before the house, and between clinking glasses and loud showings of applause, the bride-to-be heard how the Quandt couple gave voice to one of their masterly songs for the thrilled circle. The sounds roared fully and powerfully from her own mandolin.

***

Now the house was really empty. With the fall of evening, the participants of the feast had followed a demand of Captain Julius Kohlrausch, who had invited "every man" on board the "Green Herring" anchored close by the house, because he proposed as a piece of thoughtfulness to have the townspeople muster on the planks of the old vessel for the short trip home. Thus now a massive beer barrel rested on the deck, and in the light of a few colourful Chinese lanterns and surrounded by the dragging notes of an accordion, a shapeless whirl moved back and forth in the dimness between the low sides of the ship.

Only indistinctly could Richard Sell and his child, who both had remained behind alone in the deserted house, make out the blurred contours of the parting guests, and only sometimes did they smile with deep understanding when Mr Quandt, who remained behind on the shore, found far too deeply felt words of farewell for the departing guests.

But apart from that, both residents of the quiet house could not busy themselves especially with why the departure of the ship was delayed so excessively, for here too a departure was being prepared. On the upper floor, in the brightly lit bedroom of Mr Richard Sell, the smokehouse owner's chest, already varnished long ago by Kathrin, stood on the floor, and both now carried to it, in that haste and excitement which every journey causes, the merchant's bits and pieces. At the same time, they chattered lightheartedly and cheerfully over whatever came immediately to mind, discussed the administration of the house as well as all sorts of tasks which were important in the coming days, yes, meanwhile many a thankful and joyful word even fell between the dining companions who were just then saying goodbye. Nobody would have believed that both persons, who conversed so harmlessly with each other, aimed at nothing more intimate than that the curtain of space and time fell down between them once and for all so that the new thing which they had prearranged could make its beginning.

"I would like it," Kathrin said, standing next to the full chest, breathing out, "that I be informed about the result of the Stettin negotiations."

Meanwhile the smokehouse owner had set himself by the small side-window, was letting the evening wind waft over him, and followed the living shadows under the white and red spheres on the ship.

"Yes, that I will gladly do", he promised now without turning his head. "It delights me that it seems so important to you."

Still Kathrin leant in the doorway, like someone who cedes to rest now that the work is finished, but she embraced the seated man with a long look, and as she stroked down the apron she had on, she inquired further, "You have taken so much. I believe you will start your great journey straightaway from Stettin."

"That could just be if I were to be kept there past the wedding. In this case, I would travel then to the imperial capital, and continue it from there. I am just stressed over whether I will withstand for long being without an actual goal."

"And alone", the girl added, having not stirred, after a pause.

"I was always alone", her foster father contradicted, and bent down with more interest to the illuminated vessel.

Down there you heard it creaking and cracking, the sail rolled up slowly, and Mr Quandt untied the iron chain from the wharf.

Behind the observer at the window, a calm voice spoke, "When you return, I will certainly not be here anymore."

"But you have meanwhile long since found your home and your happiness", Richard Sell spoke out into the night.

And behind him something stroked with a hand over the door post, and replied clearly and confidently, "On that my hopes also stand."

***

A deep breath trembled through the stillness, but when the master of the house turned around tensely, the place in the doorway was empty, for the girl had scurried down the steps in her inaudible way.

The electric lamp was lit on the table, the smoke-house owner's bed lay ready in the corner, and a cold breeze purred from the window and through the open doorway. But the man on the chair did not feel the sudden inhospitability, for to his look, which he was still directing at the doorway, the vanished girl remained present despite everything. And now, when he pictured her figure gently leaning on the doorpost, now, when he saw in his mind the dark eyes filled with timid questions, he shook himself vigorously and blessed God that he had succeeded in stripping off all this ambiguity from himself.

"One more night," he thought, "and then the evil spirit cannot do me any harm anymore."

Yes, yes, it was certain, he had won the difficult game, and tomorrow he would again stand steady and alone in the world. Nobody could raise grievances against him anymore, he had remained the untouchable Mr Richard Sell. He closed the window thoughtfully, but at the same moment he recoiled, for in the glass a second figure was reflected. She waited close behind him, he felt the warmth of her breath on his neck, and yet he dared not turn around.

"What do you want?", he just asked calmly.

He knew those down on the ship must be able to distinguish both the figures enclosed by the window frame. And nevertheless he was not compelled to the decision to take a single step back. For he and the child and his house and the entire world were suddenly collapsing. Swaying, blurry, only readable from the reflecting glass in the window, he caught everything. A pair of hands stretched towards him, a head leant on his averted shoulder, and a weary, tuneless voice expended its last, innermost thought without great emotion, yes, almost dull and indifferent.

"I want to stay here, it is all not true. I am not afraid anymore either of the people reproaching me for my

mother. I don't know either whether you may tolerate
me here — I just want to stay here."

The stretched-out hands glided slowly down the
arms of the man, and the weary creature sank kneeling,
with head bent forward, down onto the nearby chair.

Nothing stirred in the little room. Everything remained as still as before. Only the in the sober, cool Mr
Sell, who thought himself able to figure out himself and
the world like a maths exercise, did a thousand fine
little bells begin ringing unexpectedly, bells issuing a
completely irrational answer. My God, that which
breathed here next to him, that was his youth which did
not want to be driven away. It was his work which he
had formed from tough material and whose soul he
strove occasionally to breath into. But how wondrous,
this soul must have developed more beautifully and
stronger than his own, it must hold just that which he
was lacking, for she spoke the confession for which he
had struggled so long, "I do not fear myself." Or had he
perhaps himself uttered it? And had their thoughts and
moods already long since been wedded to each other
without his knowing it?

Quickly, cautiously, he had thrown his arm about the
quivering girl, and then — the clay form of the bourgeois
existence in which the upstart had crept so long ago
burst apart. Finally, finally, it hampered the poor needy
human core no more; he drew his girl up close by the
window so that the passengers on the ship should distinctly recognise his act, and then he embraced Kathrin,
and searching, in a low voice, timidly, exactly like he
had pressed her to himself in the carriage, the proud Mr
Sell urged himself to the drink of life.

From the ship down below them, a loud cry arose. It
came flying up on the night wind, tapped imperiously
on the panes, and desired an answer. Kathrin's eyes also
solicited and begged for the same. But see there, at the
same moment, they both, holding fast in their embrace,

hear from every corner of the cosy room, from the con-
sonance of their hearts or from the swishing night wind
a hundred explaining, silver-throated little voices.

And when you have at the very end united,
And the brook flows into the streaming river,
Do not ask why it must rush so,
Devise no answer for the hearkening world.
Everything which in your close minds
Is raised to a strict demand,
At one time the wind tousled in the field
Until it tore apart.
What respectability, what daughter of a whore,
What youth and age and toxic blood!
One thing only is certain, you're good for each other,
And from that the gratifying spirit speaks,
Which shows us the way across the depths
On cords of iron and thread.

About the Publisher

Our mission is to provide translations into English of the complete works of neglected major European writers. We do not cherry-pick works that seem the most marketable, but rather seek to provide a complete collection of each writer's works so that readers can follow the writer's development and decide on its merits for themselves.

http://www.facebook.com/KANitzPublishing

http://www.kanitzpublishing.com